WOLFEATER

www.storiesfromthecave.com

Also by Anthony Mitchell

The Godsbane
The Ember Child

Tales of the Grey Crow
Wolfeater

Tales from a Domanskan Fireside
The Scars of Jorn Redclaw (coming 2021)
Glories Gone (coming 2021)

For more information on Anthony Mitchell and his books,
see his website at:
www.storiesfromthecave.com

WOLFEATER

Anthony Mitchell

First published in 2021 by Anthony Mitchell

Copyright © Anthony Mitchell 2021
Map by Anthony Mitchell

The moral right of Anthony Mitchell to be identified as
the author of this work has been asserted in accordance with the
Copyright, Designs and Patents Act of 1988.

All rights reserved. No part of this publication may be
reproduced, stored in a retrieval system, or transmitted
in any form or by any means, electronic, mechanical,
photocopying, recording, scanning, or otherwise without the
prior permission of both the copyright owner and the
above publisher of this book.

All the characters in this book are fictitious, and any resemblance
to actual persons, living or dead, is purely coincidental.

Cover art by Félix Ortiz
Cover Design by Shawn King
Map Brushes by starraven and captscott at
www.deviantart.com

Book Layout ©2017 BookDesignTemplates.com

Wolfeater/ Anthony Mitchell. -- 1st ed.
ISBN 9798581073469

For Jane,

*Who never had to touch the Blackstone
to know the answer.*

Acknowledgements

My grateful thanks to the First Reader, Jenni Mitchell, for encouraging me to walk the White Waste.

To Dyrk Ashton, for the enthusiasm and sage advice in the early days, as well as the regular reminder that the Godsbane have unfinished business.

To the cover artist, Félix Ortiz, and designer, Shawn King, for making it look so good.

And to my editor, Jonathan Oliver, for helping it all make sense.

Contents

THE WOLFEATER 15
    The First Rule 17
    The Wolfeater 35
    The Grey Wolf 57
    The Pack Survives 73
    Casting the Flame 85
    Little Sparrow 101
    One Voice, One Will 117
    The Boy from the Sea 135

BLOOD IN THE SNOW 155
    The Promise 157
    Loyalties 171
    Hunting the Hunted 197
    Old Foes 217
    The Stronger Will 235
    The Velga 251
    Voices in the Night 281
    The Crow Eater 291
    The Man from the River 311
    Defiance 333
    The Slow Death 341
    Blood in the Snow 353

THE BLACKSTONE 379
    Heroes and Villains 381
    The White Waste 401
    The *Ashan Daru* 423
    The Käda 447
    The Seven and The Eighth 465
    The Answer 481
Epilogue 499

WOLFEATER

PART I

THE WOLFEATER

CHAPTER ONE

The First Rule

Sleep is death.

That was the first rule of the Whitelands, and Senya clung to it like a drowning woman clinging to a piece of driftwood. Three days had passed since she first clambered into the saddle. Three days of harsh winds and relentless snowfall, of backache and saddle sores. Three days of loneliness.

It was the loneliness that killed, after all. Far too easy to close your eyes and drift away to darkness when there was no one there to tell you otherwise. All it took was a moment, a resting of the eyes, and then it was on you, sweeping you off to oblivion.

Not this time. Whenever Senya felt herself slipping, her father's words would echo up from the depths of memory, from the days he'd spent schooling her in the arts of surviving the White Waste. There had been so many lessons, but it was always that first one that kept calling back. *Sleep is death*, his deep voice warned. *If there's no shelter, no fire, then sleep is death.*

Senya clenched her teeth against the cold, fixed her gaze on the blackness ahead, and heeled her mount on into the frozen night. The horse stumbled beneath her, almost lost his footing on the icy rock hidden beneath the deep snow. Senya clung on grimly, her knuckles white against the reins, her heels dug in, as she muttered a prayer to the Great Hunt.

The moment dragged on for an eternity, Senya's heart in her throat as the old horse scrabbled for a hoof-hold. Then, at last, he caught himself, planting his feet and regaining some balance. The mount's breath exploded from his nostrils in a mist of relief... and then he trudged on through the snow as though nothing had happened.

Senya let out her own breath, one numb hand slapping the gelding on the neck. If anything would get her through this, it was the horse. The last thing she needed was for him to break a leg. 'I'm awake now, Rhine,' she told him. 'No need to do that again, eh?'

Senya pulled her cloak tighter about her, nuzzling into the fur. Some long hours had passed since the sun fell behind the western mountains, dragging its weak warmth down with it. The chill was sharp enough now to cut through the thick layers she wore, sinking its teeth through fur and wool and cotton, until Senya could feel it in her bones. Her hands ached with the numbness of it; the one wrapped in the reins of her mount, and the other holding her hood in place against the bitter cold winds of the North.

Even then, with the wind howling through the distant peaks like some carnivorous beast, lashing at rider and horse with waves of snow, the exhaustion was taking hold. Senya could feel her eyelids growing heavy, easing closed...

Sleep... is death. Her father's voice, tired now, less convincing.

Senya's eyes flared open as she jerked awake, almost toppling from the saddle. She peered at the sky, hoping the movement of moon and stars might tell her how long she'd been drifting for. Yet there was nothing to see up there, save for the clouds, as gloomy and forbidding as they had been throughout the past few days.

Or was it weeks now? It was hard to know for sure when each frozen day blurred into the next.

'Should have listened,' Senya muttered, admitting to herself what everyone else had known back in Haslova. It was folly, this mission. To cross the Valorian Plains during the worst winter in living memory? It was suicide.

And yet Senya *lived* for the impossible. Her father was the Ironheart, who had forged his name working the Whitelands, scouting well beyond the safety of Valorian lands. His legend dwarfed most others among the Valor, and Senya had grown tired of living in his shadow. So, with the city starving, what better time to make a name for herself? What better chance to carve her own destiny?

If she could do what no one else could, defy all expectations and deliver much needed supplies to her people, perhaps her own name would come to stand for itself? In time they would forget that she was Senya, daughter of Finn, child of the Ironheart. Instead, she would be only Senya, the Longclaw, or the She-Wolf, or whatever other title her deeds earned her.

But if not, Senya's doubts whispered, *if you die instead... you'll be lost to your father's shadow for all eternity.*

Senya glanced to the heavens again, watched the grey clouds twist and convulse overhead, her body trembling painfully in an effort to keep her warm. 'Should have listened,' she whispered.

Rhine snorted his agreement. At least the horse showed no signs of fatigue. His heavy hooves trudged through the blanket of snow without pause, his dark flanks caked in white powder. He was as strong as they came, old Rhine, unflinching and unrelenting in his desire to fulfil his mistress's demands.

'Someone had to do something,' Senya told him, patting the gelding's neck and dislodging an avalanche of snow from his shoulder. 'Without us, the city starves. With us, they have a chance. We'll be heroes, Rhine. They'll make kings of us, you'll see!'

If *you survive this*, murmured the dark voice of doubt.

Senya rode on for a while longer, violent gusts of wind battering at her, lashing snow at her chilled, red cheeks. She peered into the gloom ahead, searching for shelter, seeing none. No trees. No caves, rocks, or crevices of any kind. Just a barren, frozen wilderness...

She was drifting again. Her eyelids drawing closed with every breath. After all, why not? If she could just rest her eyes for a moment, she would soon feel refreshed.

Sleep... is... dea...

She woke on the ground. Her face half buried in the snow, her left side aching despite the numbness of the cold. She could remember nothing of the fall, only that she had closed her eyes for the briefest moment.

She struggled to lift her head, tried to look around. Rhine was standing a few feet away, pawing at the snow, digging out the treasure of grass buried below. 'Here,' Senya croaked, her throat dried raw. The horse looked up for a moment, but Senya's voice held none of its usual power, and he went back to his work, unmoved. 'Rhine!' she barked. 'Here!'

This time the horse ignored her completely. *He thinks you're a lost cause.* Senya's doubts again, relentless now. *Maybe you are?*

Not yet! Pushing her arms beneath her, Senya forced herself up. *Not like this.*

She was halfway to her feet when her strength gave out and she fell again. She lay on her back in the snow, gazing skyward. Still no sign of the stars up there, just the merciless fall of snow blotting them out, daggers of ice biting at her face.

Senya rolled her head to the left... and her eyes widened. *There.* A light flickering in the distance. *Two* lights, like a pair of glowing eyes watching her from the gloom.

She shook her head, trying to clear it. *Not two eyes; two lanterns in two windows. Uncle Velimir...*

Senya tried to stand again, but this time neither her legs nor her arms had the will to listen. Instead, her eyes betrayed her to the darkness, and she fell once more into shadow.

* * *

Crunching snow. Footsteps.

Senya opened her bleary eyes in time to see a massive figure looming over her. A bear, judging by the size of him, black fur all matted with snow. Rhine was standing a few yards behind him, still pawing at the snow.

Why hasn't he run? Senya thought distantly. *Why hasn't the beast torn him apart?*

The monster crouched beside her and Senya gritted her teeth, readying for the mauling to come.

'Stupid girl,' the bear muttered, his voice gnarled as an old oak. 'Sleep is death out here. You should know better.'

Strange, thought Senya. *Bears don't talk.*

And then the beast was gone. Melting into darkness with everything else.

She woke to the sound of sizzling meat, her mouth-watering at the scent of fried bacon. That smell took her back to her childhood, when she would sit on her father's knee and listen to Uncle Velimir's stories. Senya sighed wistfully, and when she opened her eyes it was like stepping into her memories.

Two lanterns were set in alcoves on the far wall and shadows danced in every corner, but the room was unmistakably Velimir's. Pelts and animal skulls were mounted on the walls, the trophies of a more bountiful time. Senya remembered those empty eyes from her childhood too, when they had watched her crawl about on the floor, pretending to be as good a hunter as her father was, or playing the hero in one of Velimir's tales.

'Uncle,' Senya groaned, trying to rise.

A firm hand caught her by the shoulder and pushed her back into the leather armchair. 'Rest girl, you're safe now.' It was the same rugged voice as the bear, only now Senya recognised it. Just as she recognised the troubled frown and the thick black beard of the man looming over her. For just a moment she thought it was her father, back from the grave to save her life. Then the moment passed and truth stabbed at her heart. *It's not him*, she told herself. *It's...*

'Velimir,' Senya whispered, settling back into the chair. Not her father then, but at least it was the only other man she'd ever loved. She relaxed then, letting the comfort take her. The cold was a distant memory under all the blankets piled on top of her, and with the fire blazing in the hearth at her feet.

'That's right, girl,' said Velimir, stepping back and moving to the fireplace. 'You made it... though gods know why you'd take such a risk.'

He took up a fork and started turning the bacon; Senya worked her tongue in her mouth, her stomach cramping at the prospect of tasting it.

'Can't remember the last good meal I ate,' she told him, and she winced at the sound of her own voice. Broken and weak, her throat burned with every word. 'The city is starving, Vel. That's why I came.'

Velimir grunted. Lifting the pan from over the flames, he tipped the contents into a bowl and passed it to Senya. She found mushrooms and tomatoes in there too, and bread toasting on the hearth. In food, Velimir always had a talent for the impossible, and it seemed this winter was no different. The worst winter in living memory, and here he was, somehow surviving the frozen wilderness with a pantry full of fresh goods. Senya couldn't even remember the last time she'd *seen* a tomato, let alone *tasted* one.

'How do you do it?' she asked, accepting the bowl gratefully.

Velimir shrugged his giant shoulders. 'I plan,' he said. 'Something the city folk have never been good at.'

He pressed a hand to Senya's forehead as she ate, his calloused fingers rough against her smooth brow. 'No fever,' he said. 'That's good. I'll get you some tea. Should help get some warmth back in you.'

Velimir set a pot over the hearth and settled in the armchair beside Senya. For a time they sat in silence, watching the bright flames lick at the blackened pot, only the crackle of the fire disturbing the calm. It was Velimir who spoke first. 'So, you came for my herd. How many?'

Senya groaned. It was the only question there was, but not one she wished to answer. Velimir's bison were his life and asking him to give them up was like asking him to cut off his legs. 'We need them, Vel. I wouldn't be here if we didn't. The city is starving.' *Aim high*, her father would have said, and he was right about most things when it came to his brother. So, Senya aimed high. 'We need them all.'

'All of them?' Velimir shook his head in disbelief. 'If they wanted them all, they should have sent killers instead of my brother's little girl.'

Senya shrugged. 'I'm as good at killing as any man.'

Despite himself, Velimir chuckled at that. 'Aye, girl, you can kill. There's more than one monster on these walls will vouch to that. I don't think you'll kill me though. You love me too damned much!'

'You'll get a good price, Vel.'

'Will I? And what price do they put on a man's life these days in Haslova? Because that's what I'll be giving you, if I give you my herd.'

Senya leaned forward, taking one of the old bear's enormous paws in hers. 'Not if you come back with me. We can see the winter out together back home, like the old days. I miss you, Uncle. Mother misses you.'

Velimir sighed, the memories of those old days rolling over him. 'I'd die back there, just as sure as I'd die out here.' He patted Senya's hands and freed himself from her grip. 'Not in the flesh perhaps, but in the soul, where it matters most. I lived behind those walls long enough to know what it means. Blood and death; friends and enemies hacking each other to pieces. I told myself long ago I'd never go back, and that's one promise I mean to keep.'

The fire hissed and spat as the pot of water boiled over, and Velimir pushed himself to his feet. He hunched over the fireplace and sprinkled dried leaves into the water. 'I'll give you half the herd, girl,' he said without turning back to her. 'Half the herd because you're my niece. But if they want the rest, they'll have to send the killers.'

It was more than Senya had hoped, and far more than she wished to take. But Haslova needed everything she could get, so Senya said the only thing she could. 'Half the herd, then. Thank you, Uncle.'

* * *

The blizzard that had followed Senya from Haslova had faded through the night, leaving the midday sun riding high in a clear blue sky. Still, it was bitterly cold. Senya and Velimir sat inside, drinking black leaf tea beside the fire and talking about life. Five years was a long time not to see family, and in Velimir's company Senya found herself regretting every second missed.

'You were out to make a name for yourself last time we spoke,' Velimir was saying, as he poured more of the steaming black liquid into Senya's mug. 'How's that working out for you?'

Senya grimaced. If there was one topic she wished to avoid, this was it. 'Slowly,' she admitted. She nodded her thanks for the top up and settled back into the embrace of the armchair.

Velimir set the pot back on the hearth and lowered himself into his own chair. Comfortable, he drew a mouthful from his mug and sighed with pleasure as he swallowed. Then he lowered his cup and levelled his gaze at Senya. 'Hardest task in the world, walking the White. They never tell you that. They never sing songs about it in the taverns of old Haslova. Folk back home think glory starts and ends on the wall, in the blood and sweat of warriors. They forget about the men and women out here in the wilderness, risking their lives in search of food and resources, tracking the enemy, raising the alarm when they draw too close.

'You think they care where the food on their plates comes from? Or only that there *is* food?' Velimir shook his head. 'Behind their wall they have safety and warmth, and they forget that every breath out here is a battle for survival. You'll be lucky if those selfish turds ever *hear* your name, let alone *remember* it.'

'They remember my father.'

Velimir raised an eyebrow. 'Aye, that's true. He was always an entertainer though, your old man. He knew what the people wanted, and he served it to them with bread and wine.' Velimir smiled sympathetically. 'I love you, girl, I truly do. But you're not your father. And he wouldn't have chosen this life for you.'

Senya's jaw tightened, anger flaring, and Velimir's look of pity only added fuel to the flames. She set aside her mug and stared at the old man, bristling. 'All my life, people have been telling me what my father wanted. He'd want you at home, they'd say, settled down with a good man, making babies. Do you know what I say to that, Uncle? No one knew my father like I did.'

She grinned then, her memory of the man too good not to share. 'He never wanted me to settle for the simple life. I was his only child, and it didn't matter to him whether I had a womb or a cock. He wanted me to stand on my own two feet; to face the world head-on and take everything it throws at me; to fight tooth and nail for my beliefs.'

Senya took a deep breath, emotion threatening to get the better of her. 'My father taught me to be Valor; to be the wolf, not the sheep. No words will ever change that, Vel. Not even yours.'

Velimir smiled then, a joyous grin the likes of which Senya had not seen since the days her father was there with them. Gone from his dark eyes was the pity, and in its place, she saw pride.

'I've always liked you, Senya,' the old man said. 'Even as a little girl you were full of fire. Finn would have been proud of you. He'd be proud to see the Wolf you've become.'

For the first time since her father's death, Senya slept without dreams. There were no snapping jaws lurching at her face from the gloom, no fangs dripping with bloody saliva. There were no monstrous roars to shatter her calm, no blood-curdling screams to wake her. There was nothing at all of her father's last day, only the darkness of a peaceful night, sweet and blissful.

Then Velimir was there, shaking her by the shoulder. 'Wake up, girl!' he hissed, voice tight with concern.

Senya gazed at him for a moment, her eyes struggling to adjust to the grey light of dawn seeping in through the two small windows behind him. She had fallen asleep in the armchair and her back ached with the memory of it. Velimir had kept the fire stoked though, and the room was still warm. She sat up, wiping the sleep from her eyes. 'What is it?'

'Riders. Ten of them. Coming in from the southeast.'

Senya lurched to her feet, blankets falling to the floor as she scampered across the room to the windows. She balled her hand into a fist and wiped away the condensation clouding the glass, pressing her nose to the glass and peering out.

The riders were picking a path down the steep hillside to the front of the farmhouse, only two hundred yards away. Big men on big mounts, all wrapped up in fur and bristling with steel. Senya swallowed hard. 'They only cross the river when they're heading for Haslova. And they've never come this far north.'

Velimir was busy packing food into Senya's saddle bags. 'I guess our people aren't the only ones starving,' he said, stuffing salted beef into the rear pockets. 'Desperate men do desperate things.'

Senya could feel herself looking at him as she had done a thousand times before... *a little girl lost.* 'What do we do?'

'*We* do nothing.' The old man smiled wryly. 'I'll go speak to them, see what they want. Best you slip out the back, get your horse from the stable, and disappear. You can be gone before they ever know you're here.'

Senya felt another surge of anger. 'I'm not a child anymore, Vel. I'm a Wolf. You can eat shit if you think I'll leave you here to face those bastards alone.'

Velimir sighed. 'Even a Wolf knows when it's time to run.' He finished packing the saddlebags and thrust them into Senya's hands. 'When the only glory to be found is a quick death, always better to make yourself scarce. Get you gone, girl. Before it's too late.'

Senya looked at him for a moment, into those grey, steely eyes, and knew there'd be no moving him. 'If that's what you want,' she sighed, bowing her head and taking the saddlebags.

Velimir turned back to the window and squinted out. He swore at something outside, but Senya was already moving, too intent on her own actions to wonder what the old man might have seen. She let the saddlebags fall gently to the ground, her free hand moving silently to sweep up her sword and scabbard from their resting place beside the armchair.

'You're right,' she muttered. 'No time to be stupid.' And she swung the sword as hard as she dared. The flat of the hilt caught Velimir on the side of the head with a vicious clunk, dropping the big man to a knee. Too dazed and confused to fight back, he offered no resistance as Senya struck him a second time, this time cushioning the sword hilt with her cloak. That got the job done. Velimir was unconscious by the time he hit the floor.

Senya checked him over quickly, fearful she might have cracked his skull. There was always a risk with head injuries, but there was no faster way to settle an argument. She breathed a sigh of relief. His pulse was strong and his breathing steady. He'd wake with a lump the size of an egg on his temple, but at least he'd be alive. The trick was keeping him that way.

I hope you have a plan...

Her father's voice, sounding doubtful. Senya glanced around the farmhouse in a desperate search for anything that might help. Cold sweat beaded her forehead, and she swallowed hard.

'How about a prayer to the Great Hunt?'

CHAPTER TWO

The Wolfeater

Radok waded out into the shallows of the Adalvas, his clothes tossed aside on the river bank, dark skin a stark contrast to the chunks of ice flowing south from the northern mountains. He stopped when the water reached his midriff, spreading his arms wide and taking a deep breath. The air, like the water, was fresh and bracing, and Radok smiled as his body shuddered against the cold.

Nine members of the Grey Crow watched from the safety of the shore, some already mounted, others breaking camp and packing saddle bags. They were dressed in the heavy fur cloaks and fur-lined trappings of the Whitelands, their hoods drawn up and gloves pulled tight, watching silently as their leader went about his morning ritual.

None of them understood the significance of what they were seeing, save perhaps Jorn, who had been with Radok since the beginning. He at least knew how they had found Radok, the day they dragged him from the water and made him Grey Crow. The ritual was a throwback to those days, at the start of it all, when he first learned to *walk with the Wind.*

The rest of them just saw a man standing naked in the water, his sculptured physique rigid with the cold. They saw him flex the muscles in his arms and legs, roll those powerful shoulders and stretch that muscular back. They saw flesh crisscrossed with a hundred different scars, some turning blue as Radok splashed himself with freezing water. They saw only a madman... just as Radok wanted it.

It was better they see a madman than a sick man. Sickness was a sign of weakness for the Grey Crow, and the weak never lasted long. When the coughing fits took hold, as they had done these past few weeks, it was better Radok's men remember the cold bath of the morning than turn their thoughts to darker causes. A sick man was an obstacle to be removed; a madman someone to fear.

'It's time,' Jorn called from the riverbank, dragging Radok from his thoughts. 'Let's move before we freeze to death.'

'You should try this sometime,' Radok called back, turning on his heels and wading ashore. Jorn sat his mount at the edge of the water, hands resting on the reins. His narrow eyes peered out from the shadows of a fur-lined hood, his thick black beard cracking into a smirk. Radok grinned back. 'Might wash the cobwebs from your stones and put some hair on your chest!'

'Never heard your mother complain about my stones,' Jorn countered. 'And she seemed to enjoy the smoothness of my chest when her head was resting on it afterwards.'

Radok laughed. 'That is weak, old friend, even for you.' He took up the spare blanket left on the shore and dried himself off. He was feeling the cold now, deep in his joints, but he forced himself to move calmly and confidently. 'My mother was dead the day I was born Grey Crow, and you were ten-years-old.'

'Aye, but I was satisfying women by the time I was eight,' said Jorn, straightening in the saddle.

'You'd be lucky if you could satisfy a sheep,' said Jian, heeling her mount up beside Jorn, 'let alone the woman who birthed the Wolfeater.'

Radok burst into laughter, joined by the tribesmen gathered closest. 'Oh, I like her,' he said after a moment. 'You can ride with us more often, girl.'

'As long as it's the horse I'm riding,' she said, making a point of looking down at Radok's manhood.

'Else I'd be better off as one of Jorn's sheep.' And with that, she turned her horse about and set off downriver.

This time it was Jorn's turn to laugh.

Radok cast him a wounded look and glanced down. 'It's not even that cold,' he said mournfully. Then he laughed too.

They turned north after crossing the Adalvas, away from the distant spires of Haslova, still hidden as they were among the grey mountains of the Spears. They aimed instead for the snow-clad peaks of the deeper Whitelands. It was a path few Grey Crow had ever taken, yet Radok's nine followed him without question. There were no complaints as they furrowed a track through the thick snow, battered by the elements, the morning sun little more than a ghostly orb watching over them.

Radok grunted in satisfaction at their silent obedience. Yet he couldn't help but wonder if it was loyalty that drove them, or fear of the madman?

'I hope there's good cause behind that grin,' said Jorn, reigning his mount in alongside Radok's. 'We could use a victory.'

'And we'll have one,' said Radok.

'By the Seven, I hope you're right.' Jorn scanned the landscape ahead, all whitewashed hills and frozen woods. 'They say only *Chadra* walks this far north. It's a hell of a risk we take.'

Radok glanced around, through the flurries of snow swirling all around them, to the fur cloaks dancing on the wind, the long hair and full beards snapping in the breeze.

'Does it feel like there's only one wind out here?' he asked. 'Seems like the full set to me, and they can't decide a damned thing between them!'

'You shouldn't mock the gods, Radok. We all bow to the Will, eventually.'

Radok waved a hand dismissively. 'You've always been a superstitious old bastard, Jorn... especially when times are hard! The Will favours those who favour themselves. Even Talak knows that.'

'Is that what you told him, to allow this little adventure?'

Radok groaned at the memory. Never one to enjoy his visits with the *Ashan Tay*, that last one stuck firmly in the craw. The old priest was sending men north, east, and south in search of food, yet none were going west.

'It's a mistake,' Radok had argued after forcing his way into Talak's tent. 'We're more likely to find what we need out west than we are going anywhere else.'

Yet even with Radok towering over him, Talak remained steady as a rock. He spoke calmly, reasonably, as though talking to a child. 'It's too dangerous to rile the Wolf right now. The hunger has left us too weak.'

'We won't go anywhere near the city,' Radok had promised. 'We'll swing north, towards the mountains. There is bison up there. I've *seen* them with my own eyes, *Ashan Tay!*'

Talak had grunted. 'And I have *heard* the Will with my own ears. Or do you doubt the words of the Seven?'

Radok had weighed his response carefully. While it was true all men served the Will, the *Ashan Tay* were something else entirely. They were held in such high esteem by the elders, it seemed they spoke with the voice of the Will themselves. And any man who spoke with the voice of a god had a chance to change the world. 'I doubt nothing,' Radok had said, bowing his head submissively. 'As ever, I shall heed your guidance.'

'Then ride south,' said the priest. 'Ride as far as you dare, and if you find nothing on land, bring back fish.'

Radok had backed from Talak's tent like an obedient child. From there, he rode his men south for two miles, then turned west and headed for the lands of Old Valor, ignoring everything the priest had said.

What was there to lose? Find bison and Radok would ride Talak's storm on the wings of victory, as he often had; find nothing and chances were they'd all be dead by winter's end anyway.

Radok turned back from his memories to the line of horses ploughing their way through the deep snow, and he met Jorn's gaze. 'I told him there are bison out here,' he said smoothly. 'The starving children told him the rest.'

Jorn held his gaze a moment longer. 'I hope you're right, for all our sakes.'

'Pah! You fret like an old woman.' Radok reached across the gap between them and slapped his friend on the shoulder. 'When have I ever let you down?'

'Never,' admitted Jorn, 'but there's always a first time.'

Radok rolled his eyes. 'I grow tired of this conversation. It's always the same with you, Jorn, no matter where the journey takes us. You won't relax until we're back home eating steak!'

Jorn shrugged his big shoulders. 'Can't argue with that. How else could I have kept you alive all these years?'

Radok smiled. That was true too. If it came to steel, there was no one in the tribe he would rather at his side than his old friend.

Seeking to move the subject away from their mutual admiration of one another, Radok nodded along the road ahead, to where Jian rode. She moved gracefully in the saddle, rising and falling with the mount's movement. Seemed she could have been born in the saddle. 'What do you make of our new friend?'

Jorn took a moment to study the girl before replying. 'It's a thing of beauty, watching her ride. I know that much. Even under all that fur.'

'She's a beauty, true enough,' said Radok, 'but what do you *think*?'

Jorn gave him a sidelong glance, then nodded. He dropped his voice as he spoke, so only Radok would hear him over the blustery wind.

'She'll test the men,' he said. 'When their blood is up and their loins hard... it could be dangerous for her.'

Radok had considered that himself. They were decent men chosen for his flock, but even decent men could lose themselves when the blood lust was up. 'She can look after herself,' he told Jorn, though he meant the words more than a little for himself. 'She's one of us now. The men will respect that, or they'll answer to me.'

'Why her?' Jorn asked suddenly. 'She's not the first of the Fallow to ask, but she's the first you've let ride with us. What did she say that was so convincing?'

Radok shook his head. 'That's not my story to tell. I like her though, Jorn. I like her a lot. She will do well for the Grey Crow.'

Jorn shrugged. 'If she's good enough for you, she'll do for me.' He straightened in the saddle, brushed snow from his shoulders, and swept his gaze over the frostbitten landscape ahead. 'I still don't see any bison though.'

Smoke on the horizon.

Not much, just a thin, white tendril drifting lazily to the sky, merging with the bulge of grey cloud overhead. But enough to tell Radok they had found what they were looking for.

He raised a hand and signalled for his men to draw rein, waiting as they gathered behind him. Eight men and one woman, all garbed in heavy furs and bristling with steel. They sat their mounts in silence, staring off at the distant line of smoke, wondering what it meant for them.

Means I'm right, thought Radok, cocking a wry smile. Not that he would hold their doubts against them for too long. He had known without doubt the farm existed, but even Radok knew the Whitelands had a habit of sweeping away such memories with ice and wind.

Arrogance is a gift of the young, a familiar, scalding voice muttered in his mind. *Surely you're too long in the tooth to think such victories are yours alone, Wolfeater?*

Talak's voice, Radok realised, his good mood evaporating. He glanced about him, watching the flurries of snow dance to the Will of the Seven. *As all things must dance,* Talak's voice whispered.

Radok grunted. Jorn was the pious one alright, but Radok was no fool. He knew that while a man had to do things himself to get the best from the world, it was always wise to thank the gods when things turned out well.

Radok closed his eyes and muttered a thank you, before heeling his mount over the crest of the rise and sweeping his gaze over the land below. White fields stretched out before him, as far as the eye could see, climbing and falling with the swell of the land, until they met the distant snow-capped peaks of the Whitelands. Radok smiled.

Dark, hulking forms scattered the landscape below, standing proud against the elements. Amidst it all stood the small farmhouse, thatched roof coated white, the trail of smoke rising from a single chimney.

Jorn pulled rein beside Radok with his own grin lighting his face. 'Just as you said!'

Radok clapped him on the shoulder. 'You should know by now not to doubt me, old woman.'

'What are we waiting for?'

The question came from one of the younger riders, drawing up beside them. Tiyan was a big man, tall and powerfully built, his heavy beard yet to show the first wisps of winter. 'Let's just ride down there and storm the place.'

Radok shook his head. 'We'll negotiate.'

'Negotiate?' Tiyan curled a lip. 'What is there to negotiate? How many people can they have down there? Two, maybe three? Our people are starving, Radok. We should ride down there and kill them, take the herd and head home.'

'Their people are starving too,' Radok pointed out. 'Not here perhaps, but in the city.'

Tiyan scoffed at that. 'And who cares about them?'

'*We* care,' Radok told him. 'A strong Crow needs a strong Wolf, Tiyan. Ten of these beasts will be enough for the tribe. The rest can go to the Wolves.'

Tiyan gazed at him in astonishment. 'Have you gone soft in your old age, Radok?'

'Careful, boy.' Jorn nudged his mount closer to Tiyan's, hand resting on his sword hilt.

Radok held up a hand to stay him. He could feel the eyes of his riders watching them. 'Let him speak, Jorn.'

Tiyan needed no second invitation. 'You're supposed to be the *Wolfeater*,' Tiyan raged. 'Yet here you stand, desperate to keep them happy. What happened to you?'

This time it was Radok who nudged his horse closer. 'You think I'm soft because I don't kill farmers? Because I don't leave women and children to starve? I'm not soft, Tiyan. I face my Wolves steel to steel, as the Will demands.' He leaned in closer, face inches from the younger man's. 'Now, question me again and you'll find it's the Black Wind who answers.'

Radok let that hang in the air between them for a moment, before turning back to the gathered riders. 'Follow me. Silence is the key, so no one speak unless I tell you to.'

They descended on the farmstead in single file, Radok leading the way. There was no effort to hide their approach, they just ploughed their way through the snow and kept their swords sheathed. Radok drew up a few yards from the farmhouse door and his men formed a line behind him. There was no sign of life from within, save for the wisp of smoke seeping from the chimney.

'Hello in there!' Radok called out. 'No need for fear. We only wish to talk.'

Almost a minute passed without response. 'Can we storm the place now?' asked Tiyan, restless.

Radok ignored him. 'You keep us waiting much longer, we might take insult.'

Thirty more seconds passed. Then the door to the cabin creaked open and a single figure stepped out into the crisp morning air. The door slammed shut behind him, and the farmer staggered out through the snow towards them.

Not a man, Radok realised. *A girl. A she-wolf.* His men sniggered and whistled as she drew closer, barely containing their delight. Only Jorn and Jian kept their council, while Radok studied the girl in silence. She was small, true, but lithe and bold, moving with grace and confidence despite the snow. It was most impressive.

'Silence!' Radok hissed at his men. 'Show some respect. She's a true Wolf, this one. And Wolves have teeth.'

On she came, young and pretty, long black hair flowing out behind her, caught high in the blistering wind. She wore a leather jerkin over a blue shirt and black leggings, with fur-lined boots and a heavy cloak draped over her shoulders. No sign of any heavy furs though, which was good. If she'd left them inside, it meant she had no plans to run.

She stopped some ten paces away, her dark gaze levelled at them, her face an unreadable mask. Radok waited. He wanted her to see it: big men with big furs and big beards. Men built for the cold, or forged by it. Men glistening with steel.

He smiled. So much steel. Swords and shields, axes, and knives, all hanging from belts or slung over shoulders, daggers tucked into boots. There were bows too, amongst the armoury, for there were no finer archers in the world than a Grey Crow in the saddle. Not that the Wolf would know it, for it had been an age since the Grey Crow last met the Wolves on open ground. These days the battles unfolded on the walls of Haslova, where men fought toe-to-toe on ground slick with the blood of fallen brothers...

She should have been cowed, the girl, yet it was only when her eyes fell on Radok that the colour drained from her face. That was good, too. It meant she recognised the mark of his skin, and that she knew enough to know fear.

'You're a long way from home, Wolfeater.' She tried to keep her voice calm, but Radok could sense the tremor beneath the surface.

'We are Grey Crow, girl,' he replied with a smile. 'The sky belongs to us, as does everything below it.'

'Aye, your kind like to fly.' The girl's eyes shifted back and forth along the line of riders. 'I've often seen them flying from the walls of Haslova, though more often screaming than not.'

Radok's smile grew. 'Baby Crows, perhaps. Not Crows like this,' and he took in his men with a sweep of the arm. 'We come and go as we please from your little wall, taking Wolves for snacks.'

Tiyan spoke up then, frustrated by the banter. 'Enough of this! Let's kill her and get on with it.'

Radok silenced him with a look, burning with fury. 'I promised the Black Wind would answer your next outburst, and you'll not make a liar of me. Keep your fool mouth shut!'

Radok turned back to the girl, shrugging apologetically. 'My friend here... lacks patience. He thinks we should kill you and take what we want, but I'm a more reasonable man than that.'

Radok swung down from the saddle and moved out to stand a few yards from the girl, Jorn, Jian and Tiyan joining him on foot. 'It's been a hard winter for both our peoples, no? I see no reason we can't share what we've found here, so let's make a trade. Ten bison, and we'll be on our way.'

'That's half the herd,' said the girl.

'Is it?' Radok feigned shock. 'It seems Wolves can count as well as Crows.'

The girl ignored the mocking tone. 'And what do I get?'

Radok's eyes narrowed. 'Your life, girl. You get your life. And the remaining herd. A more than generous trade, no?'

'It's not a trade when I already have everything you offer. What about *your* lives, Wolfeater? Shall we trade for them?'

Radok took a step forward. 'You think you can take us all, she-wolf?'

'I only need to take one to make the trade worthwhile. Only you.'

Radok chuckled at that. 'I've killed many Wolves in my time, but never a girl. Their teeth aren't sharp enough for my liking.'

The girl grinned back, exposing the elongated canines that marked her as Valor. 'You'll find mine sharp enough, I promise you that.'

Tiyan had heard enough. 'Let's do this!' he barked as his patience finally snapped. He lurched forward, readying to attack, but Radok's icy glare froze him to the spot.

The distraction was all the girl needed. Reaching behind her back, she drew a dagger and let it fly, all in one swift motion. It took an eternity for the blade to cover the ground between them, yet all Radok could do was watch death spin towards him...

Then Jorn stepped between them, taking the blade in his throat. He collapsed to the snow-packed earth, hands grasping at the wound as he gurgled on his own blood. For just a moment there was silence, Radok and his men watching their old friend gasp for life.

Yet before Jorn drew his last breath, Radok lifted his eyes to the girl. Their gaze met briefly, and he focused all his hatred and his fury in her direction. She bore that look for as long as she could, then she turned on her heels and fled.

She saw death in those pale blue eyes. She saw death, and she ran.

The girl turned on her heels and fled, her long black hair flowing after her as she disappeared behind the farmhouse. Four of Radok's men gave chase, their heavy mounts thundering past Jorn's fallen body.

Somehow, the old warrior still lived. His booted heels thrashed at the snow, bloody fingers grasping desperately at the dagger in his throat, trying to stem the flow of lifeblood. Radok crouched beside him and laid a hand on his friend's shoulder. 'Easy, Jorn. Easy now.'

The dying man didn't have long left, and it struck Radok like a hammer. Jorn had been with him since the beginning. Even as a child, when others had mocked and feared Radok for the darkness of his skin, Jorn had stood beside him, brothers of the Grey Crow.

He tried to speak now, but it came out as a bloody, spluttered gurgle. It was hard to see him go that way. Too hard.

'She'll pay for this,' Radok promised him. 'She'll pay.' Then he pulled the dagger from Jorn's throat and buried it in his chest. He battled for two more ragged breaths... and then he was gone.

Radok pushed himself to his feet with a heavy sigh. He looked down into Jorn's lifeless eyes a moment longer, then noticed Jian standing beside him.

'I'm sorry, Radok,' she muttered. 'Should we get after her?'

Radok glanced past the girl to the four men mounted and waiting nearby, Tiyan among them, keeping a safe distance. Radok shook his head. 'This is her country. No telling where she might lead us.' He called out to the others and pointed at Jorn's corpse. 'Get him ready to travel and start rounding up all the cattle. We won't be here long.'

'What about the men who rode after her?' asked Jian.

Radok shrugged. 'Either they'll catch her, or they won't; return or not. No point waiting for them. They know their way home.'

Jian could not hide her disappointment. 'I never took the great Wolfeater for a coward.'

Radok's anger flared then. Even now, after everything he had done, they still questioned him. He leaned in close to Jian's face. 'She killed my friend, who meant more to me than the rest of you combined.' He pulled back a little, took a deep breath and cooled his anger. 'The she-wolf will pay for taking him, I promise you that. But we'll do it my way, not hers. She knows she stands a better chance out there than she does back here, so she wants to lead us away. You don't eat as many Wolves as I have by giving them what they want.'

Radok shoved past the girl and strode on to the farmhouse.

'Where are you going?' Jian called after him.

'To see what she was hiding.'

Radok stepped up to the farmhouse and put his foot through the front door, sending it splintering from its hinges. He swept in after it, eyes taking a moment to adjust to the gloom inside. Behind him, Jian hesitated, but curiosity got the better of her and she followed him in.

It was a small farmhouse, no more than a large living room with a kitchen and dining area, offset by two smaller bedrooms, all spread across a single floor. An assortment of animal pelts garbed the walls, including sabretooths and giant elk, mountain lions and black bears. There was even the giant bear-like head of a kragan mounted proudly over the fireplace, its cold black eyes staring back indifferently.

Beyond the decoration, nothing caught Radok's eye as he moved through the main living area. It was only as he passed the second bedroom that he glimpsed a boot jutting out beneath the bed at an odd angle. He strode over and lifted the sheets aside, peering below.

'What is it?' asked Jian from the doorway.

Radok grabbed the booted foot and dragged the body out with a grunt of effort. He revealed a man well into his fifties, hair and beard thick with grey, who shared the same elongated canines as the girl. Radok met Jian's gaze and grinned. 'Nothing but a sleeping Wolf,' he growled.

Jian strolled over and crouched beside them. 'Who is he?'

Radok turned the man's head sideways. There was a lump on the side of his temple the size of a small egg. But it was the smell that gave it away, stale and well ingrained. The smell of animals, both living and dead.

'Smells like a farmer,' he told Jian. 'The bison belong to him, not the girl. She's a warrior, not a farmer.'

'She was trying to protect him?'

Radok nodded. 'She must have taken him by surprise, knocked him out cold so she could stand in his stead and meet with us. She hoped to lure us away, to the Seven knows what end.'

'What do we do with him now?'

Leave him? Take our spoils and slip away as peacefully as we came? This morning that might have been his answer, but now Jorn lay dead outside, his blood seeped into the snow, and Radok's anger got the better of him.

'We make sure she follows.'

He clamped his hand over the Wolf's mouth and nose, then slashed his dagger across the man's throat. Blood exploded from the wound in a fountain, spraying Jian's face. The shock of it brought the old Wolf back to life, eyes bulging, and he tried to rise. Radok pushed down on top of him with all his weight, holding him down, his hand still clamped tight, stifling the Wolf's cries of agony as his lifeblood pumped away.

Radok took no joy from watching the life fade from those helpless, confused, frightened eyes; no satisfaction; no sense of sweet revenge. He felt only a well of emptiness. For what was one old, toothless Wolf, next to the loss of the Grey Crow's finest? Not enough, was the simple answer. Not enough by far.

Jian was watching Radok with wide eyes of her own, blood dripping from her face. 'Why did you do that?'

Radok shrugged. 'She cared enough to hide him. Maybe she'll care enough to come find us once she realises he's dead. And when she does, she'll pay the price for what she did to Jorn.'

Pushing himself to his feet, Radok took one last look around the farmhouse. 'Burn it,' he said. Then he marched outside into the clean air.

CHAPTER THREE

The Grey Wolf

'Shit!'

Senya risked a glance over her shoulder, straining to see through the dust and snow churned up in Rhine's thunderous wake. She counted four in the chasing pack, close enough now to see their grinning, bearded faces.

Only four. 'Shit!'

She had hoped to draw them all away, to leave Velimir in peace, unscathed save for the bruise she'd given him. But there was little chance of that now. It wouldn't take them long to find him, stuffed beneath the bed. Seemed like a damned fool idea now...

'Shit!'

Only four, and not a dark face among them. Senya winced. Things might have been different had her dagger found its mark in the Wolfeater's chest. Instead, that old bastard had taken it in the throat, and now the Wolfeater was back at the farm, where Velimir was left unconscious and alone. A chill ran down Senya's spine as she saw again the fury born in the Wolfeater's eyes at the death of his friend. *The Great Hunt is nothing if not a cun...*

'Shit!'

Rhine thundered across the snowy fields, heading south, back the way they came. Senya dug her heels into his flanks, driving him on, willing his legs to work all the harder. His breath was coming fast now, smoking in the cold morning air.

Senya risked another backwards glance. The Basillians were closer now, one notching an arrow to his bow.

'Shit! Shit! Shit!'

Senya bent low into the saddle, her face pressed against Rhine's neck, making herself as small a target as possible. Up ahead, a small wood emerged from the swirling mist, just large enough to lose herself in, and Senya steered the horse toward it. An arrow whistled past her left shoulder, barely an inch from her ear, arching into the ground ahead and disappearing into the snow.

Shit, she wanted to say, but the words had dried up, her mouth drying with them.

You never feel more alive than when your life hangs in the balance. So her father often said, but it wasn't until now that she truly understood what it meant. She could feel every second passing, her heart pounding in her chest, sweat dripping from her brow despite the cold. She could even feel the weight of the snow pressing down on the huge evergreens up ahead.

Jaw set, Senya dragged left on the reins at the last moment, galloping along the tree line rather than plunging in. She gave Rhine his head for a moment, waiting to see how the Basillians reacted. They followed suit, swinging left and sticking to Rhine's tail.

Shit!

Senya rode on for a while longer, an itch in her back where she expected an arrow to appear at any moment. She counted to three. Then, seeing an opening in the tree line, she dragged right on the reins and Rhine plunged into the trees.

Senya bobbed and weaved away from the claws of low hanging branches, then drew back sharply on the reins and brought Rhine to a skidding halt. She swung down from the saddle, landing lightly on her feet, her heart pounding more than ever now. She had bought herself a few seconds, if she was lucky...

Without skipping a beat, Senya slapped Rhine on the rump and the horse set off through the trees, disappearing along the path of an old deer trail. Then

Senya stepped behind a tree and slid her sword from its sheath.

Hit fast, hit hard. More words from her father. Seemed strange that it took a day like today to bring his voice back with such crystal clarity. But then, she supposed, that was just the man he was. He had been made for days like this. *Surprise will always give you an edge in the breathless moments.*

The rumble of the chasing hooves drew closer. Senya swallowed hard as the earth trembled beneath her feet. She tightened her sweaty grip on the hilt of her sword, every inch of her tense with anticipation...

Then the first rider swept by, the wind striking Senya like a tornado as he thundered on.

Wait for it...

Senya pressed herself tighter against the tree she was hiding behind, biting her lower lip. Then a second blast of energy exploded past, and a third.

...Now!

She stepped from her hiding place just as the fourth horseman bore down on her. His eyes widened when he saw her, a silent scream forming on his face, but it was too late. Senya's sword flashed out and scythed through the horse's legs. The animal let out a terrible scream as the ruined limbs gave way beneath him, ploughing face first into the forest floor. The rider went flying from his back, his body shattering with the force of the impact, all grunts and splintering bone.

Senya charged in to finish the job, her sword slashing into the back of the man's skull with a wet thud. She looked up. The other three had turned back at the sound of their friend's demise, and, seeing Senya, they charged as one.

Senya took a deep breath. There were no words of wisdom from her father this time. Not even the great Finn had stood alone against three riders.

She'd chosen the ground well, at least. The narrow deer trail meant they'd have to come at her one at a time. Senya flexed her fingers on the sword hilt. Finn had it right earlier; speed *was* everything. If she could get her strikes in first and fall back to the trees for cover, she might actually have a chance. One slip though, and it would all be over.

The first rider closed in fast, his bearded face twisted in a snarl. 'You die now, bitch!' he called out in the harsh, guttural bark of his people, sword swinging over his head.

'Fuck you, Crow!' Senya bit back. She shifted her feet, tightened the grip on her sword, and waited.

On he came, snow kicking up behind him, earth rumbling beneath him. Senya clenched her teeth hard against the fear, legs tensing, readying for the impact. 'Shit!' she screamed as he bore down on her.

And then she moved, sidestepping to the right, away from the Crow's sword arm, and let the horse sweep by. Her sword thrust upwards, driven by instinct and skill, and slid easily into the Crow's flanks, an inch below the ribs. The sword speared upwards, through the guts and into his heart. The horse rode on, ripping the sword from Senya's hand and carrying it off down the track, still buried in her victim.

A cry of rage dragged Senya's attention back to the trail. She turned to find the other two riders closing on her fast, the first barely twenty strides away. He was kicking his mount on with venom, axe in hand, but it was the man beyond him, bringing up the rear, that caught Senya's eye. Him with the bow.

She had forgotten the bow. Yet there it was, varnished wood glinting in the sunlight. Senya could almost hear the wood straining as the bowstring drew tight on the notched arrow. She bent her knees, ready to dive into the underbrush. Then something punched into her shoulder and sent her spinning through the air.

She landed heavily in the snow, the wind knocked out of her in a great rush, agony searing through her shoulder. She hadn't heard the twang of the bow through the madness of pounding hooves and desperate war cries, but the sight of the arrow jutting from her shoulder below the collarbone was proof enough.

For the briefest moment, Senya found herself marvelling at the strangeness of it all. One moment she was eating breakfast with her uncle, and the next she was lying in the dirt, staring at a shaft of wood buried in her shoulder, grey fletching fluttering in the breeze. The pain was real enough though. No escaping that.

Senya tried to sit. She blinked as a horse appeared over her, snow and dirt showering from iron-shod hooves as he went up on his hind legs, his front legs promising crushing peace. She closed her eyes, waiting for the inevitable...

But it never came. Instead, the forest to the right exploded out in a shower of scattered snow and snapping branches, as a mass of grey fur and jagged teeth burst from the tree line. The beast collided with the rearing horse and they disappeared together into the underbrush to the left, a tangle of flailing limbs and bloody fur.

Back along the trail, the bowman drew rein, horror in his eyes. For a moment they sat frozen, staring at each other; Senya on her backside, the bowman in his saddle.

Then a second horror erupted from the trees to the bowman's flank, causing his mount to rear up in terror. The bowman fought for control, dropping his bow and clinging desperately to the reins. But the horse was done, his eyes rolling with fear.

The newly arrived beast stood on two legs, hunched shoulders thick with fur. He lashed out at the bowman and swept him from the saddle in a flash of silver and crimson. The man vanished into the undergrowth, broken and lifeless.

Senya stifled a scream as the bushes closest to her, into which the first rider had disappeared, peeled apart and a wolf's head slowly emerged. The beast was all grey, save for a streak of white fur running through his left eye - white itself, where the other was black as coal.

Senya watched awestruck as the great beast padded towards her, mouth slick with blood, eyes as cold as any killers. Yet the fear drained away the moment she saw those eyes, for she knew the wolf... and the beast he travelled with.

'Scar,' the other one called out gruffly. 'Leave her be, boy.'

The wolf whimpered a little, but he sat back on his haunches and watched Senya closely, his mismatched eyes unflinching. Senya turned away from him, and found the second beast striding towards them. Only it was not a beast at all, just a man garbed in the thick hide of a bear, giant head drawn up like a hood. Senya groaned. *Fooled by a pelt. What would father say to that?*

He was a hulking giant of a man too, wielding an axe almost as big as he was, the blade oozing with gore. All told, he needed the costume about as much as the wolf needed a sword.

With a twinkle in his eye as he met Senya's gaze, he let the bear's head fall clear and revealed his own mass of scraggly grey hair, complete with a forked beard that ran down to his chest. He smiled warmly, revealing the elongated canines of the Valor, and any doubts Senya had vanished in an instant.

It was him. It was the Grey Wolf.

'Mikilov,' she muttered, trying to rise.

He caught her by the shoulder and shoved her back down. 'Stay there, girl. We'll deal with that arrow first.'

He knelt beside Senya and inspected the damage, moving her this way and that, trying to get a better angle on where the arrow had pierced the flesh. Senya winced and grunted as he probed, her face twisting in pain when he wiggled the arrow about. She felt the arrow's shaft brush against the bone more than once, and had to bite her lip against the bolt of pain it sent searing through her.

'Not bad,' said the Grey Wolf, slapping Senya on the back. 'It's close to the bone, but the shaft has gone clean through and there's no sign of internal bleeding.' He took hold of Senya's shoulder again and leaned in closer. 'Best you ready yourself now...'

'Ready myself for wha—'

Senya bit her tongue as Mikilov gripped the arrow in both hands and snapped it off at the fletching end, sending another bolt of agony coursing through her shoulder.

Before Senya could complain, Mikilov pushed the remaining arrow through the wound and yanked it clear on the other side. This time the pain was too much. Senya shoved the old warrior away from her and screamed.

'Stop your whining,' said Mikilov, slapping her hands away. 'It's done now.'

'You bastard!'

Mikilov grunted. 'There's worse to come. Here...' Drawing a flask from the bag at his side, Mikilov pulled the stopper clear and thrust it out to Senya. 'Drink!'

Senya took down a mouthful... and sprayed it out in disgust. The spirit burned her throat like fire, the aftertaste sharp and bitter. With Senya distracted, Mikilov doused the wounded shoulder with spirit and Senya cried out again as another fire of pain lit her shoulder. She scrabbled away from him, but the Grey Wolf grasped her by the good shoulder and held her firm.

'Get off me, you bastard!'

'Aye, girl, I'm a swine. But the wound's clean now. May as well let me stitch you up so we can get on our way.'

Senya's struggle faded when she saw the genuine warmth in the Grey Wolf's violet eyes. Then her anger drained away. He was trying to help, that was all. 'Go on then,' she said softly, closing her eyes. 'Do your work.'

She offered no further resistance as Mikilov staunched the flow of blood, no complaints as he stitched the flesh back together, nor criticism as he dressed the wound. When he was done, she tested the work by rotating her arm back and forth, lifting it up over her head and stretching. The stitching pulled tight, but there was enough give to suggest she'd get some use out of it.

'Thank you, Grey Wolf.'

'Just call me Mikilov, girl. I've never liked that other name, makes it sound like I fly with the Crows.'

Mikilov set about searching the corpses of the fallen, looking for supplies or other useful trinkets. Such was the glory of survival out in the Whitelands,

Senya guessed. She grimaced as the head of one dead man lolled to the side, his neck and face a bloody ruin where the wolf had mauled him.

Scar lay nearby, head resting on his paws. When he caught her looking at him, he licked his lips as though he knew what she was thinking. Senya shifted her gaze away from him, back to Mikilov. 'What are you doing out here?'

Mikilov shrugged. 'Scar got the scent.' The wolf's head rose at the sound of his name, almost regal like. 'May have been yours, may have been theirs. Don't suppose it matters now.'

Mikilov paused over a second body, scratching his beard thoughtfully. 'Speaking of Crows,' he muttered, gesturing at the necklace of grey feathers decorating the corpse. 'This far northwest of the river...' He shook his head. 'Makes no sense. What were they doing out here?'

'Same as me,' said Senya. 'Looking for food.'

Mikilov grunted. 'Velimir then. Is that where they found you? At the farm?'

'These, and six others. I tried to lead them away - all of them - but only these four took the bait.'

'A blessing from the Hunt then. Not sure we'd have fared so well against more of them. Where was Velimir when this was happening? Don't seem right he'd let you stand in his stead.'

Senya felt a sudden pang of guilt. 'I didn't leave him much choice. Knocked him out and stashed him away. He's a farmer, Mikilov. He's not meant to face men like this.'

'And you are?' Mikilov hawked and spat. 'You're just a girl. And you would have died out here, if not for me and the wolf.'

Senya's anger flared. 'Aye, but at least I would have died like a man, eh?'

Mikilov spread his hands. 'Young, is all I meant. You're just too damned young.' He moved to a fallen tree beside the trail and sank down to a seat with a heavy sigh. 'So, you knocked him out and tried to lure them away... six stayed, you say?'

'Five,' said Senya. 'I killed one of them.'

Mikilov groaned. 'Five with a need for vengeance... Velimir is dead then.'

Senya choked back a sob. 'You don't know that. I left him well hidden. They won't find him. They only wanted the bison...' Even as she said the words, she knew Mikilov had the truth of it.

'Of course they only wanted the bison. It's been a hard winter for all of us, Wolf and Crow.' Mikilov sighed, sitting there a picture of sadness. 'Probably a farmer was exactly what they needed, and not a hot-headed girl out to make a name for herself.'

'Don't you dare!' Senya surged forward, jabbing a finger into the big man's chest. 'Don't you blame me for this. You don't know who was there.'

'Then tell me.'

Senya hesitated, as though saying the name would conjure him from the air. 'The Wolfeater,' she hissed through gritted teeth. 'He was leading them. You tell me that's a man a farmer could talk to.'

Mikilov sucked his teeth and nodded thoughtfully. 'Aye, I can see why you might act first against a man like that. Not that it matters now. What's done is done. Best we head back to Haslova and let them know what's happened.'

'Haslova?' Senya shook her head. 'No. We've got to go back to Velimir. I'm not leaving him out here with them.'

'Girl,' Mikilov laid a gentle hand on Senya's shoulder, 'the old man is dead. You killed one of the Wolfeater's own. If you think they haven't torn that place apart by now, then you're a fool. They'll either be long gone or they'll be waiting for us. We don't win by going back there. Best we can do is head home and gather more men, then we'll go back out there and see if they left us any meat.'

Senya hesitated for just a moment. In her heart of hearts, she knew the old man was right and Velimir was dead. *And it's all my fault...*

'You do what you must,' she said, 'but I can't give up on him. Not until I see the body.' She turned on her heels and set off in search of Rhine, who had scuttled off to safety when the fighting began.

To her surprise, Senya found the wolf padding along beside her. And she knew the Grey Wolf would follow.

CHAPTER FOUR

The Pack Survives

They saw the fire long before they reached the valley of Velimir's farm. By then it was growing dark, the flames turning the night sky a burnt orange.

'No!' With a hiss, Senya kicked her horse into a gallop. Scar followed after her, ploughing through the snow with big, leaping strides.

Mikilov hesitated for a moment. He barely enjoyed riding at the best of times, let alone full tilt through heavy snow and growing gloom. Yet... *the girl might need me.* He glanced down at the big horse beneath him, claimed from one of the dead Basilians. Only the strongest mounts survived the Whitelands, and none were stronger than those bred by the tribes. There was some comfort in that, at least.

'Don't you fall,' he muttered, patting the horse on the neck. Then he dug his heels in and galloped on after Senya.

By the time they sighted the farmstead, flames were roaring through the thatched roof and black smoke billowed out into the darkening sky. Even the barn was ablaze, some fifty yards beyond the main house.

There was no sign of the Grey Crow, nor the bison, for whom all this chaos had been wrought. There was only the body, lying face down in the snow, no more than five strides from the farm's door. They had stripped him naked, dragged his body out into the open, where the scavengers would find him.

Senya's face twisted in anguish and she dragged back hard on the reins, her mount skidding to a halt. She gasped suddenly, violently, and let out a long, haunting moan. It was a sound like nothing Mikilov had ever heard, and he felt his heart breaking with it.

He drew rein beside the girl, watched her grief pouring out. What else could he do? There were no words of comfort to offer, no pretty lies about how everything would be alright. That was Velimir down there and they both knew it. Nor did it take the blood-stained snow beneath the body to tell them he was dead.

Long seconds passed, minutes maybe, then Senya eased her mount forward and Mikilov followed after her. Scar reached the body first, but he made no effort to investigate beyond that. Instead, he sat on his hind legs and waited patiently for the others to approach, as though paying his respects to the fallen man. Most likely he was, for, like Mikilov, the wolf had known Velimir from back in the old days, when they ranged the Valorian borderlands together, along with Finn and his ilk. *Good days,* thought Mikilov, a deep sadness settling on him. *Days we might never see again...*

Senya drew to a halt beside the wolf and swung down from the saddle, staggering towards the body.

'Let me do that,' said Mikilov, almost falling from the saddle himself in his efforts to intercept her.

But the girl ignored him. She sank to her knees beside the body, grabbed it by the shoulders, and heaved it over. Velimir's head lolled to one side, his dead eyes gazing up at the grey sky. His throat had been slashed open, the dried blood suggesting he had been dead for hours.

Senya's shoulders sagged and her head dropped low, but to Mikilov's surprise there were no tears, no wailing. Fit to cry himself, he could have dealt with that kind of grief, but this silent devastation was a different beast entirely...

He laid a hand on the girl's shoulder and joined her in looking down at Velimir's face. The dead man looked almost ghoulish in the light from the burning farm. The smooth, sliced flesh around the wound in his throat seemed to open and close in the flickering flames.

'He was a good man,' said Mikilov, his voice soft, not really knowing where to go from there. 'He was one of the old guard. They don't make them like that anymore.'

Senya met his gaze and nodded. 'You're the last of them,' she whispered, her voice hoarse with emotion. 'And I don't know what we do without you.'

Mikilov offered her a hand and hauled her to her feet. 'You'll do the same thing every generation does. You'll survive.'

Senya looked back at the burning farm house. A timber cracked and the roof caved in, flames in the belly of the fire roaring up into the night sky. The snow continued to fall, but to Mikilov it felt like ash just then.

'Is this my fault?' Senya asked in a quiet voice.

Mikilov cast a sidewards glance at her, carefully weighing his answer. What could he say that wouldn't break her? Basillians had never touched the farms surrounding Haslova, let alone gutted one so completely. The tribes depended on Haslova as a place to blood their youngsters, and the city depended on the farms to survive. Destroying them was mutually damaging. There had never been a reason for that to change... until Senya killed the Wolfeater's friend.

And yet the Wolfeater did come with a reputation all of his own. His name alone spoke of his hatred for the Valor. Was it any surprise the girl had struck first, knowing what she knew?

Mikilov looked up and found her watching him closely, her eyes pleading. 'No,' he said at last, 'it wasn't your fault. We all know who the Wolfeater is; the things he's done. You thought leading him away would give Velimir the best chance of survival, and you were probably right. Sadly, the Wolfeater failed to take the bait. You did the best you could, girl. Velimir would have asked no more.'

'Will you help me bury him?'

Mikilov pulled the girl into a hug. 'I'd be honoured,' he whispered.

It was easier said than done, burying old Velimir. The snow was almost a foot deep when they started digging, the earth beneath it frozen solid, while most of Velimir's tools had been lost to the fire. It took Mikilov's mighty axe to break through the surface and churn it up enough for them to start shovelling.

It was hard work in the bitter cold, with a piercing chill funnelled into the valley from the north. The burning farmhouse gave them some heat, but the flames were dying now and it took the work itself to build a little sweat.

By the time they were done, the moon would have been riding high in the sky, if it weren't for the mask of unrelenting clouds rolling overhead. The snow continued too, drifting down in soft clumps that left a fresh dusting across the landscape. When Mikilov patted down the last shovel of earth, Velimir's grave was already lost beneath a white blanket.

Mikilov and Senya stood there for a spell in silence, lost in their own prayers as the fire crackled and popped behind them, the last of Velimir's home burning from the earth.

'Do you think he'll join the Great Hunt?' The girl's voice dragged Mikilov from the memories of a glorious past.

'What did you say?'

'With the way he died; defenceless, dagger across the throat. Do you think he'll have a place in the Great Hunt?'

Mikilov eyed her curiously. There was fear in her voice; *true* fear. 'Alright, girl, who are you? I dreaded asking, because it's not wise to make connections out here. But there's not many of our folk who put stock in the old beliefs these days. What do you care what happens to Velimir in the afterlife?'

'Why would I not?' she replied. 'He's my uncle.'

'Ah,' said Mikilov, as the pieces fell into place. '*Finn's* girl.' He saw it clear as day now. She had the same dark eyes and coal-black hair, the same air of arrogant surety. 'He was a good man, your father. Knew the Valor better than anyone alive. I was sorry to hear of his death.'

All at once Mikilov realised she might be asking for her father as much as her uncle. Finn, the famed scout and ranger, had died naked and humiliated at the hands of his lover's husband. Some even said he had wielded a half-stiff cock as though it were a sword...

Mikilov shook his head. Finn had brought that end on himself, but in all other aspects of his life, save perhaps being a husband and a father, Finn had been the best of the Valor. Second only to Velimir.

'It doesn't matter how he died,' he said after a moment. 'What matters is how he lived. Your uncle may have chosen a peaceful life these past few years, but he always had a warrior's heart. He'd seen his share of death, and dealt it too, before he answered the call of the land. You've seen what it's like out here... you think you don't need a warrior's heart for that too? When the time comes, Velimir will be front and centre among the riders of the Great Hunt. Side by side with his brother.'

The girl turned away, tears glistening in her eyes. *That's good,* thought Mikilov. *Tears are healing.* He left her to it then, alone with her grief and her memories. Mikilov crossed the farmyard and joined Scar near the smouldering ruins of the barn, where they had tethered their horses to a hitching rail and set up camp.

He looked back for a spell, watching the girl's forlorn shadow against the fading flames, still burning their way through the farmhouse. It was strange, Finn had never spoken of her. Mikilov had only suspected a child existed thanks to rumour and gossip, and even then he'd barely believed it. Finn had always seemed too wild and free spirited to be tied down by a wife and child. Yet he was a good man too, never afraid to step up when needed, not one to turn his back on his responsibilities. And it wasn't like the girl was simple either - she was keen and sharp-witted, with a fire in her belly to make any Valor proud. So why hide her?

'He was a shit,' Mikilov told Scar, keeping his voice low. 'Ironheart was never worthy of a daughter like that.'

Scar whined his agreement. With a heavy sigh, Mikilov turned away from the girl and made himself busy building a fire. They were well into the night now and it was only getting colder. Once the blaze in the farmhouse had burned itself out, they'd be glad for a campfire.

Scar settled down beside Mikilov once the fire was blazing, and they watched the girl together. She still stood at the graveside, lost in her grief. Mikilov thought about walking over and dragging her back into the moment, rather than leaving her alone with the heartache. But he decided against it. 'We have time,' he told Scar. 'And time is a healer.'

Mikilov yawned in exhaustion. Sleep was a healer too, they said. He closed his eyes and let the darkness take him.

He slept without dreams, deep and untroubled, but he woke with a start. The girl was sitting at the fire beside him, feeding a fresh log to the flames. It was still dark and her face was pale in the firelight, eyes bloodshot and weary. Mikilov searched for the right words, but it was the girl who spoke first.

'I'm going to kill him.' Her voice was deadly calm, spoken with grim certainty.

Mikilov raised a brow. 'The Wolfeater?'

The girl nodded.

'Not that I doubt your skills, but that chance is long gone. He'll be over the river by now, deep in Old Valirov.'

'I don't care. I'm going to follow him. I'll follow him all the way to his nest if I must. Velimir deserves no less.'

Mikilov shook his head. 'That's suicide, girl. If you think that gets you a spot on the Great Hunt, you're wrong.'

'I don't care about the Great Hunt. I only care about this one.'

Mikilov grunted. 'So it's a hunt, is it? Then we should do it right. Come back with me to Haslova. We'll tell them what happened here; how the Grey Crow took the herd. You'll be surprised how many volunteer just for Velimir, even before we get to those who'd rather fight than starve.'

'No,' said the girl. 'We can track the Wolfeater now, even with this snow. I'd wager Scar already has the scent, no?' The wolf cocked his head at the sound of his name. 'But if we head back to Haslova now, the trail will be lost and we'll be lucky if we ever see him again.'

Mikilov sighed. The girl had a point. Out in the Whitelands, when the snows swept over, you could lose a trail in a moment. For a prey as wily as the Wolfeater, it might not even take a moment. 'You can't kill him, girl. Not alone.'

'No,' she said, 'not alone.'

Mikilov's face darkened. 'Don't even think it, girl. I'll have no part in this.'

'My father told me about you. He said if he ever needed help from someone other than Velimir, you'd be the first person he'd ask. You're the old blood. You know the strength of the pack.'

'"The lone wolf dies, but the pack survives."' Mikilov smiled at the quote. He could not remember who said it, but it was as true today as it had ever been. 'You think I'm the old blood?'

'*He* does,' said the girl, stroking Scar's shaggy head. 'How many other Valor can say they have a wolf follows them about? None since the old days.'

'He doesn't follow me, I follow him. He's the reason I'm here.' Mikilov met Scar's gaze. Any other man might have looked into those black eyes and watched the light being swallowed, but Mikilov saw only the wolf gazing back. 'And what say you, shit face?'

Scar moaned a little at the insult, before resting his head gently on the girl's lap.

Mikilov sighed. 'Looks like we do things your way. I warn you now though, girl, nothing but death awaits us out there.'

'My name is Senya.'

A good name, thought Mikilov. But he only nodded. 'I know, girl. Your bloody father never shut up about you!'

She beamed at the lie, and it was a sight that warmed Mikilov's heart... even if she was determined to drag him off to his death. No point making it easy for her though. 'Get some sleep, girl. I'm not going anywhere in this light, and you're going to need all the rest you can get for what lies ahead.'

CHAPTER FIVE

Casting the Flame

Jorn lay naked atop the pyre, all his possessions stripped away so that he might return to the Will unburdened. It was strange seeing him up there like that, mounted on a stack of twisted, dried-out branches piled almost as tall as a man. He looked shrunken without his furs, his lean body pale as snow in the moonlight.

Radok took a step forward and held the flaming torch closer, his eyes sweeping the dead man's flesh. He smiled. Every scar told a different story, and Radok read them like a pathfinder might read the stars, memories filling his mind.

There was the stab wound just below Jorn's ribs, taken while saving Radok's life from their own brothers, boys whose fear of Radok's dark skin had turned them to violence. And *there*, the long viscous scar down Jorn's thigh, where a kragan had taken a chunk out of his flesh.

Radok had been the hero that time, though the beast escaped into the mist before they could kill it. Now the torchlight danced on the old wound as Radok leaned closer. The flesh had long since healed, but you could still see the jagged toothmarks, savage and deep. Jorn had never walked the same after that, but he could *stand* well enough. And he had never let Radok stand alone. No matter the odds stacked against them, no matter the reasons, Radok would find that old bastard standing beside him, no questions asked.

Radok sniffed and moved the torchlight on, studying wound after wound, remembering. There had been skirmishes against the Empty Faces, pitched battles with the Blue Eyes, raids against the Wolves; a thousand different fights against a thousand different foes, and it seemed near all of them had left a scar to tell the story.

The light paused on the wound in Jorn's chest, one of two that would never heal to scars. Here, Radok's own blade had pierced Jorn's heart, ending his brother's life. Ending all their history. He felt a wave of guilt at that. It should never have been his blade that did the deed... but what choice did he have? He couldn't let his old friend die in agony, drowning in his own blood.

Fuck no, he thought, his gaze drifting to the gaping wound in Jorn's neck. *There* was the blame. *There* was the wound that killed him. *And for what? A bite of red meat when the cold hits hardest.* He groaned.

'That fucking bitch...' As he spat the words out, Radok's anger bubbled over. In his rage, he began to hack violently, the pain of it burning through his chest like fire through kindling. *No!* he would have hissed, if he could only catch his breath. *Not now! Not here!*

But once the coughing took hold, there was no stopping it. He could only bury his face in the crook of an arm and let it run its course, every explosive cough an agony in his chest and throat and lungs.

He became suddenly aware of the crowd of men gathered behind him, come to pay their respects to Jorn. He could feel their eyes watching him, his mighty shoulders shaking with the fit, struggling to suppress each cough, and he knew they were seeing his sickness for the first time.

Sickness is weakness. Only the strong survive.

Radok focused his efforts and managed to suck in two rasping breaths, slowly cooling the fit and regaining some control. His eyes watered from the pain, every inch of his chest a burning flame...

'You still think she'll come?'

Radok jerked his head around at the question, surprised. As he turned, his gaze swept over the half circle of men gathered around the pyre, all their eyes on him. It was an impressive crowd, full of the Crows' finest, and not one man amongst them who hadn't ridden with Jorn at some point or other. They could all tell stories about the scars they shared with the old bastard, and not one of them would have a bad word to say.

It was Tiyan who stood front and centre, waiting for an answer. His eyes burned bright in the torchlight. With Jorn gone, he'd probably been with Radok the longest now. Radok was glad of the distraction, though he despised the idea Tiyan pitied him enough to intervene. Not that it mattered. Sickness was weakness, no matter how you tried to dress it up. By morning, the entire tribe would know of Radok's condition. Strength was the only answer here.

Radok straightened his back and looked Tiyan in the eye. 'She'll come.'

'None of those lads are back, the ones that followed her.'

Radok shrugged. 'They're probably dead. Like I told Jian, that was Wolf country up there, and the girl wanted to lead us out there for a reason. Wolves don't run without a plan. We won't see our lads again, but we'll see her.'

'How do you know?'

'Because of the old man. She was trying to keep him safe, away from harm. And now he's dead.' Radok nodded grimly. 'She'll come.'

He looked around at the faces gathered behind him, rough and weather-beaten, most sporting the hair and beards to match their furs. These were hard men, shaped by the hardest winter any of them could remember. They huddled in groups and spoke in hushed whispers, waiting for the burning to begin. Radok looked at those grim, unwelcoming faces and sighed.

With Jorn gone, there was no one left to talk to. Nyana could be relied on for a word or two, but she was eight years old, and she hadn't seen enough of the world to help Radok through this loss. Perhaps no one had...

The girl has. Jorn's voice, as though he'd had enough of Radok's self-pity and risen from his pyre. *There's no loss in the world greater than hers.*

The old man hadn't known of Jian's loss while he lived, but now he was gone it seemed there was no keeping secrets from him. Didn't help that he was right. Jian had lost more than most, sure enough, and there was a good chance she'd have some words of comfort...

'Pah!' Turning his back on the crowd of faces, Radok peered at the top of the pyre, where Jorn rested peacefully. 'You stay quiet up there, you old fool,' he muttered in a whisper. 'I'd not dare weigh her losses against my being rid of such an annoying pain in the arse!'

Bad enough they had seen the sickness now, without letting them know the Wolfeater needed the soft words of a woman to ease his troubled mind. And what was the death of one old man anyway, next to the loss of a child? Jian would likely stab Radok in the face for such an insult.

And why not, he found himself wondering? For softness was a sickness too... and only the strong survived.

The wind shifted slightly and the flames of Radok's torch fluttered noisily from one direction to the other. There was a change in the crowd too, their hushed voices falling silent one by one, their feet shuffling in the snow as something moved between them.

Radok sighed. It was time.

Lifting his torch higher, he watched the shadows dance on Jorn's bearded face, willing those hooded eyes to open one last time. They did not, and Radok stepped forward with a heavy heart. He kissed the fingers of his free hand and pressed them gently to the pyre. 'Goodbye, old friend.'

'So passes Jorn Redclaw,' a voice boomed out, old and sharp, crackling with an edge of ice. Radok turned to see an old man hobbling towards the pyre, crowd parting for him with awed reverence. He leaned heavily on a stick carved from bone, his right leg dragging behind him through the snow. A heavy cloak of grey fur hung from his shoulders, crowned by a magnificent shoulder piece of black and grey feathers. Radok almost missed the bird nestled on the man's right shoulder, dead eyes staring back like pieces of coal. It was a grey crow, the kind that gave the tribe their name. The man's bald head gleamed smooth in the moonlight, while beads of bone held his forked beard together. His face looked serene, almost pleasant amongst such hard company, yet his eyes, shadowed with black ink, looked as wild as any fire Radok had ever seen.

The newcomer's voice continued to bellow out as he edged through the crowd, making his way to the pyre. 'A man who flew further than most upon the wings of the Seven.' He pointed up at the corpse. 'Jorn Redclaw was the youngest of any Crow when he swam the Adalvas in his eighth winter. He saved the Wolfeater from the Old Bear, though it nearly killed him. He even defeated old Broken Tooth at the City of Wolves, threw him down from the walls and left his broken corpse lying at the gates.'

The old man drew up alongside Radok and smiled, his teeth broken and stained black from years of chewing aldar root. His name was Ilgor, *Ashan Tai* to the Grey Crow, and a medicine man without compare. Next to Talak, the tribe's *Ashan Tay*, Ilgor may have lacked spiritual power and tribal influence, but he more than made up for it in the love and respect of the common folk. 'We shall never see his likes again,' he said, his voice hoarse with reverence. Then he held his hand out expectantly, his wild eyes dancing in the torchlight.

'Never,' Radok croaked in agreement. He stared back at the *Ashan Tai's* outstretched hand, felt his own tightening around the wooden shaft of the torch, ready to pull back. Why was this so hard? He had seen this ritual a thousand times before and knew the role he had to play, yet, for the first time in his life, it felt like it *meant* something.

Ilgor seemed to read Radok's thoughts. 'Emotion is a rare beast among the Grey Crow,' he said softly, outstretched hand still waiting. 'We spend so much of our lives living in *Chadra's* shadow, we start to think of him as an old friend. But the Black Wind has no friends, Radok, and when he claws away someone we love... that's when our emotions threaten who we are. Not you though. You are the Wolfeater, and you know Jorn's time is done.' The priest's hand twitched slightly, encouraging Radok on. 'Let him go, boy. One with the Will.'

Radok swallowed dryly. 'One with the Will,' he muttered. And he handed over the torch and stepped back, taking his place among the spectators.

Ilgor lifted the torch high, the flames roaring in the wind, hissing where the snow kissed them. He swept the crowd with narrowed eyes, his brow creased with apparent grief. 'Tonight, we put Jorn's body to the flame!' His voice boomed out over the wind. 'We send him back to the ashes, so that he might return to the All Song, his strength and wisdom joined once more to the power of the Will.'

Ilgor's crazed eyes stopped on Radok, staring intently. 'Radok Wolfeater, will you cast the ashes?'

Radok cleared his throat. 'I will.'

'Then I shall cast the flame.'

And without further ceremony, Ilgor threw the torch at the pyre's base, where it clattered in amongst the piled wood. The fire caught in an instant, the oil-soaked wood working its magic, and in one great whoosh the pyre became a roaring pyramid of bright orange flames.

It didn't take long for the smell of burning flesh to fill the air, somehow as sickly sweet as it was reassuringly familiar. Radok tried to remember the first time he tasted that scent, but it was like searching for the first star born in the night sky, an overwhelming and nigh impossible task. Not that it mattered. Friend or foe, every burning meant the same to the Grey Crow. *One step closer to the Will.*

Radok took a deep breath and held it in. That smell was the very last of Jorn in this world. When the fire was done, only dust would remain. Only ash. Radok let the breath go... then coughed violently. His ribs ached with the pain of it, his lungs on fire. *Not now,* he thought, *not here!*

He clamped a hand to his mouth to slow the tide, and by some miracle he caught himself. He held in two short breaths and felt his chest loosen. The burning eased. He began to breathe normally, the sense of relief almost overwhelming.

He sensed eyes on him and slowly lifted his head. Ilgor was watching him closely, his painted eyes dancing with the firelight of Jorn's burning. Radok stared back evenly, fighting with all his fibre to hold the weakness back.

A long moment passed, until Ilgor lifted a single finger and pointed at his left nostril. Radok reached up to his own nose instinctively, pulled the fingers away to find them wet with blood. 'What the...?'

His head began to pulse, and his vision blurred. The blood was flowing freely now, pouring from his nose in a steady stream. Then his legs buckled and he fell.

He awoke to the sight of canvas rippling in the wind above him, glowing with the soft orange hue of a nearby fire. Stripped of his clothes, he lay naked beneath a pile of fur blankets, one hand above his head, the other trailing to the hard-packed earth beneath the bed. His nose flared at the bite of sweet incense and sharp spices. *Not my bed...*

Radok jerked upright as the thought struck, his legs swinging from the bed... which was as far as he got before his breath scraped to a halt inside his chest. Then he started to cough again; a vicious cough, of the kind that punches out from the stomach, clawing at the chest and hacking at the throat. The kind that tells a man something is wrong. As they had been telling Radok for months now...

'Let me see.' Radok's head jerked up at the sound of the voice. He'd thought he was alone, but Ilgor was sitting beside him, half his face cast in shadows, the other half glowing warmly in the firelight. The man's painted eyes gleamed with intrigue. 'Let me see,' he said again, his fur clad stool creaking as he leaned forward.

Radok took two deep breathes... just managing to hold them in for more than a few seconds. Satisfied the fit had passed, he drew his hands away from his mouth and held them out, palms up, for the old man's inspection. There was blood spattered all over them, glistening deep crimson in the firelight of the small hut.

'I've spilt many guts in my time,' Radok muttered, tasting the iron in the blood, 'but I've never seen a man cough them up. What is wrong with me, *Ashan Tai*?'

The old man bent in closer still, sniffing at the bloody discharge and wrinkling his nose. 'Not good,' he muttered. 'Not good at all. You have breathed the Black Wind deep, my friend. And when *Chadra* takes a hold like that... he never lets go.'

The old man held out a rag and Radok snatched it eagerly, quickly wiping his hands clean. Blood had never troubled him too much, but the sight of his own – drawn from inside of himself, not by a sword or spear, but by a *cough* - terrified him to his very core. 'How long do I have?' he croaked.

The old man shrugged his scrawny shoulders. 'How long can the eagle soar? Only so long as the Will allows it. It's not an easy way to go though, the

Rot. Better to choose a wall, I think. Better to end your life the way you lived. With a sword in your hand.'

Only so long as the Will allows it.

Radok felt a deep swell of anger at that. 'I have always served the Will,' he said. 'As well as any man!'

'You have,' Ilgor agreed.

'I've shed enough blood to fill the Great Lake twice over, and always in *their* name.'

'No one would argue otherwise.'

'I have sacrificed everything I've ever had to serve them. The *Ashan Tay* calls and the Wolfeater answers. I've done everything they've ever asked of me, and *this*...' He waved the bloody rag under Ilgor's nose. '*This* is the thanks I get?'

The *Ashan Tai* chuckled. 'Such is life, boy. Such is life.'

Radok's jaw tightened as his rage threatened to spill over. Ilgor sighed. 'Very well,' he said, slipping from his stool and hobbling towards the hearth at the centre of the hut, where the fire was beginning to fade. He took two logs from a stack piled beside the hearth and tossed them onto the fire, before gently prodding the flames back to life with an iron poker. Once the flames began to lick, the old man lowered his tiny frame to the fur blankets at his feet and nestled in for the long night ahead.

'Look around you, boy,' he said, once comfortable, and his wiry arms snaked out to take in the breadth of his hut. '*This* is the kingdom of Ilgor, *Ashan Tai* of the Grey Crow. *This* is *his* reward for ninety years of obeying the Will. I may have been too small and weak to stand as *Ashan Tay,* but I have played my part in the All Song. I have healed the sick, burned the dead, held communion with lost souls. I have taken no women, for that would have weakened my spirit. I have never tasted love, nor enjoyed the fruits of its flowering. There are no children to remember my name. The kingdom will end here, in this hut, with my dying breath.'

Suddenly the old man's eyes flared brightly, as though feeding off the fresh flames growing in the hearth. 'You speak of reward, but where is my reward for all those sacrifices? I was never given the dark skin that clads your body, marking you as special, hinting at the mysterious and exotic. I was never given the speed and power that flows through your veins, never given hope of becoming such a dangerous killer. And it's the killers our people love, Radok, not the healers. You have had your fill of women, I would wager? There may not have been love and there may not have been children, but you have tasted all the Seven could offer. You have lived life in the shadow of death, and that is the Basillian way. That is the way the Grey Crow flies.'

Radok was unmoved. 'No,' he said bitterly. 'No, I have lived death in the shadow of life. I always told myself there would be a time for love; a time for children.' He stared down at the bloody rag, felt the poison within his body dripping from his lungs. 'But there was no time, not really. Not for a man like me. There was only ever time for the Will.'

Ilgor reached across and laid a hand on Radok's shoulder. 'Pick a wall, Radok. So what if you don't die an old man lying in your own shit? Who wants that? Pick a wall and let your name live forever.'

'Why?' Radok countered, shrugging the hand away. 'So that a hundred years from now they can say I was good at killing Wolves? What difference does it make? My life has no purpose.'

'There is always purpose to serving the Will.'

'What purpose?'

It took the shaman a few moments to find the right words. 'I'm just a man, Wolfeater, and these are questions for the Seven. All I can say is that the Will is as the Will does, and our only hope is to spread our wings and fly.'

The words lit a fire in Radok's mind and for a moment the pain was forgotten. *I'm asking the wrong person the right question.*

He pushed himself gingerly to his feet, wobbled slightly, then picked a path between the scattered blankets and candles and burning incense.

'Where are you going?' Ilgor asked as Radok reached for the tent flap.

The Wolfeater paused and looked back. 'I'm going to the Blackstone. You say only the Seven can answer my questions? I'll go ask them.'

Ilgor's already pale face drained of the last ghosts of colour. 'It is forbidden,' he whispered.

Radok only shrugged. 'What have I got to lose?' Then he pulled the tent flap aside and stepped out into the cold night air.

CHAPTER SIX

Little Sparrow

The fire had guttered.

Nyana could smell it in the air, the scent of charred wood bitter against the sweet perfume of the candles. She could feel it too, the temperature plummeting as night closed in. She could *smell* it and she could *feel* it, but she *cared* not at all. In that moment, lost in the dark, oppressive silence of Radok's hut, the fire meant nothing.

That's right! Sinak's voice, sneering into the darkness. *What use is warmth to a dead girl anyway? Because that's what you are, bitch, with Radok gone. No one left in the world to protect you now!*

Nyana squeezed her eyes shut, tears spilling down her cheeks. She sobbed weakly, the sound pitiful in the darkness of her world. Huddled against the hut's curving wall, she drew her legs in closer, knees tucked beneath her chin, and rocked back and forth like a baby.

It had been Sinak who brought her the news of Radok's collapse, his every word dripping with the joy of it. 'He fell!' the boy had exclaimed gleefully. 'He cast the flame and then he fell, blood everywhere they say. Had to drag him to the *Ashan Tai's* hut and left a bloody trail even you could follow! Shame he has to die alone. But he's not the only one, eh?' He'd sounded delighted with himself at that one. 'We'll be coming for you.'

Then Nyana had balled her trembling hands into fists, nails biting into flesh, driving back the fear. 'I'm glad you've told me,' she said, keeping her voice as calm as she could. 'Small as you are, not even eyes would have helped me see you coming.'

Nyana took some satisfaction from that, listening to Sinak's friends drag him away spitting her name. At least until his words sank in.

She could handle the venom, for they'd been throwing that kind of hate at her for years, but it was the truth of the words this time that truly stung. Nyana knew she owed her place in the tribe to Radok's protection. Without him, the tribe had no use for a blind girl. Without him, she was alone.

He might yet live...

Nyana cursed her thoughts. That was a child's hope and she knew better by now. Even if he was still alive, Radok's illness was known now, witnessed by all the big names. There was no coming back from that for a Grey Crow. Sickness, especially with blood, was the worst kind of weakness. No one understood that better than a blind girl left to die by her own parents. Even now, men would be plotting their moves, eager to stake their claim for Radok's standing in the tribe.

Fresh tears rolled down Nyana's cheeks as she closed her eyes again. It was all her fault. She had known the cough was wrong. She could hear it, deep inside of him.

You should have done something, she told herself. *You should have saved him.*

But what *could* she do? Radok was the strong one, the Wolfeater; big, and brave, and unstoppable. Nyana was just a weak little girl, as blind today as she had been the day she was born. What *could* she do?

You could come for me, as I would come for you.

Radok's voice. Calm as a spring evening, cool as a winter frost. He *would* come for her, sure as the Black Wind came for them all eventually... and Seven help the man who tried to stop him.

Choking back one last sob, Nyana wiped the tears away on the back of her sleeve and pushed herself to her feet. She moved through the tent like a ghost, stepping carefully so as not to trip on the jumble of rugs, gliding past cupboards and chests, candle holders and weapon racks, making no sound as she moved. This was her realm. She had long since learned the lessons it had to teach.

But outside, things were different. The Grey Crow were a nomadic people, moving camp whenever the white snows of winter forced them on, or else when they felt the Black Wind looming over them. With every move there was a new set of lessons to learn, and Nyana would barely master the central paths before they tore the tents down and moved on again.

Right now she could find her way to the Heart easily enough, but there had been no cause to visit the *Ashan Tai's* tent and his whereabouts remained a mystery. *You can sniff him out though,* she told herself. Ilgor was nothing if not pungent. The mixture of burning incense and brewing potions made for a potent odour, bitter and acrid, yet somehow sweet. Nyana could track him down as easily as a Narg tracking blood.

She dressed in layers for the bitter cold; leather leggings beneath a linen shirt and woollen tunic, fur lined boots and, for a cloak, the pure white pelt of the snow fox Radok had cut for her. As an afterthought, she grabbed a hunting knife from one of the weapon racks and slipped it into her belt.

She was reaching for the tent's canvas doorway when it was torn from her fingers. A vast figure barged through the opening, crashing into Nyana and sending her tumbling to the fur scattered floor beside the fire. She landed heavily on her backside, tailbone taking the brunt of the damage, and stifled a cry of pain. She recognised the brute force and oak-like figure that sent her sprawling, having held tightly to it through the harshest winter nights. She recognised the smell of him too; all sweat, and blood, and steel. Even before she heard the voice, Nyana's heart soared.

'Damn, girl,' he said, the deep dulcet tones of his voice like music to her ears. 'Are you alright?'

Springing lightly to her feet, Nyana launched herself at the newcomer. This time he caught her, kneeling so he was at her level, pulling her into a tight embrace.

'They said you were dead,' she blurted out, fresh tears spilling down her cheeks. 'They said blood ran from your nose and you fell.'

Radok pulled away and held Nyana out before him, his giant hands clasped about her shoulders. 'And you believed them?' His voice sounded wounded by the thought, but, as ever, Nyana could hear the smile playing at his lips. 'You should know it would take more than a bloody nose to end the Wolfeater.'

'I never believed them,' she lied. 'I was coming to save you.'

'You were? Well, that would have been a sight to warm the heart. Even a dead one.' Radok cupped Nyana's face in his hands, his right thumb gently stroking her left cheek.

Though his hands were still cold from the outside, Nyana did not flinch. She just closed her dead, useless eyes and sighed. *This* was where she wanted to be. Held in those rough, calloused hands; sheltered by that huge, hulking frame. *This* was still the safest place on earth.

After a long moment, Radok eased himself away from Nyana's grip and pushed himself to his feet. 'See to the fire, girl. No point you freezing to death.'

She did as she was bid, moving to the fireside by memory. She prodded at the dying embers with an iron poker, felt a fresh wave of heat against her face as she exposed the glowing heart. Like Radok, it seemed there was some life left in the flames. Nyana added a fresh pile of kindling to the embers, then placed a log on top for when it caught.

Radok, meanwhile, was making as much noise as he ever had while moving around the tent. First he was digging in the clothes chest, then rummaging through the food stores, even clanging his way through the weapon racks. He was packing a travel bag, filling it with supplies and equipment.

'Where are you going?' asked Nyana.

'I...' he hesitated. 'I'm going north. To the Blackstone. There are questions I want answering.'

Nyana felt a swell of panic. 'You can't. It's forbidden. Only the Untested can go to the Blackstone, or the *Ashan Tay*.'

'Yet that's my path, girl.' In a heartbeat he was beside her, his hand resting on her shoulder. 'Others will come for me. They know my intentions. They ask you where I've gone, you tell them truth, you hear? They'll find the tracks anyway.'

You're all alone now. Sinak's voice, full of scorn. *And we'll be coming for you.*

'I'll come with you,' said Nyana, unable to keep the fear from her voice.

'A girl? To the Blackstone? Impossible.'

'Why? It's no more forbidden than you going back there!'

'You're just a girl,' Radok snapped back, his hand falling from Nyana's shoulder. 'And you're blind. The road will be long and hard enough without having to drag you along. There's a good chance I'll die out there.'

'I'll die if you leave. And you know it.'

'Don't say that.'

'Why not? It's the truth isn't it? There's no place for me here once you're gone.' She was fighting back more tears now. 'You're the only reason they let me live. I'm *nothing* without you.'

'Don't you *ever* say that!' Radok swept Nyana up into his arms, the power and speed so terrifying it almost made her cry out... until he held her to his chest and all her fears drained away. His voice was soft as he whispered in her ear. 'You think any of *them* would have survived the path you've had to walk? You're more Grey Crow than any of them. You *fly*, Little Sparrow. None of them can say the same.'

'They'll kill me, Radok. I know they will.'

Radok put her down. She could feel him watching her, thinking, judging. 'Alright,' he said at last. 'We'll go to the Blackstone together. A man for the second time; a girl for the first. Let's hope the Seven don't tear us to shreds for such an outrage!'

'Thank you!' Nyana threw herself into his arms again, hugging him tightly. 'You won't regret it!'

'I already do,' he said, but even holding him, Nyana could feel his smile. 'You have to do what I say, when I say it. You don't like being carried, but there will be times when we have to run and I'll have to carry you. There will be no arguing in these moments.'

'Agreed.'

Radok sighed. 'Then go gather your gear. Dress warm, you've never felt cold like the Whitelands. Don't pack too much though. We need to be light on our feet. There will be moments we need to move quickly and silently. Go. I'll get the food.'

Radok peeled back the tent flap and peered out into the night. A strong wind cut sharply through the channel between tents, the scattered torches lining the way flickering and hissing in the dark, or else snuffed out by the wind. Night had rolled in and there was no one to be seen outside. Most of the surrounding tents were shrouded in darkness, though a few showed light within.

Radok let the flap fall back into place and turned to face the girl beside him. Nyana was waiting patiently, her ghost eyes staring at nothing, her head cocked slightly so she could hear better.

Radok thought again about leaving her, cutting her loose and making his own way north... but the girl was right, damn her. With Radok gone, there would be those in the tribe who sought to harm her - especially once they learned of Radok's intentions for the Blackstone. He shook his head. For eight years the girl had been under his protection. He had killed her father to make it so. There was no chance he could leave her now, not even for the sake of his own journey.

'Take this,' he said, thrusting the end of the tether into her gloved hand. 'The other end is fastened to my waist. Don't tie it to you though, that could be dangerous if something happens to us. Just hold to it like your life depends on it. Follow me closely and watch your step. If you start to struggle, don't panic. Don't even speak. Give two yanks on the thread and I'll drop back. Remember: speed and silence are the key.'

'I'll remember,' she replied. 'Speed and silence.'

Radok's heart swelled at that. This girl, he realised now, was as much his daughter as anyone's, and the thought of leaving her had been a coward's thought. Even with the Black Wind at his back, there was no running from that responsibility. It was only right that he take her with him, to stand together before the gods. *Better that,* he thought, *than to make our stands alone.*

He laid a hand on Nyana's hooded head and smiled. 'Then let's go, Little Sparrow. The Seven are waiting.'

They stepped from the tent into a world of wind and darkness, Radok leading the way. He took her to the pyre first, where the last few embers still glowed despite the snow. Radok drew a leather sack from his carry bags and swept up what ash he could, careful to avoid the burning pieces.

'Sorry, old friend,' he muttered. 'You might be missing a finger or two, but I'll see you dancing with the Seven before my time is done.'

Satisfied he had gathered as much of Jorn's remains as he could, Radok set off for the camp's southern border, dragging Nyana behind him with the rope.

South seemed the wisest option. Ilgor had been a good friend to Radok these past few years, but he was *Ashan Tai* before anything else. Chances were he'd already told the elders of Radok's intentions for the Blackstone. They would be watching the road north. Best to head south first, swing east or west for a spell, then forge a path north. *Hope for the best*, Jorn would have said, *plan for the worst.*

They marched through the deep snow as silently as they could, with every crunched step sounding like thunder to Radok's ears. Yet it seemed the wind favoured them at least. It came howling through the valley of scattered tents like a maelstrom, whipping at the canvas and guide ropes as much as at their clothes, masking the sound of their advance. It came at them headfirst too, keeping their scent from anyone waiting on the path ahead. *Perhaps the Seven wish to see me as much as I wish to see them...*

'There's someone up ahead,' called Nyana, yanking twice on the rope for Radok's attention.

Radok stopped mid-stride and hunched low, peering into the darkness ahead. It was difficult to see anything through the blistering wind, but he squinted and strained all the same. 'How do you know?' he muttered back. 'I can't see a damned thing!'

'I can *feel* it. The wind moves differently around them. It tells their story.'

Radok glanced at the girl. Even now, despite everything he had seen, she could still surprise him. 'And what does it say? How many?'

'Only one. Young and afraid.'

'Then we push on.'

They took no more than twenty strides before Radok saw him, sheltered beneath the snow-laden boughs of a giant conifer. Radok swept his gaze around the area. The last tent lay several yards behind them, while the tree stood as a lone sentry at the edge of a sprawling wood. They had reached the edge of the Grey Crows' settlement. And there was no one else around.

'Who goes there?' the guard called out, his voice trembling. A boy's voice.

'The Wolfeater. Who asks the question?'

The boy stepped from the shadows of the tree just as the clouds parted overhead, moonlight painting the snowy ground between man and boy in a strange ethereal glow.

Big blue eyes gazed out from the shadows of his fur-lined hood, while the fair-haired wisps standing on his chin and upper lip marked him as a man-child. It was Vinak's boy, though Radok could not remember his name.

'They... they said you wouldn't come this way.' The fear was thick in him, thick enough to cut.

Radok shrugged. 'They were wrong.'

'They were wrong.'

Radok shifted slightly to the left, the vibrations along the rope telling the story. It was no more than a whisper of wind in a summer calm, a hunter's move, but to Nyana it felt like a rumble of thunder. She let the rope fall. If there was to be fighting ahead, best to let Radok move as freely as he needed.

'You should step aside now, boy,' Radok's deep voice pressed on. 'I'm not playing.'

'I can't.'

Nyana recognised the trembling voice and winced. It was Kian, Vinak's youngest. His brother was a mean bastard, but Kian had always been kind to Nyana. 'Pap will kill me if I let you pass.'

There was a crunch of snow as Radok took a step forward. 'What do you think will happen if you don't?'

'I don't want to see you die,' Nyana blurted out. Then she realised what she had said. 'I don't want to *hear* it, even. Let us pass, eh Kian?'

'Nyana? What are you doing here?'

'She's coming with me,' Radok answered for her. 'Now are you going to step aside, boy? Or do I need to move you?'

Kian thought long and hard about his answer, and in the silence Nyana could almost hear the workings of his mind. He was not stupid - certainly not as stupid as his brother - and he knew what it meant to stand against the Wolfeater. But he also knew his father. If Kian did anything but hold his ground, there was a good chance Vinak himself would scatter the boy to the Seven.

'Hit him,' she said suddenly. 'Hit him hard enough so they don't doubt he tried to stop us.'

Silence.

'Well, boy? Shall we play the Little Sparrow's game?'

Kian hesitated. 'You won't kill me?'

Radok sighed. 'If I wanted to kill you, you'd be dead already.'

'Aye then. Do it.'

With that, there was an explosion of sound as Radok burst into action. It painted a picture in Nyana's mind; snow crunching beneath his feet as he surged forward, closing the gap to Kian in an instant, a hissed intake of breath in anticipation, and the snapping of bone and scream of agony as Radok drove his fist into the boy's face.

Except it wasn't the face. It sounded more like a snapping branch than a broken nose.

'You broke my leg!' Kian cried out.

'I've saved your life,' Radok replied calmly. 'Now, when they come for me, you'll be left at home cursing my name. But at least your face won't be the first I'm looking for when they find us.'

The Wolfeater strode back to Nyana and placed the guide rope back in her hand. 'Let's go, Little Sparrow. There's a good chance someone heard that.'

And he set off again, loping south. Nyana followed in his wake. They passed where Kian lay sobbing in the snow.

'Farewell, Kian,' Nyana whispered to him. She would have left it at that, but the wind shifted and changed her mind. 'Bones break,' she told him, 'but spirits only harden. You'll never doubt yourself again now. No matter the foe set against you.'

Nyana stumbled on, following Radok deeper into the eternal darkness that was her world.

CHAPTER SEVEN

One Voice, One Will

Something is wrong.

Talak lifted his head from the soft fur blankets of his bed and peered about the tent, eyes still bleary with sleep. The canvas walls, painted a soft orange hue by the fire's dying flames, rippled in the breeze, yet there was no sound to it... no sound at all.

It's all wrong.

He surged to his feet, the sharp angles of his naked frame highlighted in the firelight. At his feet, Galdo and Mila slept on undisturbed, worn out by the marriage blessing. Talak would have taken a moment to marvel at his own prowess, but all he could think on was the silence. To a man born with his gifts, the All Song flowing through his veins, silence came as unnaturally to Talak as would the sun shining in the night sky. He could still remember the day he first touched the Blackstone, when the unrelenting roar of the All Song gave way to the voices of the Seven. They had been with him ever since. Until now.

Heart pounding, Talak pulled on his leggings and shirt, then ploughed out into the night air, forgetting his boots and furs. His tent sat at the eastern edge of the camp, sheltered by a copse of fir trees and partly hidden in the undergrowth. He liked it that way, away from the crowd, quiet and secluded. Talak stood at the threshold for a moment, bare feet sinking into the deep snow, looking back towards the city of tents.

Nothing strange out there. The odd tent was still lit, an island of light in a dark ocean made pale by the moonlight. The wind was still there too, flowing over and around, swaying tent and tree and man as though they were equal. *We are equal,* Talak told himself sternly. *We all bend to the Will.*

It was knowing *how* to bend that set the *Ashan Tay* apart. But what did a man do when the Seven fell silent? How did he serve the tribe when he couldn't talk them through the Will?

'Where are you?' he called into the night air, his voice smoking in the cold. 'Speak to me!'

There was no answer, only the silence of the ordinary. And was there anything worse than ordinary?

Then he felt it. A prod in the back, urging him forward. Talak advanced without hesitation, striding across the white field as though led by an invisible force. His feet burned from the cold, but he ignored the pain. There was something to see, something to *do*.

'Where are you going?' It was the girl, Mila, scurrying after him. She was still partly naked herself, her nipples standing like dark stones atop pale hills.

Talak spun on his heels to face her, his eyes blazing. 'Can you feel it?'

Confusion reigned on her face. 'Feel what?'

He turned away from her, striding on towards the settlement's centre. It was a stupid question to ask in truth: *Can you feel it?* How could she, when she was neither *Ashan Tay*, those chosen to enforce the Will, nor even *Ashan Tai*, those weak souls who could hear the Will but lacked the power to understand it? To her, the wind was just the wind - a force to be reckoned with, sure, but nothing special beyond that. She had never heard the voices of the Seven carried on the breeze, nor read the touch of the wind as guidance from the Will.

'It's changed,' muttered Talak, more to himself than to the girl, who still struggled to keep pace behind him.

Is this what it is to be one of the flock? To not hear the voices of the Seven bickering away over every little thing? To not search for the common ground between them? Is this what it is to play no part in the Will? Is this... emptiness... all people have?

It was a terrifying thought. Talak had seen the All Song break lesser men, but to him it had been nothing but a source of comfort. Chaotic as the voices were, as twisted and confused the message he had to unravel, at least he had a part to play in the great scheme. The thought he had woken to silence, abandoned and alone, shook that belief to its core. How could he survive, knowing the Seven had turned from him?

But they haven't, he thought now, the relief euphoric. *That's their hand I can feel at my back.* A firm hand. A guiding hand. It was not silence that greeted him this morning, he realised, but *quiet.* The quiet before the storm. The Seven had found their common ground without Talak's aid, and now - for the first time in his life - they spoke with one voice. *One voice, one will.*

Talak let the hand guide him, weaving a path through the mass of tents until he reached the centre. He lost the woman somewhere along the way, the cold defeating her, driving her to seek shelter in one of the tents they passed. At the heart of the Grey Crows' camp, Talak stumbled across the charred remains of the pyre, where, hours earlier, they had put the mighty Jorn to the flame.

Talak reached out a hand and laid it on a charred log jutting from the burnt ruins. He would be back here in the morning to gather the ashes, ready for the casting.

Whatever ashes the Seven leave untouched at lea...

His thoughts trailed off as his eyes fell on the ash at the bottom of the pyre. There were handprints there, big sweeping waves in the grey powder, as though someone had grabbed up handfuls of the stuff and taken it away.

'You're too late,' a voice croaked. 'He's already gone.'

Talak stretched on his numb toes to peer over the pyre's debris. Ilgor sat there, a lonely bald head sitting atop a mound of white fur, his breath misting in the cold air. His face was blank, sad almost.

'*Ashan Tai.*' Talak offered a bow of the head, but he was unable to keep a hint of disdain from his voice. It was important to remind the lower caste where they stood in the great scheme. 'What do you mean, he's gone?'

Ilgor looked surprised. 'Radok. He's been and gone. Bagged up Jorn's ashes and set off for the Blackstone. That's why you're here, isn't it?'

'I'm here because the Will made it so. And now I know why. Have you raised the alarm?'

Ilgor shrugged. 'Why would I?'

Talak felt a surge of anger. 'Because it is forbidden for anyone but *Ashan Tay* to visit the Blackstone a second time. As you well know.'

Ilgor waved a hand dismissively. 'The man is dying, Talak. I'd be amazed if he lasted a week in his own tent, let alone walking the Whitelands. He has the lungrot.'

'You think that matters?' Talak's eyes burned with a righteous fury. 'You think your friendship with the Wolfeater outweighs the laws of the Will?'

Ilgor shrugged again. 'If it's the Will he be stopped, he'll be stopped.'

'Why do you think they sent me?' Talak sighed. 'You should have told someone, Ilgor. If he reaches the Blackstone, men will be looking for blood. And not just Grey Crow; every tribe for a thousand leagues will seek his end. It's an abomination.'

Ilgor smiled. 'What if it's not? What if it's *evolution?* The Wolfeater does the impossible, Talak. He has done it time and again for the Grey Crow, all in the name of the Seven. If anyone deserves a chance to stand at the Stone a second time, to ask them why they have cursed him so, it's the Wolfeater. Him, and the girl too. She gets to ask questions too, given the path they've made her walk.'

'The cripple too?' Talak's jaw tightened and he could feel the veins popping out of his neck as his rage intensified. 'No one has that right, you old fool! No one, save the *Ashan Tay*. You think killing a few men makes you something special?'

Ilgor pushed himself to his feet with a grunt of effort, his old joints creaking and popping. 'I had my doubts,' he said, as he started to move around the pyre towards Talak. 'But then I came here and I *sensed* it; I *sensed* the Will. This is *supposed* to happen, Talak. You must see it?'

'You *sensed* the Will?' Talak laughed scornfully. 'You've never heard them, have you, Ilgor? You've never woken to the sound of their voices bickering in your mind. You open your eyes and you *sense* what needs to be done. Sometimes you're right, sometimes you're wrong; the consequences small and insignificant.'

Ilgor stood before Talak now, almost a foot shorter, his winter grey eyes staring up into Talak's. Talak sneered down at him. 'You've never had to weigh up the arguments of Seven gods in an effort to find the right path. You've never held the fate of the tribe in your tiny hands. That's been my life for thirty years. But today is different. Today the song is pure and clear, and seven voices have become one.'

'One voice?' Ilgor's eyes widened, suddenly fearful. 'Do you know what you're saying?'

'One voice, one will,' Talak muttered to himself, turning from Ilgor and striding away.

'*Chadra*!' Ilgor called after him. 'It's the Black Wind you hear, not the Will!'

But Talak was already beyond hearing. And he knew what had to be done. *Radok must die.*

The hand had barely touched her shoulder before Jian was awake, knife drawn, blade tip pressed to her attacker's throat.

Only... there was no attacker. There was only Tess, as calm and unflinching as ever, unmoved by the blade at her throat. It was not the first time Jian had greeted her so, nor was Jian alone in sleeping with such a deadly partner. For some in the Grey Crow, it was the only way to survive.

'The elders are waiting,' Tess said calmly. 'They're gathering a hunt.'

Jian took a moment to wipe the sleep from her eyes. 'And what are we hunting?'

Tess's eyes flared with excitement. 'Not what, *who*. It's the Wolfeater, Jian. They want him dead.'

Jian's blood ran cold as the words sank in. She'd felt sick when she heard Radok had collapsed at Jorn's burning, but now this? What had happened that would turn the elders against him? Where was he going?

Before she could ask any of these questions though, or a dozen others flooding her mind, Tess was gone, disappearing behind the fabric hanging between Jian's room and the main tent. She rose quickly, dressing in her travel gear of leather leggings and tunic, fur lined boots, and the black bear pelt that was once her father's. Then Jian armed herself with her sword and bow, adding a couple of knives for good measure. Satisfied, she stepped from her room into the main tent.

Only the Long Eye was present, sitting cross-legged by the fire, long, bony fingers stretched out to the smouldering flames, warming herself. The old woman looked up as Jian entered, a knowing sparkle in her weary eyes. 'You can't save him,' she said, her voice cracking and creaking like an old tree. 'He seeks to break the laws of the Seven, and they can't let that stand.'

'I'll hear what the elders have to say,' Jian told her. 'Then I'll decide where I stand.'

'You stand with the Grey Crow, girl, as you always have.' The Long Eye sighed. 'Just remember one thing. The Wolfeater may have saved your life once before, as he has saved many others in his time. But he's a killer, through and through. Nothing you can say will change that. He's killed more men than you can count, and in his stubbornness more will die before his time is done.

'He dances with the Black Wind now, and all such flames burn brightest before the end. Make sure your flame isn't snuffed out with his, child.'

Jian nodded slightly, unsure what to say. Then she made to leave, crossing to the tent's exit. The Long Eye caught her wrist painfully and Jian looked down to where she sat.

'The elders are fools,' the Long Eye said, whispering as though she might be overheard. 'They'll do all they can to hold to the old ways. Rather, they'll do what they're told. Obey them where you can, but let not their words burn through your own knowledge.' She drew Jian closer, her putrid breath and yellowed snarl barely an inch from Jian's face. 'And beware Talak. He knows not what he is.'

She released Jian as suddenly as she'd grasped her, waving her hand dismissively. 'Go then. Go see what task the fine, brave men of the Grey Crow would set you next.'

Jian needed no further encouragement. She stumbled from the tent and set off into the light mist of early dawn, traveling along the camp's main thoroughfare. Abused and broken, Jian had found a sisterhood with the women of the Fallow, but she had never felt comfortable in the old woman's company. The Long Eye was given the name for a reason. She saw deeper and further into a woman's problems than anyone had the right.

Well she can keep her crooked nose out of my life, thought Jian. *There is only one person I would share it with... and now they want him dead.*

She pressed on for the Heart, the giant tent where the elders did their work. It was tough going. While a fresh layer of snow covered everything else, the paths along the way were churned to slushy mud, and more than once Jian almost lost her boots to the earth.

She heard the noise before she saw the tent. Hundreds of voices demanding to be heard, full of outrage and disbelief. Then the canvas hall reared up out of the mist, a vast round tent with a sloping roof, patched together from the hides of a hundred wild beasts, each patch marking its own story. The history of the Grey Crow was written there, in those tattered patches, and it never failed to swell Jian's pride.

How much of that history was written by the Wolfeater, she wondered? More, at least, than had been written by the fools now holding council beneath its roof. More, probably, than any living man. *And now they want him dead?*

Jian thrust herself into the tent without pause, fury driving her on. She found herself wading through a crowd of men and women, abuse hurled after her as she shoved past. She had never seen so many folk gathered in one place that wasn't a battlefield. There must have been half the tribe gathered there, eager to hear the Wolfeater's fate.

'We all know what Radok has done for the Grey Crow.' It was Lokar talking, hands held up for calm from the crowd. He was standing at the centre of the tent, the Heart's Fire burning behind him, sweat beading his bald head, his pointy beard seeming to grow greyer by the second. 'No man can question it. But does that give him the right to ignore the laws of the Seven?'

'No!' the cry rang out.

'And what does the law say of the Blackstone? A man may only touch it once, unless the Will flows through him. Radok had his chance and the Seven turned him back. Yet our friend, Talak, brings word that the Wolfeater sets out for the Blackstone once more.'

A cry of outrage from the crowd at this, along with murmurings of disbelief. 'Worse still,' Lokar went on, 'he takes a girl with him, so that she might stand the test herself.' More gasps of horror. 'Women are forbidden from the Blackstone for good reason. Their frames are too weak and too fragile to survive the Crossing. That's why they were blessed with the gift of life instead.'

Jian bit her tongue. *The old shit thinks the pain of childbirth a gift? I'd like to see him squeeze a boulder out between his legs! Then we'd see who is weak and fragile.*

'*That* is the Will,' the old fool continued. '*That* has *forever* been the Will. To break it is blasphemy.' He made a point of staring at the faces gathered before him. 'He must be stopped.'

Jian had stopped moving. With the crowd pressing in on all sides, it was impossible to get any closer to the Heart's Fire. She stood on her tiptoes to get a better look. The other elders, Hanuk and Graal, were sat huddled in their chairs off to Lokar's left, while Lokar himself pranced about before the fire, waving his arms like a performing bear.

Jian's eyes flickered to the man standing in the shadows behind them, his wild eyes dancing in the firelight. Talak played the part of a loyal servant of the Grey Crow, yet there he stood... holding the bear's leash.

'And why should we believe *him*?' called Jian, straining to be heard over the din. Lokar glared back at her, Hanuk and Graal shifting in their seats.

Talak stepped forward, half his face suddenly lit up by the orange light of the Heart's Flame. He rubbed a hand over his bald head. 'You don't need to believe me,' he said evenly, though Jian could feel the hatred behind his gaze. 'Ilgor will testify to Radok's intentions. You'll trust the *Ashan Tai*, won't you girl?'

'More than I trust you,' Jian muttered under her breath.

'Talak speaks the truth,' said an older voice, sagely wise. Pushing himself from the crowd near the front, Ilgor climbed onto the dais and stood beside Talak. *Ashan Tay* and *Ashan Tai* side by side, the two voices of the Will. Two voices that rarely spoke as one.

Ilgor pressed on. 'Radok is a sick man. Heavy with the lungrot. He feels the Seven have cursed him, despite serving them all his life. Now he means to reach the Blackstone. To stand before the Seven and ask them why.'

'The arrogant fool!' snapped Talak. 'The Seven have a plan for all of us, but the Eighth always finds a way.'

'I told him as much,' Ilgor said calmly. 'But only after I told him he had weeks to live... days even. I fear he was not himself after that. Anger has gotten the better of him.'

Jian caught a nod passing from Talak to Lokar, and the elderman stepped forward. 'Yet laws are laws, Ilgor. Without them, all is chaos. Without them... the Black Wind rises.'

Ilgor bowed his head. 'Laws are laws,' he sighed. 'But I would add one thing. Whatever is decided here, Radok is already dead. If the lungrot doesn't kill him, the journey will. It's not an easy task at the best of times, making the Blackstone, but this is the worst winter we've seen for a generation. In these cold, bitter days, the Whitelands earn their name more than ever.'

'Swear it,' said Talak, the *Ashan Tay* stepping up to stand face to face with the *Ashan Tai*. 'Swear that Radok will not reach the Blackstone and we'll leave him be.'

Ilgor considered this for a long moment. Talak stood there, towering over him, almost a head taller, yet the medicine man stared back unflinchingly. 'I cannot,' he said at last. 'This is the Wolfeater we speak of. For him, nothing is impossible.'

'Then he must be stopped.'

Lokar raised his hands and turned his focus back to the crowd. 'Who would volunteer for this honour? Who will fly for the Grey Crow and bring the Wolfeater home? Dead or alive, we must turn him back from this foolish quest. And when he does die, we will cast his ashes to the Seven as his legend demands - with a fire hot enough to burn this winter away!'

Hands went up amongst the crowd, more than Jian would have hoped, but no less than she should have expected. Radok's name carried more weight than most amongst his people, even as a born outsider. There would be great honour in being the one to bring him to his knees. Though the feeling would be bitter sweet for the tribe.

Tradition demanded seven names be picked out for the honour of serving the Will, and Lokar wasted no time picking out the Grey Crow's finest from the sea of hands that went up. Tess was first amongst them, deadly as she was with the bow. Then it was Garda and Talgar, veterans who had served with Radok many times over. Vinak, Ingram, and Dakar followed, all seasoned hunters, who, like Jian, had ridden with Radok just a day earlier. Even Pican, the youngest of the group, had made a name for himself as a hard man to kill.

Jian's stomach tied itself in knots as each name was called out. In his prime, Radok would have proven a challenge for even this group of hardened killers, but sick as he was, with a child weighing him down?

'And her,' Talak called out, and Jian watched in horror as his bony finger pointed her out. 'Jian Stormcrow.'

'You have your seven. I'll play no part in this,' she called back. 'I owe Radok my life.'

'Exactly!' the *Ashan Tay* hissed triumphantly. 'Why else would I choose you? You will be our witness, prove our purpose. You'll show there's no vendetta against the Wolfeater, no watering of egos for those that hunt him. We merely seek to uphold the laws of the Seven, to which the Grey Crow have held true for a thousand years.' He smiled fiendishly. 'To you, girl, I put a simple question. Where does your loyalty lie? With the Grey Crow, or with the man who betrays us?'

Jian felt her heart sink. The bastard had trapped her. She felt every eye in the tent fixed on her, daring her to side with the Wolfeater. *And if I do, they will tear me apart.* 'I am Grey Crow,' she said at last. 'And I fly where the Will commands.'

'Even if it means Radok's death?'

Bile rose in Jian's throat, but she swallowed it down. 'Even then,' she said. 'Always.'

CHAPTER EIGHT

The Boy from the Sea

It was a remarkable sight – the city of tents. Close to a thousand shelters littering the valley below, standing like small islands amidst the sea of mist rolling in from the western mountains, built in all shapes and sizes and crafted from animal hide and canvas. Senya could barely believe her eyes as she took it all in. It was hard to imagine that there was only one tribe down there, and that there were a thousand more just like it scattering the plains of Basilla.

Senya sank back on her haunches, deeper into the undergrowth of the copse of trees her and Mikilov were hiding in. Her throat was tight, her fingers bristling. He was down there somewhere, the Wolfeater. *Velimir's killer.*

'We should have moved last night,' she said with a heavy sigh. 'We might have had a chance slipping in unnoticed in the darkness, but now...?' Even if the mist held, the chances were slim.

'Peace girl,' Mikilov soothed, shifting his weight beside her. 'Do you know nothing about the Great Hunt? We watch, and we wait. Sooner or later, an opportunity will present itself.'

The big man pointed at the vast tent in the centre of it all, made up of three distinct chambers, each supported by its own giant mast. 'That one,' he said. 'That's where the Heart's Fire burns.'

Senya gazed at it curiously, noting how it seemed to eat the mist away, a thick column of smoke drifting free from a hole in one of the chambers. 'The Heart's Fire?'

'Each tribe has their own,' explained Mikilov. 'It's just a fire really, but it holds great weight for the Basillians. Every fire and torch in the camp is born from it, and they never let it burn out. Even when they move camp, somehow, they take the flame with them. If it ever dies... they say the tribe dies with it.'

Senya snorted at that. 'If it were that easy, I'd head down there with a bucket of water! I'd tour the whole bloody world and put out as many of their fires as I could!'

'If only it were that easy...' echoed Mikilov, a sad look in his eyes.

Senya eyed the great tent again, chewing her lower lip. What if it *was* that easy? What if she slipped down there in the dead of night and poured cold water all over their giant fire? Would that be the end of the Grey Crow? Would they fade away like the mist, never to trouble the Valor again?

Not all of them, Senya knew at once. *Not the Wolfeater.*

Her father once told her that some men were born to ride the storm, while others were crushed by it. There was no denying that the Wolfeater was such a man. Senya could still feel the power resonating from him, as she stood before him outside Velimir's cabin. He exuded an almost elemental force, and standing in his shadow, those piercing blue eyes staring back at her, Senya had felt like ice wilting in the sun. There was no shifting a man like that, fire or no fire.

'Here's a chance,' Mikilov whispered, guiding Senya's gaze. Nine figures had emerged from the giant tent, weighed down by heavy furs and thick pelts, trudging slowly north in single file. Women and children gathered to see them off, waving and kissing, while the men watched too, silent and sombre.

Senya frowned. 'Where do you think they're off to?'

Mikilov scratched at his beard and shrugged. 'Dressed like that, with no horses? Can only be north, into the Whitelands. *Frit* knows why though. There's nothing up there but death.'

'Should we follow? What if the Wolfeater is with them?'

Mikilov watched them for a while, dark eyes narrowed. 'He's not.'

'How do you know? Even black as he is, they all look the same from up here.'

'I've seen the Wolfeater scale walls in the blink of an eye; seen him tear through my friends - all good men, all good with a sword - yet I've seen him tear through them like a whirlwind. When you've seen a man do that, it's hard to forget how he moves. You can pick him out from a crowd, sure as night follows day. And believe me, I *wish* he was down there.' Mikilov took a deep breath. 'Better to face the nine of them than the whole bloody tribe.'

'Might be best I go alone...'

Senya had given it some thought and that was starting to feel like the wiser option. The Wolfeater was down there somewhere, with no idea of what was coming. Surprise was the only edge they had, and any slip would raise the alarm, killing their hopes of ending the bastard.

'You think you have it in you, girl?' Mikilov eyed her curiously. 'You think you can slip in there unnoticed? Think you can sniff out the Wolfeater's lair? Think you can kill him? Alone?'

'Doesn't take much to gut a sleeping Crow,' said Senya, 'and I reckon I'd have a better chance doing that alone than with you at my back. You're not as sharp as you used to be, Grey Wolf.'

Mikilov smirked at that, his curled lip revealing one of his sharp canines. 'And I suppose age makes fools of us all, eh, girl? It just depends on which side you're standing as to who seems the most foolish: the young or the old. I may be grey and long in the tooth, but I can still ghost when I need to. Right, Scar?'

There was a light touch on Senya's shoulder and she almost screamed. Jerking around in horror, she found the wolf's giant muzzle resting on her shoulder. His warm breath blasted her in the face, smelling of the blood and meat of a fresh kill. Scar's black eyes stared back at Senya, looking like pebbles set in snow and yet deep as a well. Without warning, the wolf licked Senya's face and then padded over to where Mikilov sat.

She watched a moment pass between the two of them, of a meaningful look and a silent conversation, then Mikilov turned to her. 'We're not alone,' he said.

They followed the wolf back through the trees, careful not to step on fallen branches or dried leaves, ducking under the overhanging foliage of the evergreens above. It was hard going for the most part, in the grey light of dawn the wood was a dark and brooding place, the air close and thick with the smell of the earth. Every step they took was slow and deliberate. So far they had managed to avoid the patrols circling the Basillian camp, but if Scar was leading them to such a group now, it seemed best not to warn them.

They reached a clearing some hundred yards into the small wood, but before they could take in the scene the wolf bounced forward into the open. Mikilov whistled for him to stop - a short sharp sound, more bird than man - but Scar ignored it, bounding on regardless.

Senya drew a knife, the blade hissing from its scabbard. Mikilov held a hand out to stay her, but she saw his grip tighten on the haft of his axe, the creak of his leather gloves almost deafening in the silence of the wood.

'That you, woman?' he called out, his voice echoing through the trees. Senya winced at the noise of it, half expecting an army of Grey Crow to burst into the clearing. She could see it now, opening out before her, an open patch of ground covered in a thick carpet of snow.

It looked like it might have lain there for a generation, that snow. Untouched, save for the heavy paw prints now marking its centre, every inch an ugly scar. Senya's gaze followed the tracks until they settled on Mikilov's great beast. He was lying on all fours, surprisingly calm after his charge, staring up at the stump of a gnarled oak...

Only it wasn't a tree stump at all, Senya realised suddenly. It was the hunched figure of an old woman dressed in grey rags and holding to a staff of twisted wood. Her matted, grey hair hung down over her face in wiry strands, and her weathered features looked old as the mountains themselves.

'Of course it's me,' she muttered in a hoarse, craggy whisper. She lifted her head, looked directly at Senya. Though her eyes were little more than yellowed-white orbs behind the tattered veil of her hair, it seemed to Senya they pierced straight through her, digging down to her soul. 'But who is this, leading you astray?'

'No one leads me anywhere,' said Mikilov, breaking into the clearing and striding to where the woman sat. 'This is Senya, Finn's girl.'

The old woman looked surprised. 'Finn? Now there's a name I've not heard for a long time.' She eyed Senya carefully, or at least it felt like she did, with those blind eyes of hers. 'He was a great man, your father. A true Valor. It must have been hard growing up in the shadow of such a legend. A tough name to live up to. Eh, girl?'

'I've never needed to live up to anything.'

'Of course not,' said the old woman, her voice suddenly growing more serious. 'Why else would you leave the safety of Haslova to trek about in the wilderness during such a bitter winter? Why else would you wander into Basillian lands on the trail of one of their greatest ever killers? Not because you're tired of your father's shadow, obviously. It must be because you're an idiot.'

Senya stepped forward, bristling. 'Easy, girl,' said Mikilov. He tried to put a hand on her shoulder, but Senya pushed him away.

'What do you know of it?' she stormed. 'You don't know my father and you don't know me.' She paused, the strangeness of the moment finally dawning on her. 'Who even are you?'

'This is the Wanderer,' said Mikilov. 'Sometimes called the Grey One, sometimes the Old Lady of the Wood.'

With a scoff, the old woman pushed herself to her feet, her joints popping with the effort. 'My name,' she sighed, offering a small curtsy, 'is Elgamire.'

Senya stared at her, open-mouthed. It was all she could do. Elgamire was a myth, a throwback to the old days, when folk believed the gods walked amongst them. And yet there was something in those strange, empty yet overflowing eyes that made Senya doubt herself. *'Impossible,'* she said at last.

Mikilov lifted her jaw with a finger, closing it and bringing her back to the moment. 'You get used to it,' he said with half a smile. 'This crank has been hounding my trail for years.'

'And I'll keep hounding it until you stop making a fool of yourself!'

'But you're a *god*!' Senya blurted out.

'No, girl, I'm not.' She looked at Senya afresh, a trace of fondness in her gaze. 'I am old though, so very old.'

'Too old to be out here,' said Mikilov, patting Scar ruefully on the head. 'To what do we owe the pleasure?'

'This is still Old Valirov, is it not? This is my realm and I come and go as I please. The real question is... what are *you* doing here?'

Mikilov bowed his head like a scolded child about to confess his sins. 'We've come for the Wolfeater,' he muttered.

'No,' said Senya, anger temporarily overpowering her disbelief. 'We're here for justice.'

'Justice is it?' The old woman raised her eyebrows. 'Justice for what?'

'Murder. The bastard killed my uncle, just as he has killed a thousand like him.' Senya jerked a thumb over her shoulder, back towards the treeline and the city of tents. 'He's down there somewhere, waiting for my blade.'

'*Murder.*' The old woman let the word hang in the air for a moment, testing its validity. 'Is it murder, killing to survive? That's what he does when he stalks the battlefield. The Wolfeater is no different to any true Valor.'

'No different! How can you say that? The man is a monster!'

The old woman sighed heavily. 'Spoken like a pup,' she muttered, turning to Mikilov. 'What about you, long tooth? Where do you stand?'

'I stand with the girl,' Mikilov told her without hesitation. 'Finn was my brother once, and Velimir too for that matter. Senya is the last of their kin. I'm duty bound to protect her.'

Elgamire laughed scornfully. 'And to do that you would ride down into the Grey Crow's nest?'

'I'd rather not. But she's going down there with or without me, and I won't let her go alone.'

'I'm standing right here,' said Senya, blushing. She was deeply moved by Mikilov's words, yet it was irritating beyond belief that they should talk about her as though she were a child.

'Indeed you are,' said the old woman, switching her gaze - those seeing yet unseeing eyes - back to Senya. It was a hard stare to live with and Senya licked her lips nervously. Every time those milky white eyes swung back to her, it felt like the weight of ancient wisdom might crush her. 'Tell me, girl, do you even know who it is you mean to kill?'

'Everyone knows the Wolfeater.'

'Everyone knows the *legend*,' said Elgamire. 'What about the man himself?'

'That he's a Basillian dog.' Senya was growing tired of the conversation. 'What does it matter?'

'Nothing at all.' Elgamire started to turn away, then turned back, a single raised eyebrow. 'Though... you do know he wasn't born Basillian? He was born on Agaron, a small island in the southern sea. That's why he has black skin. He is not diseased or accursed, he is merely different. His people herald from a distant land, where the sun burns brighter and hotter than you can imagine. Their dark skin protects them from that. The people of Agaron may have left the sun behind, but the skin will stay with them for generations to come.'

'What does this have to do with anything? I don't care what colour his skin is.'

That wasn't entirely true. Not entirely. There was no point denying that the man's skin had deeply unnerved Senya when she first stood before him. She had even been expecting it, for it was all a part of the Wolfeater's legend. He was the Black Crow, after all; the one who carried the Black Wind with him. To stand before him, they said, was death. Yet none of that had struck Senya's thoughts when she stood before him at Velimir's cabin, seeing that dark skin for the first time. She had only thought how strange it was, for a man to be marked so different, yet appear so natural.

'I don't care about his skin,' she echoed. 'It's his black heart that troubles me.'

'His black heart?' Elgamire shook her head incredulously. 'Let me tell you about his black heart! The Radok you know was born in the water. They found him washed up on the Silver Shores of the south, his frail arms clinging to a piece of broken timber, his legs tangled up in the silver seaweed that gives the beach its name. There was no other wreckage, no other bodies. Just the boy. He was no more than six years old at the time and the piece of wood he clung to was all that remained of his old life, everything else taken by the sea.

'Each Basillian tribe is different, but they all hunger for the same thing: fresh meat for their neverending wars. That's why they steal children. The young are easier to break, easier to shape and mould. *That's* why they took Radok. It didn't matter to the Grey Crow that he was different, that his skin was darker than any they had seen before. They cared only that he was brave and strong, and that his mind was keen for honing.

'It didn't matter that he was different,' Elgamire's eyes narrowed, 'or at least that's what they told him. But Radok was born to a different tribe - a different people - and on those rare occasions he forgot that, there was always someone ready to remind him. Always the outsider, he had to fight every day of his life to gain the respect of those born Grey Crow. It wasn't enough that he be the fastest, or the strongest, or the bravest. He had to be the best too. And so he is. He is the best of the best the Grey Crow have to offer. They worship him now as a hero, yet there are still those who wish to tear him down. He lives with that knowledge every day. Every time he strides into battle for those people, he knows there are those praying for him to fall.

'And yet there is still room,' the old woman's lip curled into a sneer, 'in his *cold, black heart* for those less fortunate. While Basillians have no time for the weak, spurning their crippled and broken, Radok saved a child born blind - even as her own father wanted her dead. The Wolfeater risked it all to stand for the broken girl. She lives with him still, raised as a daughter. And when the Black Wind finally sweeps him away, I would wager her grief for the Wolfeater will be no less than yours for Velimir.'

'Enough!' snapped Senya. 'I don't give two shits about the Wolfeater's blind hatchling, or that he was stolen as a babe! He has been killing my people for as long as I've lived. He killed my uncle and he would have killed me if I hadn't run.'

'Would he?' Elgamire's tone suggested she wasn't so sure.

'Of course he would!' Senya barked back. 'He's the Wolfeater! You claim to be the Wanderer? The Grey One? Elgamire? Then the Valor are your children. How many of us have to die before you consider him the enemy?'

Senya turned angrily to Mikilov. 'I'm done listening to this fraud,' she told him. 'I'm going down there with or without you. He has to die, Mikilov. I owe it to Vel.'

With that, she turned on her heels and stalked away, back towards the treeline overlooking the Grey Crow's camp. Her heart was heavy as she went. Perhaps the old woman was right. Perhaps there was more to the Wolfeater than the legend suggested. Back at Velimir's farm, he had said it was only the bison he wanted, perhaps he'd been speaking the truth? Until she killed his man and everything changed. Perhaps it was her fault Velimir was dead...

No, she shook her head forcefully, as though that might clear the doubts. *He is the Wolfeater. He killed my uncle. He would have killed us both, and burned the farm, if he'd had the chance. The bastard must die!*

'The girl has a point.' With a wave of his hand, Mikilov gestured for Scar to follow the girl and watch her. The wolf went willingly, only pausing long enough to nuzzle at Elgamire's side. The old woman patted him obligingly and off he went.

'You think that matters?' she asked, her voice betraying her own thoughts. 'This is about life and death, Mikilov. It's suicide to go down there, you must know that? The girl may be warped by thoughts of vengeance, but what's your excuse?'

Mikilov shrugged. 'You heard what she said. She's going down there with or without me. I can't let her go alone.'

'Then you'll die.'

Mikilov nodded. 'Then I'll die. Seems as good a place as any.'

'Well,' the old woman sighed, 'it won't be down there.'

'What do you mean?'

'He's not down there. He slipped from the camp last night, going south first but heading north. The party you saw earlier is a hunting party. They want the Wolfeater dead too.'

'What? Why didn't you tell us this earlier?'

'Because you needed to let him go - *she* needed to let him go. Radok's a dead man walking, Mikilov. There is a sickness in him that will kill him before long. That's why he travels north. He's going to one of their sacred places, deep in the Whitelands, where their gods hold council. He seeks answers for his condition, but revisiting the Blackstone goes against everything the Grey Crow believe. It has turned Radok's own people against him. They will stop at nothing to keep him from reaching that holy place.

'So, you see... if his illness doesn't kill him, the Whitelands will. And if not the Whitelands, then his own people.'

Mikilov rubbed at his tired eyes. 'Senya will never believe any of that. She thinks you're a fraud.'

'But you know better,' she said, smiling a weary smile. 'You need to convince her.'

'I'm not sure that I can.'

'And yet you must. Or let her go alone. If you follow her into the Whitelands... if you chase a dead man into that white abyss... one of you will die. And it won't be her.'

'And if I let her go alone, will she live?'

The sullen silence and bowed head were answer enough. 'I will try to talk her out of it,' he said. 'But if she goes, I go with her.'

'You'll do what you must, Mikilov, just as you always have.' Turning away, the old woman started back for the western treeline. She was leaning heavily on her gnarled staff as she shuffled away, her grey robes dragging through the snow that covered the clearing. She paused and glanced back. 'I will pray the day never comes when I have to remind you of this conversation.'

And then she was gone, the sound of her passing fading with her into the trees. There was a time Mikilov had tried to follow her, but she had an ability to disappear as swiftly and alarmingly as she appeared. It was one of the reasons he had no problem believing she was who she said she was.

He turned his back on the clearing himself, heading back through the trees towards their spot overlooking the Grey Crow camp. Senya was hiding back in the undergrowth, the only sound she made the gentle rasping of her blade on a whetstone. There were several hours to go before dusk and the girl was nervous. She sat like a ball of tension, waiting to explode.

Mikilov took one last look at the tents filling the valley below, thousands of them, as far as the eye could see. Not for the first time he imagined bringing back a horde of mounted Valor, to ride roughshod over the camp and crush the Grey Crow once and for all. *How many lives would be saved,* he wondered? *How many days of peace bought?*

But such an act would change the very nature of the Valor. They would become the aggressors, the murderers of women and children, of the sick and the old. And if it worked, and the Grey Crow were gone for good, there would be those who wanted to do it again. How many tribes would they have to kill before the Basillians stopped coming? And if the tribes learned what was happening, how long before they finally wiped Haslova from the face of the earth?

'We're leaving,' he said suddenly holding his hand out for Senya.

She gazed up at him angrily, her face dappled with sunlight as the day slowly brightened. 'I told you I'm not leaving until the Wolfeater is dead.'

'He's not here. He's heading north, for the Whitelands. That party we saw are out hunting for him. If you want to catch him before they do, we should go now.'

Senya looked dubious. 'She told you this? And why should we believe her?'

'Because she is Elgamire and she does not lie.'

'She's a fraud, Mikilov. The Wanderer is a myth, nothing more. That's just an old woman playing mind games with you.'

'Aye,' Mikilov replied calmly, 'I can see why you might think that. But you've not seen the things I've seen, Senya. This woman has dogged my life. I've known her since I was a boy, yet she has never aged. Her eyes are as useless as a bent blade, yet she *sees* everything. I've even walked a thousand miles since last I saw her, yet here she is, in the right place at the right time. Can you honestly tell me that's not a voice worth listening to?'

'Then let us say it's true, let us say she *is* Elgamire... you know what the stories say about those she sinks her claws into?'

Mikilov could only nod his head. They said the Wanderer would thrust greatness upon those she infatuated over. Greatness and torment. 'It doesn't matter,' he said. 'What matters is I believe her. The Wolfeater is not down there. He's heading north, to some sacred place for the Grey Crow. He's sick, and his own people want him dead. Either we leave them to it or we risk our lives and follow.' His gaze met Senya's. 'We're here because of you and I'll follow your lead in this. But if you mean to kill the Wolfeater, we follow him north.'

At last Senya took his hand and he pulled her up from the underbrush. She took a moment to dust herself down from dirt and snow. When she finally met his gaze again, Mikilov could see the steely determination running through the core of her. 'Even if I'm not the one to kill him,' she said softly, 'I have to see him die. I owe that much to Velimir. If you say he's going north, we'll go north. But I can't let him go.'

Mikilov nodded slowly. 'Fair enough. Scar, check the way, lad. We go north.'

The wolf moved at once, nose to the dirt as he searched out the best path. If there were Grey Crow close by, the wolf would sniff them out. He would choose the safest path for them to follow, a path safe from exposure, with lots of cover. This was what he was made for; the hunt his way of life.

Mikilov set out after him, Senya a step behind. 'Stay close,' he said over his shoulder. 'Scar will show us the way.'

PART II

BLOOD IN THE SNOW

CHAPTER NINE

The Promise

Radok paused in his stride and looked back, squinting through the swirling sleet. His tracks cut across the open plains of Basilla like a scar, the freshly churned snow shining silver in the moonlight as it snaked away into the darkness.

He held his gaze there for a while longer, watching for any sign of movement. At last, satisfied, he breathed a sigh of relief. *Nothing.*

'We'll be safe a while longer,' said a soft voice.

Surprised, Radok turned his head awkwardly, trying to see the source. It was the girl's voice, tired and weak, muffled into the fur cloak he wore. She was pressed against his back, her arms wrapped around his neck, his own looped under her legs, holding her in place. Exhaustion had gotten the better of her hours earlier and he was surprised to find her awake. 'What was that?' he asked.

'The Seven are with us,' she mumbled. 'We're safe for now.'

And then she was gone again, her head sagging back against his shoulder. Radok chuckled. He wished he shared the girl's confidence, but then he'd never had that kind of faith. Not even in the old days, when faith was all a man had.

The Seven won't help a man who don't help himself, Jorn used to say, and that was as true as anything out on the Whitelands. A man served the Seven as well as he could, but every kill he made was to keep himself alive. *Pious or faithless,* thought Radok, *the Black Wind takes us all.*

A cough struck then, viscous and gut-deep. Radok tried to brace himself against it, not wanting to shake the girl too much, but his broad shoulders quaked with the effort. He hawked and spat once the fit had passed, blood spattering the snow.

Perhaps that's what this illness was? A punishment for underestimating the Seven and their influence.

Only one way to find out. Wiping a gloved hand across his mouth to clear the bloody spittle, Radok began walking again, his eyes fixed on the horizon. The Blackstone was still a long way off, but it was out there somewhere. Waiting.

*   *   *

They reached the rocky outcrop as the sky began to darken, thick grey clouds rolling in from the north to slowly blot out the moonlight. Radok stretched his back and grimaced. If he was alone, he might have pushed on, eager to add more miles to the impressive amount already covered. But he wasn't alone, and he couldn't carry the girl another step.

His body ached too much. Every step felt like he was wading through water, his arms and legs heavy as stone. Even the girl, limp as she was, hung like a weight around his neck. It was all Radok could do not to drop her. He summoned his strength, shifted her weight slightly for a better grip, and trudged on for the rocks up ahead.

It was a vast outcrop, most of the stones tall, and thin, and sharp. They jutted from the earth like shards of ice carved from granite, weathered by a thousand years lived in the path of the Seven. Picking three slanting stones resting against each other, Radok squeezed his way in through a narrow fissure between them. He found a small cavern inside, sheltered from the wind and sleet running wild outside.

Radok tried to set the girl down, but she was plastered to him, their fur cloaks matted together and frozen solid where the girl had pissed herself. It took some effort to tear her free, but Radok finally laid her down against the wall, as far from the small opening as he could get her. The relief in the small of his back was almost instant and Radok slumped to the ground, exhausted.

To sleep is to die.

He couldn't remember who had told him that one, but it was as true as anything out on the Whitelands. Close your eyes out here, even for a moment, and there was a good chance the cold would kill you.

To sleep is to die.

With effort, Radok pushed himself to his feet and looked around. There was barely enough light to see anything in the small cavern, but he spotted a small pile of branches and logs stashed in one dark corner, whispering of hidden warmth.

'Seems we're not the first fools to call this place home,' he told Nyana, who slept on in silence.

The fuel was a good mix of logs and branches, straw and leaves for tinder, all bone dry. Radok gathered up a selection of each and wasted no time building a fire. As he worked, he found himself wondering about those who came before. How long ago was it? Would they be back this way?

Given how many times he had passed this way before, Radok was surprised he'd never found it himself until now. Perhaps it had been the hold of some Grey Crow from a different age? Or some other tribe, far from home? Perhaps it was a Wolf even, from back when this was their land?

Radok struck his flint over the tiny pyre, looking for a spark. 'Not that it matters,' he told the sleeping girl. 'No one has been in here for a dozen years or more. And those who follow us will have a *cold* night.'

A spark struck from the steel and fell onto the tinder, where an orange glow took hold. An instant later, flames burst through the dry leaves, licking at the kindling. 'Not us though, Little Sparrow.' He bent closer to the fire, blew softly on the smouldering fuel until the flames began to eat into the kindling. Then the fire burst into life and Radok smiled. 'Tonight, we sleep like the Wolves in their stone houses. Safe and warm.'

Radok dragged the girl closer to the flames, enough so that she would benefit from the warmth without the risk of rolling in. Then, pulling his hood into place, he eased himself back out through the opening and stepped into the cold air outside.

After the cramped, smoked filled air of the cavern, the freshness outside hit Radok like a slap to the face. He breathed it in deeply, watching the flurries of snow dance to the tune of the wild winds howling and raging amongst the rocks. He smiled. Snowfall was good. In an hour their tracks would be completely buried, lost to anyone giving chase.

He turned back to study the cavern entrance. The orange light of the fire could be seen flickering on the sloping walls of the opening, but it was only a soft hue, most of the light contained by the shape of the shelter and the placement of the fire. Still, in the dead of night, even a faint light would stand out like a beacon in the sweeping blackness of the Basillian Plains. There wasn't much Radok could do about that, but at least the other rocks in the formation provided some additional cover. Chances were, someone would have to stumble into the outcrop themselves to spot the light, and by then it would be too late to do anything about it but fight.

And I can't fight without sleep, thought Radok, his eye lids feeling suddenly heavy. He looked back to the growing blizzard, how it swayed and whirled in the wind. 'Do what you will!' he called to the Seven. 'I'll find my way to you, one way or another!'

The Seven were listening, it seemed, for the words had barely left Radok's mouth when the gods stole his breath away. He began coughing as he gasped for air, a dry rasping cough from deep in his core. *You will pay a price for that vow*, a voice whispered in Radok's mind, and all he could do was cough, and hack, and retch.

He staggered back through the opening and made his way towards the light and warmth of the cavern, one hand pressed to the smooth surface of the leaning rock to hold him up, the other covering his mouth, as though that might keep his guts from spilling forth...

Radok's vision began to blur, his lungs burning from a lack of air, yet he stumbled on regardless. He could see the fire now, bobbing up and down before him, a glowing orange blob beckoning him on.

Is that blood...?

Before he could find the answer, the ground shifted beneath his feet and Radok fell hard. He tried to lift his head, eyes still straining in the direction of that orange glow. He watched in horror as the passageway to the cavern grew longer and longer, until at last only darkness remained.

He woke sometime later, warmth in his cheeks. When he opened his eyes, he saw he was lying beside the fire, the flames bright and hot against the empty darkness of the cavern. He was still bundled up in his heavy furs, almost too hot for comfort, and with a groan of effort he pushed himself to a sitting position and glanced around.

Nyana sat opposite, holding a cooking pot over the open flames, the smell of stew filling the cavern and making Radok's stomach grumble.

'How long was I out?' he asked, rubbing the sleep from his eyes. His back ached and he could feel crusted blood around his face. The bitter taste filled his mouth, the smell ripe in his nostrils.

'Two hours,' the girl replied. 'No more than that. It's still dark.'

Radok stared across the fire into the girl's empty eyes, watched them glowing like molten lava in the firelight. It still amazed him, the things she could do. She knew he was awake before he did. Even in the black void of her world, she knew when the sun rose and when it fell. She had the nose of a fox and the ears of a wolf. Sometimes it seemed the Seven had gifted her almost as much as they had cursed her. Radok shook his head. *Such is the Will.*

He glanced back along the passageway leading into the cavern, where he remembered falling. It was quite a distance. Ten yards at least. 'Did you drag me here?'

'I tried,' said Nyana, lower lip quivering, 'but you were too heavy. You dragged yourself in the end, moaning and muttering.'

Radok nodded. He'd seen such things himself in days gone by. A man, broken by exhaustion or crippled by wounds, dragging himself to safety through pain and delirium, against all the odds. 'The need for survival can be a powerful friend,' he told her. 'I'm sure you helped, though.'

The girl surged to her feet, leapt over the fire and threw herself into Radok's arms. 'I'm so sorry!'

Radok held her close, one arm holding him upright, the other wrapped around her. 'Oh, Little Sparrow. What do you have to be sorry for?'

'Sorry for being weak,' she said, her little body shaking with sobs. 'I didn't want to slow you down. I didn't want you to carry me all this way. I'm sorry!'

Radok pulled back from the girl, holding her at arm's length. He gazed into her eyes, though he knew she couldn't gaze back into his. Those pale orbs were as blank as ever, but the soul was there, the heart and wonder you could find in any child's eyes.

'You're not weak, child. You've barely had eight summers in this world, yet here you are, side by side with the Wolfeater. You know how many folks would have chosen to walk the Whitelands with me? Folk with eyes, no less? None. Just you.'

And I never should have agreed. Should have left you back home... should leave you now, let the hunting party find you. They might even let you live...

But instead he went on. 'I've got forty years on you, Little Sparrow. I have a man's strength and the use of my eyes to help me along. And I've walked this path before. You're not too heavy a burden I can't carry you awhile, when you need to rest your legs.'

'You promise? You promise you won't leave me behind?'

'The thought never crossed my mind,' Radok lied.

He looked around, found his travel bag beside the fire and delved inside. He produced a small knife from within, no more than a jagged piece of iron really, with a smooth bone handle well worn by years of use.

'Here,' he said, drawing the blade across his palm, cutting just deep enough to draw blood. Then he took hold of Nyana's hand and pressed her fingers to the wound. 'You feel that?'

'You're cut,' she gasped, her fingers gently tracing the wound.

'Now you.' Radok grabbed her hand and flipped it over. He paused a moment, waiting for her face to rise expectantly. Then he sliced a small cut in the girl's palm. She winced at the pain, but she never pulled her hand away nor let out a sound. She took it like someone twice her age. She took it like the Crow she was.

Radok pressed her palm to his, closed his big meaty fingers around her delicate hand. 'Now we are bound by blood,' he told her. 'I am your father; you are my daughter. I'll not leave you behind. No father would.'

'Mine did.'

There was truth in that, but the greater truth lay in the quiver of her voice. Nyana had only ever known one father... and now she knew he felt the same.

'It takes more than planting the seed to raise the crop,' said Radok. 'And I'm not him. We'll reach the Blackstone together, you and I. Or we'll die in the effort. That's my promise to you, Little Sparrow. I vow it to the Seven and the Eighth.'

Nyana pulled her hand free of Radok's and threw her arms around his neck once more. They held each other for a long time, the silence of the rocks broken only by the popping fire.

Together or not at all. Radok shook his head at the idea of it. *You stupid old fool!*

'Radok!'

The cry echoed off the stone walls, dragging him back from a deep sleep. He sat up groggily, arms and legs still aching from the previous day's work. The fire was burning low, most of the fuel gone up in smoke.

'Radok!' His name hissed this time, urging him outside.

Radok pushed himself to his feet with a groan of effort and made his way to the cavern entrance. Nyana was standing there, silhouetted against the soft grey sky of predawn, heavy furs rippling in the breeze. Beyond her, the snow continued to fall and a thick, white blanket now shrouded the landscape.

Radok cursed softly, angry that he'd let the girl wake before him. She was the one who needed to rest. She was already slowing him down and the journey to the Blackstone was only going to get harder.

'How long have you been awake?' he asked.

She ignored the question, instead pointing south, back the way they came. 'They're coming.'

Radok shielded his eyes and gazed off in the direction indicated, barely able to see anything through the swirling snow. He knew better than to doubt the girl though, who had a talent for knowing such things. Another of her gifts...

He laid a hand on Nyana's shoulder. 'You sure?'

'You'll see,' she said.

And he did. For a brief moment the wind shifted just long enough to glimpse beyond the snowfall, like peering through a tear in the veil. Radok saw a line of black dots slowly winding their way down the side of a vast hill on the distant horizon, like soldier ants marching down a mountain of sugar. Around ten he counted, before the wind shifted again and the tear closed.

'Half a day,' he muttered. 'Less, if they're eager.'

'Who would be eager to face the Wolfeater?'

Ah, the faith of the young! Radok smiled. 'They'll have been promised their weight in gold to catch us,' he said, 'let alone the glory they'll get for ending the Wolfeater. And all for killing a dying man and a blind girl.' Radok laughed bitterly. 'They'll be fighting each other to be the first to reach us.'

'Not all of them,' said Nyana, but Radok had already turned away.

'Get your things, Little Sparrow, we need to move. And remember our agreement. What I say, when I say. You'll be up on my shoulders and there'll be no complaints. Make your peace with it.'

CHAPTER TEN

Loyalties

They reached the stone outcrop as the sun reached its zenith. Not that you could *see* the sun, just a smudge of light burning through the veil of thick, grey cloud overhead. Jian watched the snow falling heavily around them, swirling about in a maelstrom of cold wind that came howling through the rocks from the north.

'They were here,' said Talgar, emerging from the cavern with a flaming torch in hand. 'The ashes are still warm.'

'Then we can catch them,' said Talak, a gleam of triumph in his eyes. 'Let's move!'

Jian ignored him. She grabbed the torch from Talgar's hand and ducked into the shelter of the leaning rocks. She ignored Tess too, who called after her like a concerned mother. *Let them wait. Radok deserves a little more time.*

She had taken only a few strides over the threshold of the shelter when the torchlight caught something on the ground, dark and glistening. As she knelt, Jian pulled a hand from one of her gloves and reached out. When she drew it back, her fingers were sticky with congealed blood. Her heart sank at the sight of it. Radok's blood, she had no doubt. It was true then. The Wolfeater was dying.

'I'm sorry, old man,' she muttered into the darkness. *What a shitty waste.*

'Did you find what you were looking for?'

Jian rose sharply, turning on her heels and bringing the torch to bear. Talak was standing behind her, his wild eyes bright in the torchlight. 'What are we doing here, *Ashan Tay*?' she asked him. 'What's the point of it all?'

Talak took a step closer, his top lip curling into a sneer as his eyes narrowed. 'What's the point? It's the Will, girl! The law of the Seven! No man can touch the Blackstone a second time. None save *Ashan Tay*. That has been the Will for as long as men could walk.'

'Things change,' said Jian. 'There was a time no one touched the Stone. A time before the Grey Crow, the Empty Faces, or the Broken; a time before any of the tribes were born. Someone must have been the first.'

Talak glowered at her. 'Aye. And *he* was *Ashan Tay. He* set the law because that was the Will, child. We question that, we question the Will. And if we question the Will... the Black Wind rises.'

Jian shook her head. It was hard to believe there could be so much fear in a man of Talak's faith. 'You fear the impossible,' she told him. 'You've gathered the finest hunters the Grey Crow can offer and set us the task of killing an old man already walking the road to death.' She thrust her fingers under Talak's nose so that he could see them in the torchlight. 'Look at his blood, Talak. Smell it! Radok is done. The blind girl he takes with him is done. We'll never see them again. So, *what's the point?*'

Talak stared at her for a moment before answering, perhaps letting his anger settle. 'What was it your friend, Ilgor, said? Ah yes! "This is the *Wolfeater* we speak of. For him, *nothing* is impossible." If it's true he's dying, then he has been touched by *Chadra*, and the Black Wind follows wherever he goes. If such a man touches the Blackstone, where the Will of the Seven is born into this world, who is to say what might happen? Perhaps that is all that's needed for the Black Wind to assert his power. And then what, girl? What if the Blackstone falls and the Eighth becomes the Will? When death reigns, do you have the power to stop it?'

Jian almost laughed at that, but she could see the fear in Talak's eyes. 'Everyone dies, *Ashan Tay*. The Black Wind stalks us all from the moment we're born, waiting for his time. That has never stopped the Grey Crow from touching the stone before.'

Talak raised an eyebrow, eyes glistening with the gleam of madness. '*You* would lecture *me* on the workings of the Seven? You think you know more about the Eighth than Talak Thunderhead?'

I grow tired of this, thought Jian. It seemed she had spent her life arguing with fanatics. *No more,* she decided. *Let the mad fool say what he must. The sooner he's done, the sooner we can leave this place.*

'You speak it true,' Talak droned on. 'There can be no life without death. The Black Wind is always there, lurking in the shadows, waiting for the moment to strike. It is the flame of life that holds him back, the warmth and light keeping him at bay. Yet all it takes is for the flame to flicker, even for a moment, and the Black Wind will snuff it out.' Talak's eyes narrowed. 'And Radok's flame flickers, girl, you can be sure of that. He is nothing more than a candle in a storm.'

And some candles can burn the world before they're done, thought Jian, though she kept it to herself. She was done arguing. Meeting Talak's gaze, she felt the anger and contempt flowing through him. He was such a small man, bitter and twisted, like a weed growing in the shadow of a great oak. He lacked the passion and charisma of a man like Radok. Yet the Grey Crow had chosen to follow him, in turn abandoning the man who had fought and bled beside them, who had lifted the tribe to new heights. They had found Radok in the ruins of a shipwreck, and now it seemed they were all too happy to throw him back.

'I will kill Radok,' she said after a moment, 'if you tell me that is the Will. But it only weakens the tribe, Talak. It will cut the heart and spear the soul of the Grey Crow. The Wolfeater is the best of us. When he dies, a part of us all will die with him. Even you, *Ashan Tay.*'

Talak considered her words for a long moment, fixing her with his wild eyes. Then he smiled and shrugged. 'It is the Will. Radok must die.'

The girl awoke with a start, just as Talak knew she would. Now that the Seven had settled their arguments, he could hear the voice of the Will as clear as if the gods were standing beside him, whispering in his ear. They had told him exactly where to be and when to be there. And they were right.

Her eyes searched the night desperately, seeking whatever horrors she had woken from, or at least trying to find something familiar to quell the fear. *You'll find both right here, girl. The monster and the haven.*

When she sighted him in the darkness, a crooked figure highlighted by the campfire, her eyes widened in surprise and fear. Talak held a finger to his lips. *Silence!* Then, turning the finger to her, he gestured for her to follow. *Come!*

She hesitated a moment, glancing down at Jian, who lay asleep beside her, their arms and legs a tangled mess. Then she began to work herself free, moving carefully so as not to disturb her lover.

Good, thought Talak. *That's good.*

He turned on his heels and walked away, leaving behind the three fires that made their camp in favour of the dark shadows of the surrounding trees. The other Grey Crow lay scattered about the fires sleeping, but Talak weaved a path through them with ease, guided by an unseen hand.

The pine wood where they had made their camp was almost silent, though the boughs of the trees creaked heavily under the weight of snow bearing down on them. Talak could hear the faint trickle of a stream in the distance.

He made his way towards the sound, stepping carefully over tree stumps and fallen branches. Every step felt instinctive, but Talak knew they were guided by the Will.

The narrow stream was only shallow, perhaps an offshoot of the Velga, trickling south. It was so cold the water was frozen in places, snow settling on the surface and chunks of ice drifting by. It smelled good. It bore the fresh, crisp scent of winter, carried all the way from the Whitelands, fresh enough to cut through the damp rot of the woods.

Talak stood at the riverbank and waited. Before long, he heard the girl moving up behind him and turned to face her. She was younger than he remembered, little more than a girl really. Big doe eyes looked out from the shadows of her hood, glinting in the moonlight. Her skin was almost as pale as the snow, though it was more likely from fear than from the cold. Talak appreciated that. It meant the girl had a healthy respect for the Seven and for those who served them.

He offered the girl a nod in greeting, a respectful gesture to help ease her in. 'Greetings, Tess.'

The girl offered a bow of the head back, though her eyes averted from Talak's gaze. 'What can I do for you, *Ashan Tay*?'

Talak took a moment before answering. 'Which of the Seven favours you, girl? Do you know?'

'*Dacra*,' she answered, no hesitation.

Talak nodded thoughtfully. He had known the answer before he asked the question, but there was no need for the girl to know that. It helped too that *Dacra* was the best answer she could have given, for any *Ashan Tay* worth his blood knew those driven by *Dacra*, the wind of love, were the easiest to bend to the Will.

'And Jian is the one you love?' he asked.

The girl shifted uneasily from one foot to another. 'She means a lot to me, yes.'

'Then it would concern you to know the elders question her loyalty to the tribe?'

At last the girl found the courage to meet Talak's gaze, her eyes flashing with anger. 'They're wrong. Jian would die for the Grey Crow.'

'She may indeed, if I cannot convince the elders she serves the Will. Tell me of her relationship with the Wolfeater.'

The girl looked confused. 'He saved her life... but that was a long time ago.'

'Ah, yes,' said Talak, remembering. 'She was the one who lost the child.'

'She didn't *lose* anything,' the girl said, her face flushing red. 'Her man, Grava, beat her near to death and the babe died as a result. She killed him in self-defence and ran for her life.'

Talak nodded understandingly, masking his own anger. 'And Radok killed the hunting party, men with families of their own, doing their duty for the tribe, seeking truth and justice.'

'The only justice they sought was Jian's head.'

Which would not have been enough, thought Talak, though he managed to hold his tongue. No point arguing the laws of the Seven with one of the Fallow. They seemed to think the loss of their wombs and the protective wing of the Far Eye set them apart, but the Seven would find them all eventually, as sure as if they were blades of grass in an open field. *Even mountains crumble before the Will. It is only ever a matter of time.*

'So, the Wolfeater saved her, and now she hunts him. You see my dilemma, girl? When the time comes, how can I be sure she will do what needs to be done?'

'She is Grey Crow,' the girl answered. 'She will do whatever the tribe needs.'

Talak was silent for a moment, the quiet disturbed only by the trickle of the stream and the rush of the wind as it cut through the trees around them. Talak stepped in closer to the girl, his voice low. 'And what will you do if she is not what you think she is?'

The girl gazed back evenly, her eyes fearful yet defiant. *Almost too defiant,* thought Talak, suppressing a smile. *Like she knows which way Jian will go.*

'Whatever the Will demands,' she said after a moment, her voice solemn. 'I will do whatever the Will demands.'

'Then let us hope Jian's faith holds as true as yours.' Talak nodded back the way they had come, towards camp. 'Go then. Tomorrow we will take the Wolfeater, dead or alive. Best you get some rest before then.'

The girl needed no second invitations. She turned on her heels and scuttled away. Talak watched her go, her slender figure weaving a path back through the trees, until he lost sight of her amongst the shadows surrounding the distant campfires.

Talak felt a wave of relief wash over him as he watched the girl go. The din he had once thought beautiful, which he'd somehow mistaken for the song of the Will, seemed to follow the girl away, and a sudden stillness filled the air around Talak. The woods fell silent in the sudden calm, and even the faint trickle of the stream grew muted.

Talak glanced up at the trees and waited. It only took a moment for him to see it. A powerful breeze blew in from the north, the trees rustling in its wake, bending slightly towards Talak. *As we all must bend to the Will.*

Then the gust hit him, and he staggered back. It was *cold*. Colder than any wind Talak had felt before; cold enough to catch his breath. And the message it carried was loud and clear.

The girl must die.

Talak smiled. It was not Tess the voice wanted dead, he knew, but Jian. *If only it were that simple...* Bowing his head into the wind, he dropped to a knee, his fur cloak whipping about him in a fury. 'The men like her,' he called out. There was no fear he might be overheard, for he knew the Will would wash away his words long before they reached unworthy ears. 'They respect her, Radok saw to that. If I make a move against her, there is a good chance it will cost me my life.'

The wind struck him again, staggering him back another step, this time the falling snow sharpened into needles of ice that bit into Talak's flesh. *Then test her,* the voice said. *Let the Grey Crow judge her worth.*

And then the wind was gone, the last of it crashing past Talak and sweeping south, leaving the snow to resume its gentle fall, landing softly, unchallenged.

Talak felt a deep sense of emptiness settle upon him in the quiet that followed. It was a strange feeling to be left alone, the desires of the Seven resting on your shoulders. Always there had been a guiding hand, a chatter of voices to help him choose the right path. No more, it seemed. Now, there was no choice involved. The Will had laid the path before him and it was up to Talak to see it done. *One voice, one Will.*

The Will. Talak could still remember the first time he heard it, standing at the Blackstone as a boy. He smiled at the memory. The Stone itself had seemed so small and insignificant after everything that came before.

They had to battle their way through the elements to reach it, battered every step of the way by the very worst the Whitelands could throw at them. Then they climbed the *Käda,* known to the southerners as the Last Rock, a vast mountain sitting alone in the white wasteland.

Talak's fingers had bled that day. He lost three toes and two friends by the time he reached the summit. Even then, there was worse to follow. At the summit the peak lay ahead of them, accessible only by the slimmest of ridges, flanked on either side by a drop of hundreds of feet down to cold, jagged rock and certain death.

The Blackstone lay at the other end of this ridge, standing no more than ten foot tall; a needle of black rock jutting from the ground like a tooth. In every other way the Stone was unremarkable, save that it stood in the centre of a vast cave mouth, like a sentinel standing guard. The cave itself was something else entirely; a chasm of darkness that opened on the mountain top, yet fell away deep into the mountain's core, and from its mouth it seemed all the wind in the world spilled forth, roaring around the Stone and hammering at those who had dared to climb the mountain.

'Time to test your mettle against the Will,' Calimon had said, their guide on the journey. He had to shout to be heard over the cacophony of the wind. 'Walk the ridge and touch the Stone, and you will find your place in the All Song.'

Though it was no more than twenty strides long, it had taken Talak almost an hour to cross the ridge. Even before he stepped onto it, he had watched two of his friends swept from the path by the sheer force of the Will, their fragile bodies shattered on the rocks far below. Still, he held his nerve and stepped out.

The wind buffeted him from every side, the brunt of it striking him face first, like a relentless scream of defiance bellowed out by the cave. Talak had leaned into that scream, edging himself forward. Every step he took was marred by crumbling rock, or threatened by slick ice.

Yet inch by inch, the Blackstone grew closer. Talak could feel the eyes of his peers and their *Ashan Tay* guide fixed on him, willing him on, but he dared not look back. He knew that would mean death for sure.

He dived the last few paces, landing at the foot of the Blackstone. In the shelter of the Stone, the wind never touched him. He could hear it, bellowing all around him, and he could even *see* it, whipping around the Stone, given form by the snow and dust caught in its stream. But the pain and numbness that came from the incessant battering of the wind subsided almost at once.

He pushed himself to his knees and peered up at the Blackstone, now within arm's reach, seeing it with fresh eyes. Up close, he could see the Stone's surface was almost smooth, yet there were thin tendrils of white cutting through it like veins through flesh. Without knowing what he was doing, Talak removed the glove from his right hand and reached out.

His bruised and battered fingers pressed softly to the Stone, the palm close behind. And then his world had changed...

Forty years on, Talak could no longer remember *how* life had changed, only that it had. The Stone was warm to touch, he remembered that. Despite the setting - so deep in the Whitelands that a man's piss would freeze the moment it left his cock - somehow the Stone was *warm*. It had made *him* feel warm.

Yet that was nothing compared to the change in the wind. In an instant, what was once a meaningless rush of sound became a song, rhythmic and beautiful. And when he listened closely enough, Talak could actually hear *their* words weaving through it; the words of the Seven, giving voice to the Will.

They had been with him ever since, the Seven and the Will. Until now. And in the silence they had gifted him, Talak began to understand the truth of faith. It worked both ways. All his life, he had put his faith in the Seven and in return they had shown him the way. Now, suddenly, *they* had shown their faith in *him*, trusting that he would find the way himself.

Talak smiled. It was a liberating feeling, to be free of their constant bickering; to know what had to be done without being led there by the hand. With that thought, chest swelling with pride, Talak made his way back towards the campfires.

Circling the fires and the sleeping bodies to the left, he stopped beneath a tall tree looking out over the northern plains. Talak gave a short, low whistle and waited... until the branches overhead began to move drastically, and a massive figure swung down to land beside him. Dakar was a big man anyway, but in his furs he looked like a bear.

'What is it, *Ashan Tay*?' he asked, his booming voice tamed to a whisper.

'I take it you saw us?' Talak kept his own voice low, glancing furtively in the direction of the fires.

'I saw you and the girl move away.' The big man shrugged. 'Didn't seem any business of mine, so I left it at that.'

'A wise choice.' Talak leaned in a little closer. 'The girl has raised concerns about Jian's loyalty to the cause.'

Dakar raised an eyebrow. 'Tess said that?'

Careful, Talak. This is not their first hunt together, but it is yours. 'It's not so much what she said,' he said smoothly, 'but what the Seven whispered between the words.'

'I wouldn't worry about Jian, *Ashan Tay*. She's never had it easy, but she's Grey Crow to the core. I'll vouch for her, if that's what you need?'

'Oh, I believe you.' Talak offered a wry smile. 'But the Seven need more than words, Dakar. Jian owes Radok a life debt, and that's hard to turn your back on at the best of times. She's already spoken out in defence of him. Who knows what she'll do when the time comes?'

'She'll do as the Will commands.' Dakar met Talak's gaze and sighed. 'She's here, isn't she? What more does she have to do?'

'She has to prove herself.' Talak paused for a moment, pretending to rub at tired eyes. 'I know you like her, Dakar. By the Seven, I like her myself! But if she betrays us, it will be at the last possible moment, when the damage will be at its greatest. We can't let that happen.'

After a long moment, Dakar shook his head and rolled his eyes, resigned. 'What must I do?'

'On the morrow, when we come to ride, you will challenge me. You will argue that Radok is already dead and it would be a waste of life to pursue him. You will argue convincingly.'

'That won't be hard,' said Dakar, 'I half believe it already.'

'As does Jian. Knowing she has you on her side may convince her to make a move against me... against the Seven. If she does, then we end her. If not, then we'll know she can be trusted and all will be forgiven.'

'And what if everyone else throws in with me and Jian before you get chance to reveal it was all just a test?'

One voice, one Will.

Talak smiled. 'Have a little faith, boy.'

*   *   *

'And what did you say to that?'

Tess lifted her head from Jian's chest and gazed up at her. 'I told him I would do whatever the Will demands.'

Jian felt her tensions ease a little. 'Very wise,' she said softly. Her hand caressed Tess's back, fingers running through the fur blanket draped over the pair. 'Talak is a dangerous man, Tess. The Long Eye tried to warn me about him, but I didn't listen. There is something... wrong with him.'

'What did she say?'

'She said he has no idea what he is.'

Tess looked suddenly fearful. 'What if he plans to kill you?'

'If he could kill me, I'd be dead already.' Jian's gaze drifted back to the campfire beside them, crackling and popping in the silence. 'He can't kill me for the same reason I can't kill him. The group has too much respect for us both. I've earned it through the blood we've shed together, he's earned it as *Ashan Tay*. It makes anything that follows... unpredictable.'

'Then what will he do?'

Jian took a moment to consider the question. 'If he wants to kill me, he'll need to break the respect first. He'll try to make me look small in front of the men; probably with some kind of test.' She nodded at the thought. 'A test of loyalty.'

'I'll kill him now,' said Tess, attempting to surge to her feet. Jian dragged her back down.

'You'll do no such thing.'

'I don't care what they do to me. It would be worth it just to see the surprise on his face as I run my blade through him. He doesn't even have the respect of the wind that comes out his arse, much less the Seven!'

Jian laughed at that. 'Stupid girl,' she said, kissing Tess's forehead. 'You may be right about him, but not everyone feels the same. Give him no reason to doubt you. And the next time you find yourself alone with him, just give him what he wants.'

Tess let her head fall gently to Jian's chest, where she rose and fell with Jian's breathing. 'He wants you, Jian,' she said after a long moment. 'He has always wanted you.'

Jian closed her eyes and let her breathing deepen. Tess was right, of course. Jian had felt the old man's eyes raking her body on more than one occasion, even when her man was still alive. Not that Talak did much to hide his desires. As *Ashan Tay*, he seemed to think he could have whatever he wanted.

That Jian had refused his blessing on the day of her marriage only made matters worse. No one ever spurned the blessings of the *Ashan Tay*. No one.

I told you what would happen, Talak had said the day the babe died. *I warned you that* Chadra *would seek him out. Next time you will beg for me to lay with you!*

Squeezing her eyes tighter, Jian felt tears rolling down her cheeks. There had never been a next time, not for her. No man wanted to lay with a husband-killer. And even if they did, the babe's death had cost Jian her womb. There would be no more children for her. No more men, for that matter. She'd had her fill.

'He knows where I am,' she whispered into Tess's ear, 'if that's what he wants. And I hope he does. For the one-eyed snake knows no tougher prey than what lies between my legs!'

She felt Tess smile at that, and they hugged each other tightly, until they fell asleep, locked in each other's arms.

Jian awoke with the dawn, dragged from sleep by the high-pitched call of a bird echoing down from the heavens. She glanced up to see three silhouettes wheeling majestically overhead, their great wings flapping effortlessly through a calm, clear sky. Grey crow, of course, watching over their kin.

She relaxed then, watching the birds soar overhead, her grip slackening on the bone-handled dagger she'd pulled from beneath her blankets.

Tess was beside her a few moments later, thrusting a hunk of toasted bread and a slice of salted beef under Jian's nose, along with a flask of steaming water to wash it down. Grunting her thanks, Jian made short work of the offerings. It was a lesson hard learned over the years in the wilds, but this close to the Whitelands nothing stayed warm for long.

All around the small camp, men were beginning to rise. Jian ran her eyes over them. She saw Pican dunk his head in a bowl of hot water, and when he emerged he looked like a demon of old, steam rising from him like smoke from the flesh. She watched Dakar clearing his throat of what seemed an inhuman amount of phlegm, and she saw Talgar yawning and stretching and then...

...Talak, standing in the midst of it all, dark and brooding, ominously silent. He pulled his hood clear and turned his face to the heavens, his arms rising at his sides. The hunters fell silent as they watched him, drawn into a circle around him. Even Jian, pushing herself to her feet and pulling her fur cloak into place, joined them in the circle. She watched the *Ashan Tay* with a growing sense of unease.

'The wind,' whispered Tess, her hand slipping into Jian's as she stepped alongside her. 'It's not touching him!'

Jian's eyes narrowed as she took a closer look. The wind moved all around them, rustling through the treetops overhead, snapping and flapping through cloaks, and hoods, and jackets, and hair. It came howling through the trees and battered at the party from every direction. Yet Talak stood unmoving in the centre of it all, as though he alone marked the eye of the storm. Jian would not have believed such a thing, were she not seeing it with her own eyes.

Tess is right. Not a single hair on his head dances to the song.

'What the hell is he?' muttered Tess, sending a shiver down Jian's spine, as the words of the Long Eye echoed in her mind.

'He knows not,' she whispered back.

'The time has come!' Talak barked at the crowd, his arms waving enthusiastically through the still air. 'Today, we catch the Wolfeater. Dead or alive, his journey to the Blackstone ends!'

'He's dead anyway!' a voice called from the crowd. 'There's no coming back from the lungrot. Why should we throw our lives away for his?'

It was Dakar speaking. Loyal, steadfast Dakar. *So, this is the test?* Jian rolled her eyes. *How disappointing.*

'Ah,' said Talak, 'the voice of dissent. You're not alone in your doubts, Dakar. Jian has already shared her thoughts on the matter.'

'That's right,' said Jian, pulling free from Tess's grip and making her way through the crowd towards Dakar. 'I've already said this mission is folly.'

'You see!' Talak cried triumphantly. 'All she needed was a second voice. Now she seeks...'

His voice trailed off as Jian struck out, stiffened fingers catching Dakar in the throat. The big man fell to his knees, gasping for breath, and Jian's dagger point found its way to his throat.

'I raised my concerns,' Jian continued smoothly, 'and Talak eased them. Radok must be stopped. That is the Will.' She looked purposefully at the *Ashan Tay*. 'We are crossing into the Whitelands, and if we start questioning each other's loyalty, then we're all doomed. We follow Talak. That's what the elders demanded, that's what we'll do. And the Seven will judge us in the aftermath.'

Talak gazed at her, astonished. After a moment he cleared his throat. 'Indeed. I should never have doubted your commitment, Jian. The Grey Crow are fortunate to be blessed with such a heart.'

He made to turn away, but Jian called out to him. 'What about this one?' she asked, twisting the dagger point in Dakar's neck. He looked up at her helplessly, then back to Talak with pleading eyes.

Talak took a moment to consider, and in that moment Jian saw a spark igniting. A spark of malice, given light by the smile playing on his lips. 'Kill him,' he hissed. 'There is no place for non-believers on this quest. Best to cut it out before the Will turns against us.'

Jian's heart sank. Her hand was sweating she realised, despite the cold, and the dagger felt suddenly heavy in her grip. For just a moment she had thought she'd outsmarted the *Ashan Tay*, but perhaps this was his plan all along? Perhaps *this* was the test?

She laid a hand on Dakar's shoulder, leaning in closer, her mouth an inch from his ear. 'I'll see your ashes cast, Dakar,' she whispered. Then she leaned closer still. 'And I'll kill him for this.'

She drove the dagger into his neck, severing the artery, then drew it back and plunged it into his heart. It was quick and painless, and he was gone before he hit the ground.

Talak showed no emotion as his puppet's blood ate into the snow. 'Well done, girl,' he offered, before turning his attention back to the rest of the party. 'On then. I want Radok before the day is done. That is the Will.'

Jian remained by the corpse while the others gathered their belongings and made ready to march on. The sun was still low, but the day had brightened and the snow was holding off. The fires were still burning too, she was pleased to see.

As the party moved out, Tess at Jian's urging, only Talak paused to look questioningly in Jian's direction. 'Girl?'

She gestured at Dakar's corpse. 'I told him I'd see his ashes scattered, and I'm nothing if not a girl of my word.'

Talak nodded. 'So be it... though it's more than he deserves. We won't wait for you though, Jian. Radok is out there somewhere, drawing ever closer to the Blackstone.'

'I know,' said Jian. 'I'll catch up to you.'

Talak nodded his head and turned away, leading his line of warriors back through the trees and out to the plains, which ran away north, vast and white and dangerous. Some of the men nodded respectfully to Jian as they passed. That was something, at least. It was one thing to keep Talak onside, but something else entirely if it meant forming a rift with those Jian hunted with.

She found herself staring after Talak as he disappeared through the trees, her anger growing. She had always despised the man and recent events had done nothing to ease the distaste. Arrogant and dogmatic, he represented everything that was wrong with the Seven and their disciples. Their vision left no room for compromise, no room for mercy or charity. In their mind there was only the Will, and the Will was law.

Grava had thought the same too, before Jian killed him. But like so many of them, he had confused his own will with that of the gods. She wondered if he had seen the error of his ways as she choked the life out of him?

Probably not, she thought. *Most likely he'd blame me for having the gall to fight back, just as he blamed me for the child's death. Some men's minds are so small, they think the world serves them.*

Talak was no different. True, he wore the mantle of *Ashan Tay*, but did the Seven truly want Dakar to die, or was that only Talak's will?

We'll find out, decided Jian, still watching the hunters filter through the trees. When they were gone, she looked down at Dakar's corpse. *I have more than one promise to keep to you, my friend.*

CHAPTER ELEVEN

Hunting the Hunted

'There were two of them in here.'

Crouching beside the charred remains of the campfire, Mikilov ran his fingers over the surrounding dirt, reading a story only the ground could tell. 'Aye,' he muttered, 'only two.'

'Yet you said there were more outside, maybe a dozen?'

'Aye. But only two or three of them took a look in here, and by then the two with the fire were already gone.'

'What does all that mean?'

Mikilov tugged at his beard thoughtfully. 'It means our hunters are closing on their prey.'

'The Wolfeater?'

Mikilov gazed at Senya through narrowed eyes. 'The day you can tell me which bird shat on my head two years ago, is the day I'll need no more than a footprint to say who laid it. We'll find out once we catch up to them.'

'That's all you had to say,' said Senya, smiling. She couldn't help herself. She had been travelling with Mikilov for five days now, and in that time she had found her liking for the man growing immensely. He reminded her so much of her father. Not in looks, perhaps, but in the things he said and how he said them; down even to the way he moved.

It was said the Valor shared their blood with the wolf, which went some way to explaining the elongated canines and heightened sense of smell, the keen ears and prodigious strength. In most cases that was where the similarities ended, but not with the likes of Mikilov and Finn.

Those two seemed to share the instincts of a wolf. They moved with grace and cunning, looking every inch the killer, yet once you got to know them, once you became a member of their pack, you knew you would find no safer haven, nowhere with such warmth, or love, or loyalty.

There could be a home here, Senya thought suddenly, *with this one and his wolf. A new pack...* But then the guilt would kick in, driving the thought away. This was no time to think of what *could* be, only what *had* been, only what was *taken*.

'Let's keep moving,' she told Mikilov. 'We've wasted enough time here.'

Mikilov gestured for her to wait a moment. 'Scar!'

The wolf appeared at the tomb entrance, his huge frame blocking out a good part of the sunlight. He padded softly down the tunnel, nuzzled into Senya on his way past, and stopped with his head resting beneath Mikilov's hand. The gnarly warrior scratched the wolf's ear, and gestured to the scuffed dirt around the campfire's remains. 'Get the scent, lad. Go find!'

Scar wasted no time. Sweeping his nose over the ground, the wolf circled the charred mound twice, before moving back up the tunnel and heading outside.

'He has them,' said Mikilov, following after him.

Senya lingered a moment longer, looking around the tomb one last time. On the far wall, barely visible in the faint daylight slipping in through the tomb's entrance, a dais had been carved into the rock, along with three thrones of equal stature. A body sat slumped in each of the stone thrones, their skeletal remains dressed now only in rags, and dust, and rot. Senya's eyes drifted to the central corpse. His head was gone, toppled from the shoulders and resting now half-shattered in the dirt.

There were no riches to be seen; no treasures glinting in the dark. They were long gone. Tomb raiders had found this place centuries ago, stripping it of any worth. Age had taken the rest, as it would one day take the bones.

The kings of old, thought Senya. *Nothing but dust in the wind.* That was how it always went, she supposed. Rich or poor, powerful or weak, time took everything in the end. Except when it didn't.

Sometimes it was men that took it all. Men like the Wolfeater. *He doesn't get to wait for time to take him,* thought Senya, *or even this bloody illness. When he dies, he'll be looking into my eyes. And he'll know the reason was Velimir.*

Leaving the dead behind, Senya turned on her heels and made her way back up the tunnel to the tomb's entrance. She stepped outside into the cold midday air, greeted by heavy flakes of snow carried on a soft breeze. Grey clouds were hanging low overhead, but the sun shone brightly behind them, almost burning through.

Scar was already some distance away, following the trail of churned snow that let out from the tomb's entrance and meandered its way north.

'That path won't last long in this snow,' Senya muttered.

'It won't need to,' said Mikilov, tossing Senya's saddlebag to her, which she caught deftly and slung over her shoulder. 'Scar has the scent now. They'll not escape.'

'You sure?'

'He's a wolf.' Mikilov smiled, those sharp teeth of his adding to the sense of confidence. 'The hunt is all he knows! You can take my word for it, girl. Scar will not stop until he has them.'

Senya made to follow the wolf, when Mikilov grabbed her by the shoulder, drawing her to a halt. She glanced at his hand, then met his gaze, an eyebrow raised.

'*He* won't stop,' said Mikilov, 'but *we* should. There is nothing in the Whitelands save death. Not for them, not for us, not for anyone.'

Senya hesitated. For just a moment she was almost willing him to drag her back, to save her from whatever precipice this was. But then she saw again the smoke rising from the charred remains of Velimir's hut, the blackened, twisted ruin of his corpse, and the moment passed. Senya let out a sigh. 'I can't stop,' she said. 'Not until he's dead.'

And so they fell in behind the wolf, following him north. They didn't run, much as Senya wanted to. The snow made it impossible in places, and dangerous everywhere else. The same reasons they'd left the horses behind. But they marched to a healthy pace, Senya keeping stride with the much taller Mikilov. She kept to his back though, using his tall, powerful frame as protection from the wind and the snow. They walked in silence for the most part, as the world around them slipped into empty, cold bleakness.

It changes nothing, Senya told herself as the frost closed in. *The Wolfeater lies ahead. I'd follow that bastard into the coldest hell to give my blade a taste of his blood.*

Smoke again.

This time drifting lazily from the centre of a small wood, the white trail standing out clearly against the soft blue sky that had broken with the morning sun.

Scar crouched low to the ground and Mikilov held up a clenched fist, signalling for Senya to stop. The three of them stood there silently, staring ahead at the distant column of smoke rising from the clump of evergreens.

'We should take cover,' said Senya, suddenly feeling very exposed out on the open white plains of Basilla.

'Take cover where?' asked Mikilov. 'Those trees are the first we've seen for two miles. If they were going to see us, they'd have seen us by now. And if they'd seen us, they'd be on their way to kill us.'

He whistled to the wolf, who looked up at him expectantly. 'Go see,' Mikilov told him, and Scar darted off to the right. Keeping low to the snowy ground, he skirted the wood's edge, before finally plunging into the trees on their eastern flank.

'What if they're in there?' asked Senya, her voice barely a whisper. As eager as she was to kill the Wolfeater, she was not a fool. She had no wish to stand toe-to-toe with a dozen Basillians.

'They won't see him,' Mikilov assured her. 'This is Scar's world out here. And this is not his first hunt.'

Mikilov led Senya on, crossing the open fields and drawing closer to the woods. The snow grew deeper with every step, their fur-lined boots crunching through the crisp surface and sinking to the top of the foot, to the ankle, to the knee. Senya winced as the sound of each footfall echoed out across the great whiteness, the only sound to be heard over the howling wind.

Once they finally reached the tree line, Senya and Mikilov ducked into the woods and headed for the centre, from where the smoke was rising. Senya had always thought herself light on her feet, but next to Mikilov she felt as subtle as a kragan with the scent of blood. The veteran warrior moved through the trees like a ghost, ducking and weaving between low hanging branches and avoiding ground debris with uncanny skill.

It wasn't long before the fire came into view, orange flames winking at them from between the trees. Slowing their approach, Mikilov gestured for Senya to fall back behind him, and only then did he crouch low and edge slowly forward. Senya stayed close behind him, doing her best to peer over his shoulder.

The light grew brighter the closer they got, and Senya began to smell what was burning. At first bitter and acrid, like burning hair, the woods were soon filled with the scent of roasting meat. Food had been scarce these past few weeks, and the smell was mouth-wateringly delicious.

'Smells like they're cooking a feast,' she whispered, stomach cramping at the thought of it. 'Smells divine.'

'Don't savour it too long,' said Mikilov, easing the underbrush aside and pushing forward. 'It's human flesh.'

Bile rose up in Senya's throat and she almost vomited. *He's right,* she thought, disgusted. She could smell it now. It was roasting meat, sure enough, but there was something off about it, an underlying trace of humanity.

Mikilov swung his axe free from his shoulders and brought it to bear. He was almost at the clearing, staring out at the fire in its centre. Drawing her sword, Senya joined him there and gazed out.

They saw a single figure standing with their back to them, gaze lost in the flames. A second figure lay in the fire itself, flames licking up over the charred flesh. Senya winced. There was that smell again, somehow appealing and offensive in equal measure. *Damn this hunger,* she thought. *Whoever knew a man could smell so good?*

'Basillian,' whispered Mikilov, 'and alone.'

'What's she doing?'

'Burning the dead, looks like.' He turned to look Senya in the eye. 'Follow my lead, girl. Don't let your anger get the better of you. We need to know what we're walking into, and this is our best chance. You hold your tongue.'

Before Senya could defend herself, Mikilov surged through the undergrowth and into the clearing. Cursing, she followed after him, her sword at the ready.

Hearing their emergence from the foliage, the Basillian spun around to face them, a dagger appearing in her hand in a blur of motion. Mikilov held his axe out to one side, his free hand out to the other, open palmed in a gesture of peace.

The gesture did no good. The Basillian sprang forward, lips drawn back over gritted teeth, her dagger thrusting forward. At that moment, a large shape exploded from the trees on the right, showering the girl with broken branches and chunks of snow. Scar crashed into her an instant later, his powerful jaws locking onto her arm. She cried out, her dagger falling to the snow, and the wolf was on her, dragging her to her knees and holding firmly by the limp arm.

'Easy, girl,' said Mikilov, taking a step towards her. 'We come in peace. Do you speak the common tongue?'

The girl stared dumbly at the two Valor, her eyes flickering between them, her tongue licking at dried lips. She was young, in her twenties perhaps, with long black hair and a cleft lip that set her face in a permanent sneer. Her eyes were dark too, and watering from the pain of Scar's hold.

Mikilov spoke again, this time in a guttural tongue Senya could not understand. The Grey Crow did though, and she replied in the same language, though it rolled far more fluidly from her tongue, even with the edge of steel she added to the words.

'What did she say?' asked Senya. But Mikilov held his hand up for patience, and spoke again. The girl replied, her words once more seemingly meaningless, and Senya felt a surge of frustration. 'What is she saying?' she snapped, turning her anger on Mikilov.

'What is she saying?'

There was fire in the question Mikilov did not appreciate. He'd asked the girl to hold her tongue, to let him find out what they needed to know, but it seemed she just couldn't help herself. More and more it was beginning to look like Senya's anger would be the death of her. *Most likely the death of us all.*

He levelled his gaze at her, letting his own anger simmer on the surface. 'This one is not the Wolfeater,' he said as calmly as he could muster. 'Let me speak to her. I'll find out what she knows.'

Senya huffed and puffed, on the verge of arguing further, but at the last she let out a sigh and nodded.

Mikilov let his gaze linger on her a moment longer, then turned his attention back to the Basillian. Here was another one too young to be out here. With long black hair and dark eyes, dressed in a thick bear-hide that engulfed her slender frame, Mikilov put her at no more than twenty-five.

She was plain-faced, save for a cleft in her upper lip. Whether that was from birth or a wound of some kind, Mikilov couldn't tell. Not that it mattered all that much. Battle scarred or not, she was Basilian. That meant she knew her way around a blade.

Mikilov's eye was drawn to the necklace of grey feathers hanging around her neck. *Crow feathers.* He knew then she was one of those they'd been tracking.

'My friend here thinks I should kill you.' Mikilov tried his best not to butcher the Basillian language, but it was far easier said than done given his lack of practice. In recent times, he had traded far more blows than words with the tribesmen of Basilla. *'But I've killed enough of your kind to last a lifetime. Tell me what you're doing out here, woman, and I'll let you live.'*

'You're a long way from home, Wolf.' The girl winced as she spoke, glancing at her arm, still clamped in Scar's mouth. She tried to pull free but Scar held firm, his cold black eyes staring back at her. He hadn't broken the skin yet, but he let her know he could by squeezing a little tighter.

'I wouldn't do that if I were you. He hasn't eaten yet.'

The girl looked up at Mikilov scornfully. *'Kill me then. Be done with it.'*

Mikilov spoke slowly, searching for the right words, not entirely sure he was finding them. *'You... are... Grey Crow, yes? We are not here to kill you. We come for the Wolfeater.'*

The girl laughed heartily.

'What did you say?' asked Senya.

'I told her we want the Wolfeater.'

'You should run home, Wolves. There is nothing out here for you save the Black Wind.'

'She was there!' said Senya, suddenly surging forward, realisation dawning on her face. 'You were there!' She grabbed the Basillian by her feathered necklace and pulled her up slightly, thrusting the tip of her blade under the girl's chin, the steel biting into the flesh. 'Where is he? Where is the Wolfeater?'

The Basillian grinned up at her, the broken lip twisting it into a sneer. *'I remember this one,'* she said. *'She was at the farm. She was the one killed Jorn.'*

'What's she saying?' asked Senya. 'What are you saying?'

'Let her go,' said Mikilov, striding forward.

'Tell her we wanted to trade,' said the Basillian. *'Tell her the old man would have lived, if Radok had his way.'*

'Tell us... where... he... is!' As she spoke, Senya twisted her sword so that the blade bit deeper into the Basillian's throat, slicing into the flesh and drawing blood.

Mikilov grabbed Senya's arm and pulled her away. He dragged her back with such force that Senya lost her footing and fell onto her backside in the snow.

The Basillian burst into laughter, so Mikilov back handed her across the mouth, stunning her to silence. 'Enough!' he stormed. *'Enough!'*

All the while Scar maintained his grip on the Basillian's arm, without even a whisper of a growl.

Mikilov glowered down at the wolf's prisoner, towering over her with his great axe gripped in both hands. *'I give no shits about who you are, girl, nor the games you like to play. We want the Wolfeater. Either you can tell us where he is and we let you live, or we can kill you now and let the wolf eat your remains. You will never burn; your ashes never cast to the Seven Winds. Your choice. Just make it fast.'*

The girl gazed up at Mikilov with fresh new eyes. There was all the hatred there that you would expect between two peoples who had been killing each other for as long as any of them could remember, but where there had been contempt and distrust before, there was now a healthy dose of respect.

'I know you too, Grey Wolf,' she said. *'They say* Chadra *circles your blades; that you can even bend the Will to your way of thinking. But out here you're just another man waiting to die.'*

'Then give us what we want so we can go home. Before I freeze my damned stones off!'

'Tell your friend to let me go and I will give you what you want.'

Without hesitation, Mikilov granted her wish. *'Scar.'*

The wolf let go of the Basillian's arm and trotted away to stand beside Senya, who had picked herself up and recovered her sword. There was still anger in her face, but there was more control to it now, a more focused rage.

After a moment, the Basillian also picked herself up. Testing the use of her arm, making sure there were no cuts or breaks where the wolf had grabbed her, she brushed the snow from her furs and picked up her dagger.

For a moment Mikilov thought she might charge at him, for which both he and Scar were ready. But instead, the Grey Crow sheathed the dagger and offered Mikilov a rueful smile.

'The Wolfeater travels north,' she said at last, *'to the Blackstone. He goes against the laws of the Seven, and for that he is outcast. We have been sent to stop him, one way or another.'*

'Why the Blackstone?'

The Basillian shrugged. *'Radok is dying and he wants to know why. He hopes the gods will tell him.'*

This is the same story the Wanderer told, thought Mikilov, shaking his head at the madness of it all. It didn't help that Senya was even less likely to believe it from this source than she was from the old woman.

'The sickness must be in his mind then,' he told the girl. *'When you have seen as much death as we have, you should know better than to think the gods have any answers.'*

The girl shrugged again. *'It matters not, he'll never make it. Either the sickness will kill him, or we will.'*

'Is he alone?'

'No. There is a girl with him, a child. She's blind and she'll slow him down, but she means a lot to him.'

'And how many tracking them?'

'Nine.' The girl flicked a glance at the smouldering corpse in the fire and grimaced. *'Eight, now.'*

That is true at least, thought Mikilov, who had counted as many when he and Senya watched them setting out from camp. *What odds the rest of it is true?*

Pretty good, given that both the Basillian and the Wanderer were spinning the same yarn. While Mikilov might have good cause to distrust the words of the former, he had no reason to doubt the latter.

'Go then,' said Mikilov. But the Basillian only gazed at him, startled. *'You kept your word. Now I keep mine. Go.'* Still she didn't move, instead stealing a glance at Senya, who was watching the conversation with her arms folded across her chest, her face a picture of thunder. *'I'll deal with her. Go, before I change my mind.'*

Still the Basillian stood her ground, this time glancing at the burning body. *'I promised Dakar I would cast his ashes to the Seven,'* she said.

'Some promises are easier kept than others.' Mikilov sighed. *'But we'll keep the fire burning. You can cast the ashes on your way back through, or else I'm sure one of your Winds will take care of it.'*

The girl hesitated for a moment... then gave a nod of her head. She backed away slowly, then turned on her heels and ran. She disappeared into the trees heading north.

'You let her go,' said Senya. She did little to hide her anger, a righteous fury simmering just below the surface. 'She'll tell them we're following. We've lost the edge of surprise. That's everything in the Great Hunt!'

The words hung in the air for a moment, dripping with scorn. Mikilov waited for the silence to grow, then said softly, 'Hatred is a powerful ally when you need to kill. For anything else, it's a weakness.'

'What does that mean?'

'You think they wouldn't have known we were coming if she never made it back to them? You think they're not watching like hawks for her return?'

'At least it would have been one less sword to face.'

'Aye true, but I gave her my word we'd let her live if she told us where Radok was, and my word is iron, even to one of them.'

Mikilov saw a little of the anger fade at that, replaced with hope. 'And what did she say?'

'That he's dying. He's out here, roaming the wilderness, because disease is rotting his core and he doesn't know why. He hopes his gods will have the answer, but all he'll find in the Whitelands is death. He has broken the laws of his own people and even they want him dead. The girl and her friends were given the task of tracking and killing him. And that's what they'll do, if the sickness doesn't kill him first.'

Senya shook her head. 'I don't believe her.'

'Elgamire said the same thing.'

'And I don't believe *her*!'

'Senya,' Mikilov said softly, 'there's a good chance we die out here. All to kill a man who'll be dead inside a week anyway. Why? Why throw away our lives when we could be back at home in warmth and comfort?'

Senya took an angry step towards Mikilov, grabbing his jacket and pulling him close. 'Why? Because I have his answer, Mikilov. When I drive my dagger into his heart, he'll know why he's dying. For Velimir. And for all the others like him.'

'You think Vel would want you dying for this? You think he was that small?'

'I'm not the one who's going to die. And I'm tired of having this argument. Go home, Mikilov. I know it was duty that dragged your arse out here, but you've done enough. Go home. I'm going on.'

Senya left the clearing, following the Basillian's tracks into the trees. Mikilov watched after her for a time, thoughts melancholy.

Elgamire's voice echoed into the silence, words from their last conversation. *If you follow her into the Whitelands...* the old woman had said, *if you chase a dead man into that white abyss... one of you will die. And it won't be her.*

Scar, sitting at Mikilov's feet and gazing after Senya, let out a soft whimper. Mikilov sighed. 'Fine, wolf. But if we die, it's on you.' He nodded after the woman. 'What are we waiting for then? After her!'

CHAPTER TWELVE

Old Foes

The snow gave way beneath Radok's feet and he stumbled. It almost threw the girl from his back, but she clung on grimly, her bony arms tightening around his throat, cutting the air off. Radok scrambled around for a foothold, trying to lift the girl higher to ease the pressure on his throat. Bad enough he could barely breath from all the running, without her choking the life from him.

'Loosen up, girl!' He grabbed Nyana's arm and yanked it away from him. 'I'll be no use to anyone if you don't let me breathe!'

Finally realising what she was doing, Nyana let some of the tension ease from her body. Radok shifted her weight higher on his shoulders and the pressure on his throat disappeared.

He stood for a moment with his hands on his knees, sucking in great breaths of frigid air. His head began to clear, and Radok turned back the way they had come, eyes narrowing against the distance.

Behind them the plains of Basilla rolled away towards the distant horizon, where they were swallowed by the growing shadow of nightfall.

It was difficult to make out any details in the growing gloom beyond the shapes of tree clumps and rocky outcrops, steep hills and shallow rivers. But *there* they were, in the far distance: seven dots moving towards them, descending the steep incline in single file, each carrying a flaming torch.

'Still there?' asked Nyana.

'Still there. Stuck to our tail like fleas on a dog's arse.'

'What do we do?'

Radok turned north again, judging the road ahead. Not that there was a road this far north. Not one that wasn't buried by history, at least. Or snow. Or both.

They stood at the edge of their own steep descent - a downslope of trees that levelled off slightly some twenty feet below, only for the land to fall away completely at the edge of a cliff. In summer months Radok knew he would have heard the song of the Velga drifting loud and clear from far below, but for now he could barely hear a whisper of the white rapids. The river border between Basilla and the Whitelands had fallen silent beneath winter's touch.

Lost in his thoughts, Radok jumped as Nyana touched his arm. 'Can you smell that?' she asked.

He sniffed at the air. Between the snot flowing from his nose and the chill in every breath, it was too cold to smell anything. 'Smell what?'

'Smells like death,' the girl muttered.

Radok grunted. He could have told her that. Things were starting to look pretty grim. At their current pace, Radok figured the hunters would be on them within two hours. Long before the Blackstone was even in sight.

Not for the first time the thought struck him that it would be better to take his chances and stand his ground than to die the slow death. He would only need a narrow passage, a place where they had to come at him one at a time. Radok fancied his chances at that game, even with the lungrot turning his guts to black tar. Sadly, he lacked the knowledge of the area to find such a place. The river waited below them, with a scattering of trees on either bank, but there was nowhere they couldn't flank him.

And there was the girl to think about too. It was one thing to throw your own life away, without knowing someone else's went along with it. Radok knew he was a dead man walking, but the girl's life was only just beginning. She deserved as much time as he could give her, and that meant doing everything they could to stay alive.

'We need to keep moving,' he said at last. He hooked his arms under the girl's legs and hoisted her up into a better position, higher up on his back. 'Hold on as tight as you can, Little Sparrow. You choke me if you need to. It's going to be a bumpy ride.'

Radok took a deep breath… then set off down the steep slope, half running, half sliding. He could have found an easier path given enough time, but time was everything just now, and straight ahead was always the quickest option. The girl laughed maniacally as they went, as though the air rushing past them was telling jokes that only she could hear.

The ground was part snow, part ice, part scree, and it was all Radok could do to stay on his feet. He weaved from tree to tree, crashing into each trunk just in an effort to stop himself, before bouncing off for the next safe haven.

Rogue branches loomed at him from the growing darkness, but Radok stooped below them or swerved around them at the last second. A couple of times he was too slow and took a branch to the face, or ducked just enough so that Nyana took the brunt. Not that she complained. She just went on laughing, perhaps overcome with the thrill and exhilaration of it all. For a moment even Radok laughed, revelling in Nyana's joy.

That was when he fell. Not because of the snow or the uneven terrain, but because of the disease. First his lungs started to burn, then his chest began to ache, until finally his knees gave way beneath him and down he went. There was no outside force, this was just another sign of his body failing.

He lost Nyana in the fall. She went flying from his back, landed heavily, and started rolling down the slope, picking up speed as she went, snow and debris from the trees kicked up in her wake.

On his feet in an instant, Radok dived after the girl, his fingers closing on thin air, missing her ankle by a whisker. Still, he scrambled after her, throwing himself down the slope, clawing at the snow and pushing with his feet, flapping after her like a fish out of water.

By the time they reached the foot of the slope, there was no stopping them. The girl was the first over the edge, flying into the air and plummeting towards the river far below. With a bellow of rage, Radok followed after her, planting his feet at the edge of the cliff and launching himself into the air.

His instinct had taken over, as it always did when it mattered most, and time seemed to slow to a crawl. He watched his hand stretch out, reaching for the girl; watched it close around her belt, stopping her fall; he felt too his right hand reaching back behind him and grasping something solid - a tree root jutting from the cliff wall. And in that moment time returned to normal. Both of Radok's arms snapped tight, pulling him in opposite directions, and he slammed back against the cliff face, grunting at the impact.

He looked down at Nyana, saw that he'd caught her belt at the rear. She dangled limply below him, her arms and legs hanging uselessly. *Thank the Seven she's blind,* thought Radok, seeing the white expanse of the Velga some fifty feet below, part frozen, part moving.

'Are you ok?' he called to her.

She turned her head slightly towards the sound of his voice. Her face was pale, filled with fear, but there were no wounds that Radok could see. 'I'm not sure I like flying,' she declared, offering half a smile.

Radok chuckled, as much with relief as anything else. 'Nor me! Hold tight, Little Sparrow. I'll try to get us out of this mess.'

The tree root creaked as Radok turned his face upwards. It was thick and strong, snaking out of the brittle rock above before disappearing back in again. Stones around the edge of it crumbled away when

Radok shifted his weight, but it felt strong enough to hold firm.

The cliff top was no more than two feet above them, but even that was too far to lift the girl. Radok searched for handholds in the rockface, but there was nothing to see in the growing dark and his hope slowly faded. 'Fuck...' he muttered.

'Looks like you could use a hand,' growled a deep voice, low and guttural, and with it a hand appeared from nowhere, dancing before Radok's face. It was no more than a skeleton of a hand really, stripped of skin and flesh and muscle, and it was posed in such a way as to receive another hand, as though to grip wrist to wrist. The yellowed bone had a shine to it, toughened by some secret varnish or oil, toughened to look as solid as rock, ready and willing to take Radok's weight.

Radok looked past the bony arm to the arm holding it, this one thick and clad in grey furs, and beyond that the face of the man owning both arms. Though he had expected it, the face that greeted Radok's gaze was most disturbing.

It looked every inch the face of a man. There were eye sockets, though the bright blue eyes sat deeper than they should have, as well as two nostrils and the line of a mouth, even stubble around the mouth and jawline. Yet it was featureless somehow, as though flattened down and stretched out over a skull too large to fit it, the flesh having the look of old leather. It was a mask, Radok knew, crafted from the face of a real man.

The Empty Face. He cursed inwardly. He should have listened to the girl. When she said she smelt death, this was what she meant...

'Take the hand, Grey Crow. I'll haul you up.' The man's voice was muffled by the mask, but his eyes glistened in the dark sockets.

Radok looked at the hand holding to the tree root, his knuckles white with tension, his arm aching from the strain. Then he turned and looked down at his other hand, holding grimly to Nyana's belt, the girl swinging limply below him, and far below her the dark waters of the Velga.

Radok had to chuckle. They really were cruel bastards, the Seven. Fall and die, they'd said, or put your lives in the hands of the cannibals. For Radok, that was no choice at all. While the fall meant certain death, at least the Empty Face offered a chance at life... and a chance was all the Wolfeater ever needed.

'You take the girl first,' he called up. 'And if you harm a hair on her head, I'll kill every last one of you.'

Muffled laughter drifted from behind the mask. 'You're not really in a position to threaten, Wolfeater. But fret not. The girl is safe with us.'

With a groan of effort, Radok lifted the girl high, so that she could reach out and grab the stripped limb. 'Take the hand, Little Sparrow. And hold tight!'

Latching onto the skeleton's arm, Nyana hugged tightly to it. 'Alright,' Radok said softly, 'I'm going to let go now and they'll pull you up. I'll be right behind you, don't let go.'

And he let her go. She sagged a few inches, and the Empty Face grunted as he took the weight, but both of them held tightly, and slowly the girl was pulled up. She disappeared over the cliff edge, back to the safety of solid ground, and for a terrible moment Radok thought that was the last he would ever see of her.

But then the Empty Face reappeared and Radok breathed a sigh of relief. The man's head tilted slightly, like that of a curious dog, before he offered the hand of bones once more. Radok grasped it by the wrist, and the Empty Face hauled him up.

By the time they dragged him back onto solid ground, away from the cliff edge, Radok was exhausted. Every muscle in his body ached, from his arms up to his shoulders, across his chest and around his back, and even down into his legs from all the running. And none of that said anything about the disease tearing at his innards. He took a moment, just sprawled in the snow and the dirt, to gather himself. He would have stayed there all day if he could, for eternity perhaps, but he felt eyes watching him. Lots of eyes.

Radok struggled to his knees and looked around. The Empty Face with the skeleton hand stood over him, head still cocked like a dog. He was dressed in heavy furs - bear, it looked like - and daubed in bone trinkets. He wore a necklace of small, sharp bones, bracelets of rune engraved teeth, and there was even a skull hanging from his sword belt, the weapon in the scabbard bearing its own bone-handle.

A dozen men were gathered in a tight semi-circle around them, each wearing the same kind of mask as the man with the skeleton hand. Those leathery faces were just as lifeless, just as empty as the first, yet some also bore the scars of old wounds, were striped red with war paint, or else still carried the beards of the men they were taken from. They were ghosts of those killed by the Empty Face; Radok may even have known some of them, back in a different life.

Nyana was standing front and centre of this crowd, her unseeing eyes full of concern. One of the Empty Faces stood behind her, hands resting on her shoulders.

'You alright, Little Sparrow?' asked Radok.

He saw relief flood her face. 'Aye,' she said back, 'no harm.'

'What about you, Wolfeater?' asked skeleton hand. 'Even with that black skin of yours, you look pale as snow. Not long now before the lungrot takes you.'

'What would you know of it?'

The Empty Face grinned. Not that Radok could see it through the mask, it was more of a feeling than anything. 'I know I wouldn't eat you! Come, there is much we need to discuss... and your friends are getting mighty close.'

The Empty Faces led them down a narrow ledge of rock that wound its way naturally from the clifftop down to the banks of the Velga. They moved in single file, Radok centre of the line, Nyana up on his back again. The Empty Face had offered to carry her, but neither Radok nor the girl wanted that. There was only so far you could trust a cannibal.

Once they reached the riverbank, they walked half a mile west along the river's course, retracing the tracks the cannibals had left earlier. Eventually the path led them to the water's edge. Even the swift moving Velga was largely frozen by the harsh winter. Ice floated on the surface, with only a few pockets of open water visible on the half-mile expanse of the river.

'This is where you cross,' said the man with the skeleton hand.

Radok gazed out across the water, the ice giving it a hint of silver in the fading light. He guessed there was two inches of ice at its thickest, but he could still see the water flowing freely beneath the frozen surface.

'It's too dangerous,' Radok replied. 'There has to be a safer place to cross. Further downriver, perhaps?'

'There is, but you'll never make the Blackstone if you go that way.'

Radok swallowed hard, the words sending a shiver down his spine. 'And how do the Empty Face know where the Grey Crow flies?'

'I am *Ashan Tay,* my friend. If the Will knows it, I know it.' The man pulled his mask clear, taking with it a head of long black hair. Beneath the mask he was younger than Radok imagined, smooth faced and bright eyed, with his true hair tied back into golden braids. He offered a bow of his head. 'My name is Hadal, and these are the finest warriors the Empty Face has to offer.'

The eleven men standing around them remained silent, letting their masks do the talking for them.

Radok shrugged. 'Most impressive. But why would you help us when one of your brothers is doing everything in his power to stop us?'

'Talak?' Hadal grinned. 'The man is a fool. Every single one of the Seven could appear before him and slap him across the face, and he still wouldn't understand the Will.' The smile faded slowly. 'He serves the Black Wind now, though he would never think such a thing possible.'

Radok raised an eyebrow at that. '*He* serves the Black Wind and *you* serve the Will? That's... hard to believe. Your lot are cannibals. If anyone benefits from the touch of the Black Wind, it's you.'

Hadal looked anything but offended. 'As I said, Talak has never truly understood the dance of the Eighth. It does not surprise me that he has filled your head with nonsense, nor that he has fallen for the song of the Black Wind. We eat flesh, that much is true, but so do you, Grey Crow. Not man flesh perhaps, not even Wolf meat, but all meat is just meat in the end. To eat flesh - to eat anything, for that matter - requires that something else dies. And in that way it can be argued that death sustains life... yet even the Empty Face knows it works the other way too; that there can be no death without life.

'*Chadra* knows this too. He knows that his song, the song of the Black Wind, would fall to silence if the Seven - his brothers and sisters - were gone. He knows this, yet he cares not at all. All he wants is an end, one way or another. He longs for the empty silence. That is the nature of the beast.'

'Perhaps,' said Radok. 'But that's not Talak. He's a shit, true enough, but his heart moves for the tribe. He would never do anything to harm the Grey Crow.'

Hadal nodded sympathetically. 'You can say that because you've never heard the song. But believe me when I tell you, a lifetime of the Will pounding at your mind, with all the voices of the Seven pulling you in every direction, can wear on a man's soul. And then you hear a different song, *one voice* telling you exactly what to do, filling your heart with joy and purpose. When you hear *that* song, it starts you thinking that perhaps this is the Will and everything that came before was a lie. There is great power in that. It may destroy everything you thought you knew, but it also sets you free. That is where Talak stands now. Instead of seven voices, he has chosen to listen to one. The wrong one.'

Radok glanced around again at the Empty Faces and their empty faces. 'Then you're here for him, not for me?'

Hadal smiled. 'My dear man, we're here for *her*.' And the *Ashan Tay* turned his attention to Nyana. 'What about you, Little Sparrow? What do you hear?'

Radok's innards took a turn at that, the sight of this cannibal moving his focus to Nyana, even using the name Radok had given her. He took a step towards them, ready to intercept Hadal, but each of the Empty Faces drew their blades, bearing an inch of steel, and Radok froze where he stood.

'I hear the wind,' answered the girl, a slight tremble in her voice.

'And what does it say?'

'There are no words,' said Nyana. 'Just... a feeling.'

Hadal knelt beside the girl, his voice soft. 'And it tells you what to do?'

Nyana shook her head. 'It shows me the way. It makes it so that something feels right, or it feels wrong.'

'A rare gift, for one so young. And *a girl*, no less.' Straightening, Hadal turned back to Radok. 'No girl has ever touched the Blackstone, but this one must. If her mind could be opened to the full power of the Will, she could become the first female *Ashan Tay*, not just for the Grey Crow, but for all Basilla. Are you truly the man to get her there, Wolfeater?'

'Well,' Radok's hand found its way to the sword sheathed at his waist, where it waited patiently. 'She's not going without me.'

Hadal nodded. 'And what about you, Little Sparrow? Do you want to carry on this flight alone with the Wolfeater, or would you like some company? What does the wind say about that?'

Nyana cocked her head in much the same way the *Ashan Tay* had, though it was more in concentration than curiosity. *She's listening,* Radok realised. 'We go alone,' she said at long last. 'That is the way it should be.'

Hadal smiled knowingly, as though he had known the answer all along. 'So be it.' He gestured to the river, the frozen surface glowing red in the dying sun. 'We spent some time searching and this is the best place to cross. The ice is strongest here, though not strong enough for all of us. Best you two go alone. We'll stay here and... distract your friends.'

Kneeling before Nyana again, the *Ashan Tay* removed his bracelet of teeth and placed it in Nyana's hand. 'Keep this with you,' he told her. 'If you ever find yourself in need of the Empty Face, show them this and tell them Hadal sent you. They'll give you anything you need.'

The girl said nothing, but Radok watched her closely as she ran the teeth gently through her fingers, and then carefully tucked the trinket away beneath her furs.

'It's a shame the Seven still have a use for you,' said Hadal, almost wistfully, pushing himself to his feet and turning his attention back to Radok. 'We've none of us ever tasted dark meat before. I should have liked to have tasted yours, Wolfeater.' Grinning like a fool, Hadal lifted his mask back to where it belonged, disappearing behind its cold, deathly stare.

'A true shame,' Radok agreed, easing his hand away from the pommel of his sword. 'Try not to die too quickly, eh? We need all the time you can get us, but these Grey Crow know how to bite back.'

'Don't worry about us,' said Hadal, his voice once more muffled by the leathery flesh of the mask. 'We know our part in the All Song.' Some of his men shifted uneasily at that, the first reaction they had shown of any kind. 'Well, *I* do,' he added with a smile. 'Best you be going now, Wolfeater. Tread carefully. Ice is a treacherous beast at the best of times.'

Radok needed no further encouragement. Taking hold of Nyana's hand, he walked to the edge of the river and paused. When he looked back, the twelve Empty Faces were watching them go, their dead, barren faces more disturbing than ever. It looked like twelve corpses brought back to life to haunt them.

Taking a deep breath, Radok stepped out onto the ice. It creaked and groaned beneath his weight, but it held firm. He thought about lifting Nyana to his back again, but it made little sense adding more weight to his footfalls. 'Let's go, Little Sparrow. Hold tight to my hand and if you feel any give in the ice, you let me know.'

By the time they had taken several strides, Radok could see the water still sloshing about a few inches below the frozen surface, flowing east. Further downstream he could hear the great falls, quieter now than in the summer, but still a crushing sound in the distance. A fall through the ice would mean certain death, and a bad one at that.

If you give me anything, he found himself praying to the Seven, *give me this!*

CHAPTER THIRTEEN

The Stronger Will

Talak reached the foot of the cliff as the last fingers of sunlight disappeared behind the western mountains, a ball of light being swallowed by a mouthful of sharp teeth. Still, even in the twilight he could make out the trail of their prey, heading west along the banks of the Velga. Not that it was hard. They had made no efforts to hide their tracks, nor was even the slowly building snowfall making a dent. *By the Seven,* thought Talak, *even Radok's girl could track these fools.*

'There's at least a dozen of them now,' said Talgar, as ever pointing out the painfully obvious.

'You smell that?' Vinak, sniffing at the air, his nose scrunched up in disgust.

Talak breathed in through the nose, tasting the air. It was there alright; the copper-like scent of blood, the sour tang of decay. Smells of death. He was so lost in the thought of it, so distracted, that he didn't realise, for the first time since touching the Blackstone himself, the wind was blowing against him.

'Empty Face,' he hissed, and the sound of ringing metal filled the air as his men drew their blades.

'There's no sign of a struggle,' said Talgar, finally offering something useful. 'If Radok and the girl go with them, they go willingly.'

'Of course!' Talak almost jumped for joy at the revelation. He searched the faces of his merry band, and saw that Jian was still missing, left behind to burn Dakar. So instead, he settled his gaze on Tess, the woman's closest ally. 'No tribe favours the Black Wind more than the Empty Face. They want to see the Wolfeater touch the Blackstone. That should tell us all we need to know about their union.'

'Then we have to stop them,' said Tess. 'Any way we can.'

'You should remind Jian of that, when she finally shows her face again. I fear the woman is too fond of Radok to see the threat he poses.'

Tess's lips tightened and she lifted her chin, defiant. 'Do not fear for Jian. Surely Dakar proves she will do what's right when the time comes?'

'Well, she might not get the chance,' said Vinak, gesturing ahead with his thick bearded chin. Talak squinted in that direction, peering through the falling snow and into the gloom. A large fire was burning in the distance, along with several torches set out around it in a circle.

'Come on in, Grey Crow,' a voice called from the darkness. 'Join us for dinner!'

Laughter boomed out at that, muffled slightly; a hollow, haunting sound that caused Talak's men to shift uneasily. Their weary eyes darted all around, as though they half expected the night to come alive and take them.

Talak might have let his own fears get the better of him, if not for the hand at his back driving him on. For that's what it was now; no voices, no wind, just an unseen hand urging him forward. There were no more arguments to settle, no confusions to untangle, no decisions to resolve. *Follow your instincts,* was all the Will seemed to say now. *Follow your instincts and we'll follow you.*

Right now, Talak's instincts led to only one place. 'Damned cannibals,' he muttered. 'Grey Crow, with me!'

Despite their fears, they fell in behind Talak without hesitation, the group marching along the frozen bank in grim silence. Say what you would about the Unblessed, at least their faith gave them all the courage they needed.

Faith, whispered a voice upon the wind, *and fear. They fear you more than they fear even the Empty Face. Show them the wisdom of that,* Ashan Tay. *Kill them. Kill them all.*

Talak swallowed hard, his throat dry as desert rock. The voice of the Will had never been so clear, so... *singular*. Yet what were they asking of Talak now, when they said to "kill them all"? Was it just the Empty Face they wanted dead, or even the Grey Crow too?

He looked around at the men following in his wake. With Dakar dead and Jian still missing, there were six of them remaining. They were all hardened warriors, battered and weathered into shape by their time on the plains of Basilla, and they had been fighting side-by-side for as long as any of them could remember. There were raids against the Valor, skirmishes against the Empty Face, bitter feuds with the Blue Eyes, and all-out war with the Cran. Some had even fought against the children of the One God, far to the east. Even the girl, Tess, had the look of a killer. Her face was carved from ice, sharp featured and deadly cold.

They were all of them seasoned killers, and while any *Ashan Tay* worth his salt had his own skills with the blade, Talak had no desire to put his to the test against his own people. He would give the Seven the

Empty Face, as they asked, but nothing more. Not yet at least...

Tess had brought her bow to bear, arrow notched, but Talak gave her a shake of the head. 'Don't loose until I give the signal. I need to speak to them first.'

'You can't reason with cannibals,' said Talgar, coming up on Talak's left. 'Best we attack first.'

Talak ignored him as the circle of light drew ever closer. The smell of smoke burnt his nostrils, and his skin prickled at the first waves of heat from the fire. 'This is the Will,' he muttered, as the light and warmth enveloped him.

The Empty Faces were gathered by the fire, one of their number sitting cross-legged in the snow facing the direction of the newcomers. The others were standing behind him, hands resting on their own blades. Their masks - the faces of the dead, dried and hardened through some unknown magick - were even more disturbing in the orange glow of the flames.

Halting before the man with the crossed legs, Talak raised a hand, signalling for his own men to stop. The Grey Crow drew up behind him, facing their counterparts as warriors did back in the old days, when feuds were settled in the pit.

With the help of a staff that had been resting in the snow beside him - a smooth shaft of wood topped by a skeleton hand - the sitting man pushed himself to his feet. He was dressed in the thick hide of a black bear, with bone trinkets for decoration, including a necklace of small, sharp bones and a skull hanging from his sword belt. Though the mask bore no emotion, Talak had a feeling the face beneath it wore a smile as wide as the Velga.

'Greetings, Talak,' he said, his voice muffled by the mask. 'It's been a long time.'

'Not long enough,' replied Talak, though he offered a nod of the head in greeting. 'Well met, Hadal.'

'What brings you this far north, old friend? This is Empty Face land up here, lest you forget.' He looked past Talak at the gathering of Grey Crow, nodding slightly. 'Looks like this winter has taken its toll on your lot, but you'll find nothing up here but cold and emptiness.'

'You seem to be doing well for yourselves,' Talgar pointed out.

'Keep your fool mouth shut!' Talak barked at him, but Hadal only smiled.

'There is always food to find, when you have the stomach for what has to be done.'

Talak grunted. 'We have stomach for more than you know, but we're not here for food. We are tracking two of our folk, currently headed for the Blackstone. Unless... you're about to offer us something special for supper?'

'Something special?' Hadal frowned. 'Like your friends? What kind of monsters do you think we are?'

'The kind that eats babies.' Talak waved it away. 'No matter. Have you seen our friends?'

'The Wolfeater and his Little Sparrow? Aye, we've seen them. They've crossed the Velga. Two weeks, perhaps, and they'll reach the Blackstone.'

The wind seemed to hiss in Talak's ears, and a flame of anger sparked inside him. 'They mean to touch it, Hadal. They mean to touch the Blackstone.'

Hadal shrugged carelessly. 'Let them, if that is the Will.'

'I *am* the Will!' Talak snapped. The Empty Faces and their ridiculous masks offered nothing, but Talak realised what he had said when he felt the Grey Crow shifting uneasily behind him. 'I was sent by the Will,' he smoothed over, 'to stop them before they desecrate the laws of the Seven and touch the Stone.'

Hadal took a step closer. 'Yet I was sent by the Will to stand in your path. A strange turn of events, no?'

'Pah,' scoffed Talak, 'you who listens to the Eighth before you hear the Seven?'

Hadal raised his eyebrows. *'I listen to the Eighth? Tell me, Talak, how many voices do you hear these days?'*

One voice, one Will.

'Enough,' said Talak. And he surged forward, dagger sliding from its scabbard in a smooth arc.

Jian watched the scene from twenty yards away, shrouded in the growing dark, her breath smoking in the cold night air, short and bated. She had no idea who the Empty Face was standing toe-to-toe with Talak, but he carried his rank with as much splendour as he hid his face. It was written in the garb he wore, the grim baubles decorating his outfit, and Jian found herself smiling.

Outside of a Gathering, it was a rare thing indeed to find two *Ashan Tay* in the same place at the same time; rarer still for both to survive such an encounter. *With any luck, the Empty Face will do us all a favour...*

Usually it would seem all manner of wrong to cheer on a cannibal, but in Talak's case Jian was willing to make an exception. The arrogant bastard had dragged them up here after all, to risk their lives on foiling the dreams of a dead man. It had already cost Dakar his life. How many more had to die to soothe

Talak's ego? Radok and the girl at least, but now it looked likely more blood would be spilt.

If the *Ashan Tay* did go after each other, their tribesmen would do the same, and say what you would about the Empty Face, those mad bastards had never been easy to kill.

'Fuck,' muttered Jian, who was still Grey Crow, despite it all. She had no desire to see any of her people harmed, but especially Tess, who was down there in the thick of it. Easing her sword from its scabbard, the soft glide of metal against leather loud in the silence, Jian started forward.

And that was when everything changed. Talak moved almost in unison with Jian, surging forward and drawing a knife from some hidden place. The Empty Face - no doubt a fine warrior, judging by the trophies jangling around him - had no time to react as Talak's knife slid up under his chin and into his brain. The man collapsed backwards, taking the knife with him, blade buried up to the hilt below his chin.

Jian staggered to a halt, her own jaw agape at what was unfolding before her. The world slowed to a crawl and every detail burned itself into her mind. She watched the remaining Empty Faces draw their swords and sweep forwards; watched Talak raise a hand to his Grey Crow companions, telling them to hold their ground, while he moved to meet the charge head on, alone.

She watched him dance among them with quiet fury, his sword flashing in the firelight as he moved from one opponent to the next, weaving between their blades, ducking and swerving each slash. Talak moved like a storm, every flick of his blade marked by the clash of steel or a flash of crimson blood.

And like all the worst storms it was over in an instant. Once the dust settled and the calm returned, Talak was left standing alone amidst the ten bloodied ruins of his opponents. One curt wave of his arm later and the Grey Crow swept in, putting those who still lived to the sword.

By the time the final blow was struck, Jian was striding into the circle of firelight, her eyes fixed on the *Ashan Tay*. 'By the Will, what the fuck was that?'

Talak's gaze snapped to Jian, as though he awoke from a daze. 'Our favourite sister returns! *That*, my child, *was* the Will. The Seven, working through me to do their bidding.' He took a deep breath and cast his arms into the air, turning slowly on his heels, face lit by pure ecstasy. 'Such a beautiful thing... I have never felt such power...'

Jian looked around at the other Grey Crow - at Vinak and Talgar and the rest, and at Tess when the girl appeared beside her and gave a squeeze of Jian's hand - and she saw the same fear there that she felt growing in her own heart. They too had never seen such power... but they had heard of it. *And the Black Wind rises...*

'Have you found them?' asked Talak, snapping from his reverie.

'No sign,' said Vinak.

'There is,' put in Talgar, gesturing towards the Velga, 'out on the ice. Two sets of tracks; one larger, one smaller.'

'The ice?' Tess shivered at the thought. 'That's suicide.'

'This whole thing is suicide,' muttered Jian. 'What now Talak?'

The *Ashan Tay* gazed off towards the river, kneeling to absently wipe his blade clean on one of the fallen. 'You can go home, Jian, as you have long wanted.' He swept his gaze over the remaining Grey Crow, all gathered in a circle around him, and smiled. 'You can all go home. I don't need you anymore. I never have.'

And with that, Talak strode to the edge of the Velga and stepped out onto the ice. He walked with confidence, never hesitating, not even when the ice groaned and cracked beneath his weight, until at least he faded into the dark mist and was lost, the Grey Crow watching after him in silence.

'It's not the Will that drives old Talak,' a voice spoke out. It was Garda, a well-wintered brute of a man kneeling over the body of the first Empty Face Talak had killed. He lifted the man's mask aside with the tip of a knife, revealing a shock of blond hair framing the youthful face below.

'What's that?' asked Jian.

Garda looked up, his dark eyes grim and serious. 'You don't get to my age without seeing some men who can swing a sword, and I've seen some of the best. The Wolfeater is good, true enough, but he's nothing next to the Outsiders - those bastards that fight beside the Wolves. I tell you, I've never seen anyone who can kill like that... not until today at least.' Garda waved his knife in a circle, taking in the scattered corpses of the Empty Face. 'Only the Black Wind could help a man do this.'

Jian shivered herself, but not through the cold. 'What are you saying?'

'I'm saying Talak serves the Eighth.'

'No,' said Jian. 'I have as much reason as anyone to despise that little rat, but Talak has always done right by the Crow.'

Pushing himself to his feet, Garda walked over to stand before Jian. He towered over her by some distance, though Jian felt no panic standing in his shadow. Quiet and methodical, he had always been one of the good ones. Here though, now, he was making his move for leadership.

'You saw his eyes,' he said softly. 'He only now realised the truth of it himself. But do you think him cowered by it? Or did he seem eager to embrace the power the Black Wind offers?'

Jian found herself struggling for an answer. Talak had enjoyed every moment of the slaughter, there was no escaping that. *You can all go,* he had told them afterwards. *I don't need you anymore.*

'Then what, Garda? What do we do now?'

Garda shrugged. 'You know what happens to those moved by the Black Wind. Killing becomes the only thing they know. Men, women, children... it doesn't matter to them. They would butcher the world just to hear the dark whispers of the Black Wind.

'The Will says a man like that must die. That's the law of Basilla and the law of the Grey Crow. I will not allow him to burn our name. I say we kill him, or die trying.' Garda looked around at his fellow warriors, sent to kill a hero but now facing a different choice. 'Who is with me?'

The question was met with silence. Tracking and killing a dying man and a blind girl through the Whitelands was one thing; tracking an *Ashan Tay* at the height of his powers was something else entirely.

It was a task no one wanted, not even the Grey Crow's finest.

'What about the Wolfeater?' asked Jian, genuinely curious.

Garda only gave it a moment's thought before answering. 'The elders' judgement was based on the twisted words of Talak. If they knew the truth as we know it now, would they have stood in Radok's way? Let the Seven deal with Radok as they see fit. We'll deal with Talak.'

Jian met the big man's gaze and knew he spoke the truth. *By the Will,* she thought, *he rode with Radok for as long as any man would care to remember. If I owe the Wolfeater my life once, Garda probably owes it ten times over.*

'If it's truly Talak you want to kill,' she said, 'I'll follow you.'

Garda looked stunned for a moment... then burst out laughing. Jian scowled at him, suddenly conscious she may have been made the butt of some unfortunate joke.

'I'm no leader,' he said after regaining some composure. 'I know one when I see one though, especially one worth following.' He smiled a little wider. 'If *you're* going after Talak, Jian the Breaker, *I'll* follow *you.*'

Jian wasn't quite sure what to make of that, but her confusion only blossomed further when the other Grey Crow threw their backing behind her. Tess was there in an instant, of course, announcing her love as well as her loyalty. Vinak, it turned out, had always been impressed by her spirit, Talgar by her strength and wisdom. One by one they all backed Jian, ready to follow her into the Whitelands in pursuit of a madman.

Jian shook her head. 'It's impossible. The elders won't stand for it. Not a woman. Not one of the Fallow.'

'They won't have a choice,' Garda assured her. 'The young will back our choice, and it's the young that rule the day.'

'Why me?'

'Why not? Some would say you owe the Wolfeater. He put his faith in you and so will the tribe. Starting today.'

Jian considered it for a moment. Garda had struck the truth of it sure enough. She owed Radok more than just her life. When the rest of the tribe had been ready to exile Jian, it was Radok who found a place for her in the Fallow, who had even trusted her enough to let her ride with him...

And now he was somewhere out there in the White Waste, dragging a blind girl and his own half-dead body to whatever fate waited for them at the Blackstone. If anyone deserved a chance to reach that hallowed place, to stand before his gods and look them in the eye, it was the Wolfeater.

'You're right,' Jian said at last. 'Talak has no right to stand in Radok's way, whether it's the will of the Seven or the Eighth he listens to. Nor do the two Valor currently dogging our tails. If I am to lead this merry band of hunters, I say we kill them all and let the Will take care of Radok. Are you still ready for me to lead, Garda?'

The big man swept his arm out towards the river. 'Lead on, Jian the Breaker. Lead and we will follow.'

CHAPTER FOURTEEN

The Velga

Though the fire had burned low by the time they reached the banks of the Velga, its orange glow shone like a beacon in the deep dark, drawing Senya and Mikilov to it like moths to a flame.

They approached slowly at first, having no idea what lay in wait for them, but it wasn't long before their apprehension gave way to curiosity and they made the last few yards at a run.

It was the smell, more than anything. If the light drew them on, the smell would have been enough to turn them back, if not for Senya's burning desire for revenge. As it was, the pungent stench of emptied bowels and spilt guts was just another sign they were moving in the right direction.

Senya staggered to a halt as she broke into the circle of firelight, breath catching in her throat. Bodies littered the ground around the fire, ten of them at least, some slashed across the belly or chest, some with their heads near severed, and others with less visible wounds. 'Who are they?' she asked as she carefully picked a path between the corpses.

Mikilov pushed one of the bodies over with a gentle shove of his boot. The dead man's hand rolled away from his side, letting his guts spill out as it flopped lifelessly into the snow beside him. There was a dark, congealed pool of blood seeped into the snow beneath him, part frozen despite the nearby fire. *Long dead then.*

The man's face was a strange, pale mass of flesh bereft of any emotion or real detail, glowing like bronze in the firelight. It was a mask, Senya realised, though somehow both more and less realistic than any she had seen before.

'Empty Faces,' Mikilov grunted. 'The worst kind of Basillian. They are nothing more than butchers and cannibals, cutting parts from the dead and eating them, or else wearing them like trophies.' He kicked the leg of another dead man, watched it rock away and back again, lifeless. 'No Grey Crow though. If our friends did this, it didn't cost them anything.'

Just then a whimpering cut into their conversation. At first, Senya thought it was one of the fallen, still alive, but the sound was drifting to them from further away, closer to the river's edge. *Scar,* she realised, and she followed Mikilov to where the wolf sat at the edge of the frozen water.

He was peering into the darkness ahead, staring across the river towards some unseen threat. Taking a few steps out onto the ice, Mikilov crouched low to inspect the thin layer of snow coating the surface. 'Tracks here,' he said after a moment. 'Lots of tracks.'

Senya nodded. 'Our friends crossed the ice.' It was hard not to respect such a bold move. 'They must be fearless.'

Mikilov shook his head. 'Mad, more like.' He turned away from the river and walked back to the fire, where he started feeding fresh fuel to the flames from a stockpile gathered nearby.

'What are you doing?' Senya asked, eager to keep moving.

'What does it look like? Keeping this fire alive.'

'We need to keep moving. They're already hours ahead of us, we can't let them pull even further away.'

Mikilov raised an eyebrow in her direction. 'If you want to try crossing a river as wild as the Velga on a shell made of ice, with the dead of night closing in, you know where to start. But I'll be waiting here for daylight, warm and comfortable. The Grey Crow can't fly all night either. We'll catch them when we catch them.'

With the fire freshly stoked, Mikilov slumped to the ground beside it. He set to routing in his travel bags for his blanket and his cooking utensils, and Scar padded over to join him beside the fire. Senya's heart sank. When even the wolf took Mikilov's side in the argument, she supposed the old warrior must have a point.

Rolling onto his shoulder, Mikilov awoke with a start, a sharp pain shooting up his arm and into his chest. 'Fuck,' he managed to gasp, before the pain curled him up into a ball. It seemed an age, but finally the pain subsided and he rolled onto his back, breathing heavily.

'You're getting too old for this.' Senya's voice, cutting through the blurriness of broken sleep.

Mikilov lifted his head. There was daylight, but it was still early morning judging by the crisp taste of fresh air carried on the southernly breeze. He pushed himself to a sitting position and rubbed at his tired eyes. Then he swept his gaze around the campsite.

The dead were still there, sleeping their eternal sleep, but the place seemed different in the daylight. The fire had burned low, down to the embers, and the cold was seeping into everything. There was a freshness to it though that was difficult to escape. The cold had killed the smells drifting from the dead, while the snow, growing thicker and heavier with every fall, had buried what it could beneath a blanket of purest white.

Senya was already packed, but she was working Mikilov's pans over a small cook fire and she grinned when Mikilov grimaced at another back spasm. 'Too old by far,' she offered helpfully.

It was difficult to disagree. In his prime, Mikilov could have slept on such hard ground for weeks at a time without his body making a single complaint. Now though, it seemed every part of his body ached... or at least the parts not yet numbed by the cold of the Whitelands.

'Our friends kindly left us some supplies,' said Senya. 'How does eggs and bacon sound? At least... I hope it's bacon.'

'What happened to wanting to get moving?' asked Mikilov, signalling for her to toss the meat over.

'I realised you were right. We'll catch up to them eventually. If not before they get wherever they're going, then on the way back at least. There's not many options for him out here.'

Mikilov grunted. 'Not many options for any of us out here.'

Senya tossed the meat through the air, and Mikilov caught it deftly. It was heavily salted, wrapped in dried lembas leaf from the north, but it sure smelled like bacon.

'Scar,' said Mikilov. The wolf, who had slept the night beside him, lifted his head and yawned. Mikilov dangled a slice of the meat in front of his nose and Scar sniffed at it. After a moment of consideration, the wolf lay back down and closed his eyes.

Mikilov tossed the pack of meat back to Senya. 'Breakfast then! Scar has no taste for pigs, but he'd bite your hand off for a slice of man.'

'What a relief,' muttered Senya, frowning at the wolf. Then she gestured around at the dead bodies. 'Just make sure I'm not around when he decides to tuck into one of these delights.'

With the bacon sizzling over the remains of the fire, Mikilov made his way to the river's edge, where he took out his manhood and set to emptying his bladder. He watched the golden piss eat into the ice, doing his best to keep it concentrated in one spot - a task easier said than done, given the amount of shivering he was doing. By the time he'd ran dry the ice was holding firm. A few inches deep then, at least. That was a good sign. The one danger of making the crossing in daylight was the extra warmth of the sun weakening the crossing.

They ate in silence for the most part, both looking out over the Velga, the thoughts of what might lie ahead running through their minds. It was obvious enough where those thoughts would take Senya. Vengeance had a way of simplifying things like that. She would be thinking of Radok, every line of his face burned into her memory. She would be imagining what it would feel like to drive her sword through his heart once they finally caught up to him.

As though it would be that easy. As though the Wolfeater - one of the greatest warriors Mikilov had ever seen - would simply stand there, while a girl of limited experience tried to run him through. As though there were not a thousand other things between here and there that could kill them in an instant, long before they ever caught sight of their prey.

Mikilov shook his head. That was vengeance for you. Delightfully simple, and wonderfully short-sighted.

Sometimes you had to think deeper than that. Sometimes you had to think about how you might survive the crossing of a frozen river. You had to consider the miles of wilderness lying ahead of you, the bitter cold dogging your steps, the other hunters lying between you and your prey. You had to put your mind to the task of killing a man a thousand others had tried to kill before you. Tried, and failed. Most of all though, you had to consider how you'd get home once it was all done.

That was Mikilov's part in the piece, at least. He didn't give two shits about the Wolfeater, only that Senya survived to see the beckoning walls of Haslova once it was all done. That was the promise he had made to the ghosts of Finn and Velimir, and he meant to give his all to see their girl safely home. Yet it was a task that was growing more difficult with every step they took deeper into the Whitelands. This was not a place for vengeance. Not when the land itself wanted to kill them.

There was no telling the girl that though. Her heart and mind were set on the path they were taking, and Mikilov was done arguing with her. 'It'll hold,' he told her, nodding at the ice. 'Time to get moving.'

Senya looked surprised. 'What? No last-minute arguments? No attempts at convincing me to turn back?'

'Too tired for that,' grumbled Mikilov. 'You won't hear it anyway. You need to see the Wolfeater's corpse before you go back home, so the sooner we get it done the better.'

'At last! You understand!' But Senya's smile quickly slipped, her fears suddenly bubbling to the surface for the first time in Mikilov's company. She met his gaze with big, sad blue eyes. 'Can we do it, do you think?'

Mikilov stared back at her for a moment, a spark of hope in his heart. Was this an opening? Could he convince her to turn back after all? Would she finally listen? But then he saw the truth of it, deep in her eyes. She was a woman struggling under the crushing weight of duty. Velimir had been one of hers and she had failed to protect him. Vengeance was all she had. The Wolfeater had to die so that Velimir might rest more easily. There would be no turning back for her, not even if she longed for it herself.

Give her what she needs.

Mikilov pushed himself to his feet, and offered Senya his hand. 'Anything is possible,' he answered, locking wrists with her and hauling her to her feet. He laid a hand on her shoulder for a moment, holding her gaze. 'Radok will die, I promise you that. And whatever follows, we'll face it together.'

They stood at the river's edge, their boots touching what was once flowing water, now turned to solid ice by winter's coldest breath. Mikilov peered out across the white expanse. A thick layer of snow quilted the frozen surface, and he could have almost believed there was no river at all, save for the sound of the

Velgan Falls rumbling on in the distance, a sign that the river's lifeblood still flowed just a few inches below the surface.

'Are you sure about this?' asked Senya, glancing sideways at him. She looked tired. There were bags under her eyes and her skin was pale, her rosy cheeks the only bright spot about her.

'The Empty Faces were,' he said, tossing a thumb over his shoulder towards the corpses. 'And they know this land better than most. It might take us a few days to find a better path.'

Senya chewed her lip, still uncertain.

'Only one of us can call this off,' he told her. 'Say the word and we go home.'

The silence stretched out between them, and, for a moment at least, Mikilov found himself hoping once more...

...only for it to be snuffed out a second later, like a candle in the wind.

'No,' said Senya, shaking her head as though that might clear the doubts. 'We're wasting no more time. If the Wolfeater dies out here, it has to be for Velimir. I have to be the one who finally puts him out of his misery.'

Mikilov raised a brow. 'For Velimir?'

'For Velimir.'

He sighed. 'Best be about it then,' and he nodded at the ice sheet. 'After you.'

Senya took a careful step out onto the ice, hesitated for a moment, and then began to walk. Mikilov watched her go for a spell. She was lighter on her feet than he was, and better balanced on the ice. If anyone was going to fall through, he thought, it was likely him. Better to fall through alone than drag the girl down with him, and if she went in first, he had a better chance of pulling her out than she did him.

He glanced down at Scar, sat at his heels, head cocked as he watched Senya making her way out across the frozen span. 'Go on then, lad. Stay close to her.'

Needing no second invitations, the wolf padded down to the water's edge. He paused there for a moment, pushing his nose out to sniff at the cold air. Then he touched one paw to the ice and snatched it back, as though the cold burned. Perhaps it did.

Scar's gaze flickered from Senya to the ice and back again, and Mikilov smiled. He could see the wolf's struggle. Protect Senya, or stick to the safety of solid ground? It was not an easy choice to make, for man or wolf.

Scar sank to his haunches, whining, all the while watching Senya stride further and further away, and Mikilov's smile widened. He had never seen the wolf so smitten. That Scar had chosen to walk with Mikilov was only ever about respect, but with the girl it was different. There was affection there, pure and unbridled. It was quite a thing to see in a wild beast.

'What kind of wolf are you?' said Mikilov, brushing past the wolf and setting off across the ice after Senya. Scar followed a moment later, bounding onto the ice and scrabbling after them, the layer of snow just enough to offer his paws some much needed grip. It took the wolf some stones to make that leap, but Mikilov suspected it was more shame than courage that drew him on.

Ten strides further on, where the water deepened, Mikilov's heart skipped a beat as the ice groaned and cracked beneath him, threatening to split open and plunge him into the murky depths below. He held his nerve, maintaining a steady pace. Too slow and he'd leave his weight in the wrong place for too long; too fast and his weight would be striking the ice quicker, and in smaller areas, weakening far more of the surface. *Slow and steady*, he told himself. *Slow and steady*.

His heart was in his throat for most of the journey, but Mikilov kept his fears at bay as best he could. His nose was red raw from the chill and the rubbing. Snot flowed freely. He pulled his gloves tighter as he walked. It was as cold out on the ice as anything Mikilov had ever felt while walking the Whitelands. Away from the banks, where there were no trees or rising slopes to offer shelter, the biting wind tore at them with hungry relish.

On they marched, snowfall swirling around them like ash from a fire. It caked their furs, the damp seeping through to their clothes. Even Mikilov's beard felt heavy with the weight of it, tugging at his face whenever the wind picked up. His fingers and toes felt numb too, the flesh around his eyes and nose burning from the relentless gales.

Senya seemed to share his thoughts. 'I never knew the cold could burn,' she called over her shoulder.

'Pain is good,' he called back. 'Pain will keep you alive out here. It's when the pain stops you need to worry.'

They walked most of the way in silence, tension hanging over them like a bad moon. The distant sound of the falls had been lost to the roaring wind, but Mikilov knew they were still out there, rumbling on. Even here, less than a foot below them, the Velga continued to flow, water rushing eastward to that magnificent drop.

The north bank edged ever closer, the steep incline crowned with snow covered evergreens and a backdrop of white mountains. It was the first true sight of the Whitelands they had seen, and in this most bitter of winters the name seemed more fitting than ever.

'I didn't know a place could be so cold,' said Senya, still having to raise her voice to be heard over the wind.

'It'll only get worse,' Mikilov told her. 'When we make land, best stay close to me, eh? The ground out here can betray you at the best of times... and these are not the best of times. Even the weather can turn quickly. If a blizzard or fog rolls in, it's best we can reach each other before we lose ourselves.'

'Have you been out here before?' Senya kept her eyes fixed on her feet as she spoke, alert for any sign of give in the ice.

'Once.' Mikilov swallowed hard at the memory. 'A long time ago. Back when I knew your father, in the days we hunted the King Killer.'

Senya froze in her stride, spinning back to face him. 'The Jarl? The last of the Jagged Horn?'

Mikilov nodded with a grimace. *Bloody bards. Everyone knows some version of the story...*

'I knew my father was there, but you too? Tell me about it,' Senya urged hungrily. 'Not the way the bards tell it. Your way, Mikilov. Tell me the truth.'

Mikilov grunted. Odds were, the truth would be the last thing she wanted to hear. 'Talk as we walk,' he said, waving her on. He was almost level with her now. 'We need to get off this ice as quick as we can.'

The girl turned on her heels and marched on, but Mikilov stayed closer to her this time, close enough so that she could still hear his voice over the wind.

'Why don't you start us off?' he asked her. 'Tell me the story you know, and I'll fill in the gaps.'

Senya thought about if for a moment, then shrugged. 'I can try. Where shall I start?'

Mikilov shrugged back. 'Same place as the bards, I reckon. Start with the snow.'

'They always say it was the worst winter Haslova has ever seen; that a man would freeze to death if he stayed still for too long. Is it true the snowdrift was fifteen feet deep in places?'

'At least. Whole villages were lost out in the wilds, buried in the snow. It was a desperate time for the Basillians. They always had a knack for killing each other, but I think that winter was the first they turned to cannibalism. No doubt that's where it started for the likes of the Empty Faces. Some tribes were wiped out entirely, lost to the cold and the hunger.'

'And then came the Jarl,' said Senya.

'And then came the Jarl,' muttered Mikilov.

The girl bristled at the interruption. 'Are you telling this story, or am I?'

Mikilov chuckled. 'Fine, girl, you tell it.'

'One day, in the midst of this winter, the city watch glimpsed shadows moving through the fog in the valley far below the city walls. One by one, the bells rang out...'

Mikilov closed his eyes as the memories came flooding back. He could remember it as though it were yesterday: the smell of coals burning in the brazier when he stepped out onto the ramparts; the clanging bells sounding the alarm; the confusion as the fog washed over him, thick as soup, shrouding the sights and muffling the sounds.

'The Jarl brought men from twenty tribes,' Senya was saying, 'two thousand strong at least. No one can say how he led them across the White Waste, only that he did.'

'Desperate men do desperate things,' muttered Mikilov, though he knew that was unfair. There was nothing desperate about the Jarl. He was a formidable foe and an inspirational figure among the Basillians, a man whose ambitious plans offered hope at a dark time. He had sought to use the weather to his own advantage, taking Haslova by surprise in a daring raid. That so many tribes had thrown manpower behind him was a testament to the Jarl's will.

'Spare me the details,' Mikilov told Senya. 'I was there. Just tell me what you know.'

As Senya recounted the story the bards had shared a thousand times before, Mikilov's memories dragged him back through the truth of that day. *Not so pretty as the songs. Not so glorious.*

He had thought it a test when the alarm went up, an order from the powers above to assess the alertness of the guards. But then he saw the lights on the horizon; the orange orbs of torches blurred in the fog, filling the valley below. Two thousand men at least, and even that a stingy estimate.

The journey through those conditions would have broken lesser men. That the Jarl had brought so many of them through in such good order spoke not only of his leadership, but also of the determination of the tribesfolk. You had to respect an enemy like that. It made them worth killing.

'The siege lasted days,' Senya was saying, 'each bloody assault turned back by the stout defenders...'

Mikilov rolled his eyes. 'That's enough nonsense,' he muttered. 'The *siege* barely lasted three hours, let alone three days. You think they would have made that journey if they had the provisions for a siege? It was the hunger that drove them to attack when they did. It was a damned raid!'

They walked on in silence for a spell, both watching the ice at their feet, ready to react at the first sign of weakness.

'Well,' Mikilov said at last, 'if you want a story told right, best to tell it yourself, eh? It was a brutal, bloody mess that day. They got a foothold on the ramparts easy enough, but only because the archers couldn't see a damned thing through the fog, not until they were right on top of us, and by then it was too late. The blizzards had battered the city for the better part of two weeks, too strong and too frequent to keep the snowdrift in check. By the time the Basillians made the wall, they were practically knee height against the battlements. They just had to step over.

'We fought them tooth and nail on the ramparts, your father and I standing beside the king. Finn already had a name for himself, even back then. One of the king's favourites. I was there as the king's shieldman, an honour passed down from my own father.' Mikilov sighed as the last moments of King Ornov played out in his memories. 'Alas, neither of us could do anything about the arrow that took the king's life.'

Senya nodded. 'They say it was an impossible shot.'

'At least the bards got that much right. It was the Jarl himself who took it. He was still outside the walls, maybe three hundred yards away, with thick fog, heavy snow, and blistering winds between him and his target. I caught him in the corner of my eye as he loosed, and I knew as soon as the arrow took flight it would find its mark. It flew strong and true, and it took the king in the neck.' Mikilov shook his head as the image faded. 'By the Great Hunt, you'd think the wind itself had carried it home. And just like that he was gone. Ornov, the last Valorian king, slain by an arrow.'

'Was that when the king's son led the counterattack, to reach his father's body?'

Mikilov arched an eyebrow in Senya's direction. 'Victor? No, there was no counterattack. The Basillians forced their way to the livestock and food supplies, though it cost them a lot to get there, but they only stole what they could carry and then retreated. It was only when he heard of his father's death that Victor gathered fifty men to him to pursue the Jarl on horseback, your father and I included.

'They'd lost the bulk of their force in the attack and most of the survivors had come on foot, so it was easy enough to ride them down. What few mounts they did have were piled high with the stolen supplies and driven on ahead. A force stayed behind to slow us down. We managed to finish them off, but the Jarl was nowhere to be seen. He'd gone on ahead with their spoils. A sharp mind, true, but a cowardly one.'

'So, you tracked him?' Senya was watching Mikilov eagerly now, seemingly forgetting the fact they were walking on ice.

Tread carefully now, Mikilov told himself. *Sometimes the truth can cut deeper than a sword.*

'We did,' he said cautiously, his eyes narrowing. 'Victor wanted revenge, and we were young and eager enough to follow after him. We crossed the Adalvas into Old Valirov; fifty of us, skirting the Whitelands and ploughing headfirst into the bitter winter. The Jarl knew we were after him, so he just kept pressing on, dragging us deeper and deeper into their land.

'We snapped at his heels and he snapped back. Bodies littered the trail behind us like breadcrumbs marking the way. Some were killed in ambushes and skirmishes, others it was the cold that got them. The frost can seep into a man's soul and snuff him out before he knows what's happening.

'On a journey like that, it's only a matter of time before the line between right and wrong gets blurred. Soon enough it didn't matter to us *who* we were following, only who crossed our path. We burned two Basillian camps along the way, butchering men, women, and children. Two tribes, wiped from the face of the earth.'

'No,' said Senya, her face suddenly pale. She had staggered to a halt, staring at Mikilov with open disgust. 'Father wouldn't do such a thing.'

Mikilov stopped a few yards from her, offering a pitiful shrug. 'And yet he did. I led the first attack, when the blood lust was still high. I was the king's shieldman and I had failed him - I hungered for redemption. But after that, after the things we did...' Mikilov sighed heavily. 'Guilt got the better of me and I was no use to anyone. It was left to your father to lead the charge the second time. I remember him screaming the king's name as he doled out slaughter.

'Somehow it was worse that second time. The first had happened too fast for thought, swift and brutal. But by that second time... ah, we knew exactly what business we were about.' He shook his head bitterly. 'Knowing that, it still shocks me how few of us held back.'

'They don't sing about this in the songs,' said Senya.

'Well,' Mikilov shrugged, 'there's no glory in butchering women and children. Not even Basillians.'

Senya's face paled even further. She looked grief-stricken. 'How could he do such a thing?'

'How could any of us?'

They started walking again, Senya leading the way and Mikilov following once a gap had built up. Scar padded along beside them, a silent shadow on the ice.

'The truth is I have no idea why Finn took up the mantle,' Mikilov continued. 'It wasn't hatred of the tribes, I know that much. When you fight them long enough, you learn to respect them. They are a brutal people, true, but they live in a brutal world. They have to be strong to survive, and we are the fire against which they test themselves. Your father knew that as well as I did... more even, having spent time in their world.'

'He never spoke to me of them,' said Senya, and Mikilov was surprised to hear the tremble in her voice. *Sometimes the truth can cut deeper than a sword.* 'Even when I asked him, he would always deflect, change the subject. They were stories for another day, he would say, though he never got chance to share them.'

'The Jarl changed him,' said Mikilov. 'Finn loved Ornov as a son loves a father, and, when the Jarl killed him, a part of your father died with him. He was consumed by the red mist. Revenge became everything to him, and Victor's bloody quest gave him the best chance of getting it. What was more dead Basillians against that?'

Senya's jaw jutted out suddenly, her eyes blazing, and Mikilov winced. He had pushed too hard. 'A small price to pay,' she said, 'to end the threat of the Jarl. I see what you're trying to do Mikilov, but you won't change my mind. The Wolfeater must die. That will be my revenge, for Velimir, and for all the others that damned Crow has killed. And if what you say about my father is true, at least I know he'd be standing with me.'

'That's where you're wrong,' said Mikilov. 'By the end, your father realised the same truth I did. Once you've seen enough of the world, enough *death,* you start to realise what vengeance is truly worth. And it's not worth the dirt you piss on, girl. Not a single bit of it.'

'Well... maybe we'll get chance to find out,' said Senya, pointing ahead.

A single figure had appeared on the riverbank, little more than three hundred yards away now. The wind whipped about him, kicking up snow and tugging at his fur coat, but even at a distance Mikilov could make out the band of grey feathers hanging around the man's neck.

'Grey Crow,' he muttered, pulling up alongside Senya. 'Now it begins.'

* * *

They stood like statues for the longest moment, staring at each other across the icy expanse. Mikilov and Senya's breath caught in their throats as the surprise washed over them, only Scar's growl rumbling on in the silence. Up ahead, the Basillian cast a forlorn figure standing at the river's edge. Behind him, the evergreens cresting the river bank swayed majestically in the wind, which rustled through the tribesman's heavy furs and danced through the large grey feathers of his necklace.

'Grey Crow,' muttered Mikilov. 'Now it begins.'

Senya cursed under her breath. There was no doubt in her mind where the blame lay. 'I told you we should have killed her. That bitch has warned them we were coming.'

'I'll not apologise for letting an unarmed woman live. She's done no less than we would have done, had we walked in her shoes.'

'Say what you will,' snapped Senya, 'your mercy may have killed us.'

'Or your hate.'

The retort stabbed at Senya's heart. Before she could reply, a surge of movement killed the words forming in her throat.

The Basillian strode out onto the ice, swinging a giant axe from his shoulders as he moved. He paused long enough to look up at them, his wild eyes peering out from a tangle of hair, thick beard split by a gash of gritted teeth. He swung the axe up over his head, then brought it down viciously, the blade hacking into the ice and sticking fast. The sound followed a second later, a howl of effort followed by the sharp clang of steel biting into ice.

Pulling the blade free, he brought it down again... and again. By the third strike, a vast crack opened up in the ice, splitting open where the axe struck and shattering outwards in jagged lines, like a bolt of lightning hurled at the feet of the Valor.

'Scar!' Mikilov barked.

The wolf's first few strides were a struggle, his claws scrabbling furiously for purchase on the ice, but then he was gone, darting across the frozen river like an arrow loosed from a bow.

The Basillian showed no fear as the wolf charged at him. He pressed on with a steady rhythm of raising the axe over his head, then bringing it down with a dull, wet thwack, chunks of ice sent flying as fresh cracks broke out from the source of the impact.

'And you, girl. Move!'

The sharp command cleared Senya's mind and she glanced at Mikilov, who urged her on with a wave of his arms and a thrust of his head, panic in his eyes. All around them the ice was starting to crack and groan, as though the water below was rousing from a great sleep.

Senya had no idea what to do. Press on in the direction they'd been heading all along, towards the axeman and the shattering ice? Or flee in any other direction and try to outrun the breaking ice?

In the end, she chose the path she thought would get them to solid ground the quickest; the path that led to the man with the axe. She ran as fast as her legs would carry her, the ice shifting and crackling beneath her, threatening with every step to plunge her into the cold, eternal depths below. There was no point holding back now, no guarantees the ice would hold even if she stood her ground. So she ran... and she prayed.

'Don't stop, girl!' Mikilov called after her. 'No matter what happens, you get to solid ground!' Senya winced every time the big man's bulky boots struck the ice behind her, heavy crunch followed by heavy crunch. She could hear his laboured breathing, his every grunt and groan, as he shifted the weight of his powerful frame after her.

Not once did Senya glance back, not even when she heard him stumble. The Great Hunt would end when it ended... no need to tempt the fates with hesitation.

Scar flew across the ice ahead of them, his paws skittering across the surface as though he barely touched it. The Basillian started working faster as the wolf closed in, panic taking hold. His axe rose and fell in weaker, less rhythmic strokes, barely making a dint as the wolf locked in. *Twenty yards now. Ten. Five...*

The Basillian's eyes widened in horror as the wolf leapt at him. Scar's jagged jaw tore out the tribesman's throat, blood spraying on the scarred ice where he'd been hacking at it, and man and beast toppled through the air. They landed heavily, skidding across the surface in a snarling, screaming tangle, the Basillian's axe clattering away out of his reach.

Senya breathed a sigh of relief. For the first time she let her eyes focus beyond the axeman, scanning the riverbank and the tree line above. *Nothing.* No sign of any other enemies waiting to strike.

She glanced back at Mikilov, the big man still striding after her, no more than ten paces behind. 'I think we'll...'

Before Senya could get the words out, the ice gave way beneath her. She plunged through the surface like a hammer punching through glass, her right foot going first, dragging the rest of her down with it. She fell screaming, though the sound cut off sharply once the freezing water pierced her clothes, stealing her breath and replacing it with a wheezing gasp.

Down she went; feet, legs, midriff sinking into the black waters of the Velga. It was only when her chest struck the ice that the broken remains of the surface held. Senya's gloved hands slapped down on the ice ahead of her, scrabbling desperately for a grip, even as she felt herself slipping ever deeper into the water.

She thought it was over, the end of both the Great Hunt and the hunt for the Wolfeater. The cold would numb her body as the heavy fur clothes that had been keeping her alive dragged her down to the riverbed. The water would burn her nostrils and her throat and her lungs, until she could take no more. And then she would sleep.

Sleep is death.

Her father's voice, reminding her of the laws of the Whitelands, as he had reminded her not so long ago. Velimir had found her back then, dragging her out of the frozen dark and into the light and warmth of his cabin. But her uncle was gone now, ended by the Wolfeater. *That's why you're here*, she reminded herself, anger warming her blood. *For Velimir.*

Digging her fingers into the ice, Senya tried to pull herself from the water. She cried out with the effort, but slowly she managed to lift her head and shoulders above the water and drag herself up onto the ice.

That was where her strength failed. Shivering uncontrollably, her arms gave way beneath her and her face slapped down on the frozen surface. Senya felt herself sliding back into the water, the Velga drawing her on like an old lover.

Then Scar was there, the grey fur around his mouth dark with blood, his teeth dripping with it. At first, she thought he was about to tear her face off, but instead his bloody maw closed tightly on her fur coat and he dragged her from the water.

Senya took a moment to gather herself. She was shivering violently from the freezing water and exhausted from the brief battle to escape its clutches. Glancing ahead, she saw the Basillian lying prone on his back, blood scattering the snow all around him. She looked back, and horror stabbed at her heart.

A vast section of the ice had broken apart in her wake and Mikilov was nowhere to be seen. Where the ice had given way, it revealed the Velga was not asleep after all - that only the surface was frozen. Below it, the river flowed east as swiftly as it ever had... and it had swept Mikilov away to his fate.

Senya screamed out in pain and anguish. The Great Hunt had spoken, and Mikilov was gone.

CHAPTER FIFTEEN

Voices in the Night

His was the only face she had ever known.

Her fingers traced every line of it, rising and falling with the creases, sensitive to the bumps and blemishes, the scars of battle and the wrinkles of age. They found his beard, usually close cropped, but longer now, wild from weeks in the wilderness. She could even tell the grey hairs from the black, reading the march of time in a single touch.

He was old now, but not so old as those grey hairs told her. That was the illness, she guessed, rotting him from the inside out.

There was a time he would have woken at even the slightest touch, though he'd lay still, letting her fingers poke and prod at his flesh, sculpting his face in her mind's eye. Not now though. Now he failed to stir. He slept on, tired and broken. That was the illness too, she knew, grinding him down and wearing him out.

With a sigh, the girl slid away from Radok and shuffled out from under the boughs of the pine, emerging into the cold night air.

Though her world was as dark and empty as ever, Nyana could still feel the moon on her skin, bathing her in silver light. Closing her useless eyes, she focused her other senses, letting them paint the picture for her. More trees surrounded them, the breeze rustling through their branches and needles, the smell of pine somehow comforting in a world where the snow had buried everything else.

It was still snowing now. Big, heavy flakes landed on Nyana's face, making her flinch, carried on the ever-shifting wind.

Yet, when it came to the wind, it was not the snow that interested Nyana, nor even the rustling trees or howling plains. It was the voices hidden within, whispering of the past and the future, the living and the dead. Squeezing her eyes closed even tighter, Nyana strained to hear the words.

No woman can hear the Will, Talak had told her once, laughing at the absurdity of the idea. *Certainly not one so young and blind and useless as you!*

Nyana feared that old bastard more than anyone, but his scorn had never been enough to stop her from *listening.* Men like Talak thought the gods belonged to them, but Nyana knew better. The Will of the Seven applied to all, whether man or woman, boy or girl, or even blind or all-seeing. And so their words were there for all to hear... so long as you were brave enough to listen.

Try. The word was little more than a whisper slipping from a screaming throat, but it was there, hiding beneath the roar. *Try,* it said again.

He wants you. Nyana was less certain of this one. The voice was deeper and stronger, but the words were muffled, half buried in the constant howl of the northern winds.

Nyana stepped further into the clearing, felt the wind grow stronger around her. She spread her arms wide and lifted her face to the heavens, turning slowly on her heels. The wind washed over her, snaking around her limbs and caressing her skin until she tingled with the touch. And the Will filled her ears...

Try, it said again.

'Try what?' Nyana called back.

Grey Wolf.

Nyana huffed. What did that mean? What did any of it mean? No matter how hard she listened for the Will, the few words she could pick out from all the bluster of the howling wind meant nothing to her.

The Blackstone.

That one she did understand. Once she reached the Blackstone and laid her hands on its smooth surface, everything would change. The chaos of the eternal wind would give way to the All Song. Those broken words and empty phrases would become whole and beautiful. For the first time in her life she would know the true voices of the Seven. She would know the Will.

And the Eighth... A different voice, lower, more sibilant.

Run. The first voice, low and soft, barely a whisper.

He is coming. The darker voice, sinister and triumphant.

Somewhere in the distance a crashing sound started through the trees. The wind seemed to fall silent as snapping branches and broken needles filled the night air, along with bending barks and crushed snow. Nyana had frozen mid-turn, ear cocked to the new sounds, while an unstoppable wave of destruction flowed towards her, growing ever closer.

Run now!

Turning on her heels, Nyana darted back to their makeshift shelter and dived beneath the tree. She grabbed Radok by the shoulder, shaking him fiercely. 'Wake up!' she screamed. 'He is coming!'

It was only on the fourth attempt that the big man stirred. Nyana felt him lift his head and peer about. 'What is it, Little Sparrow?' he asked groggily. 'Who is coming?'

'I don't know. But he's here. We need to run.'

The crashing sound was closer now, undeniable, and it was enough to get Radok moving. 'Go, I'm right behind you.'

Do what I say when I say it, he had told her, and Nyana had given her word to obey. Without argument, she left Radok to gather his sword and their belongings together, while she slipped out from beneath the tree. The sounds of destruction were almost on top of them now, drawing closer with every passing moment, moving in an unstoppable wave towards her.

Gritting her teeth, uttering a silent prayer, Nyana turned away from the approaching doom and ran. It didn't matter that she was blind, nor that every step was a risk. It only mattered that she put as much distance between herself and whatever was coming as was possible. That was the Will.

She ran with her arms stretched out before her, ducking and weaving at the touch of overhanging branches. It was harder to account for the feet though, and it was only a matter of time before a jutting tree route snagged her foot and sent her crashing to the ground. She landed heavily, ploughing face first through the thick snow.

She tried to scramble to her feet, but the fall had knocked the wind out of her and she was struggling to find a grip. She heard the trees being shoved aside behind her, branches bending and snapping with the force. Heavy footfalls slapped down in the snow behind her, drawing closer... closer...

Nyana closed her eyes then, instinctively. What else was there to do, when the end was upon you? No chance for her to be scattered to the wind. Even in death, the Will would pass her by.

She screamed as something grabbed her about the waist, hauling her up. Hands, she realised. A man's hands. Then that familiar smell of stale sweat mixed with the iron of blood and the steel of business. A good smell. *The smell of home.*

'Up, girl, on my back.' Even as he spoke, Radok practically heaved her up there. Nyana locked her hands across his chest, and hitched her legs up around his waist. Then they were moving again, Radok's giant strides eating up the distance.

'What is it?' she gasped down his ear.

'A kragan,' said Radok. 'Big bastard too. Might be the one Jorn fought off, back when we were young. We never did catch him.'

Though a kragan was just one of many things Nyana had never seen, she had heard enough stories to paint a picture of them in her mind's eye. They were said to be vast in size - twice as large as even the biggest bear, and twice as vicious - with teeth and claws the size of daggers, and a roar that could shatter bones.

As though the beast could read her thoughts, a blood curdling roar filled the darkness of Nyana's world. She screamed, part in fright, part in pain, as the sound vibrated through her, her hands clasping over her ears for protection.

'I've got you, Little Sparrow,' said Radok, though Nyana could feel him slowing. Their escape path was taking them uphill and his stride had faltered with the climb, his breathing laboured.

'Leave me,' she told him. There were tears in her eyes, but she knew he couldn't see them. 'I'm only slowing you down. You can make the Blackstone without me.'

'You're right!' Suddenly, Radok swung her down from his shoulders, grabbed her by the waist and lifted her high. 'Grab the branch and haul yourself up.'

Sure enough, Nyana felt a branch hanging over her head and she was able to drag herself up onto it. 'You can climb higher, there are good branches above you.'

This is it then, he's done with me.

'I don't blame you,' she told him. 'I can't believe you've carried me as far as you have. You have always carried me, Pappa. I love you.'

Silence followed, for what seemed an age, but then she felt his hand squeeze her foot. 'I'm not leaving you, Little Sparrow. I promised we would touch the Blackstone together, and I mean to keep that promise. You stay here now. I'll lure the beast away. If I'm not back before nightfall... wait a little longer. I'll come back for you.'

For a moment it seemed he would say more, but in the end Radok's hand slipped from her foot and she heard his footsteps moving away.

The kragan wasn't far behind him. Nyana's tree swayed with the force of his passing, the shuddering impact of his great lumbering strides almost tearing Nyana from her perch. *He smells like winter*, she thought as he swept by. *Cold and damp and hungry.*

Then they were gone, both man and beast, lost to the white noise of the forest. Nyana climbed higher in the tree, feeling her way carefully amongst the stronger branches. Finally, she settled back against the tree's trunk and lost herself in the foliage. Now she would wait.

You cannot wait.

The wind was back, if it had ever been away, and the voices were as loud and disjointed as ever.

Run, they were saying. It was all they ever seemed to say. *Run.*

He is coming.

CHAPTER SIXTEEN

The Crow Eater

'Any sign?'

Garda blew warm air into his hands as he crouched beside Jian, his question hanging in the air like the ghost of his breath. They had climbed the highest hill they could find on the Velga's northern bank, and now Jian sat on a rock gazing south.

In truth, it was difficult to see anything in the darkness, but every now and then the moon would peek out through a break in the clouds overhead. When the silver light painted the landscape below, Jian would lean forward and hold her breath. Her gaze would sweep from the trees of the north bank to the hills of the south, and then glide up and down the weaving, silken line of the river itself, looking for any sort of movement. Then she would breathe again, and sigh.

'Nothing,' she told Garda. 'My first bloody decision as leader was to leave Vinak behind, and now where is he? You want to take back your vote?'

'And lead myself? I'd rather cut out my eyes with a wooden spoon!' Garda smiled. 'Don't get me wrong, decisions I don't mind. It's living with the consequences I have a problem with. But you're stronger than that, girl.'

'Am I? I've only ever had to worry about myself.'

Garda still looked amused. 'Tell me your story.'

'What?'

'Tell me your story.'

'You know my story.'

'Aye, I do, but I want to hear it from you.'

'Why?' asked Jian.

Garda laid a hand on her shoulder. 'Because Vinak is dead, and you need to know why.'

Jian frowned. 'Even if he is dead, what does my story have to do with it?' Garda did not reply. He just kept staring at her, that half smile playing at his lips. Jian shrugged. 'I was Grava's woman until I lost his babe. Then he tried to kill me, but I killed him first. That was when the Fallow took me in. I've been with them ever since.'

Garda shook his head. 'That's not your story, Jian. Grava the Fearless was your man until the day you lost a babe in childbirth. Instead of joining you in grief, as he should have, Grava's rage got the better of him. He tried to kill you, aye, but your heart was too strong and the Eighth took Grava instead.

'That should have been the end of you. To lose your child and your sworn man in one stroke, to be told you could have no more children... a lesser woman would have faded and died after that. But not you. Even with the tribe set against you in those early days, you stood tall and proud. Radok saw it when no one else would. That man has a liking for lost causes, but he has never stood with someone he didn't believe in. And he stood with you.

'The laws of the Seven say a woman who killed her sworn man should die, but together with Radok, you moved the Will to spare you. The Wolfeater found a place for you in the Fallow, with other women left barren by the Will, to serve the Grey Crow on the battlefield. It seems even the Long Eye knows there is a place for you in the All Song.'

Garda squeezed Jian's shoulder. '*That* is your story, girl. And *that* is why Vinak stayed behind. He stayed because *you* asked it of him. And you are our leader now.'

Jian shook her head. 'I can't...'

Garda pressed a finger to Jian's lips to silence her. 'The mark of a true Grey Crow is how strong they fly through the storm. Your storms have been worse than any, yet still you fly. You should be dead, yet still you live. You should be weak, yet you are strong. You should know fear, yet none are braver.' The warrior shook his head. 'No more doubts, girl. We don't need to hear what you can't do, we only want to see what you can. Show us that, and I promise we will follow you to the end.'

Garda winced as he pushed himself to his feet, his knees popping like a knot of wood in the fire. 'Another reason I'm happy to follow,' he said. 'Hard enough keeping my body in one piece without worrying about you lot.' He gestured for her to follow him. 'Time to forget Vinak, eh? Either he'll catch up to us or the Wolves will. We don't have the bodies to worry about them all. First we deal with Talak, and then we think about the rest.'

They moved to the north side of the hill, where the rest of the hunting party had ducked amongst the snow-covered boulders and wind blasted bushes, watching the path north. Below them, the trees gave way to a vast ocean of snow; the open steppes of the Whitelands, glistening silver in the faint measure of moonlight slipping in through the cloud cover.

'Anything?' Garda asked, slipping in to sit amongst them.

'Nothing,' said the hard-faced Ingram, hawking and spitting. 'Though it's hard enough to see anything in this damned light.'

'You think they're out there already?' asked Jian. 'Or back here, in the trees?'

'Radok?' Garda scratched at his beard thoughtfully. 'He's seen the same things we have. He knows it's too open down there to move in daylight. He would have been waiting for this. This is his moment.'

'And Talak?'

Garda shrugged. 'I doubt even the Seven know what that crazy bastard will do next. He wants Radok though. If we find Radok, we find Talak.'

'Look!' Talgar jabbed a finger at a clearing in the trees to the west, where a figure briefly appeared, heading towards their hill.

Jian leaned forward, squinting, but the figure was gone as quickly as it had appeared, lost beneath the snow-capped trees below. 'Who was it? Did you see?'

'Some big bastard!' muttered Pican, who had the best eyes of any of them. 'Moving too fast though.'

'Radok?'

'Hard to say. It wasn't that scrawny prick, Talak, that's for sure. And who else would be out here?'

The man-wolf had been a big bastard too, Jian remembered, but even if Vinak had failed in holding them up, there was no chance they would have gotten so close so quickly. *It has to be Radok!*

Jian's heart began to beat more wildly. They had been sent to kill Radok, but Jian was starting to hope there might actually be a way to save him. She owed him more than enough to try.

'We can cut him off,' she said after a moment. She looked at the faces of the men around her, and at Tess who had slipped to her side. They looked tense, but could see the same hope she felt in her own heart. 'Stay close to me. Once we find him, try not to kill him. Maybe we can talk him down.'

'And if he doesn't want to talk?' Garda asked softly.

Jian hesitated for just a moment. 'Then we do what has to be done. Talak is all that matters now.'

Radok's strength was failing him. In truth, it had been failing him for months now, ever since the coughing began. Somehow, he'd always managed to battle through it, to find an edge just when he needed it most. But things were different now.

He'd been on the move for less than a minute when the pain started to take its toll. His arms and legs grew heavier with every step, turning to weights of stone that he struggled to drag along with him. Every breath was a battle. The frigid air stung at his nostrils and hacked at his throat, but it was the lungs that hurt most of all. Despite the cold, they burned with fire.

Radok could hear the beast closing in behind him, shattering the silence of the wood as it rumbled after him like thunder; a giant, crashing force following in his wake, sweeping trees and rocks aside with effortless ease. Squawking birds took flight as their shelters were shook to the core, or else torn up by the roots entirely. There were moments when the beast seemed so close Radok would have sworn he could feel its breath on the nape of his neck...

As he ran, sucking in painful gasps of air, his knees beginning to quiver, Radok risked a glance over his shoulder. The kragan was charging on all fours, shouldering trees aside and throwing up dirt and snow in his wake. Lines of saliva and spit flew out from a mouth full of sharp teeth, some long as daggers, and when his cold, black eyes met Radok's, the beast let out a blood curdling roar.

Radok turned away from him and felt his stomach tighten. He had seen this monster before, he was sure of it. It was the same beast that had mauled Jorn all those years ago, the one they called the Old Bear. Patches of white fur were missing from the left side of his face, the exposed flesh left blistered and twisted - proof of the flaming torch driven into his maw.

Radok would have laughed if not for the terror gripping his heart, if not for the sheer exhaustion. The Will had always had a wicked sense of humour, and sending this monster to finish him off was all the proof he needed.

Focusing back to the road ahead, Radok glimpsed two trees off to his right that were growing closely together near the base, their trunks forming a v-shape. He angled his run towards them, slipping slightly on a sheet of ice but somehow staying on his feet. Radok flinched as the kragan's claws whispered past his left ear, brushing the fur of his trailing cloak.

He leapt through the gap between the two trees, landing softly on the other side. Radok kept moving, wheezing hard now, legs ready to buckle beneath him. He'd hoped the beast was close enough behind him to follow him through the narrow gap and take some damage... but this wasn't the kragan's first hunt. Sighting the two trees, he pulled up short and side-stepped the obstacle, unleashing another terrible roar before powering on after Radok. The dance had slowed him by a second or two, but nothing more.

Radok was beginning to fear the worst. His lungs flared painfully with every breath, his stamina all but spent. He knew his legs were ready to buckle beneath him, but he was almost ready for it. When the beast's jaws closed around his head, finally bringing an end to the suffering, Radok thought it might actually be a relief. *At least the girl is safe. At least I did that much right...*

Using his arms as a shield, Radok pushed himself through a thick wall of foliage and burst into an empty clearing. He took two strides across the virgin snow before movement caught his eye up ahead. A girl had exploded into the clearing opposite him, and when their gaze met they both staggered to a halt in shock.

For just a moment Radok forgot about the pain of breathing... forgot to breathe at all, so lost was he in the vision of the woman. My *woman, if the Will had only deemed it so...*

Jian was well suited to her surroundings, daubed as she was all in white. Her close-cropped hair was dyed white to match her furs, and the top half of her face had been painted in chalk. Only the band of black paint across her eyes offered any break in the camouflage. That highlighted those eyes in stunning clarity and Radok was lost in them.

It reminded him of the day he'd fallen in love. He had found Jian surrounded by all the powerful of the Grey Crow, her hands dripping red with blood. Having lost her babe in childbirth, she had killed her man in self-defence after he turned grief-mad. After that, she would have lost her own life, if she'd let them take her. But Jian was a different kind of woman, and Radok had known it that day, when he first looked into those stunning hazel eyes. She stood her ground against the baying mob, and Radok stood with her.

Jian was staring back at him, her panting breath smoking in the frosty air. Radok thought again about all the chances he'd had to tell her how he felt. But how could he, given everything she'd lost? Would there ever be a right time to tell her?

Now, perhaps?

Even as the thought struck, Radok remembered where they were, and why, and the moment passed. *She's here for me. She's here to stop me.*

She was about to speak, but Radok, who wanted nothing more than to hear her out, spoke first. 'I'm sorry,' he told her, before hurling himself into the underbrush to his left. Behind him, the kragan burst from the trees into the clearing, and his mighty roar shattered the quiet of the night.

Jian's blood ran cold as the kragan's roar thundered out. He was standing on his hind legs, stretched to his full height, chest puffed out, the sound powering out from deep within him. Jian winced in pain, the noise was so loud. He was a monstrous beast, twice as tall as a man and almost four times as broad.

And he was hungry. Despite his thick white fur, Jian could see the shape of his ribs as he stretched and bellowed.

All at once the beast dropped to all fours and began charging in Jian's direction. His face bore a terrible scar, fur all burnt away, flesh blistered and pussy, and it twisted with savage relish as he closed the gap between them.

Before Jian could even register the threat, the Grey Crow moved to intercept. An arrow flew over Jian's head and buried itself in the kragan's shoulder. The beast didn't flinch, just kept pounding on towards Jian, snow and debris kicked up behind him. Then Pican and Talgar were there, Ingram and Garda, hacking at the monster with their swords. The kragan roared his frustration, then swung at this new prey with vicious claws, giant arms swinging left and right.

The youngster, Pican, was the first to die. The kragan's right paw swung back and connected fully with Pican's head, snapping the boy's neck like a dry twig. His broken body flew through the air and crunched sickeningly against a tree to Jian's right.

Talgar, Ingram, and Garda continued to dance around the beast, their swords nicking and slicing at him, turning patches of his coat a dark pink where they drew blood.

Another arrow appeared in his flank, but that only seemed to anger him. Ingram lingered a bit too long within reach, and the kragan's claws sank into his flanks. Drawing him into a crushing hug, the beast sank his jaws into Ingram's shoulder, tearing the flesh from him right up to his neck, blood gushing everywhere.

Ingram screamed as his life was torn from him, the sound of it rousing Jian from her awe-stricken trance. She realised she was offering nothing to her friends, two of whom were already dead; men she had promised to lead. *You can't lead the dead*, she told herself. And then she drew her sword and made to charge...

A hand grabbed her by the shoulder, spinning her around to face Tess. A look of terror gripped the young warrior's face as she leaned into Jian. 'Run!' she hissed, shoving Jian back into the trees and away from the beast. 'Everyone, run!'

Jian had no idea if the others escaped or not, but she followed Tess through the trees, back towards the hill. Jian stumbled through the snow and ice, the rocks and foliage. It was brighter now, the sun beginning to rise somewhere over the trees, so that Jian could see where she was going.

As she ran, Jian's mind was a jumbled mess of thoughts. Radok was first and foremost amongst them. He had stood before her, mere feet away, and the sight of him had broken her heart. Pale and withered, he was a shadow of the man she had ridden with to the farmstead near the wolf city. He had been her rock in the dark days, something to cling to when the storm was at its worst, but it looked like all the strength was gone now and he was the one that needed holding.

I'm sorry, he had said, moments before the kragan descended upon them. *What was he sorry for,* Jian wondered? *Did he bring that thing down on us? Did he do it knowingly?*

Pushing those questions to one side, she tried to focus on the only thought that mattered right then: survival. They needed to stop Talak, and *she* needed to see Radok again, to talk to him. And to do that she needed to live.

Tess crested the hill and spun around, Jian catching up to her a second later. The pair of them stood with their hands on their hips, sucking in deep breaths of cold air.

'What... now?' Tess panted.

Jian moved to the vantage point they had been using earlier, when they first spotted Radok. She swept her gaze over the trees below, hoping for a sign of movement. But there was nothing.

'I can't believe they're dead,' said Tess. 'I've never seen anything like that.'

'We have to kill it,' said Jian absently. 'He has our scent now, and a taste for blood. He won't stop hunting us until we're dead.'

'How can we kill that thing?' Tess looked scared. It was the first time Jian had seen her show fear for anything other than the *Ashan Tay* or the Far Eye.

Jian gave her arm a squeeze. 'Everything dies, Tess. You just have to stab it in the right place.'

A scream sounded out from below, shattering the silence, but there was nothing to be seen down amongst the trees.

'By the Seven...' muttered Tess. 'It sounds like he got another one.'

Jian's frustrations boiled up. These men had voted her leader, and now most of them were dead, or soon would be. They had barely taken their first steps together and already she had failed them.

That was when she screamed. She was too sad, too bitter, too angry to hold her emotions in check, so she let them go in a long, primeval cry of anguish. The sound echoed out across the empty foothills below, washed away with the southern wind.

It did not take long for the kragan to answer. His roar was full, deep, and drawn out. And then he was moving. The trees towards the Velga started swaying in a wave towards them, like the trail of a fish cutting through water.

'Fuck,' muttered Tess, swinging her bow from her shoulder and notching another arrow.

Jian glanced around. The hilltop was bare, save for a handful of trees on the southern slope and a few rocks littering the ground. There was a boulder amongst the smatterings, almost head height. Jian waved Tess towards it. 'Get up there. I'll keep him distracted; you fill him with arrows.'

'I'm not sure there are enough arrows in the world,' said Tess, but she tossed her bow on top of the rock and began to climb. Fairly nimble, it didn't take her long to swing her trailing leg onto the rock and take up position. Crouching low, she drew back on the bowstring and took a calming breath.

Jian tested the weight and balance of her sword, stretching her arms and loosening the muscles. She had always felt cumbersome fighting in furs, and today was no different. They might keep you alive in the cold, but in a fight their weight and bulk were just as likely to get you killed. *Can't take them off,* she thought. *Not enough time.* Hell, even if there was, there was a good chance she'd freeze to death before getting them back on.

'He's here,' said Tess, just as the kragan's head appeared over the crest of the hill. The beast was moving quickly, charging on all fours, strings of bloody saliva dangling from his snarling, bloody teeth.

The earth trembled beneath Jian's feet as the monster bore down on her, yet she did not run. She held her ground, her sword gripped tightly in one hand, and waited.

Tess loosed her bowstring with a dull twang, and the arrow soared over Jian's head. It was on course for its mark until the kragan threw up an arm and swatted it from the air. With a cry of rage, the monster leapt the last few feet, his huge paws balled up and raised over his head.

Jian sidestepped the attack, hair fluttering in the breeze as his giant fists crashed down into the snow where she'd been standing. Even as she dodged, Jian slashed her sword across the beast's side. The blade bounced harmlessly from his ribs, nowhere close to cutting through the thick hide. She dodged two more attacks while the beast towered over her, then threw herself into a forward roll, narrowly avoiding a left hook. She sliced at the kragan's hind quarters as she rolled by, but the cut lacked the strength to draw blood.

The snow slowed Jian's roll just enough for the kragan to catch her before she could regain her feet, clubbing her across the back and sending her sprawling into the snow.

She came up dazed, the blurry figure of the kragan towering over her, ready for the killer blow. Another arrow punched into the beast's shoulder, just short of his throat, and with a roar of pain and outrage he turned from Jian and charged at the boulder where Tess was standing.

He hit the rock shoulder first, the force of the impact enough to shift the giant stone under Tess's feet, throwing her off balance. She fell hard, cracking her head on the stone and falling limply to the snow below.

'No!' screamed Jian, forcing herself back to her feet. Before she knew what was happening, she had drawn the knife from the sheath in her boot and hurled it at the monster's back. It was a poor throw and it struck the kragan hilt-first, just below the left shoulder, from where it fell harmlessly to the ground and sank deep into the snow.

Poor, but effective. It did enough for the kragan to forget all thoughts of Tess and turn his killer's gaze back to Jian.

'Come on then, you shit!' Jian taunted him. 'I'm right here.'

The kragan's roar bellowed out in reply, the sound of it stinging Jian's ears. *Run*, that roar said. *Run for your life.*

But Jian had never run. Not even when the mob came for her after Grava's death.

Glancing down, she saw her sword lying at her feet, and she grunted as she bent to pick it up, her back still aching from the blow she'd taken. Her vision had started to clear, but it wasn't entirely comforting given the sight of the beast bounding towards her for a second time.

Jian's hand tightened on the sword hilt, the creaking leather drowned out by the kragan's thunderous charge. She shifted her feet, ready to spring clear at the perfect moment. Jian smiled then, a deep calm settling on her. She couldn't run even if she wanted to. Tess's screams would haunt her to the end of her days. And if this was how it ended, then so be it.

The kragan's gaze drifted beyond Jian and his charge suddenly faltered. Much to Jian's amazement, Talgar and Garda ran past on either side of her, roaring their own battle cry. She followed without hesitation, falling in alongside them, not just holding her ground but joining the attack.

The kragan stumbled to a halt, stunned by the sudden turnaround. The three Grey Crow hacked at him in a blur of steel, every sword stroke followed by a curse of some description.

'Die, you whoreson!' screamed Talgar, his blade biting in above the kragan's hip.

'The Black Wind rides for you, bastard!' cried Garda, blade slicing through the flesh beneath the kragan's right arm.

'I'll eat your fucking heart!' Jian hurled at him, spit flying from her mouth. She had aimed for his throat, but the tip of her blade did no more than catch the underside of his chin.

Only the fur at the top of the beast's head remained the white of snow; the rest of him had been painted a pinkish red, right down to his paws.

Now that he was on the defence and Jian had a chance to really look at him, she could almost feel pity. The kragan looked gaunt and tired, half-starved by the king of winters, and for all his bravado and menace he was as weak as they came; a shadow of what he must have been back in his prime. The thought was enough for Jian's hand to pause... and the moment's hesitation was all it took for any hint of pity to be wiped away.

Seizing even the slightest opportunity, the kragan lashed out at his three attackers, his claws raking across them all in one fell swoop.

Garda took the brunt of the attack, the kragan's claws slashing across his stomach, heading upwards the chest. Jian was next in the line, but she leaned back just at the right moment, the razor-sharp claws grazing her chest and throat. She saw Talgar catch the end of it, his face torn open, and the three of them hit the ground together.

Rather than finish them off, the kragan turned on his heels and lumbered away. Seemed he'd taken enough damage for one day. He looked back only once, making sure he wasn't followed.

'Aargh!' Talgar writhed in agony, half buried in the snow. He was holding his hands to his face, but Jian could see the blood flowing freely between his fingers. She gave his arm a squeeze. His good looks were gone for good, but at least he'd live.

The same could not be said for Garda. The old man was finished, torn up across the belly, his guts spilling out like spoiled fruit. He smiled as Jian loomed over him, taking his hand in hers. 'Only the best for the Black Wind,' he muttered, through bloody, gritted teeth. 'Toe to toe with a fucking kragan.'

And then he coughed his last cough and was gone.

CHAPTER SEVENTEEN

The Man from the River

The screams echoed out in the growing gloom as Radok stumbled through the trees. He kept glancing over his shoulder, but there was no one following him, nor any sign of the kragan giving chase. Nothing besides the sounds of death, at least.

He staggered to a halt, his lungs burning up into his throat, bile sitting on his chest. The last time he walked the Whitelands he remembered seeing smoking mountains far to the east, which had turned the skies orange of a night. 'Volcanoes,' the *Ashan Tay* had explained. 'Below the ground the world burns, and those mountains are where the fire escapes.'

That's what I feel like right now. Like there is something bubbling up inside me, waiting for release. And this fire will eat away at me until there is nothing left to burn.

Radok started moving again, pushing the fears and the pain to one side. He knew the Eighth was hunting him - had been hunting him for most of his life, in fact - but it was as close now as it had ever been. Radok could feel the Black Wind's cold caress on the nape of his neck, even as the fire burned within.

'Not yet,' Radok muttered into the wind. 'I save the girl first, then we touch the Blackstone... and then you can take me.'

What about me? Jian's voice, as strong and challenging as ever. *You left me behind with that...* thing*!*

Radok could still see Jian's eyes widening with horror as the kragan burst through the trees behind him. He had led the beast straight to her, then abandoned her to deal with the consequences. After everything she had lived through, everything she survived, it was heart-breaking to think he had visited such a terrible end upon her...

She made her choice, Radok told himself, driving the voice away. *She chose Talak. Now she's on her own.*

He made his way back along the tracks that had taken him up the hill; his own tracks, demolished by those of the kragan. It was growing darker now, with the sun starting to slip behind the western mountains, but Radok eventually found his way back to the tree where he had left Nyana.

'Little Sparrow,' he said, his gaze sweeping the branches above. 'We're alone now. Where are you?'

No answer.

Circling the tree, Radok performed another sweep of the surrounding area, searching for any sign of tracks in the snow beyond those he'd left himself. He found a set of small footprints heading southeast, back towards the Velga. *The girl. Running, by the looks of it.*

'I told her to stay put.' With a curse, Radok set off in pursuit. He followed the trail of footprints through the trees, only starting to run when he saw the second set of prints, off to the left, moving parallel.

They were larger than the girl's, Radok noticed, and he judged them most likely a man's boots. Like the girl's though, there was only one set and he found himself wondering who might be out here alone.

He thought back to the encounter at the top of the hill, when he had been almost blinded by Jian's appearance. Radok still had enough wits about him to pick out the other faces in amongst the trees. There were all the usual suspects - Garda, Ingram, Talgar, even Tess - but there was one face missing that should have been there. *Talak*.

As *Ashan Tay* to the Grey Crow, there was no chance Talak would have missed the opportunity to join the party charged with stopping Radok from returning to the Blackstone. And if there was anyone in the world Radok wanted to keep away from Nyana, it was that righteous fool. Talak had wanted the girl dead from the moment she was born; one reason amongst many that he and Radok shared such bad blood.

Run, girl, Radok willed her, even as his lungs started burning afresh. *Run as fast as your legs will carry you. I am coming.*

The sound of waterfalls drifted to him as he moved further south; a rushing, churning sound that grew steadily louder with every step he took. He followed the trail down a steep incline, half running, half sliding on his way to the bottom. At the foot of the slope the trees ended and Radok stepped out onto the stony shores of the Velga.

To his right the waterfall glistened orange gold in the fading sunlight, water thundering down the side of the icy cliff in three big steps, each slightly larger than the last, until at the foot of the falls the water eased into a slow meander east, where eventually it would spill into the vast frozen lake that bore the same name.

Radok gazed up at the falls for a moment, marvelling at the volume of water pouring down toward him. It was hard to believe that the river had been frozen up there, while down here the heart still pumped and the river's lifeblood flowed as true as ever.

Radok turned to the east and gazed along the river's length. His heart skipped a beat as he caught sight of something floating in the water further downstream. He cursed, and started to run again, his eyes fixed on the distant object. The fire had spread to his chest and throat now, not to mention his arms and legs, and every other part of his wretched, dying body, yet he ran on regardless. He tried not to imagine the worst - that it was his girl floating down there, the Little Sparrow - but he imagined it anyway.

The Blackstone faded from his mind. The Seven and the Eighth fell silent. Their voices, which Radok had never understood anyway, still washed over him as he ran, but he could not hear their whispers, only the sound of blood rushing to his head. Even the pain tearing at his insides dulled to a weak throb as the body in the water drew closer.

And it *was* a body. Radok could see the arms and legs now, bobbing on the surface. Big arms. Big legs. *A man!*

Relief flooded Radok like a tidal wave and he almost staggered to a halt, almost collapsed such was the force of the realisation. Yet instinct drove him on, and he waded out into the Velga. The ice-cold water caught his breath, but Radok pushed on, finally grabbing the body by the shoulders and turning him face up. Long, wet hair, covered the man's face, but there was no gasp for air as he turned over - no sign of life at all.

Radok thought about letting the body go, allowing the current to carry it away downstream, for he barely had the strength for anything else. But he had come this far, and if there was a chance the man lived, there was also a chance he might have information Radok could use. Grabbing the body under the arms, Radok began dragging the man back ashore.

He hauled the body from the water and staggered onto solid ground. The man's hands and feet left trails in the shingle, where they dragged lifelessly along, until Radok collapsed under the weight, coming to rest with his head on the man's chest. He waited for a moment, listening. But there was nothing to hear. No breathing. Not even a heartbeat.

Radok peered up at the man's face, brushing aside the dark, greying hair for a better look. His mouth hung open slightly - a crack in the midst of a wild, tangled beard - revealing two sets of sharp canines, glistening menacingly top and bottom.

'Valor,' Radok muttered, hawking and spitting. His dagger was drawn before he knew what was happening, ready to make sure the Velga had done its work. *It would not be the first time I had to end a sleeping Wolf...*

Yet there was something familiar about this Wolf that gave Radok pause. His hand hesitated, the dagger point barely an inch from the man's throat. Radok leaned in closer, studying the lines around the man's eyes. Recognition finally dawned. *It's him. It's the Grey Wolf.*

Radok had seen enough action on the walls of Haslova to recognise one of their finest warriors. He had watched countless friends cut down by the Grey Wolf, both young Crows and old, yet had never seen any malice in the man. He was a killer, aye, but a fair one. And in this world, it was rare to find such an honourable foe. That was why they called him the Grey Wolf. Not because he was grey himself, though he had reached that age, but because they saw him as one their own... a Crow born on the wrong side of the wall.

Radok sheathed his blade. The Grey Wolf deserved better than a dagger through the throat. *By the Seven, he deserves better than drowning!*

Radok's fist thumped down on the Valor's chest with as much strength as he could muster, but there was no reaction. The Grey Wolf lay still, his head lolling to one side, his mouth slightly ajar. The fist struck down a second time, but again there was no reaction. Radok sighed. What was the point in it all, he found himself wondering.

It was the same question that had dragged him out into this wilderness, where nothing but death waited. *If I am to die,* he had decided, *the gods can tell me what it was all for. I will stand before the Blackstone and demand an answer...*

Yet the Blackstone seemed as far away as ever, and Radok was no closer to his answer. He had brought the girl out into this world and lost her, with little hope of her surviving without him. And now this? The Grey Wolf had done as much for his gods as Radok had done for the Seven, yet he too had ended in obscurity, stripped of honour and dignity. The gods were cruel indeed, to offer such rewards for the lives spent in their service.

'What is the *fucking* point?' Radok's rage spilt over and his fist slammed down a third time... causing water to explode from the Valor's mouth. The man Wolf sat bolt-upright, sucking in a great gulp of air. He tried to catch his breath, but every gulped air ended in a coughing fit that was painful to watch. *I've been there.*

'Breathe,' Radok told him, resting a hand on his shoulder. 'You're back now. Stay calm and breathe.'

Slowly, the Grey Wolf's breathing eased and his senses started to return. Radok studied him closely. There was a blueish tinge to his skin and he was shivering badly. 'What happened?' he asked, his eyes trying to focus on Radok. Then they widened. 'You!'

The Grey Wolf tried to rise, but he fell back, his head striking the shingle hard, and slowly drifted to unconsciousness.

'Me,' said Radok.

Mikilov drifted in a world of darkness, vaguely aware of his aching body, battered and bruised from his journey over the falls.

He should have been dead. After falling through the ice, he had plunged like a stone, dragged down by his weapons, the thick fur coat he wore soaking up water like a sponge. He'd never had much talent for swimming, and the extra weight he carried made the feat almost impossible. Even where the water ran shallow, he had lacked the strength to reach the surface and break through the ice.

Just before his lungs failed him entirely, Mikilov hit the falls. Three vast steps, each higher and rockier than the last, and Mikilov was dragged over all of them. It was a reprieve from drowning at least, but more than once his body was smashed against the rocks and only the fur coat played a part in holding him together.

Finally, the white rapids had given way to the calmer, placid current of the lower river, and it was there that Mikilov's exhausted body shut down. He floated for a spell, watching the grey clouds drifting overhead. And then the darkness had taken him, hiding him from the pain.

Not all darkness, he remembered suddenly. *The Wolfeater!*

He saw again the black face leaning over him, a dagger in one hand. It was a face he had seen many times before, but only ever across the battlefield. They had killed countless men between them, but never stood face-to-face.

With a groan of effort, Mikilov forced his eyes open and sat up. It was dark, but a fire was burning beside him, its light and warmth offering some solace in the circumstances. He winced as a log popped in the fire, sending up a flurry of sparks. The sound echoed off hidden walls beyond the darkness. A stale, damp smell clung to the air, and Mikilov could taste it with every breath. The sound of dripping water drifted from somewhere close, and the earth rumbled with some unseen force. *A cave then*, Mikilov reasoned. *Not far from the falls.*

He glanced down. There was a fur blanket draped over him, but beneath it he was naked. His clothes lay by the fire, drying, and there was no sign of his weapons. He moved the blanket aside for a moment, inspecting the damage. He was covered in bruises and grazes, his skin ranging in colour from yellow, to purple, to red. *Nothing broken though. Thank the Great Hunt!*

At least that was what he thought until he breathed, when a sigh of relief turned into a groan of agony. When his lungs pushed up against the ribs, pain seared from his chest. Wincing, Mikilov tested the area where the pain had struck, his fingers tracing the curves of his ribs on his right-hand side. He found two he was sure were broken, and another two severely bruised at least.

'You're lucky,' a voice drifted from the other side of the fire's glare. 'You should be dead. You smashed your head up pretty good too.'

Mikilov reached up instinctively to the right side of his temple, wincing again as his fingers landed on a lump the size of a child's fist. Then he felt the pain that accompanied it; a dull, throbbing ache deep in his mind.

'Wolfeater?' he asked, though he knew the answer.

The man shifted around the fire and crouched before Mikilov, a white smile breaking his dark face. Even having seen this face before, even having its origins explained to him by Elgamire, it was still the strangest sight Mikilov had ever seen, made all the stranger by the flickering light of the fire. 'You can call me Radok,' said the Wolfeater. 'And you, Grey Wolf? What is your name?'

Mikilov thought about lying, about arguing, about throwing insults, but in the end he only sighed. Whatever his reasons, this man had saved him. The least Mikilov owed him was an honest answer. Besides, he had no idea where his weapons were stashed. In his current condition, Mikilov knew it would be a difficult task to kill the Wolfeater without a blade. 'My name is Mikilov.'

Radok nodded. 'Well met, Mikilov. You should know that I have seen you many times before, on the walls of Haslova. I have watched that axe of yours cut my people to shreds. It's quite a sight to behold.'

'As I have seen you,' said Mikilov. 'Hard to miss the black crow in amongst the grey. You're always the first to get a foothold, leading the way for your young ones. I've always wondered, why don't you push on? Once you have the wall it wouldn't take much to topple Haslova.'

Radok grinned. 'You Wolves think the world will end with you, but you're nothing in the All Song. Have you ever been east, Grey Wolf? Have you ever looked upon the wall of the One God? *That* is where the world begins and ends, and that is the wall we want. That's the truth for all the tribes of Basilla. We live for that wall, and one day we'll take it. Haslova is practice for the real thing, nothing more. And that is why we stop.'

Mikilov grunted. 'And what a life we all live, eh? Wondering if each day will be our last... knowing that it probably will.'

Radok's smile slipped. 'Aye. What a life.'

'Why did you save me?' asked Mikilov. 'You knew who I was and the things I've done... and you saved me anyway. Why?'

'Why not? All my life I've been killing men like you. Some deserved it, some didn't. I thought I was doing it for the right reasons, for a cause greater than myself. I was doing it for the Seven. I was doing it for that *fucking* wall.' Radok shook his head. 'My reward for all those dead? The lungrot, eating me from the inside out. I'll be dead soon enough, Grey Wolf, I can feel it coming. But I won't spend the last of my days killing Wolves for the Seven. Not until I've stood before them and asked them why.'

For the first time since waking, Mikilov allowed himself to relax. The tension eased away, and he lay back. 'You know why I'm out here?'

'To kill me,' Radok said without hesitation.

'No,' said Mikilov, 'that's why the girl is out here. I'm here for her.'

'The girl?' Radok mused. 'The one from the farm?'

'Would you have killed him? The man with the bison. Before the girl got involved, would you have killed him?'

'That wasn't my first choice. I wanted to talk first, to see what happened. That's what I told my men, and that's what I would have done.'

Mikilov sighed. 'You don't sound much like the Wolfeater to me.'

'Nor you, Grey Wolf. They tell stories about you around the fires of the Grey Crow. The Grey Wolf who stalks the walls of Haslova, *Chadra* swirling around the blades of his great axe. They say you've killed more of our people than the plague.' Radok patted the knife sheathed at his waist. 'Why haven't you dived at me yet, grabbed this knife and buried it in my chest?'

'That's right,' said Mikilov. 'I've killed Grey Crows, and I've killed Empty Faces too. I've killed

Crawsmen and Blue Eyes, Hardings and Blood Sworn. I've killed a thousand different men from a hundred different tribes, most I've never heard of. You think it makes a difference to me, adding one more name to the list?'

'You think it doesn't?' Radok's smile returned. 'The both of us forged our names when we were young, fired by the hate between our people. We are revered as heroes by our own kind, and feared as butchers by the enemy. But every kill we make takes us closer to the great truth. That is why we are able to sit here now, as old, wizened men, and talk about it. No swords, no anger, just words.'

'And what is the great truth?'

'When I stand at the Blackstone,' said Radok, 'I'll have the answer. Until then, nothing will stand in my way. Not even your girl.' The Wolfeater stood suddenly, as though only to take the dagger from Mikilov's reach.

'I'm sworn to protect her,' said Mikilov. He tried to rise, but his ribs shifted, and he fell back in agony.

'If she's ahead of us, it's already too late. Best you turn back, Mikilov. Your people need you. And right now, there's a girl that needs me.' He turned to leave, but Mikilov grabbed his leg.

'Don't tell the girl,' he pleaded. 'About the farm. She already blames herself, no need to drive that blade any deeper.'

Radok stared down at him for a moment, then nodded. 'The girl killed my friend and she'll pay the price for that. But I'll hold to the guilt for the farmer. It was my anger that killed him. You have my word.'

And with that, Radok pulled himself free and backed away into the darkness, leaving Mikilov alone in the haunting quiet of the cave.

It took Mikilov almost an hour to build up enough strength to force his way through the pain and climb to his feet. Though his clothes were still damp to the touch, he dressed as quickly as he could, then carried out a quick search of the cave. He found his weapons stashed between two rocks at the back and quickly armed himself, axe slung across his back, daggers belted to his waist.

By the time he stepped outside, thick storm clouds had consumed the night sky and were poised ominously overhead. Hoping to find his bearings, Mikilov worked his way towards the sound of the falls, an endless crescendo of water tumbling down over those three vast steps. It was distant now, that incessant roar, but unmistakable. He could hear the river too, though only faintly over the sound of the wind that came blowing through the trees. The river would be flowing southeast, but the falls would point the way north. And it was north that he would find Senya and Scar.

Stumbling across an old deer trail heading in the right direction, Mikilov followed it through the trees. It began snowing as he walked, big soft flakes floating down through the gaps in the canopy overhead. It was hard going. The snowdrift was already banked up in places, and Mikilov had to fight his way through to the other side. It didn't help that he was hampered by his injuries. He walked hunched over, shielding his broken ribs, and every breath he took jabbed at his lungs with fresh pain, partly because of the ribs and partly because of the cold.

While he walked, he found himself wondering about Scar and the girl. Would they have tried to follow him downstream, or pressed on without him, leaving him for dead? It was more a question for the girl really. Tough to know what meant more to her, friendship or the need for vengeance? Most likely the latter, given the choices that had brought them here.

The wolf, on the other hand, was much more predictable. He would mourn Mikilov, of course, given that they had spent so much of the Great Hunt sharing the road together. But he was wise enough not to risk lingering for a lost cause. He would follow the girl, whether onward or backwards, for Scar was nothing if not a realist. He had to be, in order to survive the wild. There was no place out in the wilderness for dreamers or romantics.

'Then why are *you* out here?'

Mikilov spun at the sound of the voice, dry and creaky as an old door. The old woman gazed back from the hood of her ancient rags, those haunting white eyes hidden in the shadows. Behind her, there were no tracks in the snow, despite her rags trailing in the ground behind her.

'Elgamire,' he muttered, offering a nod of the head. 'How am I not surprised to see you here?'

The old woman shrugged. 'Because I've developed a bad habit of saving you from your own stupidity? I asked why *you* were here.'

'You know why.'

'Ah, yes. To kill the Wolfeater.' Elgamire shook her head. 'So many lives wasted on killing a man who is already dead. Yet you missed your chance. How was your meeting with our forsaken rival?'

'I'm not here for him.' Mikilov felt a twinge of pain, and exhaustion suddenly got the better of him. He found a fallen tree beside the trail and took a seat, breathing heavily. He was shivering violently again, the cold gnawing at his core. Yet he recovered long enough to meet Elgamire's gaze. 'I'm here for the girl.'

'Ah, yes. The girl.' Wandering over to him, Elgamire cupped his chin in one wrinkled, arthritic hand, and she smiled fondly. 'What was it about romantics?'

'I'm a realist too,' Mikilov told her. 'I know what it means to be out here, but I couldn't live with myself if I let her face it alone.'

'You're a damned fool,' she said softly, but there was a fondness behind the words. 'Too noble for your own good. I suppose that's why I like you.'

She laid a hand on Mikilov's shoulder and he felt warmth flowing through him, emanating from the place where she touched him. He hadn't even noticed his teeth were chattering until they started to slow, and soon enough the shivering stopped entirely. He could even feel his clothes drying on his body, as though her touch drained all the cold and damp from him. Finally, she laid her free hand on Mikilov's right flank. He winced as she pressed her fingers to the broken ribs, yet he felt the warmth again and the pain quickly evaporated.

Finally, her hand fell away and she sagged heavily on her gnarled, oaken staff. Mikilov felt strong again, rejuvenated, his clothes somehow warmed and dried.

He tested the ribs again, breathing deeply, stretching left and right, and they felt as fine as they ever had.

Yet Elgamire's face was ashen, her energy and vitality drained away. For someone who had always looked old - *ancient* even - today was the first time it truly showed.

'What have you done?' he asked, moving to her side and guiding her back to the fallen tree.

She sank to a seat and gave a sigh of relief. 'I have saved your life for a second time,' she told him. 'I fear there will not be a third.'

'Why?' he asked. 'Why do you keep helping me?'

'Because you are the last of the Old Valor, the *true* Valor, and you alone will pave the way for the generations to come. That's not this story though.' The old woman's white eyes drifted off to gaze into nothing, as though she was talking to herself rather than him. 'Few will care what happens to the Wolfeater. Only the Sparrow has a part to play in the years ahead.'

'The Sparrow?'

Elgamire blinked. Her blank, yellow eyes shifted back to meet Mikilov's gaze. 'Radok's girl. All being well, you will know her before this journey is done. She must live, Mikilov. If you take anything from this meeting, take that.'

'You didn't even want me out here, now you want me to save some girl?'

'I only try to point you in the right direction,' said Elgamire. 'You decide the role you play. Go now, this storm will only get worse.'

'What about you?'

'I will rest here a spell.' Elgamire smiled fondly. 'The cold does not trouble me, but you are not an easy friend to keep alive.'

'Will I see you again, old woman?'

'Oh, do not doubt it.' She took his big hand in hers and squeezed. 'Go now.'

Mikilov did not look back as he set off up the slope. He could see the falls rising up above the trees, plumes of mist filling the air like smoke. There was no time to look back and check for the old woman. It was time to climb.

CHAPTER EIGHTEEN

Defiance

For the first time in her life, doubt gnawed at Nyana's mind.

Radok had told her to stay where she was and he'd return for her once the kragan was drawn away. But then the wind told her to move. Not one voice, but many, all pulling in the same direction. It was the Will, Nyana was sure of it, and so she did the only thing she could. She ran.

Now the voices had fallen silent, lost to the confusion of wind and rushing air as she ran, while she had left Radok, her only constant, far behind. Suddenly Nyana could not be sure she had made the right choice. What if it was not the Will that guided, but the whispers of the Eighth? What if it was the Black Wind, *Chadra*, leading her astray?

Nyana ran on, wincing as trees whistled by on either side of her. Branches snagged her clothes and scratched her face... but not once did she hit a tree. When she sensed their great bulks looming before her - and she did sense them - she would swing aside and choose a different path. Radok had always said she had good instincts, but Nyana knew there was more to it than that. She could *feel* the guiding hand of the Seven in every decision she made. Even now, with her doubts at their strongest.

The mass of trees suddenly gave way and the land opened up before her, revealing a vast expanse of empty country. Though Nyana lacked the eyes to see the sweeping dunes of snow lying ahead, she saw it in her mind. The wind was wilder out here, battering at her tiny frame from all directions, like the tide breaking on a lonely piece of driftwood.

The snow was thicker too, falling in heavy clumps that stuck in Nyana's ears and nose, or else landed in her eyes and mouth. It made running almost impossible. Nyana struggled to pull her feet free of the deep blanket of snow and lift them high enough to keep powering herself forward. The effort quickly sapped her energy.

Still, she kept moving. What was it Radok had said? *Sleep is death, out here.* She thought it must be the same for standing still too. She could already feel the cold seeping through her clothes, made worse by the cutting wind.

'Where are you running to, child?'

The voice cut through the howling wind like thunder through silence, and Nyana froze to the spot, her stomach lurching sharply.

She made no reply, hoping against hope that the voice had been a trick of the mind. But then the wind shifted and she caught his scent; a strange concoction of stale sweat, fire smoke, and the sweet perfume of Kamra's Whisper, the flower from which the *Ashan* castes drew their visions. The smell, when paired with the voice still echoing in Nyana's mind, sent a shiver of fear down her spine. *Talak.*

Perhaps it *was* the Eighth then, delivering her to his servant. *Or perhaps it's a test,* she thought suddenly. *Perhaps I need to prove myself...*

The *Ashan Tay's* footsteps drew him closer, crunching through the snow, until he stopped a few feet away. The wind eased sharply, as though the Seven and the Eighth were holding their breath, watching.

Nyana licked her lips. Talak had always terrified her, for one reason or another, and she'd tried her best to avoid him like the plague. Even now, her legs felt weak at the thought of his cold eyes staring back at her. In another life she would have run, fear breaking her courage. But that life was done now.

You heard the Will, a voice whispered. Not a voice on the wind this time, but a voice in her head; Nyana's own voice. *You have heard the Will, and he never has.*

Nyana held her ground.

'I asked where you were running to?' said Talak, his craggy voice carrying even more of an edge than usual.

'Where the Will leads me.' Nyana's own voice sounded tiny and afraid out on that frozen tundra, little more than a whisper.

'*The Will...*' Talak sneered, his voice breaking into a cackling laugh. 'I have followed the Will for most of my life, girl - almost fifty years, man and boy - and it never brought me anything but pain and loss. You're better off without them.'

And just like that, Nyana's fear of the man melted away. He had always hated her, she knew that. From the moment her mother died in childbirth and he saw the ruin of her eyes, Talak had declared her an abomination, urging the Grey Crow to end her life before she could taint the rest of them. Back then, even as now, it was only Radok who stood for her. He was the only one with enough influence to stop the Grey Crow from holding to Talak's version of the Will. Yet Talak *was Ashan Tay,* and in the eyes of the tribe he spoke for the Will. Nyana knew the day would come when they took up his call, with or without the Wolfeater's backing.

That was the fear Nyana had lived with until now. Now she saw the truth and the fear was gone. Now she was free.

'I'm not afraid of you anymore,' she told him. 'I thought you were special, a true *Ashan Tay*, and I was always terrified that what you said of me was true. I actually believed the Will might want me dead.'

'But now you know better, eh?' said Talak. Nyana could still hear the sneer in his voice.

'Now I know better,' said Nyana. 'I know you're a weak, bitter, twisted old man. You might hear the Seven, but I don't think you've ever *listened* to them. You're no closer to knowing the Will than anyone. And now you follow the Eighth...'

The sound of lurching steps in the snow cut Nyana short. '*You* would lecture *me*?' spat Talak, his words dripping with venom. 'You're just a child! What do you know of the world? What do you know of suffering? Even forgetting your eyes, you've *seen* nothing of this world!'

Though every inch of her wanted to turn and run, Nyana stood firm. For a moment she was lost for words, but then she remembered the winds had fallen silent and the words were already waiting for her.

'You're wrong, *Ashan Tay*,' she heard herself say. 'What do *you* know of suffering? You had a mother and father who loved you, who made you strong enough to touch the Blackstone and join the All Song. You have a tribe that respects you, and a people who would do whatever you ask. And you have your eyes, to see the world and all the beauty it holds.' Nyana shook her head. 'I have none of these things. They were taken from me the day I was born, and I've been outcast ever since. You dare to tell me you've suffered more than I have, but that belittles the both of us. Pain and loss *are* life, Talak. That's how we *feel* it. That you would turn your back on that, for whatever small reward the Black Wind offers, is a sign of just how small you are!'

That struck a nerve. Talak cried out in fury and grunted as though hurling something. Nyana felt a tug on her left sleeve and side-stepped in that direction. She felt something hard and cold brush against her right cheek as it flew past her, the ring of metal following after it.

There was the crunch of snow again as Talak charged forward. She heard him draw his sword, icy fingers of fear closing about her heart...

And then it happened. A loud crack shattered the silence of the snowy waste and Nyana felt the ground giving way beneath her. She stepped back sharply, just as a great chasm opened up between her and Talak. Snow and ice split apart and crashed away into the void below, debris raining down after it. For just a moment, Nyana allowed herself a small moment of hope that Talak had gone down with it.

But then the wind swept back in, bringing with it a blizzard so fierce Nyana had to shield her face from it. It burned at her skin and roared in her ears. She turned back from the chasm, away from the worst of it, and felt a shove against her back, as though the wind had formed a hand to push her. She staggered away, back towards the Velga, and the pressure eased almost at once. She tried to turn back, but the blizzard lashed at her harder once again. *Not yet,* a voice rose above the crowded whispers. *You must take a step back before you can move forward. You're not ready to stand against him.*

'You best run, bitch!' Talak's voice cried out, barely audible over the storm. The hope died, and Nyana ran.

Talak glanced down at his feet, the tips of his boots standing at the very precipice of the new chasm, his toes sticking out over the edge.

Below him, snow drifted down into the deep dark that had almost claimed him. He lifted his gaze to look across the ten-foot expanse, squinting into the swirling snow of the blizzard, trying desperately to spot the girl. She was gone, scurried away to safety by the Seven.

Smiling, he turned slowly in a circle, arms spreading wide. The blizzard continued to rage around him, but he remained untouched. An unseen barrier stood between him and the winds, shielding him from the snow and the hail. It was like he stood in the centre of a sphere of glass and nothing the world threw at it would break through.

It's not glass though, thought Talak. *It's the Eighth; the Black Wind, protecting his servant. And his will is mightier than the Will of the Seven.*

'What now?' asked Talak, though he did not expect an answer. *Chadra* had chosen him because he could think for himself, because he could make the hard choices. He turned on his heels and headed north.

It mattered little where the girl was fleeing to, nor even where Radok was. What mattered was the Blackstone. That was their goal, and it was there that he would wait for them.

CHAPTER NINETEEN

The Slow Death

He found the girl's trail easily enough, though more by luck than by skill. With the snow as deep as it was this far north, he would have struggled to miss the trench the girl left behind. It wound its way through the trees in a meandering path that only a blind person would have taken, though somehow missing every tree along the way.

Still, the snowfall was near constant now and it wouldn't take long for the trail to be buried. Radok picked the pace up. He felt good, for a change. He had feared the time spent helping the Valor from the river would cost him massively, but the respite had done him good. He was rejuvenated, energised. His chest still felt raw, like a deep breath would be too much for his lungs to bear, but he was breathing freely.

Climbing one gentle slope with ease, Radok half ran, half slid down another, before finally reaching the northern edge of the Velgan trees. From here, he gazed out across a vast, open expanse. He expected to see the rolling white plains from which the Whitelands took their name, but it was too dark and the blizzard too heavy for him to see anything.

The wind was driving in hard from the north, relentless as the tide. Radok ducked beneath the needled branches of a fir tree and pressed himself up against the trunk, peering around to watch wave after wave of harsh snow crash into the woods around him. He groaned.

She was out there somewhere, Nyana, lost in the middle of that storm. The thought of it terrified him. If he waited long enough for the storm to pass, there was a good chance he'd find her half buried in the snow, frozen to death. He pictured her blank eyes staring back at him, as lifeless as they were useless. *No,* he told himself. *I can't let that happen.*

He pushed himself from the tree and stepped out from the woods, into the swirling snows and wicked winds of the northern plains. For a moment it was like plunging his head beneath the surface of the water during those naked swims in the Velga, but then the cold truly hit him. The wind chill cut through his furs like a sword through paper, the snow and ice lashing into his face with the burning force of boiling water. He fell back again, slinking back into the shadows of the tree.

He cursed himself a coward. *How many times have you stormed the walls of the Wolf men? And now you're beaten by the weather?*

He pictured Nyana's face again. They could see nothing, those eyes, yet they held more soul than the eyes of any other living thing Radok had ever known. The day he saw them lifeless would be the day he died himself.

He stepped out again, arm shielding his face, and strode forward into the wind. It hit him like a forge's hammer, blasting him again and again, but this time he rode it out, driving himself forward step by step, inch by inch.

The shock of the cold made it hard to catch his breath, and he felt his lungs starting to burn again. He managed some ten steps before he fell to his knees, trying desperately to breathe.

It was the Will, he knew. The Seven would do their damnedest to keep him from the Blackstone, but they had not accounted for the girl. Radok had never realised it before, but everything else paled into insignificance next to her. And now that her life was in danger, the gods would have to burn the flesh from his bones to keep Radok from saving her.

With a grunt of effort, he pushed himself to his feet and staggered on. He was leaning into the blizzard, his clothes flapping about him, a layer of snow slowly building across his body. The wind roared in his ears, angry and defiant.

Radok staggered on. The pain was fading now, his body starting to numb, but he could still feel his ears burning and his eyes watering. That was when he felt blood trickling from his nose. He looked down. His front was covered in it, red seeping into the white layer of snow covering his chest.

'Radok!'

A voice on the wind, faint and barely audible over the raging storm. Radok shook his head. It was a trick of the mind, nothing more. *There's no time for it,* he told himself. *The Little Sparrow is out there, somewhere, and she needs you.* He took another laboured step forward.

'Radok!'

There it was again, that voice, only it was louder this time, harder to ignore. Radok glanced back over his shoulder. Once again it was difficult to see anything through the snow and the dark, but when the clouds shifted he caught a glimpse of three figures standing in the shadows of the trees, like ghosts given form by the moonlight.

'No,' he grunted, turning back into the wind and forcing another step. He wouldn't be fooled by his imagination. There was nothing back there for him. There was only the girl, lost in the whiteout up ahead.

His left leg buckled beneath him and he dropped to a knee. He took a deep breath, blood still trickling from his nose, and pushed himself up once more. He managed two more steps before he fell, landing face first in the snow.

He thought he heard the voice again before the darkness took him.

'Radok!'

He stank of death.

In truth, he had always stank of death. Each time he went away, whether on a hunt or a raid, he would return with the smell of death clinging to him, soaked into his furs.

Yet this was different. This was not the smell of the quick death - the bitter, iron scent of splattered blood and spilt guts, or the pleasant hint of smoke from the fires of battle - but the rank, unpleasant stench of the slow death. There were no wounds to see, no injuries of any kind, but the smell was enough to tell Jian everything she needed to know. *He is dying. And the end is close at hand.*

With a sigh, she sank to her knees beside the Wolfeater and took his hand in hers. They had managed to drag him back to the trees, dumping him with his back up against a tree trunk, unconscious, while the blizzard continued to swirl around them.

'He's rotting away,' said Talgar, uselessly. He was standing over them both, pity in his eyes. Or what you could see of his eyes, at least, through the scraps of blood-stained cloth wrapped around his head, holding his face together. 'How long ago was it,' he muttered, 'that farm raid? Three weeks? No more than a month, surely, yet he's already half the man he used to be.'

'And still prettier than you.' Tess appeared beside Talgar, grabbing him by the arm and pulling him away. 'Let's give them a moment, eh?'

Jian nodded her appreciation to Tess as she led Talgar away, out from the shelter of the tree and into the snow. Tess nodded back, that same look of pity in her eyes. That hurt more than any of it. This was the Wolfeater; the finest Grey Crow to ever live, loved by his own folk and feared by their enemies in equal measure, a legend on both sides of the All Song. He deserved more than pity. And he deserved a better end than to be wasted away by some wretched disease.

Jian felt a squeeze on her hand and looked down. Radok's eyes slowly opened. They struggled for a moment to focus... then his dark gaze met hers and he smiled. 'It was you calling for me,' he said, his voice cracking from a parched throat. 'I thought it was my mother, calling me home.'

'Your mother died a long time ago,' Jian told him.

'She never stopped being my mother,' said Radok, before being gripped by a sudden coughing fit.

Jian winced. It was painful enough just watching him sputter and wretch and hack like that, without even imagining how bad it must feel to go through it. She waited for the fit to pass, then, digging her flask out from the folds of her coat, where she kept it close enough to her body heat so that it might stop the water from freezing, she removed the stopper and pressed it to Radok's lips, tilting his head back so that he could drink.

The Wolfeater swallowed what he could, though most of the water spilt down his chin. Once he'd had as much as he could stomach, he knocked the flask away weakly with a wave of his hand.

Radok let his head rest back against the tree trunk. His eyes shifted beyond Jian to take in the swirling snows and blistering winds rushing through the surrounding trees. 'I'm tired, Jian. I've given all I can.'

'No one has given more.' Jian felt tears in her eyes as she spoke. 'The gods are cruel, Radok. You taught me that.'

Radok nodded. 'I wanted to ask them why. That's why I dragged you all out here. Even Nyana... I promised her she would touch the Blackstone, but I should have left her back home, where it was safe.'

'The blind girl? I know you love her Radok, but the tribe see her only as a burden. She was only ever safe with you.'

'And now she's lost in this storm...' Radok's face creased up in a spasm of pain.

'There's still time,' said Jian, watching the pain slowly pass. 'You can find her, you can still touch the Blackstone.'

The pain lines on Radok's face were replaced by surprise. 'I thought you were here to stop me.' His eyes flickered to the dagger sheathed at Jian's belt. 'I'm ready for you to stop. I'm so tired, Jian.' This last was almost a whisper, and it broke Jian's heart to hear it.

'You think I could do that? You saved my life, Radok. You were there for me when no one else was. Talak forced my hand to join this bloody quest of his, but I would have killed him before I stood against you.'

'Don't say that,' said Radok, 'not even to me. Talak is *Ashan Tay*. He speaks the Will and the Grey Crow follow. That's how it has always been - how it *must* be. My journey has led me down a different path, but the Grey Crow always fly true.'

'You wouldn't say that if you'd seen the things we've seen,' said Jian. 'Talak has fallen, Radok. He serves the Eighth now.'

Radok forced himself into a sitting position, though it obviously pained him to do so. 'I don't believe that. He's always been a self-righteous shit, true, but I've never doubted his grasp of the Will.'

Jian shook her head. 'We met with the same Empty Faces you did, back at the Velga. Talak butchered them like a wolf tearing through sheep. And then he left us, saying he didn't need us anymore.'

'Maybe he was right,' said Radok. 'After handling a few cannibals, I'm sure he fancied his chances against a dead man and a blind girl.' He laid his head back once more, his tired eyes sliding closed. 'What does it matter? Let me sleep, woman. I'm done now.'

'No you're not,' hissed Jian. 'Don't you understand? It wasn't Talak, it was the Black Wind working through him. And if he wants to stop you reaching the Blackstone, then the Seven must want you to make it. You have to do what you set out to do. *That* is the Will.'

Radok's eyes flared open and Jian knew she had made a mistake. 'You think I give two shits what the Will wants! I gave my life to them, and this is what they gave me...' He hawked and spat, and a thick blob of congealed blood landed in the snow. 'I'm done answering their call.'

Jian's shoulders slumped in defeat. Of all the men she had ever known, she thought Radok the unbreakable. 'You're not the first person to suffer,' she said softly, her hand moving subconsciously to her belly. 'You're not the first whose body has let them down. But suffering is a part of life, Radok. It's what sets us apart from the gods. I would wager Nyana knows the truth of this. She is out there somewhere as we speak, suffering. No doubt Talak will put an end to that the first chance he gets.'

Jian gave Radok's hand one last squeeze. 'You rest a while,' she told him. 'We'll find the girl and lead her to the Blackstone. We'll keep your promise, even if you can't, because we are Grey Crow, and that's the least you deserve.'

Jian made to move, but Radok held tight to her hand and drew her back to him. 'Promise me you'll look to the girl once I'm gone. Her heart is pure, and she needs a place in this world.'

Jian nodded.

'Then get me up,' said Radok. 'I won't make it to the Blackstone alone.'

Jian signalled to Tess and Talgar, and together they heaved Radok up onto his feet. He stood for a quiet moment, sucking in great gulps of air, seeming to grow taller and sturdier with every breath, as though the cold air restored a fraction of his strength.

They heard a bestial roar carried on the wind, echoing from somewhere in the distance. But while the sound froze Jian, Tess and Talgar to their spots, it spurred Radok into action. He stepped out from the shelter of the tree and set off north once more, into the biting cold and the raging winds. 'Come,' he said over his shoulder, a smile somehow lighting his face. 'Crows fear only the slow death.'

And so they followed. On to the Blackstone.

CHAPTER TWENTY

Blood in the Snow

Gripping tightly to the fur at the nape of Scar's neck, Senya let the wolf lead her on, deeper into the blizzard. He had stuck close to her following Mikilov's fall, but he showed no sign of the loss beyond that.

She thought there might be some hope in that. A bonding between man and wolf was rare these days, but it was said such relationships were powerful enough that both sides could sense the pain or death of the other, even over great distances. Perhaps Scar's lack of mourning was a sign that Mikilov had survived his plunge into the river. *By the Great Hunt, let it be so...*

Senya had considered turning back, of course, perhaps following the course of the river in the hope that Scar might pick up the old man's scent. But in the end, she decided against it. They were here for justice against the Wolfeater, and they had come too far and risked too much to put it on the line for a fool's hope. *Better to push on and get the deed done*, she'd thought. *If, by some miracle, Mikilov did survive, he'll find his way out of this mess I've created.*

They soldiered on, pushing deeper into the woods on the Velga's northern bank, eventually stumbling across a scene of carnage. They found themselves in a clearing where the snow was churned up and scattered with blood.

In the middle of the scene a corpse lay face down in the snow, his throat and shoulder torn out. They found a second body wrapped around a tree a few feet away, his broken frame twisted in unnatural angles. Though Senya lacked Mikilov's talent for reading sign, she knew enough of the basics to see in her mind's eye how events had likely unfolded.

She saw that the Basillians had come down from the hill to the east, their seven sets of footprints moving at speed to the clearing. There they met the maker of a second trail coming in from the south west, back towards the river. The second trail had been more difficult to read, due to the churned snow, but Senya found a few massive paw prints and tufts of white fur snagged on nearby trees to hazard a guess at the maker.

She had never seen a kragan in the flesh before, only the stuffed head mounted on Velimir's wall, but even that massive trophy was enough to fill her with dread. A bear would have been bad enough, but a kragan was something else entirely. The beast had made short work of the two Basillians in the clearing, while the others had fled for their lives.

Knowing it wouldn't do to linger, with the beast likely to return at any moment to feast on his kills, Senya had allowed the wolf to lead her away. Scar followed the kragan's trail west, back towards the Velga. Senya tried to turn him around, knowing the Wolfeater was heading north, but the wolf was stubborn and she decided to trust his instincts.

He led her to a third body, this one torn in half, his guts sprayed across the white earth. Beyond this they reached a tree around which Senya found two sets of prints. The first set, the larger of the pair, merged with the kragan's chaotic trail, heading off through the trees to the bloody clearing. The second set of prints were much smaller and now half buried in the steadily rising snow. This trail did head north, and it was the trail Scar followed, his nose pressed to the earth.

Senya had hesitated for just a moment. They were supposed to be hunting the Wolfeater, not a child. And yet Scar had been following Radok's scent from the beginning. If this was the way he pointed, what choice did she have but to follow?

She fell in behind him, leaving the shelter of the trees for the open plains of the Whitelands, where the blizzard swept in hard and fast. She had grabbed the scruff of Scar's neck, bowed her head into the wind, and followed him out into the great White Waste...

Back in the present, the wolf pulled up sharply and Senya almost fell over him, dragging her thoughts back to the swirling winds around them.

'What the...?'

The wolf was crouched slightly, staring north into the blizzard, his head square to his shoulders, ready to pounce. Senya drew her sword instinctively and stepped up beside him. She couldn't see a thing through the darkness, not with the snow lashing at her face, but she felt a presence closing on them, some remarkable, unseen force.

They seemed to wait an age, unable to hear anything over the wailing wind, until, at last, a shape began to form from the darkness. The child materialised as if from nothing, a dark silhouette emerging from a dark horizon.

Slowly, the figure advanced on Senya and the wolf, details growing clearer with every step towards them. It was a girl, judging by her figure and her gait, wearing grey furs with a hood drawn up. She stopped perhaps ten feet away, cocking her head in a way that almost mirrored Scar's own flare of curiosity.

That was when Senya noticed it. The snow was barely touching the girl. It seemed to dance around her, drifting close and then swerving away, as though an invisible force protected her. *It's the wind,* thought Senya, staring in astonishment. While it blasted her and Scar with ice-laden waves, the girl's clothes barely whispered with movement. She should have been coated in a layer of snow like the rest of this god forsaken place, but she was dry as a bone.

'Who's there?' she asked, a knife flashing into her hand. 'I can hear you breathing.'

'I doubt it,' said Senya, who had to strain just to hear her own voice over the raging wind. Yet what if the girl spoke true? What if the force protecting her from the elements also shielded her from the sounds, letting her hear only what she needed to hear? What kind of girl could hold that sort of power?

It reminded Senya of the old woman they had seen while overlooking the camp of the Grey Crow. She had appeared from nowhere, dressed in rags and talking in riddles, with unseeing eyes that seemed to see everything. *The Wanderer,* Mikilov had said. *El-gamire.*

It was a name of myth and legend, and Senya had refused to believe it. Yet there was no denying the sense of awe she felt when standing in the old woman's company. It carried with it the same kind of elemental force she felt now, watching the snow swirling around this statuesque girl, never touching her.

'Who are you?' she heard herself ask. And in her mind, *Some kind of god?*

Stepping forward, the girl drew back her hood and revealed a plain, round face and a pair of blinded eyes. As soon as she saw the eyes, Senya thought it *was* Elgamire, only younger somehow.

'I am Nyana,' the girl said, lifting her chin defiantly. 'I am Grey Crow.'

She tried to match Senya's gaze, as Elgamire had, but this one lacked the piercing vision of the older woman, the feeling that those unseeing eyes saw everything. They instead missed their mark, the girl's head jerking left and right as though searching for the right spot. *Just blind then,* thought Senya. *She must be the one Elgamire spoke of: the Wolfeater's cur...*

Overcome by a sudden swell of anger, Senya drew her sword and strode forward. The girl should die, she decided. For once in his life, it would be Radok who endured the bitter taste of loss.

Hearing this sudden advance though, the girl's bravado disappeared in an instant. She stumbled back terrified, almost tripping over her own feet. It was heart-breaking to watch, and it gave Senya pause. Her sword arm sagged suddenly, the blade feeling very heavy. *Just a child,* she realised. *And a blind one at that.*

'What are you doing out here, girl? Where is the Wolfeater?'

The girl straightened, the grip on her dagger tightening. 'You'll never stop him reaching the Blackstone.'

'I don't care if he touches some rock... so long as he dies. He killed my kin.'

'You are Valor?' The girl nodded sympathetically. 'Radok has killed many Wolves.'

'And now it ends,' said Senya.

The girl cocked her head again, as though straining to hear something over the roaring wind. And then her dagger fell away. 'You are right,' she said. 'Everything must come to an end. You should come with me to the Blackstone. All our paths lead to the same place.'

Senya considered it for a moment. She didn't like the idea of scouring the Whitelands for the Wolfeater, especially not with conditions the way they were, and only likely to worsen. That the girl meant something to Radok only added weight to the idea of playing along. At least she'd be something to leverage, should Senya need an advantage over the Wolfeater.

Before Senya could answer, though, it was Scar who made the choice. Having stayed at Senya's side throughout the whole encounter, he suddenly strode forward and sat at the girl's heel. Even sitting on his haunches, he still towered over her, yet he nuzzled at the girl's free hand with a softness that belied the difference in size. The girl hesitated, then, a smile growing on her face, she patted him on the head. 'You can come too, wolf. The wind touches all.'

'Out here it does,' muttered Senya. Then, louder, 'We'll come with you, girl, but know that I mean to kill the Wolfeater.'

'I understand,' she replied. Her head twitched again, turning her ear south, listening. 'We should go now. He is coming.'

'Who is coming?'

But the girl had turned on her heels and started north, Scar padding along beside her. Senya glowered after them, their figures fading into the dark, washed away by the blizzard swirling around them. She looked back over her shoulder to the dark outline of the trees. There was shelter back there, and, somewhere, maybe even alive, was Mikilov. Or onward into the storm, with no knowing how long it would last or how bad it would get?

He killed Velimir, she told herself for what seemed the thousandth time. *There's no stopping until he's dead.*

And so she walked on after the girl and the wolf, leaning into the blizzard and tracing their footsteps. Behind her, drowned out by the roaring wind, a different kind of roar split the night air.

He was coming.

They walked slowly across the open white, their feet crunching ankle deep into the snow. The day warmed slightly as the sun rose, but the blizzard kept on. It wasn't so bad for Nyana, who could feel the Will weaving its power about her, shielding her from the worst of the storm.

'How are you doing this?' asked the woman, walking a pace or two behind her.

'Doing what?' asked Nyana.

'This... bubble? There's a blizzard raging all around us, yet somehow it's barely touching us.'

Nyana had no answer. This was as new to her as it was to them. She'd even wondered herself if the protection of the Seven would extend to her new friends, and here was the answer. In the end she said the only thing she could. 'It is the Will.'

The wolf strayed a little closer, his right flank brushing against Nyana's hand. She smiled at the touch, turning her hand over to run her fingers through his fur. Strangely, the beast reminded her of Radok. There was a familiar scent of the wilds for one thing, but mostly it was the sense of power radiating from him that Nyana recognised. It was like she could tell instinctively when they were close, even before her other senses gave them away. It was comforting, that power. Almost as comforting as the Will.

'He likes you,' the woman said. 'Most Basillians, Scar rips their face off before they get chance to pet him.'

'I am not most Basillians.' If the words were meant to scare Nyana, they failed. Something in her bones told her the wolf was safe. 'His name is Scar then?'

'Aye,' the woman said. 'Most of his coat is grey, but three white lines mark his fur on his left side. Mikilov... my friend... tells me it was from a wound when he was a pup. The name has stuck.'

Scar pulled away, perhaps tiring of the attention, and moved off ahead of them, edging out into the blizzard. Nyana turned all of her focus to the woman walking beside her. 'And your name?'

'I am Senya. And you are Nyana of the Grey Crow.'

'You shouldn't be out here,' said Nyana. 'There is nothing in the Whitelands but death and the Blackstone, and the Valor have no business at the Blackstone. Your kind serve different gods.'

'No gods,' said Senya. 'Only the Old Ones and the Great Hunt. And we don't call it the Blackstone. We know it as the Last Rock, because there is nothing else in the white waste beyond it. Death sounds good, though. Death for the right person.'

'Radok is already dying,' said Nyana.

'People keep telling me that, yet he's still breathing. My uncle is not so lucky. Radok killed him and stole his bison. That's why I'm here. For justice.'

'This is about bison?' asked Nyana, surprised. 'Then your friend must have killed Jorn, that was why Radok killed him. Justice is done.'

'Vel didn't kill anyone. He gave up his sword a long time ago. Not that it stopped the Wolfeater from slashing his throat open.'

There was a quiver in the woman's voice, though only Nyana's keen hearing could have caught it. *She killed Jorn,* Nyana realised. *Then she must have run and Radok killed her uncle in revenge. She blames herself.*

The wind shifted slightly, the tremors in the air surrounding Nyana filling her mind with sighs and whispers. As ever, it was difficult to know for sure what they were saying, but Nyana found herself understanding more and more the further north they travelled, as though they were closing in on the source. *Of course we are. The source of all things lies at the Blackstone.*

Heeding the whispers, Nyana said no more on the subject of Senya's dead uncle. This was a volatile woman, the Seven warned, and Nyana would need her for whatever lay ahead.

'What about you?' the woman asked. 'What are you doing out here? The Whitelands are no place for a blind girl, not even with...' Nyana imagined her gesturing around at the surrounding blizzard, still held back by the Will, 'whatever *this* is. Why would the Wolfeater bring you out here? He must have known you'd only slow him down.'

'He had no choice,' said Nyana.

'There's always a choice,' said Senya, and Nyana heard the smile in her voice.

'Not for someone you love,' she replied. 'It would have been the end of me once Radok left. The Grey Crow have no use for the blind. They would have banished me, maybe even killed me, so long as they were left with one less mouth to feed. Radok knew it too. That's why he brought me with him.'

They walked on in silence for a time, only the sound of their feet sinking into the snow or else the muffled howling of the blizzard following after them. Nyana almost fell twice, her feet getting stuck in the snow and almost tearing the boots from her feet. She could feel the ice-cold dampness starting to seep through the leather cladding of her fur-lined boots, and her toes were starting to ache.

The third time Nyana would have fallen, face first into the powdery white, but Senya caught her by the elbow and held on until she straightened. 'What next?' Senya asked when she finally let go. 'What happens when you reach this Blackstone of yours? When the Wolfeater finally succumbs to his illness - if he hasn't already - what becomes of you then?'

Nyana stifled a gasp. It was almost painful to think of a world without Radok, and yet that day was coming. There was no escaping it. She had sensed him melting away these past few days, knowing his great coat was starting to outgrow his shrinking frame, imagining his ebony skin growing paler with every passing moment. It was only a matter of time.

'I learn to fly alone,' she said, 'or I die with him.'

'And you will learn this at the Blackstone?'

Nyana nodded. 'Once I touch the Blackstone everything will become clear. I will know if I'm *Ashan Tai,* or *Ashan Tay,* or... nothing at all. I'll know my place in this world.'

Senya remained unconvinced. 'And how can a stone tell you that?'

Nyana considered her answer carefully. She was still learning the great truths herself, how could she explain it to an outsider? 'It's not just a stone,' she said carefully. 'The Blackstone stands where the wind is born, where the All Song pours into this world.'

'The All Song?'

'The song of everything,' said Nyana. It felt like she was talking to a child. She supposed, in a way, she was. 'We can all hear it, even you. Every time you hear the sigh of a gentle breeze, or the roar of a wild storm? That is the All Song, flowing all around us.'

'No,' said Senya, 'it's not. It's just the wind.'

Nyana bristled at that. 'You wouldn't say that if you heard the voices. But they are there, Senya, for those willing to listen. The voices of the Seven, and of the thousands and millions of souls to ever pass through our world.' She paused, hesitating over what she wanted to say next, but it was not something to be hidden. 'Only the Eighth sings a different song. He sings the End Song.'

She heard Senya tut. 'The End Song? The All Song? It's all just noise, little girl. Stories they tell children to keep them in line. There are no songs, only the wind.'

'Tell that to Talak,' said Nyana, a shiver running down her spine at the memory of their last encounter. *Is he waiting for us up ahead*, she wondered? Then she remembered that Senya had no idea who Talak was. There was only one she cared about. 'Tell it to Radok.'

Senya sighed with exasperation. 'Fine, then let us say it's true, these songs of yours. Where does the Blackstone fit in?'

Nyana's mouth opened to answer, but no words came out. If Senya couldn't hear the song, how could she understand the power of the stone?

No one can understand the Blackstone until they have pressed their hand to its cold surface. Ilgor's voice, *Ashan Tai* to the Grey Crow and Nyana's own teacher. *But you know the theory, Little Sparrow. Use it.*

'Touching the stone focuses the mind,' she explained as best she could. 'Countless voices make up the All Song, but there are only really seven worth listening to - the Seven we worship: *Life, Destiny, Fate, Chance, Desire, Love,* and *Time.*'

Nyana closed her eyes, as pointless an exercise as that was, and focused her hearing. 'Right now, I can catch the odd word or phrase uttered by one of the Seven, but most of their words are lost in the song, amongst all the other voices.' Her eyes peeled open again, unable to resist, as a smile crossed her lips. 'But once I touch the Blackstone... ah, the many will fade for the few and I will hear them loud and clear. I will know the Will.'

'And you will become *Ashan Tai* or *Ashan Tay*... one of your priests?'

Nyana nodded. 'If that is the Will.'

'We also have a word for those who hear voices in their head,' said Senya, her voice taking on a mocking tone. 'We usually lock them away for their own safety.'

Nyana shook her head. She would not be shamed by a non-believer. 'We don't hear them in our head,' she said, 'we hear them on the wind. Our minds are open, not broken.'

'Ah, my mistake,' said Senya, with that same mocking tone. But then the tone changed, becoming urgent and frightened. 'What was that?'

Nyana had heard it too, coming from some distance behind them, tearing out of the swirling sheets of snow. A viscous roar, loud enough to break through the sound of the blizzard and pierce the bubble of protection formed by the Will. Nyana licked her dry, cracked lips. 'He has found us.'

Senya gazed back the way they had come, across the open plains and into the blizzard, back to where the distant roar still echoed. Her blood ran cold at the sound of it, dread gripping at her heart. What kind of beast could make such a sound?

'Scar!' she called, but the wolf was nowhere to be seen. He had pulled away ahead of them, disappearing into the blizzard. Cursing, Senya grabbed Nyana by the collar of her fur coat and dragged her back behind her. She drew her sword, the blade ringing out into the crisp night air. 'Stay behind me,' she hissed at the girl.

Best to keep her safe. I still need that edge over the Wolfeater. He'll have no use for a dead girl, and he's too canny to let anger and grief get the better of him in a fight.

At least, that was what Senya told herself. But deep down she knew she had no desire to see a child torn apart before her... not even a Basillian. And she liked this one more than most. Blind and seemingly helpless, Nyana had shown more courage, more strength, and more determination than any grown man Senya had ever met. Even without the strange power that seemed to emanate from her, the girl was something formidable.

Another roar echoed out, this time much closer, and Senya felt the earth trembling beneath her. Adjusting her stance, she gripped her sword in two hands and waited. She breathed slowly, deeply, hot breath smoking in the cold air.

Then she saw it bounding through the blizzard towards them; a colossal, white figure charging on all fours. Snow had plastered itself to the beast's fur coat, but he thundered on regardless, his dark eyes and black nose standing out like pieces of coal. His eyes narrowed when they locked on Senya, lips drawing back to reveal a mouthful of long, sharp teeth. The creature picked up pace, his powerful limbs churning up clumps of snow in his wake as he bore down on them.

Senya knew that face from childhood, staring back at her from the wall of Velimir's cabin. Back then, the kragan's jaw had been locked in place and the eyes lacked the usual spark of life, yet Senya had always felt those eyes following her around the room.

She stared back now, mouth agape, hands trembling, as the beast crashed ever closer. Time slowed in that moment, and a cold certainty settled on Senya. *This is the day I die.*

The kragan launched himself through the air as he reached them, his massive arms raised over his head. Reaching back and grabbing Nyana once more, Senya threw herself to the left, dragging the girl with her. They ploughed through the snow, getting clear just as the kragan's massive paws crashed down where they'd been standing a moment before. There was a crash like thunder as the ground gave way beneath them.

Nyana went through first, Senya holding grimly to the girl's fur coat, praying to the Great Hunt that both it and she had the strength to hold on. She glanced down into the abyss that had opened up below them, threatening to swallow them whole. It was a narrow chasm that fell away some thirty feet to a mass of jagged rocks at the bottom, hidden by a shell of thick ice. Mikilov had warned her the Whitelands were full of such traps, yet it never entered Senya's darkest thoughts that her quest for revenge might end like this.

More of the ice broke away beneath Senya's legs and she had to scramble for solid ground. She managed to get some purchase between her free arm and her upper body, before the rest of her was left dangling out over the drop. She looked down, her arm aching with the strain of holding onto the girl, and watched Nyana slowly swinging back and forth below her.

The girl should have been screaming - perhaps *would* have been, if she had the eyes to see her predicament - but she stayed silent, simply holding to the arm that was her lifeline. Senya tried to lift her, but it was useless. She wasn't strong enough.

Instead, she turned her face skyward, the veins in her face and neck bulging with effort as she tried to heave herself up. If she could find a foothold and push herself up, she might have a chance...

The kragan's face loomed over her, drool dangling down from his jagged teeth, dripping onto Senya's face. When he leaned closer, Senya could see the scarred, blistered flesh making up the left-hand side of the kragan's face, where the fur had been burned away. His putrid breath was almost enough for Senya to let go, even before he unleashed a terrible roar directly in her face.

Senya squeezed her eyes shut against the sound. She wanted to clamp her hands over her ears, to fall into the abyss, anything to escape that deafening howl. But she held on with the last of her strength, clinging desperately to the rock with one hand, to Nyana with the other. Her eyes slid open and she gazed back at the kragan, willing him to end it.

The beast raised both paws over his head, and with reckless abandon he brought them down.

It felt better out here.

The one they called Scar had been born to feel the wind rustling through his coat, to taste the blizzard lashing at his face with cold claws. That was life, in the eyes of the wolf. Wild, and brutal, and relentless.

Things were different in the Small One's company. Everything seemed calmer, less unpredictable. Scar had barely felt a breeze while walking beside her, and the twisting, dancing snow had not fallen within reach.

Even the smells lacked their usual body. The cold killed most smells out in the wilds, but those that remained were often the most potent. On a normal day, with the wind at its best, Scar could track a scent for miles at a time. Yet, *with* the girl, he could only smell one scent - a blend of smoke, and sweat, and filth. Her scent. It was all so... unnatural.

Not for long, the wolf told himself. *The Grey Beard will catch up to us soon, and things will return to the way they were. The way they have always been.*

So he had walked on ahead, leaving the Long Hair and the Small One to their strange talk, while he joined once more with the Great Hunt. He found the snow again, and the wind, and all the scents of promise they held, and the elements embraced him like an old friend. Scar missed the Grey Beard, but the white plains would always be home.

Scar's ears twitched suddenly, drawn to some sound off in the distance, back the way he had come. Was it a howl, or just some trick of the wind? He stood there listening, his ears pricked up.

Just as he was about to move again, he heard something else. A voice it sounded like, yelling the name they had given him.

The wind changed direction suddenly, violently, wafting into his face. And then he caught the scent.

It was a smell of the wilds, thick with blood and earth, and a faint trace of rotting flesh. A killer.

Scar was moving at once, paws digging into the snow and springing him forwards. He didn't even notice the wind change direction again, flowing with him towards the waiting carnage.

He had pulled away from the Long Hair and the Small One further than he realised, and it took several seconds at full gallop before he sighted them through the unrelenting snow. His heart sank as the sight of them cleared. A narrow chasm had opened beneath them and they had fallen through. The Long Hair clung desperately to the crumbling edge, while the Small One dangled from her other hand, swinging over the darkness.

That was all the sign Scar needed. Charging on, he covered the ground between himself and the beast like a bolt of lightning, flashing across the white expanse. The monster ignored him, raising his paws over his head and swinging them down like a giant hammer.

Scar leapt across the small crack in the earth and crashed into the monster's chest, his jaws sinking through flesh and clamping onto collar bone. The force of the wolf's weight colliding with him was enough to topple the beast, and together they rolled away into the snow, biting and kicking and clawing.

The beast had the tougher hide, and for every chunk of flesh Scar took out of him, he took three in return. Scar's teeth sank into the meaty part of his thigh, but the beast's talons tore into Scar's flanks and he had no choice but to let go. The beast tossed him aside, sending him rolling through the snow, blood spattering the surface.

Shaking the grogginess from his head, Scar pushed himself to his feet and glared back at the beast. For his part, the monster stared back evenly, his own white coat stained with fresh blood where Scar had bitten him. He was up on two legs now, towering over them all, his breath smoking in the frigid air while his bared teeth glistened red with blood. He unleashed a terrible roar, his fists shaking with fury as his anger bellowed out.

Behind him, the Long Hair had managed to climb out from the broken earth and dragged the Small One out behind her. They were safe for now, but only for as long as Scar could keep the beast distracted.

Though his strength was fading quickly, Scar howled his defiance and charged. It was all or nothing, he knew that. Fight or flight, and he chose to fight. *The throat,* he told himself. *The secret of all life lies in the throat.*

Scar leapt through the air one last time... and the beast caught him in mid-air. Claws sank deep into Scar's flanks, but he ignored the pain long enough to clamp his mouth on the beast's throat, locking it as tightly as he could. The beast cried out in rage, and with a desperate surge of effort, he tore Scar from him and lifted the wolf high over his head, Scar's legs flailing uselessly in the air above him.

Scar knew it was over in that moment, but he also knew a satisfying chunk of flesh dangled from his mouth. *The secret of life.*

The beast brought Scar crashing to the earth with all the strength he could muster. Scar felt his bones shatter into a thousand different pieces, his body exploding with pain for just the briefest of moments.

And then the pain was gone and he just lay there, broken and still. He looked up at the beast and saw the lifeblood flowing from the gaping wound in his throat, flowing through his white fur and spilling to the snow.

Ignoring his own doom, the beast raised one massive balled fist in the air, ready to bring it down and crush Scar's skull. In that moment, a flash of silver cut across the beast's torn throat and his giant head toppled from his shoulders.

The Grey Beard appeared beside Scar, dropping his bloody axe to the ground beside them. There were tears in his weary eyes. That was a sign of pain Scar knew well, but he had never seen them from his friend before. He tried to stand, but his legs wouldn't move. Instead, he licked the Grey Beard's hand. It was all he could do.

The Grey Beard spoke softly to him, his hand stroking Scar's torn flank. Scar had been wounded there before, had felt pain ever since, but there was no pain now. No feeling at all.

The Long Hair and the Small One appeared alongside the Grey Beard, and there were tears there too. It was good that the Grey Beard had found them. *He can watch them now*, thought Scar. *I'm tired. I need to sleep.*

And he closed his eyes for the last time.

PART III

THE BLACKSTONE

CHAPTER TWENTY-ONE

Heroes and Villains

No sooner had the final breath slipped from Scar's broken body, than a quiet calm settled on the scene of his last, defiant stand. The blizzard died with the wolf. The howling wind ebbed away to a gentle breeze, and the last of the snowfall drifted peacefully to the earth. It was as though the Great Hunt itself paused to pay its respects.

Mikilov laid a hand on the wolf's head and stroked him behind the ears one last time. It was heart-breaking to see him lying there like that, motionless, patches of his flesh torn open, his blood soaking into the snow. *We have walked this earth together for almost a decade, my friend. Hard to believe that time is done...*

Slow, cautious footsteps sounded behind him and Mikilov glanced over his shoulder. The girl, Senya, inching her way towards him, looking exhausted, bone weary and dishevelled. Her clothes were torn in places, or else caked in snow. She looked every inch a woman who had lost a fight with a kragan.

He wanted to be angry at her - to hate her even - but there was too much grief in his heart to let the anger in.

Holding to Senya's hand was a young girl dressed from head to toe in fur. She wore a necklace of small grey feathers that dangled across her chest. Grey Crow. A *blind* Grey Crow. Remembering Elgamire's words, Mikilov raised a brow. *Radok's* blind Grey Crow.

He turned back to Scar, bent low to the wolf's ear, and whispered, 'You always did make the strangest of friends.'

Pushing himself to his feet, Mikilov took a deep, steadying breath, before turning to face Senya. 'Are you ok?' he asked. She looked well enough, if a little pale from shock and exhaustion.

'Thanks to Scar,' she said. 'By the Great Hunt, Mikilov, I'm so sorry...'

It was still too raw for Mikilov to deal with, so he waved his hand in dismissal and turned his attention to Senya's companion. 'And who is this?'

'I am Nyana of the Grey Crow.' The girl's voice was small out there in the wilderness, but she spoke the words defiantly, her chin held high, her eyes carrying an intense flare though still locked on nothing.

'You speak the common tongue?'

'We all do,' the girl said. 'When needed.'

Mikilov smiled, remembering their earlier encounter with the woman Crow, before they crossed the Velga. She had spoken only in the tongue of her people, apparently unable to understand the common tongue. *She played us for fools...*

'It's Radok's girl,' put in Senya, as though it could be anyone else.

'And the Wolfeater himself?' asked Mikilov.

'Behind us, somehow. If he's even still alive...'

'He was when I last saw him.'

'You've seen him?' There was a desperate edge to Senya's voice. 'When? How?'

'He dragged me from the river,' said Mikilov, 'saved my life.'

Senya's eyes widened. 'You were face-to-face with him, and he's still alive?'

Mikilov's anger finally pierced the veil of grief and his eyes blazed through Senya. 'Even now, girl? Even now you know the price, vengeance is all you crave? The man saved my life; I wasn't about to end his.'

Senya flinched back a step, shocked by the flash of anger. 'I'm sorry, Mikilov. You're right. I just don't understand why. Why would he save you?'

'The same reason you saved me.' That small voice again, somehow full of power and authority despite belonging to a child. Mikilov glanced at the blind girl, watched her smile back. 'It was the Will.'

'Don't do that,' Mikilov said to her. 'I've heard the words of enough dying Basillians to know your gods hold no power. I'll not have Scar's death put down to a lie.'

'It's the truth,' she said. 'The Will moves us all, even the non-believers.'

Glimpsing something as the girl spoke, Mikilov's hand darted out instinctively. His hand closed around her jaw, thumb and fingers squeezing into her cheeks, forcing her mouth open. His eyes widened in surprise at the sight of four fang-like teeth in her mouth, two top and two bottom. '*That's* what moved Scar,' he said, 'not the bloody Will. The girl's Valor. Or at least her mother was.'

'My father actually,' she replied quickly, pulling herself free of Mikilov's grip. 'Though he was very young when he joined the Grey Crow.'

'You mean when they stole him?' asked Senya, leaning in closer to see the teeth for herself.

The girl shook her head. 'They took a Wolf and gave him wings. They set him free.'

Her voice trembled with emotion, and Mikilov guessed at the story behind it. 'And did he set you free, girl? When he saw those eyes? Not much room in the Grey Crow for a blind girl, eh?'

'I never knew him,' she said carefully. 'It was Radok who set me free.'

'I thought we might use her,' said Senya. 'If she means as much to Radok as it seems, holding her might give us an edge.'

Mikilov's gaze shifted from Senya to the girl, and back again. 'You want to use this child, blind and defenceless as she is, for a hostage? No, Senya. The Wolfeater is supposed to be the villain here, not us. Scar gave his life for her as well as for you, perhaps even more so, and he didn't do it so we could use her for bait.'

Senya sighed, exasperated. 'What then? You tell me what we do, because I'm out of ideas.'

'We wait,' said the girl, smiling. 'Radok will be here soon.'

Mikilov considered her for a long moment, then finally shrugged. 'We wait then.'

Senya stared back at him, astonished. 'You'll take her word for it?'

Mikilov shrugged. There didn't seem much else to do. 'We can wait awhile, at least,' he said, drawing a dagger from the folds of his cloak and fixing his gaze on Scar's body. 'I have work to do.'

'What is he doing?'

Nyana tilted her head slightly as she spoke, listening carefully to Mikilov's gruesome work. Senya winced as the big man drove his dagger into Scar's stilled chest, then began to saw down along the wolf's torso.

'He's taking the wolf's hide,' she told the girl, turning away. For just a moment she was almost envious of the child's lack of vision.

'Why would he do that?' asked Nyana. 'I thought they were friends?'

Senya lowered her voice slightly, and, taking Nyana's hand, led the girl away. 'They *were* friends; the greatest of friends. That's why he takes the hide. That way, they will continue to walk the earth together. Not even death will part them.'

Nyana frowned. 'And will he wear your skin, when you die?'

Despite herself, Senya smiled. 'That's different.'

'If he does not,' the girl said solemnly, 'I will. I swear it.'

Senya stifled a laugh. Somehow, she found herself genuinely touched by the girl's grim declaration. 'Honoured, I'm sure.'

They stopped at the gaping hole through which they had nearly fallen just a few minutes earlier, and Senya peered down into the darkness below. 'What about your dead?' she asked the girl. 'What happens to them?'

'We burn them.' Nyana spoke calmly, as though this was the most natural thing in the world. 'Then we scatter the ashes to the Seven, so that they may return to the Will, as all things should.' She shrugged. 'What else can we do, once the Black Wind has had his say?'

Senya considered the idea for a moment. The Valor believed burial was the natural step once a person's role in the Great Hunt had ended, returning them to the earth. The thought of something different seemed strange to say the least. But death was death, she supposed. *What does it really matter what happens to the flesh once the soul has fled this world?* 'They teach you a lot about death in the Grey Crow, girl?'

'Life *and* death,' said Nyana. 'What else is there in the All Song?'

'Oh, I don't know...' muttered Senya, 'fun and laughter?'

Her smile faded as she studied the girl's face. Hard and lean, it was framed by the angled edges of her cheeks and chin. Even her eyes, blind as they were, sparkled with a sharpness Senya had never before seen in a child. 'You live a hard life, out here,' she said gently, 'and it's made you a hard people. But I suppose you know that better than most.'

Nyana shrugged nonchalantly. 'The *Ashan Tai* once told me life is only hard for those who don't know their place. My place is with Radok. He has given me a good life.'

Senya grunted. 'A child shouldn't have to *know* their place; the world is there for them to go *find* it. Whatever homelife the Wolfeater has given you, he's been butchering my people for as long as I can remember. He is not a good man.'

Nyana stared back at Senya in that strange way she had, as though her eyes were peering straight through Senya and into the horizon. Again, Senya was reminded of Elgamire, and she found herself wondering if all blind people had a gift for seeing through people and into the future.

'You want to kill him, I understand,' said the girl. 'But you won't. That is not the Will.'

'It's *my* will,' said Senya.

'You don't understand. But you will, once you see him.'

Senya snorted at that. 'And when will that be?'

'Now.'

Senya spun on her heels in the direction of Nyana's gaze, back towards the Velga. Four figures were crossing the white flatlands behind them. Three of them, a man and two women, Senya had no mind for, but the fourth... even at a distance she could see the dark skin that defined the Wolfeater.

In her mind's eye, Senya saw herself draw her sword and charge across the snow, striving to reach Radok and open his throat, the way he had opened Velimir's. But in reality, she simply stood there, frozen to the spot, her heart racing and blood rushing to her head.

As he drew closer, she saw that he was smaller than she remembered. His body had withered away, leaving his face gaunt and ashen. Every step he took seemed to pain him, but on he came. *It's true,* thought Senya. *He's dying.*

'Greetings, She-Wolf,' he said, drawing to a halt several strides away. Even his voice was weaker, lacking that elemental spark it had carried at their first meeting. 'Nothing to say? You've come a long way from home to hold your tongue now.'

'She was looking for a man,' said Mikilov, stepping up beside Senya and the girl. His hands glistened with Scar's dark blood, but they hung freely at his sides, relaxed. 'But it seems she's found only a ghost.'

Radok nodded a greeting. 'I'm glad to see you're still alive, Grey Wolf.'

'Thanks to you. A debt I've not forgotten.'

'Looks like you've paid it back and more,' said Radok, sweeping his gaze over the scene, taking in the two fallen beasts, before finally coming to rest on Nyana. 'Are you well, Little Sparrow?'

'I am,' she said. 'They saved me, Papa.'

Radok met Mikilov's gaze, then Senya's. 'You have my thanks, Wolves.'

Senya felt a flare of anger, enough to thaw her frozen state. 'No,' she said, 'you don't get to do that. You have to pay for the things you've done.'

Mikilov laid a hand on her shoulder. 'Easy, girl.'

Senya shrugged him off, her own hand closing around Nyana's arm and dragging her close. 'A life for a life, Wolfeater. Do you love her enough for that?'

'Oh, my life is not worth so much as hers.' Radok smiled at the girl, and Senya could see the love behind it. 'Besides, I have already paid the debt you're here to collect. Was he your kin, the old man?'

'My uncle,' said Senya.

'And I killed him, that's true enough. But only after you killed my friend. A life for a life, yes?'

'Let the girl go, Senya.' Mikilov tried to peel Senya's hand from the girl's arm, which was turning white under the pressure, but Senya shook him off again.

'He's killed far more than Velimir,' she said, her voice shrill in her own ears. 'What about *those* lives, Wolfeater?'

The dark man raised his eyebrows. 'You would have her pay for those lives too? This blind girl who has never even seen a Wolf, let alone harmed one? And you say I'm the monster...'

'Senya.' Mikilov again, pleading.

Senya could feel the moment slipping, but she had no idea why. *This is why we're here, isn't it? We came all this way for the Wolfeater, and now that we have him... we're going to let him live?*

'He has to pay, Mikilov,' she heard herself say, though her voice sounded smaller than usual. 'For Velimir. For Scar. For all of them.'

'By the Hunt, girl, look at him. He pays with every single breath.'

The Wolfeater had heard enough. 'Take it then,' he barked. Unbuckling the sword belt from his waist, he tossed it to the snow and spread his arms wide, waiting. 'If my life means that much to you, take it.'

'No!' Tearing free of Senya's grip, Nyana ran into Radok's arms, her own arms locking tightly around his waist. 'I won't let them hurt you.'

'Step aside, girl,' said Senya.

'No,' said the girl. 'He isn't done yet.'

Radok tried to peel away from her, but the girl held fast. 'It's alright, Little Sparrow. You can let go.'

'No, it's not alright.' One of the women, the older and taller of the two, intense eyes staring out from a black strip of war paint, the rest of her all in white. She drew her sword and stepped forward. 'You kill him, I kill you.'

'Then I kill you,' said Mikilov.

The man next to Radok, his face covered in bloody bandages smiled. 'And I kill you.'

The smaller woman rolled her eyes. 'And we're lucky if anyone is left alive to get this girl to safety.'

Senya's gaze flickered between them. From the three younger, healthier Basillians, to the sickly, withering Wolfeater. 'He's a dead man anyway. Why would any of you die for him?'

'Because he's not dead yet,' replied the woman in white. 'And he still has work to do.'

'What work?'

'To touch the Blackstone,' said the Wolfeater.

'We both must touch it,' added the girl. 'That's why we're here.'

Senya's fingers flexed on her sword hilt, tempted to draw it. *I'll cut through all of them if I have to, even the girl. For Velimir...*

But Mikilov spoke before she could act. 'That settles it then,' he said, lowering his axe. 'We'll travel with you to the Blackstone, and there we'll make a decision about what stands and what doesn't.'

'Agreed,' muttered the Wolfeater, relaxing.

'We can't do that,' said the man with half-a-face. 'We can't lead Wolves to the sacred place of our people.'

'Don't be such a fool, Talgar,' said the woman in white, sheathing her sword. 'We're not supposed to take those already turned back by the Stone, or girls either... yet here we are. You think it matters to the Seven who stops Talak, or only that he is stopped?'

Senya's anger bubbled over. The decision was made and there was nothing she could do about it. And now they were talking about something else entirely. 'Who the fuck is Talak?' she stormed.

The woman stared back at her intensely for a moment, something cold and deadly in her eyes. 'You'll find out soon enough, if you stick with us.'

'Are you with us, Wolves?' asked the Wolfeater. 'Or shall we make this the end of the path?'

Senya stepped closer to Mikilov, hissing in his ear. 'We can't do this. They are the enemy. We should be killing them, not joining them on some suicide march.'

'I joined you on yours.' He spoke softly, but the words cut deep. 'Scar paid the price for that decision, but he saved that girl for a reason. Elgamire told me I'd find her, and that I'd have to make sure she lived. I'm not going to stand by while she throws her life away.' He turned back to the Basillians and raised his voice again. 'We're with you, Crows. We'll see this Blackstone of yours, and then we'll decide what happens next.'

Mikilov's hands were shaking as he returned to his place over Scar's corpse. They were still stained with the wolf's blood, and, though the bone-handled skinning knife was only small, it felt heavy in his massive grip. Was it nerves from the standoff with the Grey Crow, he wondered, or grief from Scar's loss? A little of both, he guessed.

Squatting beside the body, Mikilov took a handful of fur in one hand and slid the knife in between flesh and skin once more, sawing away to free it. He knew the flesh was dead - that Scar had joined the Great Hunt in the sky - yet it still weighed heavy on his mind that this was his friend.

'I can't believe we're doing this.'

Mikilov looked up. Senya was pacing around behind him, the snow well-trodden beneath her.

'You're the one who wanted to be here,' he said.

'I wanted to kill the Wolfeater, nothing more.'

'Well, it's time you learned that actions have consequences. Scar died for that little girl, which means I won't leave her side until she's safe.'

Senya paused in her pacing. 'I was down in that hole too. How do you know he didn't die for me?'

'Did he?'

Senya held his gaze for a long moment, then she sighed. 'He died for the girl.'

Mikilov nodded. 'Then we see this through to the end. *Her* end in this story, at least. Whatever that might be.'

Senya started pacing again. 'I tell you, Mikilov: the first chance I get, I can't promise I won't kill him.'

'Why?' It was Radok's woman, the older one, striding across to join them. Groaning, Mikilov turned his attention back to Scar's corpse. 'Why are you so desperate to see dead a man you don't even know?'

'I know him well enough.' Senya's footfalls fell silent as she stopped pacing and stood facing off against the other woman, both trying their best to intimidate the other. 'We call him Wolfeater for a reason. He has killed hundreds of our people, perhaps thousands. My uncle Velimir is just one blade of grass in that field, but he meant the world to me and I am sworn to avenge him.'

'Your friend here has killed just as many Grey Crow,' said the Basillian. 'He has killed Flatheads and Long Claws, Empty Faces and Burning Suns. Is there a tribe you haven't fought, Grey Wolf?'

Mikilov shrugged. 'None that I know of.'

'What does it matter?' snapped Senya.

'It matters,' said the woman, 'because every side has its heroes and villains. We tell stories about the Grey Wolf around our fires, warn our children that he will come for them if they misbehave. But now that I see him, I find that he is just a man, not too unlike any Grey Crow. Even with those teeth, he's just a man. Do you see?'

Senya did not reply, so the Grey Crow pressed on. 'Our people have been at war for as long as even the elders can remember, and these two, Radok and... Mikilov? These two are just warriors in that great game; they have only ever done what was necessary in order to survive.'

'My uncle was no warrior,' said Senya. 'He was just a farmer, killed in cold blood. Where was the survival in that?'

'Not Radok's finest moment,' the woman agreed. 'But even he would admit as much. You had just killed his greatest friend... his mind was not in the best of places. He lost his self-control. You say vengeance brought you out here? Well that was *his* vengeance, and look where he is now.' The Grey Crow clicked her tongue. 'Vengeance is just a word, She-Wolf. It does nothing to fill the hole left by those we love.'

'You're a killer yourself,' said Senya. 'All you people are. What do you know about anything?'

'I know I loved a man once,' the woman answered. Surprised by the honesty in the voice, Mikilov let his hands fall away from his work and looked up at the two women. They were standing close to each other now, barely two feet apart.

'His life was my whole world,' the woman went on. 'He put a baby inside my belly, and I have never felt so much love as I did in those few blissful months. I know too that my body struggled with the birth, and that the babe lacked the strength to survive those struggles. I know my man - the love of my life - blamed me for the child's death...'. Her voice broke for a moment, and she took a breath. 'I can still feel the blows to the head where he tried to smash in my skull. I buried an axe in his face to save my life, and for that the tribe ordered my death.

'I know I'm alive today because of Radok. He was the only one who stood for me. Even when the elders called him off, he held his ground. Just as he held his ground when they came for the blind girl. Most would have rather seen her dead than lay that burden on the tribe, so Radok told them he would carry it himself. *That's* who the Wolfeater is, She-Wolf, so don't tell me he's just a killer.'

'Aye, he's no monster,' put in Mikilov, pushing himself to his feet. 'No more than any man, at least. Thank the Hunt, there aren't that many monsters left in this world. Even this *thing*...' He grabbed the kragan's severed head by a tuft of fur and lifted it high. The black eyes stared back empty, the burned half of his face glistening with puss in the rising sun. 'There was no evil in him, no malice. He was just an animal doing what he was born to do, preying on the weak for survival.

'We all of us must do what we can to survive, but sometimes we have to do what's right too. That's what separates us from the beasts and the animals.' Mikilov cast the head into the open chasm below them, listening to it bounce hollowly against the icy rocks below. 'We are with you, girl,' he told the Basillian. 'I gave my word that we would see the Blackstone together, and I'm nothing if not a man of my word. No harm will befall you or yours at our hands. Not even the Wolfeater.'

Senya tried to protest, but Mikilov raised a hand to silence her. 'Give your word, Senya.'

'But...'

'Your word.'

The girl's face reddened with anger, but Mikilov stared her down. At last, she lowered her face and sighed. 'No harm,' she promised. 'Not until the Blackstone.'

Mikilov turned back to the Grey Crow. 'Satisfied?'

'Enough.'

'Good.' Mikilov gestured at the kragan's corpse. 'Then you two should get to work on that. There's still a long way to go before we reach the Blackstone and we'll need more supplies if we're going to make the return journey. No point letting good meat go to waste.'

The two women looked at each other with a grimace of disgust. Whether it was the grim task they'd been set or the idea of working together, Mikilov didn't care.

'I'm almost finished here,' he said, turning back to the fallen Scar. 'Once I'm done, we'll need to get moving again. The smell will bring more hunters down on us, even out here.'

CHAPTER TWENTY-TWO

The White Waste

They were called the Whitelands for good reason; vast, open tundra quilted in perpetual snow. Yet, once night had fallen and the clouds lay heavy overhead, the name could not have been further from the truth...

Looking out into that black emptiness, back the way he had come, Talak smiled. He sat cross-legged in the snow, his hood drawn up against the northern wind, adjusting his fur coat so that it sat better on his shoulders. *The Darklands,* he thought absently. *That's what they should have called it. Home to the Black Wind.*

Out in the distance, an orange spark lit up, its weak light flickering in the deep dark, and Talak breathed a little easier. For five nights now he had sat sleeplessly, watching the back trail for sign of the enemy. Each time he sighted their little fires it made him smile.

The flames were a sign of weakness. Cutting as it was, Talak barely even felt the cold now. The Seven tried to force him back, of course, as they did anyone trying to reach the Blackstone, but the Eighth shielded him from the worst of it. He hadn't eaten for days, drank sparingly, and slept not at all. He should have been exhausted, hungry and parched, yet he had never felt stronger. *It's the Black Wind*, he thought. *It nourishes the soul.*

He didn't move as he watched the fire flickering in the distance. That's how it had been these past five days. During the hours of daylight they marched into the endless white, and when the sun fell they made their camp, where they cowered from the eternal dark.

They moved slowly, held back by the blind girl and the sickly Radok, but every step they took was forward. Talak had to give them credit for that. The Whitelands had broken far greater men than the strange band set against him.

He pictured them in his mind's eye, bunched up around the fire, leaning towards the flames, trying their best to keep warm. There were seven of them in total, including the blind and the dying. Talak had counted them on that first day, dragging each other along in two groups.

Talak had no idea who the two outsiders were, Valor by the look of it, but it was the Grey Crow in the lead group that held Talak's interest, including Radok and the girl. Of that five, the other three must have been all that remained of the hunting party that set out with him from the Heart's Fire. The two women were there, easily identified, and for the third Talak guessed at Talgar.

That these three had joined forces with Radok was hardly surprising. They had been taught all their lives, by Talak himself even, that bending to the will of the Eighth was an abomination, and that anyone found walking with the Black Wind should be destroyed. That was why they had set out after Radok in the first place, for fear *he* served the Eighth.

It was the slaughter of the Empty Faces that changed things. That was the moment Jian and her friends learned the truth, that Talak had turned from the Seven and sworn his loyalty to the Eighth. *Stupid fool,* Talak cursed himself. *You showed them too much too soon. If only they knew the power the Black Wind had gifted me, perhaps then they'd understand...*

The union that followed was inevitable. In knowing Talak now served the Black Wind, it told the remaining Grey Crow that Radok's goal served the Will's purpose, and that made him special.

But it was never about Radok, thought Talak, smiling. *Any man can wield a sword, but it takes a special kind of gift to know the Will without ever touching the Blackstone. It's the girl that's special.* Pulling his coat tighter to him, Talak shrank a little deeper into the furs, settling in for the long night ahead. *It was always the girl. That's why she dies.*

It was the strangest feeling.

Out here in the frozen wilderness, disease coursing through him and enemies in his camp, Radok had never felt so close to death. Yet in that moment, with Nyana curled up against him on one side and Jian resting her head upon his shoulder on the other, he would not have chosen to be anywhere else.

Talgar sat to Radok's right, Nyana nestled between them, his cloak draped over her along with Radok's. Tess sat to Radok's left, on the other side of Jian, her head resting on Jian's lap. And across from them all, still unsure of their new allies, even in the face of such bitter cold, the two Valor were huddled together, leaning in towards the flames.

The fire itself was something of a miracle. Talgar had brought a supply of wood with him when they set out from the shelter of the Velgan forest, his bag near full to bursting. The rest of their supplies - the dried meats, the lentils and beans, the cooking pots - were divided among Radok, Tess and Jian. Now that they had joined forces, Radok even left his pots behind, to make room for sharing the load. The Valor brought nothing to the party when they joined, though everyone did take up a share of kragan meat, packed with snow to keep it fresh.

Radok had thought the idea of fire a fool's hope, believing that the incessant snow and wind out on the open plains would make it nigh impossible for a flame to take. Yet the flame did take, and the fire roared away in the quiet night. 'It's the girl,' Tess had said. 'I don't know how, but for some reason the wind is different around her.'

'It's the Will,' Talgar had offered, always the superstitious one. 'The Seven are with her.'

'Then they're damned fools,' Radok had replied. 'If they're helping her, they're helping me; and if they knew what I had in mind for them, they'd have no part in it.'

Radok fed a log into the flames and settled back once more. That would be the last this night, he decided. They'd agreed to ration the fuel as best they could, or else it would have been burned up the first night they spent out in the Great White. As it was, they used just enough to get them through the coldest hours between dusk and dawn.

The girl, Tess, moaned something in her sleep and Radok glanced at her. Her head still lay on Jian's lap, Jian's gloved hand resting on her shoulder, holding her close. He wondered how long they had been together? Tess was already with the Fallow when Radok delivered Jian to the Far Eye. *Did it start back then, in the early days? Were her babe and her man even cold yet?*

It was a callous thought, Radok knew, but jealousy was getting the better of him. He'd hardly taken his eyes from Jian since they'd fallen back in together. In much the same way he hadn't realised Nyana's worth, Radok had been oblivious to how badly he needed Jian in his life. They were everything to him, he realised now, in one way or another.

'What are you thinking?'

Surprised by the voice, Radok jerked his head slightly, his eyes meeting Jian's where she lay against his shoulder, staring up at him. She wore that half smile she sometimes carried, a knowing smile, with the flames of the fire dancing in her hazel eyes. She'd washed the war paint away, along with the white hair dye, and the softened look made her even more beautiful.

'Stop staring,' she said, 'and tell me what you're thinking!'

Radok shrugged. 'That it's a good match,' he lied. 'You and her.'

Jian smiled. 'No cock. That's the secret.'

'It's a waste,' said Radok, offering a wry smile of his own.

Jian shrugged. 'It never would have worked between us, you know that don't you?'

'Why not? I would have treated you right.'

'No doubt,' said Jian. 'But you only wanted me because I was broken. It's the same reason you took on the girl. You're all strength, Radok, and you only want those who need you that way. But I could never stay broken. I needed to fly again, and you gave me the strength to carry on.'

Radok considered her words carefully. There was some truth in there, he supposed. His strength was prodigious, and all his life it had dictated his purpose among the Grey Crow. Yet killing the enemies of his people had never been enough to satisfy the Wolfeater. He had always felt the need to fight for the plucky unfortunates too, the likes of Nyana and Jian. The thought that it was those battles, fought for the individual, and not the wars waged among the tribes or against the Valor, that defined him had never even occurred to Radok.

'You're wrong,' he said at last. 'It's not the broken that win my heart. It's those who continue to fly even when their wings are clipped. That's Nyana. And it's you.'

As Jian struggled to find the words to reply, Radok eased himself from between her and Nyana and pushed himself to his feet. 'I need to go piss,' he said, suddenly embarrassed by the honesty he had shared.

Stumbling away from the warm circle of light offered by the fire, Radok found himself staring off into the darkness of the south, pissing with the wind. The snow was light still. Soft flakes drifted down gently from the heavens, though their swirling dance picked up pace further away from the fire - further away from Nyana. Even as that thought ran through his mind, Radok felt the sensation of being watched.

He waited for the flow to end, then shook himself off and tucked it away. Finally, he turned slowly north, his gaze fixed on the dark horizon. He walked slowly around the fire, freeing himself of the glare, and stared out into the night. He could see nothing through the darkness, and the only sounds to be heard were those of the crackling fire and the soft breathing of his comrades. Nothing.

'It's this friend of yours,' a gravelly voice whispered near his ear. 'This Talak?'

'Damn, wolf,' muttered Radok, casting a glance at Mikilov standing beside him. 'You move like a ghost.'

'Only when I need to.'

Radok nodded. 'You can feel it too?'

'Aye. He's watching us. Scar would have dealt with him by now... if he was here. Who is he?'

Radok mulled the question over. *Who is he?* Not a friend, that was for sure. But a man to be respected. Radok had always favoured Ilgor when it came to council from the Will, but the tribe preferred the talents of Talak. While Ilgor, the *Ashan Tai,* appeared fair and wise in his dealings, the *Ashan Tay,* Talak, was far more rigid and strict in his beliefs. That made him the natural choice for the elders.

'Do you have those who preach the message of your gods among the wolves?'

'Priests?' Mikilov raised one bushy, grey brow. 'Not for a long time. Hard to keep faith when every day is a struggle.'

Radok grunted. He'd never lost faith in the Seven, only his desire to serve the Will. But he could understand why a people might turn from the gods they once worshipped, especially when dark day followed dark day. 'A priest,' he muttered. 'Aye, that's Talak. A warrior priest.'

'And he's dangerous?'

Radok shrugged. 'To a man like you? Before this journey I would have said no, but my friends believe he serves the Black Wind now, that death is his friend. They say he killed a group of Empty Faces in single combat before they crossed the Velga.'

'We saw the bodies,' said Mikilov. 'He did that alone?'

'So they say, and I have no reason to doubt them.'

'Then why doesn't he come down here and kill us? What's he waiting for?'

It was a new voice that answered, soft and young. 'He wants the Seven to see it.' Radok and Mikilov turned in unison to see Nyana standing behind them, her fur cloak dragging in the snow behind her, unseeing eyes gazing off into the darkness of the north. 'He wants them to *truly* see it,' she said. 'He serves the Eighth now, and there is nothing he wants more than to shame the Seven. He will wait for us at the Blackstone. That's where the journey ends.'

Mikilov grunted, shifting on his feet in an effort to keep warm. 'I understand none of this,' he muttered.

'It's simple really,' said Nyana, and Radok smiled. Young as she was, the girl had a habit of making old men feel stupid. *One reason among many that Talak and the elders must hate her.*

'Why don't you teach him, Little Sparrow?'

Nyana tutted at the indignity of it all, but Radok saw the eagerness light her face. 'It's the All Song,' she said, in a tone that suggested she was the one talking to a child. 'It's the eternal dance between life and death.'

The girl paused and Radok chuckled. He could almost see her mind trying to work out the best way to explain her gods to an outsider. It would not be an easy task. The wolf had only ever heard talk of the Seven from men who had tried to kill him, and he wouldn't offer much slack if she lost her way. After a moment though, the girl had her angle.

'When we speak of the Seven, think of them as seven rivers, all flowing in the same direction, from beginning to end.' Radok smiled. This was the version he'd been told as a boy, back when the Grey Crow fished him from the waters of the south and taught him their words. He had heard it many times since, always through Ilgor, seeking to convert those children taken in raids and ambushes. *Now it's Nyana shining the light, taught by the best...*

'Running through it all is the largest river, *Kamra*, what you would call life itself. All living things are born from this river. We are carried along by its current, ageing as we go, until our part in the All Song is done.

'The other six flow beside it, weaving in and out, sometimes merging with the life stream, sometimes flowing far away. If we are caught in any of their currents, one of these rivers can sweep us away, our lives changing dramatically, for better or worse. Yet all seven flow in the same direction, their differences ironed out along the way, so that what is meant to be will be - what we call the Will.'

'Tell him about the Seven, girl,' said Radok. He had closed his eyes to listen. Hearing the words from Ilgor was one thing, but hearing it in the sweet song of his Little Sparrow was something else entirely. It brought Radok a deep sense of joy. *She is made for this. She is made for the Blackstone.*

Nyana sighed at the interruption, but she knew well to give the audience what they wanted. 'There is *Padra*,' she said, 'fate, for those who stick to the course they are given, and very few ever break free once she has them in her stream. *Kari*, destiny, plucks out those who strive for greatness, sweeping them up from *Kamra* as a beggar and casting them back as a chief.

'Then there's the *Idari*, the two sisters of fortune. They are the most unpredictable of the Seven. *Idra* can raise you up when you least expect, but *Idri* can send you tumbling over the falls. They are the balance that holds the Will in check.

'And finally the *Dacari*, the two brothers of desire. *Dacri* you would know as lust, and *Dacra* is love. One river we can resist if we swim hard enough, the other there is no fighting. ...Both can bring great joy or great sorrow.'

'That's the Seven,' said Radok, 'and theirs is the Will. Now tell him of the Eighth.'

Mikilov grunted. 'Him I've heard of.'

'They say you serve him,' said Nyana. 'That the Black Wind circles the blades of your axe, and in return you pay for it with the souls of the children of Basilla.'

'Then what would he pay me for yours?' asked Mikilov, a wicked glint in his eye.

'The Eighth, Little Sparrow. Tell him of the Eighth.'

'*Chadra*,' she said, 'the Black Wind. He cares nothing for the whims of the Seven, only for death and destruction. He weaves his way through the All Song in defiance of the Will, crossing the Seven and bringing death to any unfortunate souls caught in his path.'

'Sounds like any Basillian I've ever met,' said Mikilov, and the sincerity of the words pained Radok. Perhaps because he knew the truth of them.

Radok opened his eyes and gazed at the wolf. 'We kill to survive,' he said, 'but the Black Wind takes from both sides. He wants us all dead.'

'It sounds like this Talak only wants you. So why not let him?'

'It's not him,' said Nyana. 'It's me. He wants to stop me touching the Blackstone. He fears I will become a conduit for the Will like none before me, and the thought of it terrifies him. It terrifies the Eighth too.'

Mikilov looked as confused as ever, but even Radok struggled to make sense of that. 'Why?' he asked.

She fixed her dead eyes on Radok, the seriousness sending a shiver down his spine. 'Because I could change the tribes. Not just the Grey Crow, but all the tribes of Basilla. And if I change the tribes, I change the Wolves; I change the people of the One God; I change the future of nations, and, with it, all the wars to come.'

Radok sank to his knees before the girl and laid a hand on her shoulder. 'You don't expect much of yourself, eh Little Sparrow?'

She smiled shyly. 'I just read it as I see it.'

'Very well,' said Mikilov. 'First we'll kill this Talak, and then you'll touch the Blackstone.'

'You believe her then?' asked Radok.

'I think she believes it, and that's enough for now. Scar gave his life to protect her. Now I'm duty bound to do the same.'

Nyana caught Mikilov's hand before he could turn away, her big empty eyes meeting his. 'Thank you, Grey Wolf.'

'Don't thank me yet, child, there's still a long way to go.'

'Do you speak for the She-Wolf too?' asked Radok.

'Senya?' Mikilov laughed. 'No one speaks for her. But if you stay away from her, I'll make sure she keeps away from you.'

Radok nodded, satisfied. 'Then we best get some sleep. There's still a long road ahead of us.'

On the fourteenth day out from the Velga they crested a large rise, where they were met by a sight that took their breath away. For the first time on their journey there was nothing to see on the horizon; no hills or snow dunes, no rocky outcrops nor frozen trees. The long arm of the Spears, known as the Körangar mountains to the Grey Crow, loomed out of the west, reaching towards them, but there was nothing else beyond that. Only the sprawling, empty waste of the Whitelands themselves.

Senya held a hand to her brow, shielding her eyes from the bright sunlight, which bounced off the white landscape with an almost blinding harshness, and peered at the distant mountains. The jagged, snow-capped peaks of the Spears stabbed at the sky like white steel, the memory of them burning into Senya's vision. She wondered, not for the first time, how a place so cold could still find a way to burn?

'Are you sure this bloody rock of yours isn't out that way?' she asked, waving a hand at the distant mountains. She turned back to the group of Grey Crow gathered behind her, relieving her eyes of the painful glare, and slowly focused on her new companions. She found no comfort there, only the cold animosity of an enemy sworn to peace. Senya found her fingers playing at the hilt of her sword, the gesture not entirely subconscious.

'There's nothing that way,' said Radok, his voice growing weaker by the day. 'Only ice and rock, and death.'

'Still more than what's out here,' muttered Senya, turning her gaze back to the bleak emptiness of the north.

'Two days,' put in Talgar, Nyana's head peering over his left shoulder from where she dangled from his back. In light of Radok's worsening decline, Talgar had taken over transport duties of the little one, with neither of them complaining too much about it, all things considered. 'Give it two days,' he went on, 'and you'll see the Käda... the Last Rock.'

'Best we keep moving,' urged Jian. 'Daylight is already wasting.'

The party started to move off, but Radok hung back, gazing off to the distant mountains. 'Huh,' he muttered.

Following his gaze, Senya saw a flock of birds flying south, like black arrows moving across the bright blue sky, the distant sound of the cawing carried over the silent emptiness.

'What is it?' asked Nyana.

'Grey crow,' Radok told her. 'A flock of them, heading south.'

'Tell me,' the girl said, her voice anxious, desperate almost.

'There's maybe fifteen, flying against the wind, battling hard.' Radok paused, turning his eyes on the girl, watching her for a moment as she strained her own unseeing eyes toward the distant marvel. 'It's a thing of beauty.'

'I can see it,' she said, her voice almost a delighted squeal. 'The snow-capped mountains behind them!'

'That's right, Little Sparrow. That's right.' Radok smiled warmly. There was no mistaking the emotion behind that expression. It was a look Senya had seen a thousand times before, back in her father's days, when he would cast her that same smile.

It was love, pure and simple. The love of a daughter beaming out from a proud father. *And she'll never know what it looks like.* Senya felt a swell of pity for the girl, and even for the Wolfeater. Perhaps there was more to him than the rabid killer she had taken him for. He'd killed Velimir, and no displays of tenderness would undo that, but Senya was starting to understand what Mikilov and the old woman had tried to tell her. Nothing was ever black and white. It was always shades of grey.

'Where are they going, do you think?' the girl asked.

'The same place we should be going,' said Radok. 'Somewhere warm.'

Talgar was right. Two days later they got their first glimpse of the Last Rock, peeking its pointed head over the flat horizon. Energised by the sight, they marched on with renewed vigour, every step taking them a little closer, the mountain slowly emerging from the white haze of landscape up ahead.

Little by little, the lonely mountain climbed up out of the earth until it stood brazenly before them, beckoning them on like a beacon in the darkness. By the third day they could pick out the details: three lower spires of sharp rock glazed with the ice of a thousand years, crowned by a fourth peak climbing high enough to scrape at the sky above, and all crisscrossed by a spider's web of wind carved crags and ridges, ice forged ledges and passes.

The party took a break once the sun reached its zenith, taking drink from their water skins and sharing in the dried strips of kragan meat they'd gathered when they joined forces.

The water was an issue. Senya hadn't given it much thought until they were out in the frozen wastes, when Mikilov told her to ration her water. 'Why?' she asked. 'We're surrounded by water; we'll just drink the snow!'

'If old Finn could hear you now,' Mikilov had scoffed. 'How do we melt it? We'll be lucky if we see another fire before we're back south, and if you try to melt it in your mouth it will steal your body warmth and you'll freeze all the quicker.'

'Then what?'

'We share skins,' Mikilov had said. 'When one is empty, we fill it with snow and start drinking from the other. We'll carry them between the layers of our clothes, let our body warmth melt it that way. It will take a while for it to melt enough, so we'll have to ration the good one.'

That was what they did. Senya took her swig now and passed the skin back to Mikilov. 'How are you feeling?' he asked, returning the stopper and slipping the skin back beneath his coat.

He had asked the same question each time they came to a stop, and each time she had fed him the same lie. *I'm fine.* Yet the closer they got to the Last Rock, the further they were from home. And the further they were from home, the more it seemed the time for lies was coming to an end.

'It's my hands,' she told him. 'I can barely feel my fingers.'

'Frostbite,' he muttered. 'Here.' Grabbing Senya's arms, he crossed them over her chest and shoved her hands into her armpits. 'You need to keep them as dry and warm as possible. If your fingers start turning black, you'll lose them. And don't rub them. That will only make it worse.'

Radok ambled up beside them, offering a sympathetic half-smile. Gazing off toward the mountain, he said, 'We'll reach the foothills by tomorrow afternoon, and with any luck we'll meet the *Ashan Daru*. He should give us everything we need.'

'The *Ashan Daru*?' asked Senya.

'A servant of the Seven. The First and the Last. He is the gatekeeper to the Blackstone. He'll offer us shelter and prepare us for the climb ahead.'

'And if Talak reaches him first?' asked Mikilov.

'He will,' said Nyana, standing just behind them. 'But the *Ashan Daru* picks no sides. He serves the Seven and the Eighth. Talak will not harm him.'

Radok shrugged his shrunken shoulders, loosening them. 'I hope you're right, Little Sparrow. Without him, there's no way we make the climb.'

As she watched him walk on, each staggered step crunching through a layer of crusted snow, Senya knew the truth of what the Wolfeater said. Even in the short time since they had joined forces, she had watched him wilting away, like a flower caught in the winter of its life. 'I'm not sure he'll even make the mountain, let alone the climb,' she told Mikilov.

'He'll make it,' said Nyana, climbing back up onto Talgar's back. 'He still has work to do.'

CHAPTER TWENTY-THREE

The *Ashan Daru*

He found the *Ashan Daru* waiting for him, as he had known he would. The old man stood in the cave mouth at the foot of the Käda, the mountain towering away behind him. He was dressed only in a grey rag that covered his manhood, with a necklace of small bones dangling against his bony frame. Gaunt and shrivelled, he shivered in the cold air, his breath smoking as he exhaled. His pale skin had a taut, bluish tinge to it, while his small, dark nipples stood as hard as pebbles in the bitter cold. He looked every inch a man freezing to death.

Talak was about to call to him, when his breath caught in his throat. This was not the man he had known. He was dressed the same, with the same apparent indifference to his own wellbeing, but this one was younger. Much younger. There was no grey in his long, scraggly hair and his beard was more that of a youth gone wild than a wizened man's of untold winters.

'Where is Barun?' Talak called to him.

The man's face, all hollowed cheeks and sunken eyes, brightened with a crooked smile. 'Barun is dead,' he said, his voice like dried timber. 'I am Aldur. Welcome to the Käda, Talak of the Eighth.'

'You know me?'

'I live in the shadow of the Blackstone. The All Song is the only company I have. I knew to expect you, as I know to expect the others. Come...' he said, sweeping aside the heavy, tattered hide hanging over the entrance of the cave and waving Talak forward. 'There are rules we must discuss.'

'What rules?'

'The rules of what follows.'

'There is only one rule,' said Talak. 'Life or death. And I have made my choice.'

'And yet there is balance too. Before the scales are tipped in favour of one or the other, there are rules that must be obeyed. Come!'

Without waiting for a response, Aldur ducked into the cave and disappeared from view. Talak lingered a while longer, his eyes scaling the mountain beyond the cave, stopping at each of the ice-blasted spires before pushing on to the summit, where the Blackstone waited.

It sent shivers down his spine, seeing it again. Talak remembered the fear he'd felt the last time he stood there, gazing up at that monstrosity of rock. Yet he was just a boy back then, and the Black Wind was nothing but a whispered warning from the elders of the Grey Crow. Now the Black Wind was with him and there was nothing to fear. There was only the thrill of anticipation.

Inside the cave Talak found the *Ashan Daru* sitting beside a roaring fire, tending a broth-filled cooking pot with a wooden ladle. Animal hides decorated the walls and littered the floor, covering every inch of the rough-hewn rock with a look of comfort and cosiness. There was a hand-chiselled chimney over the fireplace for the smoke to escape, but most of the heat stayed within, helping to explain Aldur's choice of clothing. The sound of trickling water echoed from deeper in the cave, reminding Talak of the hot springs he knew could be found around the Käda. There was something magical about those springs, Talak knew, but he had never been close enough to see them for himself.

'I would offer nourishment,' said Aldur, 'but I know servants of the Eighth have little desire for food or drink, even as their bodies waste away.'

'I have what I need,' Talak told him, though his stomach rumbled at the intoxicating smell of the bubbling stew and he had to drive the thought of it from his mind. 'I'll take the rest from the fallen.'

'The fallen?' A smile flickered on the man's lips. 'You think you'll win then?'

Talak's jaw tightened. 'The Black Wind always wins.'

'True enough. All things die... eventually. But before then there is life, and that's not so easy to sweep away. Not when the Seven have plans of their own.'

'I could kill you easily enough,' said Talak, though he wasn't sure if that was a good idea or not. While the Eighth had left him largely to his own devices these past few days, there was always a whisper of guidance. Not so within this cave, where he could hear no trace of the All Song at all, neither the Seven nor the Eighth.

'You could,' said the *Ashan Daru*, settling back with a bowl of stew. 'But I am merely the gatekeeper. Here at the Blackstone, life and death hold the same value. Neither side has anything to gain from my death. Even if you do kill me, another will come to take my place. There will always be an *Ashan Daru*, despite what *Chadra* may wish.'

Talak thought about putting the man's words to the test and killing him anyway, but at least one thing Aldur said was true: the *Ashan Daru* stood neutral in the All Song, and there was no way of knowing how killing such a man might tip the balance of power. Talak sighed reluctantly. 'Speak then,' he said at last. 'Let's hear these rules of yours.'

Aldur took another mouthful of stew before answering, and his words trickled out slowly as he wrestled with the heat of the food. 'You must... respect the sanctity... of the Käda. Only the children of the Wind - only Basillians - can die upon the mountain's slopes. You cannot touch the Wolves.'

'And if they attack me?'

'They won't. I'll make sure of it.'

Talak considered it for a moment, then nodded his head in agreement. *The Valor mean nothing to the Black Wind, only the girl.*

Setting his bowl aside, Aldur leaned forward suddenly, his eyes bright with intensity. 'Only the girl.'

Talak's stomach tightened at the thought of the *Ashan Daru* reading his mind. His hand drifted slowly towards the hilt of his sword. 'What did you say?'

'Only the girl,' Aldur echoed, his gaze lost somewhere in the distance. Then he shook his head as though clearing it. 'If she touches the Blackstone, there is a chance the girl becomes the greatest *Ashan Tay* to ever live. That's why you're really here, no? It's not about stopping Radok or protecting the Blackstone, it's about the girl.'

Talak's fingers brushed lightly at the soft, leather-bound hilt of his sword, his hand resting on the pommel. 'That's why I'm here. The girl.'

'Then it will be *Ashan Tay* against *Ashan Tay*; servant of the Seven versus servant of the Eighth. There will be the balance.'

Talak almost laughed aloud. 'You want me to fight a blind girl? You think that's balanced?'

'Not the girl, perhaps, but a champion of her choosing. The Grey Crow have already lost too many heroes on this journey without adding three more to the list. Defeat her champion, and the girl's life is forfeit.'

Talak suppressed a smile. There was no doubt in his mind that the girl would choose Radok for her champion. A weak, dying Radok, no less. And set against him would be the right hand of the Eighth. *Death itself,* thought Talak, remembering how he had cut through the crowd of Empty Face near the Velga. What chance did one dying man have against that? Less than he would with three friends alongside, that was for sure.

'I accept,' he told the *Ashan Daru*. 'I will kill her champion, and then I'll kill her. I'll kill any the Black Wind demands.'

'Then you'll never find rest,' said Aldur. 'For so long as there is life, death will call its day. Go then,

Ashan Tay. Climb to the Blackstone and wait there for chance. The blind Crow and her friends will be here soon. I shall strike the same bargain with them, before sending them up to you.'

'No tricks,' said Talak, though he quickly realised the warning was unnecessary.

'The *Ashan Daru* always speaks true,' said Aldur, thrusting his chin out indignantly. 'The truth is neutral. Only lies take sides.'

'Then I climb.' And with that Talak turned on his heels and swept out through the covered entrance, into the cold and the wind and the snow.

It was snowing again by the time they stood in the shadow of the Käda, a wicked flurry lashing at them from every angle. Though still shielded from the worst of it by the guiding hand of the Will, Nyana could feel the tiny shards of ice flicking at her face.

Ignoring the pain, she focused instead on the looming presence set before her. Nyana needed no eyes to see the lonely mountain towering over them, a sentinel of frozen rock standing tall in the white waste. She could *feel* it. Nor did she need ears to hear the wind roaring down at them from the summit, though these she had. The sound filled her head with its awesome power, with the full glory of the All Song threatening to drown her thoughts.

'Is he mad?' a voice asked suddenly, having to shout to be heard over the wind. It was the one they called the Grey Wolf. 'He'll freeze to death, standing there like that.'

Nyana smiled. He was waiting for them, as she had known he would be. She smelled his fire long before the others saw the smoke rising from a shaft above his cave, a heady mix of woodsmoke, toasting bread and meaty stew. She could see him standing there in her mind's eye, near-naked, watching them draw ever closer. 'It is the *Ashan Daru*,' she said brightly. 'He does not feel the cold.'

She felt Radok's hand on her shoulder. 'Oh, he feels the cold, Little Sparrow. But I doubt there is a hotter place in the world than the cave he calls home. The cold is a reprieve for him.'

'I never dreamt I would see him,' said Jian. 'Not here, at the end of the world.'

'Who is he?' The other Wolf this time, the woman, Senya. 'He looks half mad.'

'Only half?' Radok's voice again, half amused. 'The *Ashan Daru* lives for the All Song. He serves neither the Will of the Seven, nor the lone voice of the Eighth, but all of them combined.'

'All of them, and none,' put in Jian. 'He is the only neutral in the never-ending struggle between life and death. He is the...' She struggled for the right word. '... arbitrator?'

'Aye,' said Radok. 'It is his role to maintain the balance between life and death, for there cannot be one without the other.'

'I suppose Basillians know that better than most,' said Senya. 'Your life *is* death.'

'Sometimes survival must be paid for with death,' said Nyana, who had heard Ilgor offer the same argument many times before. The words seemed to work well against the younglings of the Grey Crow, whenever one of their number spoke out against the violent life thrust upon them by the elders. But Nyana doubted they would carry the same weight among those they called the enemy. She let out a sigh. 'We should join him, before he does freeze to death.'

The *Ashan Daru* remained silent as he watched them approach, but for Nyana that silence spoke a thousand words. The Will faded to silence as she grew closer to him. She could still hear the wind, roaring down from the summit of the last rock like a waterfall, but the voices of the Seven fell slowly silent, as though nullified by whatever power the man radiated. By the time she stood before him, the wind was just the wind, tugging at her clothes and lapping at her skin like waves in a storm.

'Nyana of the Grey Crow,' she heard him say, his voice like grating stone. 'I've been waiting a long time for a girl to touch the Blackstone. Will you be the first, I wonder?'

'She will,' said Radok, taking her tiny hand in his and giving it a squeeze. 'We'll make sure of it.'

'Ah, the Wolfeater! Yes, I don't doubt you will play your part in what lies ahead. You've come a long way to speak to the Seven.'

'Will they hear me?'

'My dear Radok, they have always heard you. The question is: will you hear them?'

'If we're going to do this,' said Jian, 'can we at least move it inside? I hear it's quite warm in there and this cold is starting to grate on me.'

The *Ashan Daru* chuckled. 'Quite. My nipples feel ready to drop off. Come then. I offer warmth and rest, food and drink. The Blackstone will still be there in the morning.' Nyana felt his eyes suddenly on her. 'And some of you have choices to make.'

The cave felt like paradise after weeks out in the open wilderness. The fire popped and crackled, the heat and the orange glow enough to banish - however briefly - the memories of the cold outside.

Fur hides littered the place, covering the floor and hanging from the walls, while animal skulls were nailed up alongside them. Even as she stepped inside, Senya found herself reminded at once of Velimir's home. This was a little less civilised perhaps, but both homes spoke of a man firmly at one with the world around him. And with every reminder came the anger...

Senya flashed a look at Radok as he sidled in beside the fire, sinking down to sit on one of the hides laid on the ground. Her fingers brushed the hilt of her sword, tempting her, while the others moved in behind the Wolfeater, each taking a place beside the flames, each distracted by this brief reprieve from the great outdoors.

It would be so easy to do it; to just draw her blade and bury it in the Wolfeater's back. The memory of Velimir cried out for it...

'You are Senya.'

Surprised by the voice, Senya turned to find the strange cave dweller standing beside her, his emerald eyes bright with energy. In the fading light outside he had looked gaunt and unhealthy, but up-close Senya saw that he was younger than she'd thought, and lean, and wiry, and strong - a man in his prime.

'You know me?' she found herself asking, and the man's mouth twitched with a faint smile.

'I know the eyes. You have your father's eyes. He was a great man, Finn the Ironheart. One of the few

Valor to seek out the ways of the tribes, wanting to understand his enemy beyond the violence. He earned our respect by giving us his, and there were many who were sorry to hear of his death. If there were more men like him in the world, there would be no need for the *Ashan Daru*.'

Senya stared at him, dumbfounded. She knew her father had worked Old Valirov and the Whitelands, but she never dreamed of him consorting with the tribes of Basilla. Nor that they would remember him with anything but hatred, which seemed all that existed between the Valor and the tribes.

'You are Aldur of the Slow Storm tribe,' said Mikilov, eyebrows raised. 'Finn spoke of you many times.'

The man grunted. 'I was Slow Storm, many years ago. Before the Blackstone called me home.'

'The Slow Storm?' Talgar chuckled. 'More like the storm that never moves.' Jian tried to restrain him, but Talgar ignored her. 'When was the last time they joined a raid?'

The *Ashan Daru* stared back at Talgar coldly, the mask of neutrality slipping just a fraction. 'They are waiting.'

'Waiting for what? The Whitelands to melt?'

'They wait for the Thunderhead. The one who will change the world.'

A sneer twisted Talgar's face even more than the scars he now bore, and he dismissed the notion angrily. 'The Thunderhead is nothing but a myth; something you and your ilk dreamt up to keep the tribes hungry.'

Turning his attention away from Talgar, the *Ashan Daru's* gaze fell briefly on Nyana, who sat beside Radok at the fire. 'Believe what you must, Talgar of the Grey Crow. I would only warn you that the storm is closer than you think. Wait! Let me see!'

Senya, who had started to peel the gloves from her numbed hands, looked up in time to see the *Ashan Daru* bearing down on her. He snatched her hands into his and frowned down at them, squinting as he inspected the damage. Senya winced as she looked down herself. There was no pain - her fingers were numb to any feeling - but the tips of two fingers on her right hand and three on her left were bluish and splotchy. They looked dead. They felt dead.

'Frostbite,' said the *Ashan Daru*. 'Don't put them near the fire, you'll do more damage that way. Come, follow me.'

Senya glanced at Mikilov, unsure, but the big man gave a subtle nod and so she followed. The *Ashan Daru* led her through a narrow passage at the back of the cave, the sound of running water drifting out of the darkness, into a smaller, torch-lit sub-chamber. A pool of steaming water almost filled the chamber, with bubbles rising up from beneath the surface and rivulets trickling down from between the stalactites above. Senya felt her skin prickling with the warmth.

'Pleasant, no?' The *Ashan Daru* smiled as he held his hand out towards the pool. 'This water has properties that will warm your flesh and repair some of the damage caused by the cold.'

'How is it so warm?' Senya asked, astonished.

'There is fire deep within the mountain.' Lowering to his haunches, the *Ashan Daru* pressed his hand to the stone beneath his feet. 'You can feel it in the rock. Most of the caves around here have similar hot springs, some with different properties, others with powers of their own.' He grinned again. 'For anyone who walks the Whitelands, this is the place to be.'

The *Ashan Daru* held his hands out, waiting. Senya glanced at them for a moment, then back at him, and shrugged. 'Your clothes,' he said. 'You don't need them to bathe. I'll see that they get dry. There are robes over there by the pool, once you're finished.'

'I'm not stripping in front of you.'

'Child, you don't have anything I want.'

Seeing that his words failed to move Senya, the *Ashan Daru* sighed. He closed his eyes and turned away. Senya hesitated for a moment, but one look at her blackening fingers was enough to sway her. She removed the heavy layers of her furs, then slipped from her boots, her white linen shirt and her leather leggings. A moment later she was dipping her feet - the toes showing their own signs of frostbite - into the steaming water.

The relief was almost immediate. Rather than the searing heat she had expected, a gentle warmth drew Senya into a world of comfort. She sighed as the steam washed over her, clearing her sinuses and opening the pores on her skin. Taking a deep breath, she submerged herself completely, shuddering with pleasure as the water closed over her. By the time she lifted her head from beneath the surface and looked back, the *Ashan Daru* was gone, her clothes disappeared with him.

She lingered in the water for almost an hour, letting the heat slowly soothe life back into her frozen digits. Hot baths were rare even in Haslova, and Senya could barely remember the last time she had felt so clean and relaxed. Eventually, her skin beginning to shrivel up, she lifted herself from the water and dressed in one of the woollen robes left beside the pool.

She made her way back into the main chamber, where she found the others still sitting around the fire. Mikilov was deep in debate with Talgar and the *Ashan Daru*, discussing something about their gods, while Radok dozed with Nyana asleep on his lap. Jian and Tess rose from their seats once Senya emerged, moving off to take her place in the pool.

Senya found a seat for herself beside the fire, where the *Ashan Daru* brought her a plate of food that rivalled anything she had eaten before. There was sausage and bacon, fried potato and tomato, mushrooms and beans, and sourdough bread. And it was all cooked to perfection. Senya ate her fill and more besides before she had the courage to ask where it had all come from.

'The mushrooms grow here, in the shadows of the Last Rock. As I said, this is not the only spring with gifts of its own. They give extra energy and fortify against the cold. You will remember them fondly when you tackle the mountain.'

'And the rest of it?' asked Senya. 'Somehow I doubt there's a spring for hogs.'

The *Ashan Daru* laughed at that. 'No, no spring for hogs. The tribes send most of it, in tribute. Whatever they can spare.'

Senya's mind drifted back over the journey of the past few weeks. She saw again her blackening toes and fingers, freezing to death before her very eyes. She saw the bodies torn apart by the kragan, Scar among them. She felt the cutting winds of the blizzard once more, watched Mikilov falling through the ice on the Velga, swept away to who knew what end. And then she remembered how it all began, what had dragged her from behind the walls of Haslova in the first place: the harshest winter in an age.

'A hard road,' she said at last, 'during a winter where nothing is spare.'

The *Ashan Daru* considered her words with a rueful smile. 'Your friend says the same thing. But all gods need sacrifice, and none more so than the balance between life and death. It must be the same for the Valor, no? Are there no sacrifices demanded by the Hunt?'

'The *Great* Hunt,' Senya corrected, but she was already considering his words. 'No,' she said at last. 'No sacrifice is needed. We *are* the Great Hunt. We choose the life we want: hunter or prey, wolf or sheep. We live the best life we can, and when the Great Hunt calls us home, we are rewarded with whatever we deserve.'

The *Ashan Daru* frowned. 'I remember speaking to your father of the gods of the Valor. He spoke of the Old Ones; the Half Bear, the Grey Woman, all the rest. They seemed strange enough to me, but this *Great Hunt*? In my mind, a god that holds no power is no god at all. There is wind up in the hills of Haslova, no?' Senya nodded. 'Then you could do worse than touch the Blackstone yourself. It may open your mind to a greater purpose, and then you'll understand the power of true faith.'

'Oh, I think I understand the power of faith,' said Senya, as she glanced around the cave once more. 'You may live up here in a cave at the end of the world, but men risk their lives so that you can live in comfort and eat like a king while your people starve and freeze. If that's the kind of world your gods want, I'll have no part of the Blackstone.'

To her surprise, the *Ashan Daru* only smiled sadly and nodded his head. 'A wise choice,' he said. 'Not everyone is made for the cutting edge of the wind. Only Basilla. Only those forged in the Whitelands.'

One by one, the group took their turns eating and bathing, until they were all gathered beside the fire once more, their bodies free of the aches and pains of months in the wilderness. They lounged about in the simple robes the *Ashan Daru* had provided, their own clothes hanging over the fire where the heat could dry them, their weapons stripped from them but close enough at hand for them to feel relaxed about it.

Jian and Tess lay in each other's arms, looking fresh and clean, utterly at peace. Talgar had a fresh bandage over his wounded face, which the *Ashan Daru* had also dressed with some moss from another of his sacred springs, to speed the healing. Mikilov looked younger somehow, with the tangles brushed out of his hair and beard, and the colour returned to his cheeks for perhaps the first time since he fell into the Velga. He looked sad though, gazing into the dancing flames, lost in his own thoughts. *There's no bathing grief away*, thought Senya, her own heart suddenly aching. *Who knew a wolf could cause so much pain?*

Only Radok showed signs of the past two weeks. Out of his furs, the loss of weight was even starker to behold. His flesh was wasted away, his skin ashen grey where once it had been smooth ebony. It would surprise Senya if the man could stand in the morning, let alone climb a mountain.

Such a fall for such a man was something pitiful to witness, and Senya found her hatred for the Wolfeater had wasted away along with the rest of him. *What's left to hate,* she found herself wondering? *No man deserves such a fate as this. Not even him.*

The *Ashan Daru* rose to his feet at the head of the fire, raising his hands for attention. His guests fell to silence and gazed up at him, like a family waiting for their father's words. 'Tomorrow, you face the Käda - the Last Rock.' He spoke calmly, but his voice resonated with power, booming around the confined space of the cave. 'Yet there are rules for those who wish to lay hands on the Blackstone; rules that both the Seven and the Eighth must obey.'

'What rules?' asked Radok, his voice tired and weak. Kneeling beside him, perhaps even holding him upright, Nyana cocked her head to listen.

'You will respect the sanctity of this holy place. What happens at the Blackstone is for the children of the Wind alone. The Wolves can play no part.' He fixed his eyes on Mikilov and Senya in turn. 'Bear witness, Valor, but you *must not* interfere.'

'That is madness,' said Jian, sitting opposite Senya, the flames between them. 'You don't know what he can do! If Talak is here, waiting for us, we'll need every sword we can get.'

'He *is* here,' said the *Ashan Daru*, 'waiting for you. But he knows the rules also, and I have his word no harm will come to the Valor.'

'*Well*,' Jian breathed in exasperation, 'if you have his word!'

It was Nyana who spoke next, her soft voice cutting through the hot air like calming music. 'What else?'

The *Ashan Daru* fixed his gaze on the girl, a strange half-smile on his face. 'Too many have died already,' he said. 'Balance is needed now. Whatever reasons you had for starting this journey, it has led you here, to the Seven and the Eighth, to the All

Song. It will be ended the old way: *Ashan Tay* against *Ashan Tay*.'

'We have no *Ashan Tay*,' put in Talgar. 'We had Talak, but you've seen how that turned out.'

The *Ashan Daru* tutted and shook his head. 'The young think they have all the answers.' He thrust a finger out in Nyana's direction. 'The girl has everything an *Ashan Tay* needs. She can hear the Will, even now, even before the Blackstone. They took her eyes, yet still she sees far more than any of you. She is wise beyond her years, and she knew she was coming here to be reborn... or to die. Did you not, Little Sparrow?'

'You would name her *Ashan Tay*?' asked Radok, his voice little more than a rasping whisper. 'This blind girl who has never swung a sword in her life? You would have her fight Talak of the Grey Crow?'

'It is not my place to name anyone,' said the *Ashan Daru*. 'Only the Will can decide such a fate... and that requires a touch of the Blackstone. The girl has the chance to become the first female *Ashan Tay*, with the potential to become the greatest who ever lived. *If* she can only touch the stone.

'Yet such a servant to the Seven does not sit well with the Eighth, and he sends Talak to put an end to her. She represents everything he despises. A child - a *blind* girl, no less - with a greater understanding of the Will than he will ever know? That cuts Talak deep, and he will stop at nothing to see her dead.'

'And you seek to help him?' asked Jian.

'I seek the balance,' said the *Ashan Daru*. 'One against one. Him, against a champion of her choosing.'

'Agreed,' said Nyana, speaking in a voice that broached no argument.

All the other Grey Crow chirped in with their objections, but it was the near-death rattle of the Wolfeater that cut through the noise. 'You understand what it means?' he asked the girl. 'Your life would be forfeit.'

The girl took his cheeks in her hands and kissed his forehead. 'It started with me and you,' she said. 'That's how it should end.'

'And you?' The *Ashan Daru* was gazing at Senya and Mikilov again, an eyebrow cocked.

'If that's what the girl wants,' said Mikilov, 'we won't interfere.'

The *Ashan Daru* focused on Senya. 'And you?'

Senya shrugged. 'Stand in the way of Basillians killing each other? Why would I want to do a thing like that?'

The *Ashan Daru* clapped his hands together. 'Excellent! It is decided then. It will be champion of the Seven against champion of the Eighth. You should sleep now, all of you. You'll need to start out early. The blizzards are coming, and you'll want to be up and down again before they strike. Please, sleep. All is balanced.'

CHAPTER TWENTY-FOUR

The Käda

'Your gods could have sent a little sunshine to help us on our way.' Senya squinted out from the shadows of her fur fringed hood, the howling wind battering against her, swirling snow gusting into her eyes. 'You sure they want you?'

Radok cast a gaze in her direction. The hatred was gone, he saw. Replaced by... what?... pity? He groaned. Hatred was good. He could use hatred - *had* used it, whether to fire his spirit or drive his enemies to their own mistakes. But what could he do with pity? Pity was no good to anyone.

'Some of them, at least,' said Nyana. 'But they're all here, wild and uncontrolled. That's what makes the climb so hard.'

'Then let's get started,' said Talgar, who dropped to a knee and waited patiently as the girl clambered on to his back. That pained Radok, as it had pained him throughout the last leg of their journey across the Whitelands. He had even confessed as much to Talgar himself a few days earlier.

'It should be me carrying the girl,' he told the man one evening, while Nyana slept between them. 'I'm responsible for her.'

Talgar had only smiled. 'You've been carrying her all her life, Radok,' he said. 'Let me take the burden a while longer, eh? You save your strength for what lies ahead.'

'I'm not sure I'm ready to let her go.'

'Perhaps not. But she's ready to let you go, and that's the best we can hope for when the time comes. I pray my two girls have the strength you've given this one, once the Black Wind decides my time is done.'

Back at the Käda, Radok offered Talgar a nod of the head, and the warrior pushed himself to his feet with Nyana clinging to his back. He set off along a narrow path winding up and around the mountain, the two Valor falling in behind him, Tess the next in line. Jian remained a while longer, watching him.

Radok looked back towards the cave where they had spent the night before, and where the *Ashan Daru* still stood watching them, half-dressed even now. The priest raised a hand in farewell.

'Do you believe him?' asked Jian.

'The *Ashan Daru* do not lie,' said Radok. 'But the Eighth does. There's no reason to believe Talak won't kill us all given half a chance.'

'Then what do we do?'

Radok turned back to face the mountain, his eyes scaling the icy rock up to the heady heights of its snow-capped peak, lost to sight among the low-lying clouds. 'We climb,' he said. 'We climb, and we see what Talak's words are worth.'

Radok found the early going easier than expected. His lungs burned with fire at every snatched breath and his arms and legs were heavy as stone by the time he managed to battle his way through some of the higher snowdrifts, but, for all the pain, there was no denying the progress they made.

They had scaled nearly a third of the mountain before the path gave way to more difficult terrain. By then it was midday, though it was difficult to tell one hour from the next, given the swirling maelstrom of snow and hail still lingering from yesterday's storm.

'Rest here,' said Jian, raising her voice so as to be heard over the wind. 'Tess and I will scout the path ahead.'

'No need,' put in Talgar, who, along with Radok, was the only member of the company to have ever visited the Käda.

Twenty years and he still remembers, thought Radok. *Hell, it's been thirty years for me. Some things a man cannot forget...*

Raising a single finger, Talgar pointed at the wall of frozen rock where the trail ended and gestured upwards. *Here*, that gesture said. *We climb.* Six pairs of eyes followed that finger, including Radok's, climbing the rock face from its jagged footings up to the shrouded heights far above.

'There must be another way,' said Jian, a hand shielding her eyes from the falling snow as she gazed upwards.

'Not for those wanting to touch the Blackstone,' said Talgar, and Radok nodded his head in agreement.

Though the younger man's first visit to the Blackstone had taken place some years after Radok's own, no doubt guided by some other *Ashan Tay*, the experience had told them both the same thing.

'There's nothing else for it,' Radok told the others. 'We have no choice but to climb.'

Jian looked up again, shaking her head in disbelief. 'You think the girl can make that climb? You think you can?'

'I made it once before, as a boy.' Radok could still remember every inch of that climb. From the agony in his fingers, where jagged rock tore at his frozen flesh, to the power of the wind battering against his frail body, trying its damnedest to tear him from the mountainside. He said now the same thing the *Ashan Tay* had told him back then. 'Even the blade must first be tempered by fire, before it knows its true purpose. There is only one path up to the Blackstone, and this is it. Best we ready ourselves for the flames.'

The climb was made free handed, as was always the way on the pilgrimage to the Blackstone. It was, after all, a trial by the gods. There was no place for guides or markers, ropes or climbing spikes, in the final test of manhood. *All a man should need*, the *Ashan Daru* had droned out, *is the wits and wiles given to him by the Seven.*

'Then we should take our clothes off too,' Jian had argued. 'Then we'd truly be as the Seven intended.'

'Don't be a fool,' Talgar had barked back, missing the point entirely. 'It's never been the Will for us to freeze to death!'

Bloody men! Jian rolled her eyes again. In the safety of the Fallow she had almost forgotten how small a man's world could be. At least this journey had gone some way to opening her eyes to it once again, enough to have the Long Eye's words echoing in her mind.

Forget the gods, the old woman would often say. *This is a man's world. They are the ones who make the rules, not the Seven, nor even the Eighth. Men. Stupid, foolish, weak minded men. And we all must live with the consequences.*

That was the great truth Jian was beginning to understand, and the longer she spent with men the more abundantly clear it became. Men were fools to the last, and in the world of the Grey Crow the weaker sex held all the power.

Shaking her head, Jian pushed up with her right foot and grabbed a jutting rock with her left hand. Her fingers stung as they found their grip, even through the gloves, but they felt better than they would have before the visit to the *Ashan Daru's* spring. She pulled herself up slowly, inch by inch.

The climb itself was not so difficult. There were plenty of ledges protruding from the rock, plenty of cracks and crevices that made for ideal footholds and hand grips, and Jian powered herself up easily enough. It was the elements that made it so dangerous.

Almost every inch of the black rock glistened with ice, unbearably cold to touch and treacherously slippy. Snow continued to fall, big flakes whipped around by the wild winds seemingly circling the mountain. Not to mention the wind itself, grabbing at the climbers' clothes and trying to yank them from the wall.

As had been the case for days now, Jian could smell nothing. She blamed the cold for the most part, which had bunged up her nose and stifled all her senses. But in truth, there was nothing to smell anyway. Snow had buried most of the world out here, and the small patches of bare rock that resisted offered no home to life.

She could smell Talgar and the girl well enough, especially when the wind shifted and crashed down the mountain towards them like a waterfall. That wave would hit Talgar first, leading the way as he was, Nyana clinging to his back. Then it would wash over Jian and Tess behind him, Radok a few feet below, and the two wolves bringing up the rear, rocking them all where they clung. It brought with it the musty, stale smell of the well-travelled. Yet there was at least a scent of lavender and honey mixed in, offering a fading memory of Aldur's spring.

Jian glanced to her right, to where Tess was matching her rise up the mountainside foothold for foothold. The younger woman met Jian's gaze and smiled. She looked the most comfortable out of all of them. Her long, slender frame was made for climbing, while a lifetime with a bow in her hands had given her the upper body strength needed to hold herself to the mountain and pull herself up with ease. Jian gave a shake of her head, but she found herself smiling back. This was Tess in her element. And, by the Will, if it wasn't the most beautiful thing Jian had ever seen.

Time moved slowly as they made the climb. They'd made a swift start, mounting the wall in pairs and leaving enough space between them so that anyone who fell would only take themselves out. Yet the higher they climbed, the more dangerous it became, until it was clear one slip could kill them. They pressed themselves in firmly against the rock face, taking their time to choose every hand grip and foothold with great care.

Their spacing became ragged as confidence waned, and Radok especially began to struggle. The air was thin up here, and the Wolfeater's breathing grew shallower and shallower. Jian looked down at him, labouring away, then beyond to the base of the climb. Mist had rolled in from somewhere, shrouding the lower part of the mountain, but they had climbed close to a hundred feet by now, with half again still to come.

Jian bit her tongue, not sure of the best advice to give. If Radok climbed on, the risk of falling would only increase. On the other hand, if he turned back, he would face the same risk of falling, but at least the fall would diminish.

'I'll make it,' he said suddenly, as though reading her thoughts. 'I've not come this far for them to stop me now.'

'Heads up!'

The barked command took Jian by surprise, and, glancing up sharply, she was just in time to see a huge chunk of ice flying towards her face. She swerved aside at the last possible moment, even felt the ice catch the edge of her hood as it plunged past her, bouncing off the rocks below with a dull, wet thud.

She looked up to find Talgar grinning down at her. 'Close one, eh girl?'

Beyond him, where the wind thundered out over the edge of the cliff top, leaving a swirling cloud of dust and snow in its wake, Jian glimpsed a dark shape disappearing from sight towards the summit. Her gaze lingered there for a moment longer... and then she saw something new, hurtling through the air towards them. This was more a boulder than a chunk of ice, nearly twice the size of the piece that almost killed her, and it came spinning through the air at a frightening pace.

Jian cried out in horror. 'Talgar!'

But it was too late. The boulder struck Talgar on the head and exploded into a thousand pieces. Knocked unconscious by the blow, perhaps even killed, Talgar dropped from the wall like a stone, plunging lifelessly towards the rocks far below. Nyana fell too, slipping from Talgar's back and setting off on her own course to earth. She gave a startled cry at first, but she never screamed. There was something eerily calm about her.

Jian flailed at them with her free hand as the pair swept by, but they were moving too fast and too far away to reach them. Tess was just as useless. All they could do was watch, as Talgar and Nyana plummeted between them.

In the end, it was Radok who reacted first. It was always Radok. The Wolfeater was nothing, if not predictable. Even weak as he was, even half wasted away by the Black Wind, he sprang to life the moment his Little Sparrow took flight. It seemed to happen in slow motion, every detail of the moment burning itself into Jian's mind as she watched it unfold.

Radok balled himself up against the rock face, the muscles in his arms and legs bunching up and straining through the flesh until every inch of his body was riddled with tension, waiting at the edge of explosion...

And then it happened. Radok thrust his legs out beneath him and launched himself from the wall. He flew through the air with his arms outstretched, fingers rigid like claws. For just a moment, wind whipping through his fur coat, he looked like one of those giant cats found in the mountains of the west, pouncing with lethal intent upon some unwitting prey.

They seemed to hang in the air like that for the longest moment; Radok straining with every sinew of his body to reach the girl, and Nyana, though falling through the air and lost in the agonising darkness of those broken eyes, somehow serenely calm...

She knows he's coming, thought Jian, who could only marvel at the complete faith such belief required. The girl showed no fear as she plunged towards her death, just as Radok showed no fear when he leapt out to meet her. No fear, no hesitation, just the certainty of knowing what had to be done. *This is what love looks like...*

It moved Jian in a way she had not felt since the Black Wind took her child, when the love of her life turned on her so viciously. Had she ever known love like this? Even back then?

Before she could answer those questions, the moment passed and time resumed its flow. Radok grunted as his body collided with the girl. He managed to wrap himself around her and turned through the air so that he'd land first, perhaps saving her from the worst of the fall.

There was a chance, Jian guessed, that he might save her, but he had almost certainly doomed himself.

They plunged as one, Jian's heart in her mouth as they fell away from her. They were doomed, the pair of them. Until the miracle happened...

Mikilov watched them fall.

Talgar went first, his head caved in by whatever debris came raining down on him from the summit, his body limp as a child's doll.

He was followed by the girl, Nyana, who had been holding fast to Talgar's back when the rubble struck his head. As the big man's body fell away beneath her, all Nyana could do was throw herself at the cliff face and pray the gods were kind...

...and kind they were, if only for a short time.

Nyana slammed hard against the wall and a great whoosh of air exploded from her lungs. With Mikilov watching on with bated breath, the girl began to slide down the rock face at once, her feet scrabbling about for purchase, her hands hunting desperately for any nook or cranny she might use for grip.

It was an impossible task. With no eyes to guide her or strength to hold herself up, Nyana was unable to stop herself slipping from the rock face and plummeting after Talgar. She stopped trying, but there was no fear in her face as she fell, just a calm acceptance. There was barely a second between her and Talgar as the pair fell towards their death.

That was when the Wolfeater joined them. Leaping from the wall, Radok caught the girl in mid-air, clasping her to his chest and shaping up to protect her from the landing. The three of them plunged like stones while the others watched on in silent horror.

It all happened so fast. There was barely any time to think between Talgar's blow to the head and Radok's fearless leap, but that was all the time Mikilov had to make his decision. He would get no help from Jian or Tess, who had already been left behind by the falling threesome, while Senya was too far away and too torn between her emotions to offer any help. It all fell to Mikilov...

Talgar is done. That was the first decision he made. Even if the man still lived, he was too big a unit, too solid a mass, to hope of catching him, let alone to catch him and hold to the wall. *Let alone catch him, hold to the wall, and somehow climb!*

At least there was a chance with Radok. Not only had the disease wasted away the greater part of him, there was still some fight left in the old bastard. *And the girl*, Mikilov told himself. *He has the girl too. The one Scar died for...*

Mikilov swayed back slightly to let Talgar fall past him. The Grey Crow made no sound, save for the rippling of his clothes as he plummeted through the air. Mikilov felt a swell of pity at that. Though he barely knew the man, he knew enough about Basillians to know none of their kind would wish to end their part in the All Song with such a pathetic whisper.

Forgetting him, Mikilov waited a fraction longer. Then, as Radok swept by, clutching Nyana close to his chest, Mikilov's free hand shot out. He caught Radok by the ankle, his fist closing tightly around a handful of the man's leggings.

The new weight dragged Mikilov's arm down and almost tore him from the wall. He grunted with pain as his fingers - those of his climbing hand -tightened grimly on the jutting rock to which he clung. He felt the skin on his fingers tear as his grip slipped, even through the thick leather glove. Then his fingernails bent back painfully as he tried to hold himself in place.

Mikilov looked down and met Radok's gaze. While his own face was twisted with strain, his eyes bulging in their sockets, Radok looked serenely calm as he swayed back and forth over the cloud of mist hiding the rocky ground far below.

'Tell the girl to climb,' Mikilov squeezed out through gritted teeth.

Radok wasted no time, and soon enough Nyana was climbing up his leg and onto Mikilov's arm. She used their bodies like a rope, finally coming to a rest when her arms were wrapped around Mikilov's neck.

'Drop him,' Senya called from her place a few strides width from them. 'You've got the girl, no point letting him drag you all down. Let him go, Miki.'

'No!' cried Nyana, her grip tightening on Mikilov's neck, almost choking him.

'She's right,' said Radok. 'Save yourself, you save the girl. Let me go.'

'No!' Nyana's grip tightened even more.

Mikilov worked his head from side to side in an effort to free some breathing space. 'I'm not dropping anyone. We've come this far to watch you touch that bloody stone, Wolfeater, so you'll fucking well touch it!'

Mikilov still held a fistful of the Wolfeater's pants, but he knew it wouldn't be long before either his grip or the material gave way. He began swinging Radok backwards and forwards slowly, easing him into a gentle, pendular rhythm.

'Can you see the rock jutting out near Senya's foot?' Mikilov called. 'You need to grab that!'

Radok moved his head about and scanned the wall. 'I see it,' he said after a moment, every swing bringing him closer to it. 'I can make it.'

Back and forth Radok swung, each time growing a little closer to the jutting rock. At first his hands fell well short, but soon enough his fingers were brushing the stone with their tips.

Mikilov was starting to ache by then, his great shoulders burning with the effort of both clinging to the rock, and swinging Radok in ever greater arcs. With his strength fading fast, he gave one last heave and at the last second Radok caught hold of the jutting rock.

Mikilov held fast to the Wolfeater's leg, not daring to believe it... yet Radok's grip held true and he gave Mikilov a nod to let go.

As he did, Mikilov noticed Senya looking down at the Wolfeater, one foot raised in mid-air over his head. For one terrible moment he thought she would bring that foot down on Radok's head, or on his grip, and send him plunging to the earth. But at the last moment she turned her face upwards and started to climb. 'Let's move,' she barked at them. 'No saying when the weather will turn.'

Mikilov took a moment to catch his breath. 'Are you well, girl?' he asked Nyana.

He felt her nod against his back. 'Thank you for saving us,' she whispered. 'One day, when I serve the Will, I'll make sure the Seven pay this debt. I promise it.'

He could have told her it was a foolish act to make promises of the gods, but she was still blessed with the innocence of youth. She hadn't lost enough yet to the Great Hunt to know any better. *But she will,* thought Mikilov. *Before this day is done, she'll know.*

CHAPTER TWENTY-FIVE

The Seven and The Eighth

Radok's arm slammed down into the snow at the top of the cliff and he levered himself up over the lip, rolling onto his back and gazing skyward. He lay there for the longest moment, breath misting fast and hard in the air above him, every last ounce of energy given to the climb.

Is this what it is to die?

The question seemed to lurch into Radok's mind from some dark recess. He had been bloodied in battle many times before, skewered by arrows and slashed by blades, but this was the first time he had ever felt so close to death. Close enough to feel the Black Wind breathing down his neck.

Radok was almost ready to let it take him. The end would be a relief at this point. He was in so much pain. Not just the pain of exhaustion, with fatigue seeping into his bones and muscles, but the pain of the disease too. Every inch of his body burned with agony, and now not even sleep took the pain away.

We've come this far to watch you touch that bloody stone, Wolfeater, Mikilov's words called back to him, *so you'll fucking well touch it!*

The Grey Wolf had called the truth of it; there was no way Radok could let the Black Wind take him. Not yet, at least, not after they had crossed the Whitelands so that he could touch the Blackstone and ask the gods face-to-face why, having served them all his life, they would reward him with the worst kind of death?

'What is it?' It was the She-Wolf's voice, hushed and awed in equal measure.

With a grunt of effort, Radok rolled onto his side and climbed unsteadily to his feet. The others were gathered nearby, their eyes fixed ahead on the mountain's steepled peak. There, at the foot of that jagged spire, with the Cave of Voices yawning wide beyond it, stood a thin needle of smooth, black rock. It was smaller than Radok remembered it, no taller or broader than the average man, yet the sense of power radiating from that white-veined, ebony rock was as strong as ever. The wind came pouring out of the cave in an incessant roar, smashing against the Blackstone with such force it seemed the stone had to give way. But it held true, the wind washing over and around it, its path seen in the dust and snow it picked up along the way.

'The Blackstone,' Radok muttered, taking a step closer. It was strange to think that, with Talgar gone, he was the only one among them to have seen this place before...

No woman had ever set foot on the Käda, let alone set sight on the Blackstone. Now there were three of them, in Jian, Tess, and Nyana. True, Nyana would not *see* it, but she would *feel* it, perhaps more than any of them. And none of that said anything of the two Wolves, whose people had never had interest in the Last Rock, believing the gods of the tribes were nothing but fool's talk. Now they saw the truth, and they would take word of it back to their people.

Radok's eyes drifted from the Blackstone and traced the path of the slim ridge they would have to cross to reach it. Either side of that narrow bridge the mountain fell away for hundreds of feet, ending in a mass of jagged rock that had claimed the lives of hundreds, perhaps thousands, of Basillian boys down through the years. And the wind was still there, sweeping back and forth across the ridge, ready to wash away more poor souls.

It was only then that Radok noticed the figure barring the way at the ridge's threshold, watching them closely. Radok's eyes narrowed. It was Talak, still dressed in the dark furs he'd been wearing when he set out from the Heart's Flame, including the shoulder piece mounted with hundreds of grey feathers that marked him out as *Ashan Tay* of the Grey Crow.

'Time to test your mettle against the Will,' he called, though it was still difficult to hear him over the violent discord of the wind.

'Your days of serving the Will are done,' Nyana called back, and Radok's heart swelled with pride. The girl was standing front and centre of their small group, this the first time in Radok's hearing she had ever answered back a man of Talak's standing.

'The Will of the Seven perhaps,' Talak replied coolly, 'but who stands for the Will of the Eighth, if not me?'

'No one need stand for him,' said Nyana. 'His will is inevitable.'

'Not as inevitable as he'd like. Take your friend for example.' Talak turned his gaze to Radok and both men shared a meaningful moment. 'The Black Wind has been trying to take you for years, Wolfeater. Yet even now, with death coursing through your veins, you cling to life. Let go. Say farewell to your friends and make peace with your ending.'

'My end will be here soon enough,' Radok told him. 'There's just one last thing to do and then I'm his. Is that why you're here, *Ashan Tay*? For me?'

'Well,' Talak smiled, 'that's why we're all here, isn't it?' The priest's gaze drifted to Jian and Tess, and his smile seemed to widen when he saw Tess's bow aimed at his heart, arrow notched and bowstring drawn taut. 'You two were with me, not so long ago. We were sent by the withered wise of the Grey Crow to stop Radok Wolfeater from breaking ancient laws by touching the Blackstone a second time. Do you remember that?'

'We remember,' said Jian. 'They were swayed by your words, Talak, when they thought you served the Will. If they'd known it was the Eighth you served, they would have sent us after you, not the Wolfeater.'

Talak snorted derisively, before turning his attention to the two outsiders. 'What about you?' he asked the Wolves. 'He's the reason you're out here, isn't he? Did he not kill your friend? By the All Song, he's killed so many of your friends you call him the Wolfeater! And here he is, ripe for the plucking!'

'Aye, we came for him,' admitted Mikilov. 'But things have a habit of changing out in the wilds. Now we're here for her,' he added, nodding in Nyana's direction.

At that, Senya cast a sidelong glance in Radok's direction. *He might be here for the girl,* it said, *but I still have one eye on you.*

'Ah, yes,' replied the *Ashan Tay.* 'The girl.' He took two steps sideways, putting his body between Nyana and the distant Blackstone, and studied her closely. 'And what do you think, girl? Why are you here?'

'To touch the Blackstone,' she said simply. 'To serve the Will.'

Talak swayed as a great whoosh of wind swept over him, snow kicked up out of his furs. 'The Eighth does not like the sound of that. You have a gift, Nyana. It cannot be denied now. The Black Wind fears that you will tip the balance too far in favour of the Seven. I must kill you. That is why I am here.'

Nyana straightened, puffing her chest out. 'You can try.'

Talak smiled. 'I could kill you all right now, in the blink of an eye. But I am bound by the *Ashan Daru* to fight only one - a champion of your choosing. So who will it be, *Little Sparrow*?'

Radok felt a flicker of anger at that. Little Sparrow was the name he had chosen for the girl as a sign of the love between them, and to have it used by this despot in an effort to goad her was almost too much to bear. Yet before he could speak, Nyana gave her answer.

'Only one man has ever fought for me, and I would ask him to do it one more time. I choose the Wolfeater.'

She spoke calmly, a trace of pride and a brazen confidence in her voice. Not once did she turn back to face Radok. *Does she know what she asks? Are there tears in her eyes?*

Radok felt Talak's gaze pore over him. There was a time such a look would have drawn respect, awe even, but Talak only smiled. It was easy to understand why. Radok was a shadow of the man Talak had known. His once prodigious muscles had melted away like snow, leaving a shrunken, shrivelled wreck. Where once he had towered over the shaman, now they stood eye-to-eye, and it was Talak who stood the more formidable.

'I accept,' said the *Ashan Tay*, his smile glinting in the midday sun.

'As do I,' said Radok, flashing a smile of his own. 'The fact I'm near dead anyway should give the old bastard half a prayer.'

The two men stood facing each other, snow swirling about them on the busy wind. Behind Radok, his five companions huddled together and watched in silence. Behind Talak, the Blackstone pulsed with power, channelling the wind as it came pouring out of the Cave of Voices, the sound as crushing as any waterfall in the world.

Talak drew his sword. The blade felt good in his hand, perfectly balanced and hungry for blood. Beneath the leather binding, the ivory handle had been carved to fit his grip perfectly and his fingers slid smoothly into their grooves, even with his thick glove.

Ten strides away, Radok drew his own sword. The steel blade glinted in the daylight as it slid from the scabbard, long and broad. Talak's smile broadened. The weapon weighed heavy on Radok's sword arm, dragging it down to his side. He looked exhausted. His once smooth, ebony skin had dulled to a grey, pallid colour, and, despite the cold, a sheen of sweat covered his face. The man's weary, blood-shot eyes stared back at Talak with dull ambivalence.

By the Eighth, thought Talak, *he should be dead already. I'll be doing him a favour, putting an end to his misery.*

'Are you ready, Wolfeater?' Talak called to him. 'The Black Wind wishes to dance with you, one last time. You die on this mountain.'

'Of course I do,' Radok called back. 'You only have to look at me to know the truth of that. But you die first, *Ashan Tay*. And know that when your body lies broken at the foot of this mountain, there will be no one to seek it out and burn it. Your ashes will not be cast to the Seven Winds. Your soul will not join the All Song. The story of Talak ends here, with him nought but a slave of the Eighth.'

A shiver ran down Talak's spine at the Wolfeater's words. It was true, none of those gathered atop the Käda would mourn him should Radok somehow prove victorious... but the odds of that were so small Talak had given no thought to the idea of rotting away without a burning. But when he finally did fall, as all men must, who *would* mourn the loss of a servant of the Eighth?

A gust of wind pushed against him, rocking him on his heels. *You die in fire,* a voice told him. *Fire is the pure death.*

And just like that, Talak's fears were washed away. The Black Wind had told him he would die in fire, and there was no fire on the Käda. Wielding his sword two handed, he moved in on the Wolfeater, his stride eating up the snow between them in the blink of an eye.

Radok watched him come, his sword arm rising suddenly, not so tired as he had made out. Their swords clashed in the cold mountain air, the ring of steel piercing the roar of the wind. They danced around each other, their swords striking and countering in both directions, clumps of snow kicked up as they shuffled their feet.

In another life, the Wolfeater would have been too much for the *Ashan Tay*. Talak had never been especially skilled with a blade. Even though such a talent was integral to the life of a warrior priest, he had always known certain men were beyond his means. Radok was one of those men. The Wolfeater had earned his name killing Wolves, themselves vicious warriors, on the walls of their own city. Along with his devil skin, whatever gods the Seven had stolen him from had also blessed Radok with a powerful, athletic physique that made him a physical match for any man.

But this was a different life, and both men had seen a turn in fortunes. Radok had been ravaged by the lungrot, his physical presence melted away, his health a distant memory. Talak, meanwhile, had found himself blessed by the Eighth. He was still as talented with the sword as he ever was, but now the Black Wind guided his hand, sharpening the edge of his blades with death for his enemies.

Talak's sword slashed at Radok's face, but the Wolfeater deflected it away. Talak used the block to drive his own sword along the edge of Radok's blade, then flicked it back to open a slice on Radok's arm.

Blood spattered in the snow, yet Radok barely flinched. Stepping back for just a moment, he pressed in again, hacking and slashing. Talak backed away, deflecting Radok's attacks with ease. Whispers carried on the wind governed Talak's movement, as he ducked and swerved Radok's attacks.

Radok feigned a slash, then lunged at Talak's midriff with his sword. Talak sensed the move as it unfolded, ignoring the feint and swerving around the lunge. His own sword licked out, slicing deeply across Radok's left leg. The Wolfeater felt that. His leg almost buckled beneath him and he limped away wincing. He kept his sword up and his front to Talak, as he tried walking off the pain.

Talak smiled. 'Swords are the Eighth's favourite toy, Wolfeater. This is a game you cannot win.' He glanced at Nyana, who stood among the handful of spectators, looking nervous. Her face was twisted in concentration, with each of her senses trying to paint a picture of the fight that her eyes could not. Talak sneered at her. 'I hope you know how to fly, Little Sparrow.'

Radok's fury erupted like a volcano. His voice bellowed out in a roar of frustrated emotion and he charged forward, his left leg dragging behind him. The ferocity of this new attack took Talak by surprise, and it was all he could do to get his sword up in time to defend himself from the savage blows. Time and again he turned Radok's attacks aside with his own sword, his arms threatening to buckle under the pressure of the unrestrained fury.

Radok's voice boomed out between each sword stroke, 'She. Is. Not. Your. Little. Sparrow!'

As Radok spat the last word out, Talak sensed a movement in the air around him. If he'd lingered a moment longer, Talak knew it would have been the end of him. As it was, he brushed aside Radok's last hammering blow, spun to the Wolfeater's side, and slashed his own sword across the Wolfeater's sword arm. Cutting through flesh, muscle and sinew, Talak watched as Radok's sword spun from his arm and clattered into the snow at his feet. Still following the guiding hand, Talak pirouetted behind Radok and slashed his blade across the back of the man's right knee.

The Wolfeater fell to his knees, his eyes wide with horror. His friends cried out in dismay, but their voices were lost to the fury of the Seven. Talak's smile was so wide it felt like it might split his face. He had never felt so glorious, so at one with the greater power of the Eighth.

Stepping around to stand before Radok, he tilted the man's face up with the tip of his sword. They looked into each other's eyes. There was no fear there, much to Talak's annoyance. Perhaps the Wolfeater was ready to die after all?

Well, let's not disappoint him.

Talak drove his sword through the Wolfeater's chest and leaned in close, driving the blade ever deeper and getting close enough to watch the life fade from those dark eyes.

Then the unthinkable happened. Radok *smiled*. The expression unnerved Talak, who let out a yelp when Radok grabbed him by the wrists. The Wolfeater's iron grip crushed down on Talak's bones, sending a wave of agony up the shaman's arms. Radok pulled himself up to his feet using Talak as a crutch, grimacing as the action drew the blade even deeper into his chest.

Talak realised his mistake then, as Radok straightened to his full height. The Wolfeater had not shrunken away so much; he still towered over Talak, was still as strong as ever. And now there would be no dancing away from him, no escape from this trap...

The wind blasted them as they wrestled with each other, and for a brief, flickering moment Talak felt a swell of hope. It was the Eighth, trying to tear him free.

But the Seven were there too, of course, and they threw their weight behind the Wolfeater. Radok's grip held tight.

'You should have known,' he hissed through bloodstained teeth, 'not even the Eighth can kill a dead man.'

Without warning, Radok released Talak's wrists and switched his grip to the shaman's head, where he locked on with an equally crushing force. Talak screamed as Radok forced his thumbs into his eye sockets. The shaman's vision blurred at first, then turned slowly to darkness, as the soft organs were pushed back into his skull. The pressure proved too much and Talak's eyes burst with two wet pops. The sound was like thunder inside Talak's head and his agonising scream turned into something more primal.

The sound did not last long. It was cut short when the Wolfeater smashed his forehead into Talak's face, shattering nose and cheekbones. Talak sagged backwards. He should have fallen, but instead he felt like he was floating.

Was that a hand at his throat? At his crotch? Lifting him? There was no way of knowing for sure, not in the sea of pain in which Talak found himself drowning. He tried to open his eyes, but there was only darkness waiting for him. Was this what it was like for the girl, he wondered distantly? A world of eternal darkness, with nothing to cling to but the memory of light? Did she feel the same pain?

They should have killed her, he thought absently. *Better that, than a life of this.*

And then he was falling. In his mind's eye, he saw Radok hurling him out over the crevice, and then the wind was rushing through his hair as he plummeted to the rocks below. It was not the Seven or the Eighth he found, but the dead, empty wind of speed. That was when he knew it was over.

The Eighth had promised him death by fire, but the only fire was the one of pain raging in his head. That would soon be over at least. And then his bones would rot away alongside those others rejected by the All Song. It was a bitter end, for one who had given his life to service.

Before he could dwell upon it any further, Talak's body hit the rocks at the foot of the Blackstone's high perch.

He hit them hard.

CHAPTER TWENTY-SIX

The Answer

Senya let out a breathless sigh as the Wolfeater hefted the wiry shaman into the air and launched him into the abyss waiting below the Blackstone; all with the shaman's sword still buried in his chest.

The fight had been majestic at first, with the skills of both swordsmen clear to see. Even unhealthy as he was, Radok's attacks were dizzying and ferocious, as though everything Senya had seen before was just the quiet before the storm. Yet the priest proved to be a match for all of it, always seeming one step ahead, until, finally, he cut Radok down and drove his sword into the man's chest. Senya almost felt exultant at that, as though it were her own blade jutting from the Wolfeater's torso.

That should have been the end of it. Radok, consumed by disease and driven through with a sword, should have bowed his head and died. But he didn't. Instead, he pushed himself to his feet and ended Talak more savagely than any of them could have imagined. Senya shuddered at the memory of it: the sight of Radok's thumbs disappearing into Talak's skull, and the priest's screams as his eyes popped. Senya would hear those screams until the day she died.

Now, Radok lingered at the precipice for a moment, gazing down at Talak's broken body far below. Then he staggered back from the edge and collapsed. The Basillians rushed to his side, the young girl throwing herself upon him, tears flowing from her broken eyes. *That's a blessing*, thought Senya. *She wouldn't want to see him like this.* Radok had been pale and withered before Talak's sword found its home, now he looked every inch as dead as his opponent.

'You... have to... stand,' Nyana told him through broken sobs. 'The Blackstone... it's right there.'

Radok smiled, blood at his lips. 'Let me catch my breath, Little Sparrow. You go first, eh?'

'No,' the girl said with cold certainty. 'It has to be you first. You can't come this far and stop.'

Radok stroked her cheek affectionately. His thumb, which still glistened red with the pulp from Talak's eyes, left a streak of blood as he wiped away a tear.

'Don't cry, Little Sparrow,' he soothed, holding her to him. His voice remained strong, despite it all. 'I understand now. The Seven gave you nothing when they brought you screaming into this world. They gave you nothing... and then they took your folks, and your eyes, and everything else you ever valued. They chewed you up and spat you out... and still you found the strength to crawl. You have never once questioned the Will, nor doubted your part in the All Song. You're a better person than I am, Nyana Little Sparrow, and I'm proud of you, girl. More proud than you'll ever know.'

Jian dropped to her knees at Radok's side. She was crying too, Senya saw, as was Tess, who stood beside her. Only Mikilov watched the scene through clear eyes, though even he wore the expression of a man bearing witness to the passing of greatness.

Senya punched him in the arm as she stepped up beside him. 'What's wrong with you?' she hissed, keeping her voice low. 'This is why we're here, isn't it? We've hunted this man to the ends of the earth, and now his time is done. It's a moment to savour not lament; to celebrate not mourn!'

'Do you truly believe that?' Mikilov's own voice was little more than a whisper. 'Even now, after the things we've seen and heard, you think he's nothing more than the enemy?'

Senya looked down at the dying man. Jian was getting ready to pull the sword from his chest, but Radok reached out and stayed her hands. He gave a shake of the head. *It's over*, that gesture said. *Leave it be.*

Senya shook her head, driving the pity away. 'What else can he be?' she asked. 'He killed Velimir, just like he killed so many others. What else can he be?'

Mikilov shrugged. 'Just a man doing the best he can with the life he was given. You know he was a boy when the Basillians found him? Can you imagine that? Can you imagine losing everything you ever loved and being washed up on the shore of some strange world? Can you imagine your skin being a different colour to everyone else, marking you as an outsider every single time they look at you? Can you imagine fighting for those people, knowing at least a small part of them hates you? Can you imagine rising up through their ranks anyway, gaining their respect and admiration? And can you imagine, after all that, that their gods reward you with a terrible wasting disease?'

Mikilov nodded his head at the dying man. 'That's been his life, girl. At any point he could have rolled over and died, but instead he fought tooth and nail to be here. He crossed the Whitelands and climbed this bloody mountain for a chance to speak to his gods. And now that he's here, at the very end of that journey, disease ridden and weak, he has given his life for his little girl. Basillian or not, you tell me that's not a man worthy of the Great Hunt.'

Senya couldn't, and the dawning of that truth broke her heart. If she hadn't been there that day, all those moons ago, it was more than likely Radok and Velimir would have shared a hot drink and made a trade. But she *was* there, and first Velimir and now Radok were dead, and the world would be a darker place without them. 'I wish I could...' she heard herself whisper.

Radok grabbed Nyana by the shoulders, and eased her away from him, gazing into her eyes. 'Will you do me one favour, while you're out there?'

'Anything,' she said, her eyes shining with tears.

Radok produced a leather satchel from the folds of his fur coat and handed it to the girl. 'Cast Jorn's ashes to the Seven. Set him free. Send him back to the All Song.'

The girl almost broke again, but Radok held to her shoulder. 'I was there at your beginning, Little Sparrow. Fitting, you should be here at my end. Go now. Let me see you have your moment.'

The girl touched his hand and kissed his cheek. 'I love you, Papa.'

Senya closed her eyes. She felt tears flowing down her cheeks as she remembered another young girl saying the same thing to her father.

'I love you too,' she heard Radok say. 'Now go. Test your mettle against the Will. Walk the ridge and touch the stone, and you will find your place in the All Song.'

This last was spoken from memory, no doubt the same thing they were all told when they came to this insane place, but it was spoken with such sincerity it felt unique.

By the time Senya opened her eyes again, Nyana was already crossing the narrow ridge of rock leading to the Blackstone. The wind battered at her tiny frame from all sides, threatening to spill her to the distant rocks below, but she strode on regardless, somehow keeping her balance. Senya felt sick watching her go, knowing it was only a matter of time before the girl fell, yet she could not tear her eyes away.

'That's my sparrow.' Radok's voice was laboured now, but he was smiling as he spoke, watching Nyana's progress. 'I knew she could fly.'

It had taken Radok two hours to cross the ridge when he was a boy. Two hours, and three fallen friends. Nyana had only heard the story once, but she could remember it in vivid detail, as though she'd been there herself.

The ridge was no more than twenty strides long, Radok had said, but with the wind cutting across in both directions, carrying the whispers of the Seven and the Eighth, it may as well have been twenty miles.

You take your time with every step, he told her. *One slip and it's over.*

Back then Radok could see it, of course, just as he'd seen three of his companions lose their balance and fall to the rocks far below. Nyana did not live with the same fear. She saw nothing, save for the painting conjured in her mind's eye by the whisperings of the Will. The voices were gargled and distorted even this close to the source, perhaps *especially* this close to the source, with the sheer force and volume of the wind that came rushing from the Cave of Voices. The Seven and the Eighth were there, dancing around the Blackstone and sweeping back and forth across the narrow ridge, before crashing against Nyana at the other end and washing over her.

Taking a deep breath, Nyana focused her mind. She strained her ears to pick out only those voices sharing the same words. Those voices belonged to the Seven, and their combined urgings gave form to the Will. Nyana listened, and obeyed.

She stepped forward confidently, untroubled by the uneven rock that formed the ridge. In Radok's story, the boy he'd been had taken his time. With the wind howling in his face, violent gusts trying to sweep him from the ridge, he'd had to pick his footholds carefully. Nyana had no such concerns. She walked on almost carelessly, confident that every step she took would find its mark. The wind pulled and tugged at her of course, but for every swipe of the Black Wind, Nyana felt the Seven balance her out. She would sway heavily to one side, then catch herself and straighten, her next step carrying her forward.

Radok had spoken of how the ridge had been slick with ice, how chunks of the rock would break away beneath him and fall into the chasm below. But Nyana found none of that. She found only solid ground beneath every step, somehow avoiding ice like a mountain goat. The truth was clear enough. *This is the Will.*

Without thinking, she took out the bag Radok had given her and loosened the leather thong. She held the bag over her head and shook out the contents, staring up as grey powder filled the air over her, swept in every direction by the torrent of wind. So went Jorn Redclaw, cast back to the All Song as Radok had promised. Nyana let the bag fall and pressed on.

What took Radok two hours took Nyana less than a minute. She knew she was standing in the shadow of the Blackstone when she could no longer feel the wind licking at her chapped lips and numbed face, when her useless eyes blinked the snow away and could feel again, in that strange unseeing way of theirs.

It was still there, the wind, roaring over and around the Blackstone as it flowed into the world from the Cave of Voices, but the stone sheltered Nyana from its wild wrath.

Calmly, as though she had not been waiting for this moment her entire life, Nyana pulled the glove from her right hand, reached out slowly, and pressed her palm to the Blackstone.

The stone was as smooth as glass to touch, but Nyana could feel veins running along the surface like thin strands of hair. It was warm too, as Radok had said it was. She smiled then. He would be bursting with pride watching her touch the stone. It seemed somehow fitting that it should be the last thing he ever saw.

With that thought, and with the Blackstone working its magic, Nyana's world changed forever.

* * *

Radok's heart swelled with pride as he watched her touch the Blackstone.

He would have died a thousand deaths to see her live that moment; to see her stand where no woman had stood before; to see her stand there longer than any man before her; to see her become one with the Will.

'This is it,' he said, his cracked voice barely a whisper.

'What's that?' Jian was only half listening. She was too busy watching the girl; they were *all* watching the girl.

'This was my purpose,' Radok said with a smile. His vision began to blur, but he could still see her standing across the chasm from them, her hand pressed to the stone as all the might of the Seven and the Eighth swirled around her. 'This,' he said. 'Her.'

Jian took hold of his hand and squeezed it tightly, but Radok barely felt it. He barely felt anything now. Perhaps that was a sign the end was close, or perhaps the pain was just dulled by the euphoric joy of watching Nyana defy the expectations and wishes of all those wizened men who thought themselves above her.

My Little Sparrow has surpassed you all, he thought joyously. *And this is just the start of her journey...*

He felt a hand shaking him by the shoulder and realised he had closed his eyes. Forcing them open, he found Jian leaning closer to him, all her attention on him now. 'Not yet, Wolfeater. She's on her way back. It's your turn to touch the stone.'

Looking past the woman, Radok tried to catch a glimpse of the girl, but his eyesight was too far gone and the world was fading to black. 'Not for me,' he breathed out. 'I don't need them anymore. I have my answer.'

'You rest then,' she said, and there were tears in her eyes. She bent forward and kissed his brow. 'Thank you, Radok. You're the best man I ever knew, and I owe you more than just my life.'

'You don't owe me a damned thing,' he told her, returning the squeeze of the hand. She'd barely feel it too, he knew, but it was important he tried. 'It was an honour to know you, Jian. In another life, I would have made you my woman.'

She smiled, the kind that melted hearts. 'In another life, I would have let you.'

'Will you look to Nyana for me? She's something new now and the tribe won't know what to do with her. None of them will. But she can change the world.'

'I'll keep her safe, I promise you that.'

That was good. Radok closed his eyes again. There was peace in the darkness. Peace, and no pain.

He thought he heard the girl's voice as he drifted deeper and deeper into the darkness. He smiled. *There was never a sweeter sound than that.*

Through all the years of blood and death, she had been there waiting for him, ready to welcome him back from the darkness, with an easy smile and a ready laugh. He had been her hero, and she had been his.

It was just a shame that it was only now, with his part in the All Song fading away, that he realised the truth of it. The Seven had given him the greatest gift they could and Radok had never realised it. He sighed sadly. At least that voice would be the last thing he ever heard...

Farewell... Little Sparrow.

Radok was dead by the time Nyana got back to him. Jian watched his eyes slide closed for the last time, his last ragged breath smoking slowly from his mouth. And then Nyana was on him, arms flung around him, sobbing against his stilled chest.

It was too much for Jian to take. She pulled her hand from Radok's death grip and pushed herself to her feet. Tess moved in to comfort her, but Jian pushed her away. She loved Tess, she truly did, but there was something special with Radok... and it was gone now.

'I just need a moment,' she heard herself say, as she staggered away from the group, her thoughts a whirlwind. Eventually, she found herself at the edge of the cliff they had climbed earlier, looking out over the Whitelands far below.

In her mind's eye, she pictured Radok's face floating before her, dark and handsome and sharp-edged. The man had worn the mantle of husband and father without even knowing it, never expecting a thing in return. That was a rare gift among the men of the Grey Crow, who usually took whatever they wanted.

Jian sighed. *In another life,* Radok had said, *I would have made you my woman.* A part of her wished that he had. She loved Tess with all her heart, but Jian had always favoured a man's touch. Now she would always wonder what could have been...

'We have to burn him.'

Turning back at the sound of the voice, Jian found Nyana standing tall beside the body. The girl had wiped away her tears and Jian noted a remarkable change. The quiet, timid girl who had travelled with them since their encounter with the kragan had suddenly blossomed into something else since touching the Blackstone. There was an air of confidence about her now, a certainty not just to who she was, but to what she was doing. *And why not*, thought Jian? *She is Ashan Tay.*

Those were four words that had never belonged together before today - nor ever would, Jian had thought. Perhaps Radok was right; perhaps the girl would change the world.

'There's no fuel,' Mikilov told her. 'And much as I respected the man, I don't fancy carrying him down a mountainside.'

'We could throw him down,' said the She-Wolf, who had made no effort to hide her disdain for Radok. 'He's just meat and bones now.'

'We burn our dead,' said Nyana, fixing Senya with her unseeing eyes. 'And if you throw him down, you throw me down.'

'No one's throwing anyone,' said Mikilov, stepping between the scowling pair. 'We'll burn him, if that's what you want. But I still don't know how.'

Nyana smiled suddenly, visibly relaxing. 'Ask, and the *Ashan Daru* shall provide.'

Jian flinched as a bag of twigs and branches landed in the snow beside her. She turned in time to see a hand join it at the top of the cliff, followed by an arm, and then the hooded head of the *Ashan Daru*. Stepping over, she helped the holy man up the rest of the way and hauled him to his feet.

He stood for a moment, hands on hips, breathing heavily. He'd at least dressed this time, wearing a heavy, fur-lined jacket and pants. He smiled at Nyana, offering a little bow of the head. 'Congratulations, *Ashan Tay*. You have found your place in the All Song.'

'Did he have to die?' she asked.

'We all must die someday, just as we must make the most of life while it lasts. That is the balance. Something the Seven have always appreciated more than the Eighth.'

Nyana nodded. 'That is the Will.'

'Then we burn him?' asked Jian. She could barely look at Radok's body now, without the grief overwhelming her. The disease had left him a shell of the man he once was; an empty, shrivelled husk. The sooner it was done, the better.

'You'll need more wood than that,' put in Mikilov.

The *Ashan Daru* flashed him a wicked grin and winked. Picking up the bundle of kindling and fuel, he found a length of rope tied around it and traced it back to the cliff top, where it disappeared over the edge. There, he began to reel the rope in. After a few moments he drew up a second bag of fuel, then a third, and a fourth, the branches and twigs giving way to larger cuttings and small logs.

'What about Talgar?' asked Tess. She was standing off to one side, pulling her fur coat tight about her. 'We should burn him too, it's only right.'

'Don't worry about him,' said the *Ashan Daru*, and Jian thought she saw a twinkle in his eye. 'He's taken care of. Now, who will help me build a pyre?'

Jian was the first to step forward, eager to see it done, but there was none among them who refused to help. Not even the She-Wolf.

'You were right.'

Mikilov raised an eyebrow in Senya's direction. They stood away from the others, watching the small pyre burn. The flames roared up in the wild wind, flaring violently as they licked and danced around the corpse in the centre. It was quite a sight under the darkening sky, and the smell of burning flesh was sickly sweet.

'Right about what?' asked Mikilov.

'About this,' she said, nodding at the fire. 'It's not what I thought it would be.'

'And what did you think it would be?'

'I thought there would be some satisfaction in seeing him dead, for what he did to Velimir. But this? I just feel empty.'

Mikilov took a moment before replying. 'It always tears a hole in us, losing someone we love. There's never been a death can cure that ill, no matter who they are.'

Senya looked unsure. 'Perhaps I needed to kill him myself?'

'Or perhaps his death showed you a side of him you weren't prepared for? More than just the monster, the Wolfeater, you saw the man, Radok. A man who gave his life so that we might live.'

Senya grunted. 'He gave his life for the girl. I doubt he gave two shits about the rest of us.'

'Even so,' said Mikilov, 'he showed his worth.'

He could see the girl wanted to argue further, to reclaim some of the hatred that had slipped from her heart, but she could find nothing to back it up with. 'He died well,' she admitted after a moment.

'He did. Better than most I've known.'

'What will you do now?'

The question came from one of the Basillian women, striding across the mountaintop toward them. It was the younger one, Tess. Mikilov noted that her bow was strung across her shoulder, but a hand rested on the dagger hilt at her waist. He had been waiting for this moment; when the task at hand was done and the old rivalries returned. Looking beyond the woman, he could see that the others remained close to the pyre, watching Radok's remains turn to ash. The youngster's silhouette stood in the centre of the flames, flanked by Jian and the strange priest.

'Don't worry about them,' said Tess. 'This is sacred ground. No more blood will be spilt on our part. I just want to know your part.'

'We go home,' answered Mikilov. 'Or at least what's left of it for the both of us.'

The woman nodded. 'It's changed for all of us, I suppose.'

'What will you do?' asked Senya.

Tess looked back towards the fire. 'The girl is *Ashan Tay* now, which means she serves the Will. She'll go wherever it takes her, for the good of the Grey Crow.'

'And Jian?' asked Mikilov.

'Radok's dying wish was for her to protect the girl. That's what she'll do, for as long as she lives.' Tess smiled fondly. 'And I'll be there to protect her. That's what we do for those we love.'

There was a flash of anger in Senya's eyes at that, and Mikilov groaned. 'Sometimes we can't protect them,' she said softly, though her words carried a hard edge. 'Sometimes vengeance is all we have.'

Tess smiled. 'I like you, She-Wolf. Perhaps we'll meet again, if the Will commands it.'

'You'll know where to find me,' said Senya. 'And I'll be waiting with cold steel.'

Epilogue

Fire burned atop the Käda for the first time since the Forging Days, when the Blackstone was born. The flames lit up the sky over the barren wilderness of the Whitelands like a burning star, its fiery light seen for a thousand leagues in all directions.

That was the mark of Radok the Wolfeater.

In his wake, he left behind Nyana the Blindcrow, the first female to touch the Blackstone and to be blessed with the calling of *Ashan Tay*. On her tiny shoulders rests the fate of all Basillian tribes, not just the Grey Crow, for she alone has seen the face of the true enemy.

Yet she does not carry this weight alone. With her goes Jian the Breaker and Tess the Bone Arrow, who will guard her life with their own.

Their work done, Mikilov and Senya return to their own people, knowing that their journey to the Whitelands has changed them forever. The loss of Scar leaves Mikilov a broken man, but he may find his fate more entwined with the Grey Crow than he realises. Senya, meanwhile, must decide which song of the Wolfeater she keeps in her heart: the man, or the monster? Her decision could shape the future of the Valor in ways her father never dreamed.

    ... and these stories shall also be told.

THE END

ABOUT THE AUTHOR

UK fantasy writer Anthony Mitchell is the author of several stories set in the world of Domanska.

He lives on the Wirral with his wife, Jen, daughter, Penny, and their dog, the mighty Thor.

By day he works in IT, but by night he can be found in a world of swords and sandals, working towards his next novel.

You can find out more about both him and the world of Domanska at his websites:
www.StoriesFromTheCave.com
www.AnthonyMitchellAuthor.com

You can also connect with the author on:
https://twitter.com/oldmanmitchell
https://www.facebook.com/storiesfromthecave
https://www.instagram.com/storiesfromthecave

Printed in Great Britain
by Amazon